Rivers Parting

Rivers Parting

A NOVEL BY

Shirley Barker

CROWN PUBLISHERS
NEW YORK

Printed in the United States of America

For my mother and brother
Alta Leighton Barker
Hiram Leighton Barker

Contents

1. "Such glory I had in loving"

～～～～～～～～～～～～～～～～～～～～～～～

JOHN SCARLOCK felt great things astir that night, but whether they came and went in the flow of his own blood up the dark creeks of the brain, or outside him, a trouble, too, for other farm lads looking out at the star-pricked sky and the windless hazels, he could not tell. He put his head out of the low doorway in the farmhouse kitchen, and looked up at the sickle moon, down at the plowland curved with the curve of the Trent valley. No comets flashed above him, and no earthquakes rocked the ground and its waters under; outside lay only an autumn night, like a thousand others he could remember. In the room behind him, a log snapped and settled on the hearth. He turned then, glanced at old Rob and Bet nodding in their chairs, and stepped outward, shutting the door.

White rime spun a delicate mist over the grass, and looking back once as he walked up Gamwell Chase, he could see his footprints marching square and black and stubborn on the whiteness. It was a night to walk between the great crabbed trees here on the lower edge of Sherwood; a fit night to meet Old Will, if ever you were to meet him. John had walked often so, hearing the thorn twigs crackle under his bootsoles, shoving his way through the hornbeam thickets, half of him hoping to meet the family ghost, half of him not believing there was such a thing. Maybe that story was true, his father was so fond of, that the Scarlocks of Old Thorny had come down from the merry man, Will Scarlet, and that it was given to them to meet him sometimes in the high wood, slipped from his grave by Blidworth Church, alive as ever in his forest green. But more than forty years back was the last time it had happened—to Cousin

Rob, the night before he went off to fight the Armada, a warm night, smoking with fog, in the late spring. Had there been a strangeness on that night the way there was on this one? John wondered uneasily. Did it mean *he* would be going off tomorrow to fight for something he'd never quite find out all the reasons for, just as Rob had? His muscles tensed like those of a hound asleep by the fire when something unseen and trackless walks around the house, something that may be the wind for all a man can tell. Impatient at the treachery of his own nerves, he caught suddenly at a birch bough dipping toward him and snapped it off.

"The devil with it!" he said aloud. "I'll go see Joan."

Striding along the windmill ridge, with Trent flowing silver below him on the left, he kept his eyes straight ahead toward Nottingham, all roofs and chimneys and lighted panes slanting up a hillside at the sky. Out of the shadow of the forest now, his forebodings left him and he began to whistle. There were more ghosts in the wood than Will Scarlet's, and 'twas one of those old, dark things that dwelt there, passing just beyond his sight, that had been the trouble, likely; nothing to do with him. The landscape round him now looked just the way it always had; here a quickset hedge, there a barley rick, on the right, before you came to the first row of houses, a hooded malt kiln smoking. The known, familiar look of it all reassured him. Men could die and roofs fall in, but the land under them did not change. You could trust the land—even now in these declining times, in the fifth year of Charles the First, King by the Grace of God. It would feed you if you sowed it, and take you into itself when the time came for that, just as it had for your father and would for your sons after you—for his sons, he thought, his sons and Joan's.

He quickened his steps when he thought about Joan, the barmaid at the Bull's Head, brown and slim, born just sixteen years ago this fall in St. Nicholas' workhouse. But that wasn't so bad a thing. He'd rather take home a workhouse girl, pretty and warm and loving, than a cold, giggling stick like Squire's daughter, and it was time he took Joan home now. He'd loved her in every hedge this side of Sherwood, and at first he thought loving her in the hedges would be enough, but it wasn't. He wanted to marry her with a ring and take her to Old Thorny. Maybe Christmas or Boxing Day—after the winter wheat was sown and a man could rest from the fields for a bit. He could see how she'd look with holly all about her, her brown eyes shining through the glossy leaves, and the berries not so deep a red as her soft mouth. He'd kiss her mouth in a few minutes, he thought; kiss her, and then sit in and drink with the men until Jack Gambrell cried closing time, and then—his flesh quivered in his rough woolen clothes to think what would happen then— how he would be all alone under the sickle moon with the sweetness of Joan.

Just as he reached the edge of town the strangeness of the night began to trouble him again—the feel of something about to happen—something that he was to have a part in, that might be good or evil, but would be, in any course, a great thing. He had felt a little like that five years ago, he remembered, the time the woods got afire from a charcoal cart and blacked over the noon sky way to Newark. Looked as if all Sherwood might come down and half the shire be burnt over. But why trouble his blood tonight about fires and going off fighting? He'd got no use for either, and if they came again, he hoped it wouldn't be in his time. He wanted to live peaceably on Old Thorny and marry Joan. He put up his head and sniffed the night air in the way all animals test their world for approaching trouble: for the salt wind that wandered inland sometimes before a storm fell, the brimstone of mortars pounding in battle, even the faint tease of spicy airs that meant the unknown. But he smelled only plowed ground and dying leaves, the sweetness of unpicked apples rotting on some forgotten tree in the darkened fields behind him, then the reek of the tanyard and the fulsomeness of brewery malt as his feet struck the cobblestones of Nottingham.

Past the Swine Green he went, taking the short way through St. Peter's churchyard with its broken gravestones, and down into the dirty fog that rose off the sluggish waters of the Leen Ditch. Unsightly, even on a foggy night, the houses of Brew House Yard sprouted out of the hillside, like toadstools from a fallen tree. All the street doors opened into alehouses, and no one asked or needed to ask what went on behind the crazy gables. Under the floors and pavement, round caves tunneled through the red sandstone, but no man living had pried into them very far. Master Tibbalds used to tell the boys at the Free School, when John was a boy there, that the Gray Friars had made the caves to bed down men fallen sick of the plague in the old time, that the sickness still might live on there in the porous stone, for all he knew.

John had never gone into them to find out, but he'd been often

3

enough in the well-like cellar to the north, for Jack Gambrell stored casks there, and trusted his servant Joan with the key of it. Kissing in the copses could be cold work on a frosty night, but no winds raked the malt cellar, and there was clean, kind sand on the floor. In his pocket now, as he went up the tilted cobbles toward the Bull's Head, he felt a clever little copy of Joan's key that he'd got Ned Trigg to make for him. Humpbacked and finical, Ned was no good at the forge he tried to work, but he could cut an eye in a needle, or mend their London earrings for the aldermen's wives. Some said he was a rare lad for the girls before he got the fall that crippled him —close kin to Joan Sweetapple, John had heard more than once, but her mother had died in the dirty straw under St. Nicholas' with her mouth shut, not naming any names.

John stopped by the wide bow window of the tavern and looked inside. For a moment he forgot about Joan, seeing the men over their ale mugs in the firelight, and thinking of one man who had often sat there until last winter's great snow took him off. His father he thought of, and how he used to thump on the table with his earthen mug, telling bits of the family story that the whole shire knew as well as he did.

"Never said we was great folk," he'd argue, tossing his shaggy head and mumbling a little for want of teeth. "Robin Hood now, some say he were a lord's son as run away, though I've my doubts about that even. But we're not his kin, whichever way it were. We be yeomen folk from Gamwell Chase, and we come down from his man, Will Scarlet, the one who always got the deer, and warned Robin against that she-devil prioress who killed him later—likewise the one the queen out of Spain took a fancy to."

And at that he would look slyly at Joan and she would slide a full mug in front of the old man and wipe up the froth he'd spilled from the last one. How eagerly then he would lift it to his dry old mouth. Dry, dry . . . and so the dust is dry. "Dust thou art," Parson had read, the words blown away from him on the icy wind that raked the December graveyard. John's throat ached suddenly and his eyes filled.

A mirror glass hung on the opposite wall of the tavern, and John caught the look of his own face in it, a little distorted by the curved panes between. He saw a thin face, more long than wide, with gray eyes, and dark, straight brows, and wisps of brown hair tossed above it by the night wind. You wouldn't look twice at him, he thought, because there were lads all over England looked like that; good to fight the King's wars, and plow the fields, and get sons who would do the same thing over. No one to look to if you wanted someone rare and strange, a great man for a beacon on the night.

A trim brown head moved between him and the man in the mirror. It was Joan. She stepped carefully, a brimming tankard in either hand, but she could not keep her eyes from turning toward the leaded windowpanes. John raised his arm and brought it down quickly, a long sweep of green where the candlelight shone into the street. He had other coats at home, hodden gray, and plowman's russet, but it pleased his fancy to wear the forest color and Joan knew it. She had been watching for the flash of green. Her face lighted up now, and she spilled ale on her customer's sleeve as she hastily served him. There was no cold pretense about Joan. She saw her lover, and the sight made her happy, and she would go to him now as fast as she could. Almost running, she crossed the crowded room and slipped through the inner door that John knew would take her to the malt cellar. How slim her waist was, set between the full homespun skirt and the curving bodice; her shoulders were straight and slim, too, and something about the way she moved made him think of a Michaelmas daisy swaying on its stem. That was the way a girl should look, not thick like Moll at the Trip to Jerusalem, the only other girl he had ever lain in the hedges with. "Town o' Nottingham keeps Moll Doubleday for the lads to learn on," his father used to tell him. Well, Moll could teach him nothing more. He knew her ill-smelling fair hair and the grease stains on her bodice, her panting love, and the sick revulsion after. He had Joan now, and that was something the King of England didn't have. Plunging into the lightless alley that ran along the tavern wall, he came up against the stone door to the cellar and unlocked it, stepped down into the malty dark and the ring of Joan's laughter from the stairs below.

"Guess, Johnny, where I am. How many steps?"

"Don't have to guess. I know. Thirteen."

"How could you tell?"

He groped down the mossy treads toward her.

"Because you're a daft maid with no honest fear in her. Just the kind that's like to try the unluckiest number."

He counted, stopped on the right ledge and drew her to him, lost in the soft warmth of her arms and bosom, finding her mouth.

5

"Johnny!" She writhed a little. "What's in your jacket? It hurts me!"

"Only the book. I forgot 'twas there."

"Forgot! Likely! It's always by you. You're worse than Parson with Prayer Book."

"I am not. Prayer Book's high and mystical, and full of things they don't teach you at the Free School. Let Parson make what he can of it, and I'll listen to him on Sunday, but I'd not carry it around with me. This is a man's book of common sense, written down by a farming man, Thomas Tusser. I used to sit out at Old Thorny and read it every night before I knew you, and the crop's been bettered a third for going by it. Has all the learning I'll ever need."

"But it's a book! It's only paper rotting inside of leather that might ha' soled a pair of shoes."

The book still nudged its corners into her breast and hurt her, but something about the way her words had struck him lay sharper between them than the worn calfskin. He stirred restlessly against her.

"Only a book! Yes, I know. But there's a queerness on books. They've not tongues, but they can speak to every man that reads them, and they'll talk to him of things the writer never meant, things no man knows of but he."

Joan shivered. "What things? I thought it told all about when to stick hogs and drain sedge."

"No, there's other matter. It's older'n we, this book. Way before Rob went off to fight the dons, it was written. Man who wrote it's dead, Old Tibbalds says. But there's words in it that's we—that's ours—that's you and I!"

"What words?"

"'Such glory I had in loving!' Joan!" He said it over slowly, not quite clear, his mouth brushing her hair. "'Such glory I had in loving.' Doesn't that make you remember the rye hills and the saffron meadow?"

"Aye. And the oak knoll by Ann's Well."

"And the stone nest under the sycamore atop Chapel Gate."

"Oh that night! We were mad that night! All Nottingham could see us cuddling up there."

"Well, cuddling's nothing new in Nottingham. But how did Old Tusser know way back then to put in a book the thing that we . . . ?"

"Think he never walked out with a girl, Johnny?"

6

"Think it would be . . . the same?"

"No . . . no . . . I guess not . . . ever."

But a moment later she drew away from him. "Not now, Johnny. There's a spider crawling on my neck, and you saw the place was full upstairs. Jack'll box my ears if I'm out much longer. And a stranger's there, talking about—oh, you jumped! Was it the spider?"

"No. Not that. All night I've felt that there was something uncommon queer afoot and I was part of it. When you spoke of the stranger I felt it again. Come. We'll go."

They had no need to slip into the tavern by separate ways. They could enter boldly together by the street door, for all Brew House Yard knew that they had enjoyed each other's love, and Brew House Yard believed in love's enjoyment and a pox on banns. All the sin and vice and poverty of the teeming shire town seemed to draw cosily into this tilted close, but sin and vice and poverty were not really reckoned so very bad in Nottingham, with its proud memory of one merry thief who had loved the poor. And if stale, sour odors and a curse or two drifted upward on the river wind to the great houses of the merchants and aldermen, why let it be remembered there that this is, after all, a world of sin, and he who would breathe of untainted airs must look to Paradise for them. In due time the merchants of Nottingham might turn to Paradise, preferably just before the bell started to go for their last leavetakings, but now they were too busy making money. The tanners, and the brewers, and the weavers, whose craft had come down almost unchanged from their Flemish ancestors, would be early every Saturday at the Market Cross in time to welcome the farmers trundling in from Belvoir Vale with apples, wool and tallow, hides and slaughter cattle, or what's-in-season. The chapman's vans from London would be there, too, to carry away the country's richness in return for silks and silver and Eastern seasonings that would spice your porridge up so your wife herself couldn't tell what it was she'd set out to cook. City goods, too, that men would buy because they glittered, but couldn't always find a name or a use for afterward. John o' London wanted a flitch of bacon in the rind, and Jack o' Leenside Farm wanted a city waistcoat, and Nottingham would take its shilling toll from John and Jack. So long as wheels turned, ewes grew fleece, and crops ripened, all went well in market and Nottingham throve, so what did it matter if a wench below the wall liked varied company in bed, if dwellers in the foul

7

mews stole from each other and rooked unwary strangers at shovel-board? Of course the Yard stank, but so it had in their fathers' time, and their fathers had not minded it, so why should they?

As John and Joan stepped inside the Bull's Head, a dozen voices called out in greeting, but Jack Gambrell's could be heard over all the others.

"So ye're back!" he roared in loud good humor, coming out of the buttery, a ladle slung at his belt and slapping against his round stomach with the food-splashed apron drawn tight across it. "Little cool nesting in the hay, were it?"

"Ye'll not pick any hay out of my hair, Jack Gambrell," laughed Joan, gathering up the unwashed mugs and elbowing his ribs as she passed him.

"Ho, Joan!" called a rough lad half down the room. "We're right dry waiting for you to be done your loving!"

"Aw, drink up, and leave the wench alone!" called another. "Over here, Johnny."

The men made a place for him at the long table down the middle, not too near the fire. There was hardly a face there that Joan hadn't slapped in keeping herself till he came, the way she had. But they all understood that—part of a maid's ways, for which there be no accounting—and John was the lucky man, and they were all friends now.

"Come on, Jack, you robber!" called John to his host. "Mine's Northdown ale, and bring the boys the same again."

They were farmers like himself who sat around him, men with sun-bleached hair and thorn scratches on their hands, good wool coats and eyes looking straight at you. There were paler, swarthier men, too, a little furtive, smelling of the dark warrens around the Yard, quick to come forward and claim knowledge of everything, slow to pay their share of the reckoning. Joan beamed upon them all and brought ale for everybody, coming last to John. He took his drink, smiled into her eyes, and lifted the tankard to his mouth.

He saw the stranger, alone, sitting in the bow of the window.

He was a dark man, lean, not over tall, dressed in gentleman's velvet, and as he waited at the small oak table he ran his fingers along his sword caressingly, as if it were the dimpled arm of a woman. His eyes caught the unsteady light of the burning tallow in the sconces facing him, and gleamed like phosphorus in the swamp

8

pools where the Leen flows out of Sherwood; not the kind of fire that comes when you strike flint, but a colder, less cheering thing.

Jack, always proud of his own cookery, waddled in and set down a tray on the oak table.

"Got an eel pasty for ye, sir. Deer's not so easy to come by now in Sherwood, for King says they're all his, and our best poachers are not the men their fathers were, not by cock's bones. As I growed older and fathered lads of my own, I seen it more and more, how little men be what their fathers were in their time. What'll ye drink?"

"Wine, in Bordeaux," smiled the stranger, "and mead where the beehives are. But here in Nottingham—the nut-brown ale!"

"Now here's a man knows what's good," roared Jack. "I never held, man or boy, with swill out of French casks. Sells it, I do, but drinks it, I don't, for it befoggles one."

"Which ale does not," murmured the stranger, plunging his knife under the crust of the pasty and flipping a coil of white meat into his mouth.

Ned Trigg drew close to John's elbow and spoke quietly to him, under the drone of voices now filling the room with a comfortable sound.

"The key work, Johnny?"

"*You* made it, Ned. That's answer, isn't it?"

He looked down at the twisted gnome who might be his sweetheart's father and wished he could get drunk enough to ask Ned if there were truth in the story. It wasn't a thing you could ask a man sober.

"If ye'd not been out dallying with Joannie, ye'd have heard the stranger over there giving his fine talk."

"What'd he say?" asked John, slopping his ale on the table, feeling that sick uneasiness again.

"Talked about his master. Said he was a trading man o' wealth somewhere in the south—Hampshire, of course, it were—named John Mason. Seems he thinks to build himself a manor."

"Well, men have done that since the time of God. There's no fine story there."

"But this one's going over the western sea to do his building. Right square into the middle of a wood that's never had the axe put to it. Red savages, an' lions, an' tygers, an' what-all be there."

"He better build in Hampshire."

9

"Give you back your own words, Johnny. Since the time of God there's men built manors in Hampshire. This one'll take new country."

John stared silently into his ale, and Ned went on.

"Oh, he—Captain Neal, that is, over there—made a rare tale of it. Seems they're signing papers down in London now for King to let 'em go."

They watched the dark man bending to the eel pasty.

"They think to call the place 'New Hampshire,' and they're going out there in a ship, come spring. He's looking for a pack of likely lads to take with him, and he says once Mason's land's cleared and his hall put up, there's no reason every man can't go past it into the woods and take as much for himself. I'd sure go, if I was a whole man again, and twenty-one like you be. You ought to go along, Johnny."

"Me? Why? I got Old Thorny, and I wouldn't trade that for any land this side of hell. You're drunk, man."

"No." Ned shook his head. "Your farm's a tidy bit, lad, but it's not a manor. New Hampshire'll have manor lands for all that go there, and from some of the things he said, I'm not so sure which side hell it's on."

Captain Neal finished the pasty as they watched him, cleaned his knife on a gobbet of bread, and rose leisurely. He came toward the long table, his glance running like a flash of light over the men gathered there. Then he kicked up a stool just across from John, sat down on it and spoke to him.

"You've not been here all evening?"

"No," said John, his hand cupped around his tankard, staring into it.

"Then you didn't hear my story. But you look like the man I told it for. Where do you live and what do you do there?"

"I farm my own land by Gamwell Chase."

"Your own land?"

"Aye. Forty shilling freehold, down in Subsidy Book."

"You're better off than many."

"Aye."

John nursed his ale. The captain tried again.

"Close to the Forest, is it?"

John laughed then, too high and loud.

"Close to where it was. My fields run up to the Chase on the north side, and there's a good growth there, but the high wood beyond's been thinned out by too much cutting ship timber. More bilberries than oaks now."

Why should he think Captain Neal would want to hear about Sherwood when he had all those unending forests oversea to look to? But he had to go on talking because he was afraid to hear what the man was going to say next.

"You mean Sherwood's pretty well down? I'm from the home shires myself, and wouldn't know."

"It thickens up to the west. There's hornbeams by Worksop Priory grew out of seeds that our men brought back from Agincourt—first way that tree ever came into England."

"Agincourt . . ." mused the captain, his hand playing with his sword again. "I've often wished I could have been there. . . ." Then, waking from his moment's dream, he spoke sharply. "What's Agincourt to you?"

"To me? I don't know. Something I've always heard of. Mostly old men talking. Nottingham's bowmen's country, and that was supposed to be a great day for bowmen. Just another time we beat the French, I guess. It's happened often enough."

"About Sherwood, now?"

"Oh . . . Sherwood. You should see Bilhaugh where the oaks are so great and old, and gray lichens grow so thick that it's never clear day, only twilight. Or the hawthorns up by Birdley. Men say there's fifty thousand trees there. Could be. I never counted them. It's a lie to say Sherwood's down. It's thinning some."

"And I suppose that goes for Dean and Epping and the west," pondered Neal. "London shipyards, Sussex iron forges . . . it takes wood to run the world, to keep England England."

"Woods, and mostly oaks," said John, sipping at the ale Joan had brought him without being told to. "Holly's tougher, and fir's more limber, but if you was to take off all the trees and leave me only one, why leave me oak. I've seen oaks men had cut their names on, and when I read the date cut under, it were a hundred and twenty year back."

"Same name as yours?"

"What? Oh, aye. 'John' like mine. Maybe 'Rob' or 'Will.' "

"And the last name?"

"Mine? Oh. John Scarlock. 'Scarlet,' it'll be sometimes written."

"The word for red?"

"Na, na," interrupted Ned Trigg, cross with drink. "Nothing to do with red. 'Scar lock'! Means his folk been cracking pates round the shire since trees been growing there."

"I could use," said the captain slowly, "a cracker of pates from Sherwood Forest."

I knew. I knew he was coming to that, thought John. Why did he have to come to that? I don't want to go with him. His ale went down his throat like liquid dust. Neal was still talking.

"You know the way of seeds in the ground, John? And how to hold an axe?"

"Yes. I know that. It isn't much."

"Nobody ever called him 'Johnny Fool.' He's a Free School lad," piped Ned, his face sliding down into a pool of spilled ale on the table.

John flushed. He watched Joan in the alcove washing mugs. Getting married to her under the holly berries had seemed so near a little while ago. Now he couldn't see how he had ever thought he would be doing such a thing. And still there wasn't any reason why he couldn't. More men stood in to drink at every moment, for the tang of the fall night seemed to put a man in mind of ale the way an empty stomach would send him groping to the buttery.

"John," said Captain Neal, "is there any man around here who knows the things you know, who'd be glad to leave his old acres and go look for some better ones?"

"Can't say."

"You know my business here."

"It's naught to do with me."

"Will you wager that?" asked the captain, his eyes catching the light again.

John felt the green wool of his jerkin scraping his neck, and ran a gnarling finger down the skin. He was as nervous as a mare running first time in the Goose Fair race. Why was he, for God's sake? He tried to answer, but choked on his ale.

Neal leaned easily on one elbow and talked on. "Cracking pates around Sherwood since trees been growing there! Well, that's a fine past, but a man needs more than what's behind him. Comes time now when the trees are so much gone that you feel the need to boast about what's left. Isn't it time a man should go, too? Did you ever think there might be something better in the world than Gamwell Chase . . . ?"

12

"You've never seen the Chase like it is tonight. Half moon, half dark, all old time waiting there."

"Devil take old time!" rapped Captain Neal. "A man's alive today and dead tomorrow. Today's damn short, and tomorrow's forever. You're a young man with blood and muscle. Yes, I know, you had them both from the old pate-crackers, but manhood's not an heirloom to keep like a silver porringer in a locked chest. Didn't any of your kin ever leave Sherwood?"

"Rob fought the Armada."

"So? To Rob, then!"

He took the longest swallow of ale John had known a man could hold his breath for. "There must be adventure in the stock. You're not all clay like Trent bottom."

Anger stirred in John unreasoningly. "Trent bottom's ledge, not clay, as all fools know. And as for adventure, I come down from a man whose trade it were. What's yours, I wonder?"

Captain Neal stroked the brass mountings of his scabbard.

"This is my trade. It serves me well enough."

No one seemed to have any more to say. The ale dipped down the tankard sides. The autumn moon rode high over Brew House Yard and the fog had shrunken back into Leen. Inside the taproom the tallow dips burned down, the fire dwindled, and Jack no longer replenished it. The men were leaving unsteadily by twos and threes.

"John," said Walter Neal after a long silence, "when you came in here tonight, I knew you were a man I wanted. You have the strength I want, and somehow the look on your face that I like a man to have—the look that means England, whether you meet it fighting on the Rhine, or coasting North Virginia, or home here, drinking in a tavern. You know timber and seeds, and no man has yet signed with me who knows them. Coopers I have, with pegs and hammers; masons; merchants' sons to build the fur trade, and bully boys who want to kill redskins; fishermen; men to tend the salt pans. But it worries me to think whoever in God's name's to see to feeding them all. Corn out of England, Captain Mason says, but corn boats out of England have a way of going to sea bottom or New Amsterdam after Dutch prices, and the taste of game gets rank in a man's mouth before the winter's end. I say we should have fields by Piscataqua—the river there—and men to lay them out and see to tilling them. What kind of manor would it be without? And then, another thing. Cod's there, and beaver, and it would please all men

13

to find gold, but with our forests here falling off the way they are, I'm not so sure the best thing we get for ourselves won't be the ship timber. Why, Sherwood in its best days was nothing but a field coppice beside the woods I'm going to. And I want a man with me who knows trees. Yes, point for point, you're the man I'm after. And you have your mystery, too, as every man should have, and yours I wonder at. Here we've sat at the board all evening, and you've put down two ales for every one of mine. Your friend's in a sore plight" —for Ned snored in the ale puddle—"and I—I, a rare lad in taverns all over the world—I, sir, am mellow. But you sit there dry and sober as Paul's. How d'ye do it?"

John did not doubt that Captain Neal was a rare lad, in taverns or wherever he might be, even under Great Paul's in London. He felt awkward and oafish, took his leather cap out of his pocket and twisted it.

"'Tis a curse put on us in grandsir's time by an old begging woman. He moved the bottle away from her because he said she'd had enough already, and she said, 'Ye'll get no good from the grain or the grape, nor your heirs afterward.' Nor do we ever."

"You mean it's always so with you? The more you drink the soberer you grow?"

"Aye," answered John morosely.

Captain Neal shook his sleek head and a dark lock of hair hung into his eyes. "Then you'd hardly do for us. I have not seen New Hampshire, but from what I hear of it there will be times there when a man must get drunk or go mad. Sir, I'll not take you."

"So I've been telling you."

"I won't? Damme, I will. Some day when my fine colonists are lying drunk on a rock beach, caught between the salt tide and the squalling Indians, it will be well to have one sober man among us to fend off trouble."

His lean, muscled hands in their black velvet cuffs lay before him, flung outward on the table. Not drunk, but drunk enough to speak the truth, he looked at John and spoke it.

"John, I have work to do, and I was hired just as you'd hire a man to stick a hog at Martinmas or pitch hay in midsummer. If I make an ending to the business that pleases John Mason and those who adventure money, they won't enquire how I brought it about, and I'm not a man to carp and query inside myself as to whether my works are good or no. I've gone up and down England for the men I wanted, talked sly to the stoutest youths, and promised each of them the thing I thought he most lusted after—gold guineas, mostly, to buy them wenches whiter than Helen, and raise them up past what they were born to. Some lads like a fight, and God knows I could promise them that with honor. I have even promised ease and luxury, God help me. I have made New Hampshire sound so fair my men would go past heaven to get to it. I've promised them land, and enough wideness around every man so he could lift his voice and shout a prayer or a curse without his nearest neighbor knowing which it was. But to you, I shall make no promises.

"There's a safe harbor with a rocky shore. My friend, John Smith, who's been there told me that. Some of the headlands, he says, mind him a little of Devonshire. And that's just about all I know of it. The savages, they say, will tear a man's flesh like ripping rotten cloth, cut off his scalp like taking the crust off a pasty. There's wolves and worse animals, I hear; great snows, and mountains with bald, whitish tops. I've told some lads there'd be rich mines in those mountains—but I do not tell you so. I don't know what the hell is in them. There's beaver along the rivers, and cod enough to feed Pope's people till the next coming of Christ. Great trees begin at the sea's edge. I don't know where they end or what kind of soil is under them. And if you come, I don't know what you'll get out of it. Likely, a hard death before your time. Here you're a free man on your own acres, rooted in Sherwood Forest like a beech tree. You've got no trouble to run away from, and you're not all awry with the love of God, like the men who are getting a charter south of us in Massachusetts. But I'd rather have you beside me in a fight than any man I know."

Captain Neal did not put the question. Instead he waited. John looked into his empty tankard. All his life he would remember the little whorls at the bottom of it. He knew he was meant to go with Walter Neal, but he did not want to go. No man alive remembers being born, he thought, but it must be like this, a force thrusting you into life, whether you would or no, and something within yourself urging you the same way, too. Only if you can resist your birth can you resist your destiny.

The two men looked each other in the face, done with words. And then John felt a light touch on his sleeve.

"We're closing, Johnny. I'll walk out with you a little way."

Joan pulled at him, turning her face toward Walter Neal. "Jack says for you to take the candle, sir, and go upstairs. The room's straight ahead, made with clean linen and a fire laid if you want it. Himself, he's quite befoggled."

Turning away with Joan, he did not bid the other man goodnight, but he knew that the dark eyes followed him, even after the timbered door had closed between them. Joan nestled close under his arm as they threaded the crooked, cobbled streets. In the Goose Gate he asked her if she should not go back, but she only laughed at him as they stepped out together into the moonlit fields. And a little later they were lying in the bracken under a gray beech, her cloak keeping the frost from both of them. Holding her, looking into her eager face that changed with the changing flow of the light and shadowy air, he thought how wonderful, how beautiful she was. Too wonderful to be any man's love! And she was his! And suddenly all the evening's burden of strangeness and confusion slid away from him like a wool sack lowered from the shoulder. Neal was a sly man with a courtier's tongue that fooled nobody, and John Mason could put up his manor wherever he wanted to, but he would have to do without any help from John Scarlock. He was staying here—to plow Old Thorny and to marry Joan. In loving her he did not love only a woman, a warm mouth and soft flesh moving sweetly beneath him in answer to the movement of his. He loved the ground, every lift and curve of it, and every tree in the wood, and every thorn by Gamwell Chase; and as he pressed closer to Joan, he pressed closer to the very heart of England, loving that, too. And oh, and oh, he loved being alive, being a man. Manhood was not to hoard like a silver porringer. It was to carry about you—like a good sword—

"Oh Joan! Such glory I had in loving . . . !"

She stirred against him with a little sigh. "Johnny—that book! It's hurting me again."

He wrenched all Thomas Tusser's printed wisdom out of his jacket and hurled it into a drift of dead leaves. Then he put his mouth back on hers and sank his fingers into the thick turf beneath her head. Nothing could keep him from glory now, no trouble gathering in the dark air and windless hazel trees, no destiny calling him off the farms of Nottingham. He held Joan, and he held England, and for one moment heaven touched earth as love came home to love.

2. There we take England

~~~~~~~~~~~~~~~~~~~~~~

FROM OLD THORNY

JOHN slept away that night in his narrow flock bed under the eaves at Old Thorny, restless with dreams that were almost too sweet for him to bear; and stumbling downstairs in the red daybreak, he cursed himself for being so slow to make up his mind, for not having brought Joan home half a year ago. His household was ahead of him at the board, Hob and Kit trying to tease the brindled mastiffs with a bone they'd already gutted the marrow from, but Watch ignored them, thumping his tail to welcome his master, and Warn, heavy with pups, drooped one wrinkled eyelid insolently toward the young fieldhands. Bet ladled up pease porridge at the fire, and Gilly, the dairymaid, handed round the bread and ale. John sat down at table's head, petted the dogs, and greeted everybody a little shortly, for he was still sleepy. He stared across the smoky hall at a rusted suit of armor collapsed on a hook against the stillroom door. He'd never known it moved, much less worn, but it seemed to belong there, like the bunches of dried herbs spraying down from the hewn rafters, the iron spit by the hearth, or the blue tapestry wall cloth his mother wove, and he guessed he'd leave it there for his time.

"Down in East Country they'll eat measled hogs," old Jankyn, the shepherd, was telling Rob, "though we won't here. If a hot wash don't better the beast, I'd kill him and sell him for Norfolk."

Rob shifted his creaking legs to the side of the bench away from the table and bent to cinch the leather band he always wore where the Spanish round shot had shattered his calf muscles. He straightened up, grunting.

"Don't know 'tis measled," he said. "Shouldn't be, for it's had plenty red ochre and no green acorns. Bet'll look at it this morning, and Bet'd cure death itself. It's a gift them has sometimes, who hasn't much else in life."

The three men turned silently to look at the woman, who was now swinging the crane from the fire and coming forward for her own meal. Bet had a skin like a last year's quince and a shape like a hop pole, a tongue sharp as old cider, but soft hands when the cows were calving. She kept the best kitchen garden in Thurgarton Hundred, but she couldn't keep her sweetheart, not after he'd got a look at that red-haired wench up in Papplewick who married him and then killed him, part with bad temper and part with bad cooking. Bet had taken service then with John's mother, who was just breeding him, and she'd been there ever since. "Promised Mis' Cecily on her death bed," she would sometimes boast wryly, "young master John'd never lack a hot dinner nor a clean shirtband. An' he hasn't, has he?"

Wonder how she'll take to Joan, he thought as he watched her. Two women between them could ruin any man's house if they had a mind to it.

Jankyn stood up, drying his beard on his sleeve. "The lads are spoke to go with me today, Johnny. We're scrouding brambles off Colwick sheep common, and all the farmers that use it be sending aid."

"I remember, man. Told you last week we'd plan on it. Past threshing and too soon to butcher; jakes and chimney's cleaned, and fresh straw all over. They'd go idle here."

"Done plowing?"

"All but headlands—which I can do—and that little field up the Chase."

"What are you going to seed it to, Johnny?" Rob wanted to know. "It's lain fallow two year."

"I know, but it's poor land. I think maybe drink corn."

Hob and Kit began to cheer. "Hurray for drink corn! What? Wheat in the house and no barley?"

"Come on, lads," growled Jankyn, "we'll be last men at Common." He shoved the oak door open and they followed him into the yard.

Rob got to his feet, then sat down again. John watched him anxiously. He knew how the leg pained the older man, but he knew it pained him worse to feel he was useless, to sit hunched in the kitchen while the work of the farm went on without him. "Look, Rob," he said, "take your time about it, but there's harness to mend in the barn if you can get down there."

"Now that I can do for ye, lad." Rob's face brightened and he fastened his jacket.

Bet climbed on a three-legged stool to hang the bacon flitch away. "Johnny," she said, "I think 'fore Gilly gets to churning we better have her take the hogs to the wood and let 'em get another bellyful of mast, if we're to slit their gullets next week. I'm going to gather sloes to dry against the flux—and look at that hog the pother's over."

"Sounds good sense. You folk could run Old Thorny without me sure."

"We could run heaven without God," she answered tartly, "but it wouldn't be the same. Gilly! Gone to put a ribbon in her hair, likely. Please the pigs, it will. Gilly! Here, you." She set a platter of broken meat between the dogs.

John stood up from the table, drew on his leather mittens, and went outdoors. As he stepped over the fieldstone sill, he felt a shudder go all through him, a shudder that did not come from the tang of the mild air. For a moment he thought he must be sick, and he had better go back and take a swallow of the brandy Squire sent around last year when his heir came of age. Then he shook his head. It'll wear off, he thought. He crossed the packed turf of the farmyard, scored with hoofs and hobnails, and stopped by the barn door to take a look at the weather. Gray sky, come soft and low enough to put your finger into, and after a red sunrise—that would mean rain before dark. A flight of rooks in caw went beating south over the Trent, and the sight of them, even the sight of the familiar plowland lying all about him, seemed to make him feel worse.

No man can tell, he thought, the last time he goes afoot across his threshold, the last kiss he gives his girl. He remembered young men's buryings he'd gone to. Jack Collin, a great runner, won the races on the Green at last year's Lammas, and Jack got a little cut at hogsticking that left him swollen, black, and dead within the week. Tom Hedges was touched with the sun last summer, haying in the nether field, and went to lie down in the shade, and never stood up again. And others, like Rob, you couldn't kill with a cannon ball. He, John, didn't really ail; his heart just seemed to be strange and wandering a little in its beat. He'd heard that could happen to a man because of trouble in love, but he had no trouble in love, for he loved Joan, and Joan was as certain to him as night and day. No. His sickness was something else. It couldn't be that talk he'd heard last night at the Bull's Head. It wasn't that.

He stepped into the barn through the slit door at the side, and stood a moment, smelling dung and clean clover hay, getting used to the dimness of it, the wooden arcs of the low bays, the full mows bulging overhead. Here waited the chain plow and the swing plow, the cradles, and scythes, and flails, all the useful friends he knew as well as the palm of his own hand that fitted to them. Jankyn's sheep shears and reddle and marking iron lay neatly on the bench under the high window. Trust Jankyn to leave everything right—not like the lads. Here they'd gone piling the hop poles on the threshing floor, when they ought to know enough to put them in the hovel by the barley ricks. He kicked the stripped rods with bits of dry vine still clinging to them, and walked on to Meg's stall in the third bay. All the other beasts were grazing, he'd kept her here for his purpose—but maybe he wouldn't plow the little field today, after all, maybe he'd just spade headland. He didn't know what he wanted to do. Meg whinnied, and he slapped her roan flank, but he went on past her, stepped around the wains, and took shovel and mattock.

Outside again, he turned between the helms full of sheaves for winter threshing and looked into the hog pen where Rob's sick beast lay. It didn't look so well, did it? No healthy creature'd lie in its own muck. Bet would probably know a dose for it. He walked on, up through the sloping crab orchard, and out on the open land beyond the trees. It was a little field, half blown-dust and half bramble roots, but it was the first field he'd ever set the plow to as a boy, and he loved it for that. It would never feed cattle or sheep, it would never grow good corn, but if he let it go fallow another year, more than Rob would ask where his wits were at. He stood there, in the red-brown, crumbled earth of it, with his back to Sherwood, and looked about him in the mild, gray air. Below him stood the house, red sandstone with thatch curved all over, like a beehive curving down; squat chimney, stemlike, in the middle; windows small and wide apart, framed with oak. East of it, and larger, loomed the stone barn and its cluster of ricks and hovels. He could see Bet in a blue cloak, peering into the hog pen. To the south lay the gardens: herbs, flowers, and kitchen plants, no blooms nor fruit now, all a welter of brown stalks and late leaves, red-purple, dull orange, and dark, undying green. And circling round three sides, east, south, and west, lay the fields—his fields—barley, pease, wheat, and fallow, bounded with quickset and holly hedge. Now what more could a man be after in this life, he thought, and as he thought it, a wind began to blow, a strong wind out of the west, that stirred no leaf in Gamwell Chase, no drift of smoke from the farmhouse chimney, but swept the man and left him shaking, like an aspen in a water meadow.

It was a wind that said come and not go, a wind that you knew had blown more than a thousand miles and tossed acres of thick boughs and salt washes of sea on its way to find you. It poured into you like the spring eagre pouring into Trent and gave your limbs at once a weakness and a strength they had never had before; sought out the soul wherever it hides in a man's body, and spoke to it with the voice of God. Not the prim, cadenced voice he uses to talk Latin in the churches, but the voice that speaks within a man when death moves on his household, or in the hour before the women call out to him to come and name his son. The voice, awful and mighty, yet with something of your father's voice in it. The voice that says, "This is as it shall be for you. There is no other way." And that is good, for it is doubt, not certainty, that confounds a man forever.

And part of the strength in the strange wind's blowing was this: that you knew, as well as if you could see the others, how you were not alone. How men all over England were shaken with the same wind, too, as it passed among the salt nets hung up in the Devon fishing towns, or crossed over the castled hills of the Welsh border, or swooped between the spires and tiled roofs by London Wall. A country squire, dwelling by Fleet Ditch midden and homesick for the Suffolk hedgerows felt it, and went home and sold land and made plans for shipping westward. A young wife by the reedy weirs in Lincoln felt it, and left off scribbling verses to pack her books and linen in chests that were said to be proof against sea water. The come-all wind from the great west blew on England, bare wold and market town, and cleft the generation that peopled it that autumn. Those who felt it were to go and those who did not were to stay, and there was no appeal from the doom of it. It blew strong and slow, as became a wind that had ten years blowing ahead of it. It struck John Scarlock, and stirred, and filled him, and raised him up, as high as a man can be raised on this earth without leaving it, and then it dropped him, like an empty haw, down on his knees on the thorny furrow.

After a few moments he climbed to his feet, awkward as Punch in the poppet show at Goose Fair, and plodded down the slope to the house, no purpose in his mind, only surprise at where his feet were taking him. The ground fell away below the east wall, and a little opening, just big enough for a man to crawl through, led into the root cellar. At the back of the root cellar, for safety, stood the great chest, and John found his fingers springing its catch in a way that none but the heir to the farm would know. First he drew out a smaller chest full of coins, and part of them he counted into his pockets, a part he put back. Then he took out a gray-yellow, crooked thing, the crumpled horn of a milch cow. He held it in his hand for a long moment. Then he dropped it back in the chest.

Inside the horn lay curled the parchment that said Old Thorny belonged to Scarlocks. John's father had been a little wandering in his Robin Hood stories, but he was sure enough of how the land had come to them. "We had it from Peverells, and they had it from Doomsday Book. Earl William gave it to the Scarlock of his time because of the young wife he had. . . ."

"Needn't tell any more," John had cried in disgust, and begun to whistle, "Cuckholds all a-row."

"Shut your noise, boy. 'Twasn't like that at all. Earl William's wife were a poor creature with a sickly heir at the breast she couldn't feed. But Scarlock's wife took it and fed it—no lack o' milk there. So we'd the choice of Colwick farms to pay for it—for the rent of twelve drops of woman's milk a year."

"How do you go about paying that?"

"You don't, now. Been no one to pay it to, more years than I ever heard of. Sometimes I think what if some coxcomb should come by and say he was Peverell and claim all the years' back rent. 'Twould keep a deal of wenches working."

The memory brought a smile over the set mask of John's face. He shut the parchment back in the chest and crawled out of the cellar, easing his heavy pockets through the gap. Whatever he came by in New Hampshire he'd have to take for himself. Papers from Doomsday Book wouldn't help him there.

Bet and Rob stood by the hog pen as he came up to them. He could think now, not of what he had to do, but of how he must go about doing it.

"Oh—er—Rob," he said, clearing his throat. "I got to go away from here for a while—I guess."

Rob looked at him, a groove in his russet forehead, his gentle brown eyes blinking soberly. Bet stood still as a hitching post.

"What for, Johnny? Running from trouble?"

"No. Not that. Running *to* trouble, more like."

"Not like I done? You don't mean the war's gone wrong? Be them Spanish bastards off the Hoe again?"

John looked down into the pen. The hog was on its feet, he noticed, gnawing a fat, yellow root, probably Bet's medicine. He'd never know now whether it got well or not. He'd not have to worry about how to plant the little field.

"No. Not a war. I don't know why I'm going . . . except I have to."

"I know." Rob spat into the straw between his bulbous feet. "Same as I felt when Frobisher come by. He'd been up north to Finningly where he bought land after, and he stopped in the Bull's Head at supper time. It was a better house then, with none of the knaves Jack Gambrell has there. I'd gone in town for a mug of ale, but you couldn't sit an' keep on drinking once you'd listened to him— not if you was six feet of muscle, like you be now and I was then. Well, I listened, and I was back—a cripple on Old Thorny within the year. He said the dons had took to sea and was going to make war on England, mostly on the forests of her, because that's where the ship timber came from, and if there ever was one thing could make a don cry out for Christsake and a hail to Mary, 'twas an English ship with English men aboard her. He said they meant to burn our woods down and Dean was to be first. I thought quick of Sherwood, and if the others go, why what's to save it? Trees there grew out of the same land as I did. Times I'd gone among 'em and put out my hand to the bark, and felt it like another hand to mine. And ships, and ships, and ships, has sailed out of Sherwood. Half of her's gone to sea and rotted there!" His tone changed sharply. "But that was in my time, and my time's done. Where be ye going, lad?"

"New Hampshire."

"You mean Hampshire down on the Channel?"

"No. Not there. In the plantations."

"Ye better stay home."

"I know I better, but I'm not going to. Listen. I took fourth part of what was in the chest. Half part is for you and the land."

23

"And t'other fourth?"

"T'other fourth's for Joan Sweetapple at the Bull's Head . . . when she comes to you and says she wants it."

"Oh, no! Pay off your tavern wench yourself, Johnny."

"You're down the wrong furrow, Rob. I mean to marry her, and if she has a child it's mine and you're to treat it so."

"You're wise to know so much."

"And as soon as I can I'll send for her."

"You're going to settle there? Then what's for an heir to Old Thorny?"

The two men looked at each other, brown, lean-jawed, heavy-browed. John saw the scrolling lines in the old face, and for every line there he knew there would be one in his own some day . . . if he lived long enough. He spoke with a good cheer he did not feel.

"Don't worry, Rob. The land'll raise one up. It never failed us yet. I'll have boys aplenty, and I'll send you one of them."

Their hands gripped, then fell apart.

"Good-bye, man."

"Good-bye."

John looked once up the Chase, at the tangling thickets and high wood beyond. Now he would never meet Old Will under the gnarled boughs in timeless moonlight. He did not look at the house and fields, nor at Rob and Bet. He squared his shoulders and walked off toward Nottingham.

The old pair looked after him.

"I was to sea once," said Robin sadly. "I sailed with Frobisher . . ."

"Yes," answered Bet, "so I ha' heard."

"And there I met with a Swedish sailorman, white-haired and thick, weaned on salt water. He used to tell about small beasts he knew at home, like rats, they were. 'Lemons,' I think was the name."

" 'Lemons' is yellow quinces like that grows among the heathen. You can buy them in Thursday Market."

"You have got the name wrong, woman, but no matter. Anyways, these beasts live in the uplands, and now and then they come to-gether, thousands of 'em, and run full cry down valleys and town-lands like a hunt going over. Walls, an' cities, an' men can't stop 'em, till they've done what they're supposed to do, and that's to plunge into salt sea an' die. The why of it's only because they has to. Seems like Johnny's gone the way them creatures go."

"He'll not be back," said Bet. "I know—none better—the look in a man's eyes when he's not coming back. Oh, Rob, let's go and see if there's help in Squire's brandy."

He turned to look at her and saw with surprise that tears were running down her face like rain down the bole of a gnarled apple tree in the spring. He cleared his own throat harshly, guiding her back across the yard. The cowshed door flapped in the risen wind. Suddenly, inside the house, the great throats of Watch and Warn lifted up their ancient note of wailing for the dead.

FROM BREW HOUSE YARD

Joan's eyes burned dark with horror and she clenched her brown hands together, crushing the mopcloth between them till stale foam oozed out of it and dripped down her crimson skirt that she was usually so careful of. The reek of malt suddenly sickened her as it never had before. Aside a little, Walter Neal stood by, smiling, not cruel, not the man to delay himself too long for a barmaid's sorrow.

"Johnny," she said very low and quiet, "I—I didn't think you'd go away from me."

John heaved his shoulders restlessly. He knew she did not understand, and he could not explain all that had happened to him since this time yesterday, for he did not understand it himself. Maybe he never would. "Sherwood's a field coppice beside the woods I'm going to," Walter Neal had said, and he knew that he wanted to stand under those great trees and wonder at them. He had looked around Old Thorny and seen it was good, and maybe when a man sees he has shaped one thing well he feels bound to shape another like it. Maybe what he really wanted was to make all that wild riverside, Piscataqua, as tame and blooming as Trent valley. He would be inquiring into his reasons all the rest of his life, probably. And one thing he could never tell her, Joan, who believed only in the colors her quick eyes could see, in the substance of oak, and wool, and living flesh that she could put sure fingers on. She could never understand a blowing wind that did not rattle dead leaves or bend the chimney smoke. Such winds never blew on Joan. But what should he say to her? He remembered Ned Trigg's urging. If she were Ned's daughter, she might see Ned's reasons.

"We'll have a manor, Joan," he said, feeling soiled and mean, knowing he did not want a manor.

She did not look at him, not daring to. "Old Thorny were good

25

enough for a workhouse girl," she said. There were matters she'd not be the one to speak of: love, and promises, and their holly wedding last night under the beech tree. She would jump through a hoop if he held it. She would never chide him or tell him what to do. But she could not understand.

He put his hands in his pockets and shrugged his shoulders. All right, if she felt like that. It would be a long time before he could talk to her again about it, not till he had her at home abed in the house he'd build by Piscataqua—a house to look like Old Thorny.

"I'm going, anyway. Half of what's mine I left with Rob, and he knows it's for you when you want it. And you'll be coming to me."

"Will I?"

"Did I ever lie to you?"

His gaze went into hers, speaking with such deep intimacy that she had to accept and believe. "Yes . . . we'll be together again . . . in good time . . . but no more now for a while. I promise you we shall be together. Parson in church may lie to you; maybe stars at night over Gamwell Chase will lie. But you can believe me when I tell you this."

"Go on, then, Johnny," she said, twisting her mopcloth. "I'll be here when you want me."

John took a step toward her, then drew back and turned to Walter Neal.

"So . . . now?" he said.

Neal smiled and motioned to the open door.

The two men stepped out of the Bull's Head into the street. Joan sank down on the settle and put her head in her lap. First their voices died away beyond the bow window, then the beat of hoofs rang fainter and fainter, dying too. A thin, seeping rain began to fall on Brew House Yard, where it seemed to her the sun would never shine again.

As John rode with Captain Neal over the brick causeway that spanned the crocus meadows reaching south to Trent, he did not look back, but the captain turned somberly. He saw the ramparts of the old town that remembered the Danes and Lion Heart, and the square castle and spired churches where a doughty sheriff must have worshiped before he went off to Sherwood to do his duty and be carried home with a cracked pate. The man beside him belonged to all that, and it belonged to him, safe and sure in possession. Then he thought about a slate-colored, houseless coast, dripping and low in the water; of salt swamp rimmed with hemlock trees, thrusting their gaunt roots like the feet of old men into tidal mud; of black-green wood stretching under the northern lights, unbounded and alien, full of unknown terror. And worst of all, in that country, when a man's spirit in extremity cried out for the comforting presences of the well-remembered dead, it would cry in vain.

"John," he said impulsively to the man riding beside him, " 'fore God, I think you better go back. 'Fore God, I think it's not fit for me to meddle so far with a man's destiny."

John rode with his head down, but his low answer carried. "If it hadn't been you, it would have been another," he said soberly. "I was meant to go."

But Walter Neal shook his head. He often boasted that he had never believed in God after the bloody welter of his first battle, but he had been a child in the old faith. He made the sign of the Cross and muttered to the rainy wind, "Mary forgive me . . . now and at the hour of my death."

FROM PORTSMOUTH IN HAMPSHIRE

John Mason, the portly merchant, sat back from his writing table and smiled as he poured out two glasses of choice Madeira. He was a man of achievement; he had been governor of Newfoundland, and he had written a sonnet, the one readily and well, the other with much labor. Not old, but old enough to sit peacefully in a warm room and plan adventures for other men, he settled back on the turkey cushions and gave his attention to his companion, who was reading aloud from a legal paper. December twilight thickened beyond the panes, blurring the gables across Portsmouth high street, and a maidservant moved in the room now, lighting up the silver sconces. Fire crackled on the hearth, and a tortoise-colored cat padded down the crimson carpet, rubbing against Mason's velvet knee and croaking softly. Up the stairwell drifted the thin, uncertain music his wife, Ann, was learning to make on her new virginals.

"What was that again, Walter? It sounded so fine. Let me hear it over."

Walter Neal turned back a page and read, skipping and choosing. " 'The Laconia Company . . . one body corporate and perpetual. Soil, ground, havens, ports, rivers, royal mines of gold and silver, pearls, precious stones, woods, quarries, marshes, waters, fishings, huntings, hawkings, fowlings, commodities, hereditaments, together with all prerogatives, jurisdictions, royalties, privileges, franchises and prehiminences . . . to Captain John Mason and his heirs and assigns . . . now and forever . . . to be governed as he sees fit. . . .' "

Mason took another swallow of wine. "Fine—again! And the limits to my power?"

Neal looked down mockingly at the page before him.

"You must govern according to the known laws of England."

"Well, I don't know of better ones. Ordered Newfoundland like that and made money. Anything else?"

"You can't give it away to any foreign prince."

Both men laughed. Neal reached for his glass. As he looked into the merchant's face, the pleasant fatuousness dropped away from it, like a mask laid aside, and a young man eyed him back again, sharp, keen, honest.

"All right, Walter. So much for precious stones and hereditaments. Now what's really there?"

"I've never seen it, sir."

"I know you haven't, but you're thicker than three abed with one who has. What does your friend John Smith tell you?"

"He says in his book that there is good land behind the crags." John Mason poured out more Madeira.

"Never mind his book, or his map either. What does he say of it over a glass?"

"Says the time of year makes a difference on it. Cherries may grow in Kent, but you'll find none there at Christmas."

"Can't you speak plainer than with proverbs, Walter?"

"He said he'd promise no gold mines."

"Or leave a kiss within the cup . . ."

chimed a girl's voice at the virginals, high and clear. Mason's eyes lighted. He'd forgotten his married daughter Tufton was coming for supper. Then he turned back to his captain.

"What else? Devil, it's like drawing your teeth, man."

All right, thought Neal, let him have it. Let him take his money out if he wants to. There'll always be wars abroad I can get my bread by. He lowered his empty glass to the carved stand at his elbow and fixed his eyes on a tapestry against the far wall.

"He said he had seen land more fertile, but it will nourish man.

He also said he never got a shilling out of it but what cost him a pound, and for himself he wouldn't own a foot of it."

Somewhere in the house supper was cooking. Neal could smell the fragrance of roast goose and herbs he did not know names for. The virginals were still.

Mason spoke broodingly. "All that means is this: we must put away fine schemes for my province of New Hampshire. It will not be a Spanish Potosi flowing silver. But I want my manor there—a hall built and fields cleared. And I want what the other adventurers want—my money back and more. Fish and furs should do it, and we look to you to find the Laconia Country within the year and start running the beaver off the great lakes there."

"I wish I could get you to think about ship timber."

"You've been Bedlam-mad about trees ever since the King let you go into the New Forest and sell off those rotted oaks to pay your company. I doubt we can better Riga fir anyway. No, it's the cod and the beaver I look to for our return from there."

"And those vineyards you were talking about last time I was here?"

"Now I'm not so sure about the vineyards as I was. I thought to plant both black and white muscadine, but John Scarlock says it's scarce warm enough for them in England, and—he's not so chary with truth as you are, Walter—he says he hears it about the docks that all America's a frozen swamp."

Walter Neal smiled and his eyes glowed deeply.

"So you're listening to John Scarlock now? I told you he was a lad to watch."

"I don't know that I grant you that. He's useful in stocking the ship, and he has that about him that should you put him down on a bare rock he'd be able to scratch a living there—but so would most yeomen. I do not find him so out of common. Couldn't go from here to shire's edge without meeting twenty like him."

"Nor could you. That's the glory of him, sir, and the glory of King's England—the men who are not out of common. Why, I could go out on the downs and pick up a lump of sod, frozen over for winter now, but all alive with roots and quick to come again in March—furze, gorse, rosemary, what you will—pick it up and carry it across the sea and set it into the shale and clay between the great pines of Piscataqua. It would be a richer land for putting the old and the new together."

"That I see, but damme if I see the point you're making."

"The point's John Scarlock. Wherever we take him, there we take England. There we take a great, solid, root-gnarly lump of English earth to build into our new country. Do you see it now? I treasure him for all that he is and the wise use we can put him to."

"There we take England," mused John Mason into his ruddy glass. "Yes. We take all you say when we take John. But we take something else you have not reckoned with. Something that I am not sure of. Will he always yield kindly to our wise use, do you think?"

Wind blew up from the freezing harbor, rattled at the casements.

"Last night I had a dream, and in it I was stone-blind. Stone-blind, and made to sit and sign my name forever on leaves I could not read!"

Neal drew down the corners of his mouth. "I would not like to dream that," he said.

"But I think now that perhaps it was less a dream than truth. We set our names at the bottom of all kinds of high schemes without ever knowing quite what they'll come to, or what will come of them that can change the world. In my dream I was afraid, Walter."

Neal made no answer, and after a moment his host stood up. "There'll be supper downstairs," he said, and then added, staring into the lighted gables across the street, "Well, come March or April, the ship'll be ready for you, and the goods, and the men. Take England, if you will. You can't very well go without her, since there's something in every man of the land where he was bred, more in some than in others. But know what it is you're taking. I love it too, but it's a stubborn country, bitter and unruly, and its course you cannot always predict. If you doubt my word, go up to Whitehall, and ask King Charles about it."

3. The Book of Joan

I was Joan," she thought, telling herself a little running story, half past, half future, to comfort her, as she huddled on a heap of dirty linen and tried to forget the icy rain tapping on the deck overhead. "Always Joan, because I had no right to any other name. And I lived in St. Nicholas' workhouse behind the broken hedges, where the old men drooled, and the old women scolded, and the young, swollen girls were always weeping. I lived there till I was tall enough to carry round ale in Jack Gambrell's tavern, and then one day a man came there whose name was Johnny, and when I looked at him I knew the why of everything. And Johnny and I were married and had a fine house and many children, and lived together all our lives, and died together one night in our sleep when we were old. But once I did a fearsome thing, a thing to make you tremble and take the breath out of your body. *I came all alone across the great sea.* Only once in my life did I do anything like that, high and awful."

She had not been at all afraid when she set out from Nottingham on a rainy day, just like the day Johnny had left her, all Trent valley dank with mist and the coach wheels spinning in the blue, greasy clay of the London Road. She had not been afraid when they passed Land's End and the scent of burning gorse died away on the wind behind them. Not when the *Pied Cow,* a small but ungainly ship, lumbered across the path of an autumn hurricane, not when her bedmate broke out with the running sores of smallpox, not when the crew got drunk and roared through the women's cabin had she been afraid. But it would all be over in a few hours, and she was wondrous afraid of it now.

She shivered and drew closer to Alice Goble, who lay burrowed in the quilts beside her. Alice moaned a little.

"Oh . . . ! Did I hurt you, or have you got the pains again? Mistress Catherine says her brother Fernald will know what to do for them when we get to the shore. He was a ship's surgeon in the King's Fleet, she says."

Alice, still bearing in her body the wounds of childbirth made months before, smiled wanly in the dim light that sifted through the cracks in the planking over them.

"I doubt he saw much of my trouble in the King's Fleet," she said.

She looked at the girl beside her, then at her own baby daughter asleep on a soiled blanket across her knees. Some day they would know what troubled her now, the awful deathlessness of being a woman: how love, and hard work, and childbearing drained the life out of you, till you'd think after a while it would be done, and there'd be an end of it, but no—more life kept coming in you to pour away. She clasped and unclasped her wasted hands, drew her breath shrill and quick.

"Or are you grieving for Adam?" asked Joan, trying to be wise and comforting.

For Adam Goble, master carpenter of Cripplegate Ward by London Wall, had died at sea, and gone down, sewn up in sailcloth with two charges of round shot, somewhere between here and there— somewhere about forty-five degrees north latitude, Captain Stephenson said, after he'd finished reading the Prayer Book, and two half-drunk sailors had bundled the poor corpse over the side. Oh, your man need not be buried with kings in an abbey—if he's laid at St. Mildred's, Bread Street, or Allhallows, Staining, or Michael's in Cornhill, or Martin's-in-the-fields, you can go and sit by him of a summer evening, when all London's abroad in the streets and the grassy spots for air. Even if he's laid with his own folk by the church in the little country town he came from, you can go there once a year with a decent nosegay in your hand. But how can you go back through all that heaving water and seek for a soul that's laid down at forty-five degrees north latitude?

With a sudden impatient need to escape from her sorrowful destiny and the ills of her body, Alice struggled to her feet. There was not enough room between the deck and the rocking floor for her to stand upright, so she sank back again, but her movements had awakened the child, who began to wail dismally.

"Hush, Bessie, love," said Joan, lifting it in her slim, strong arms. "I can't suckle you, but I'll get you some broth maybe."

Walking with her head bent low under the worm-eaten timbers, she stepped into a larger cabin where half a dozen women were gathered around an iron pot of coals trying to warm themselves. Mistress Catherine Warburton, eighteen years old, come of a noble family somewhere in the west country, was just lifting a brass piggin of stew from its nest in the heart of the pot. Shaking her head at the odor rising from it, she turned to Joan.

"We'd best not go about the ship, Captain Stephenson says, for the men have been at the strong waters again. He tries to govern them, but there's more drunk than sober, for they're as glad as we to see land. How is Alice?"

Catherine was lovely, Joan thought, for all the dark waxiness under her blue eyes, the tiny salt sores on her lips, and the stains on her rich velvet.

"Not well. What's to become of her when we get to the shore, mistress?"

Joan looked at the other women, goodwives all of them, and older, worn and bedraggled from weeks of sickness and fright and bad food and no way to wash themselves, but lighted inside, somehow, like candles glowing behind the rood screen in the great London church she had gone to just before they sailed from Gravesend. By sunset they would be with the men they loved, just as she would be with Johnny, and she knew that she was glowing, too. Only Catherine, spoiled with too many suitors to give her heart to any, had come out of England a free woman.

"When we get Alice to the shore," she said, answering Joan's question, "the first thing is to cure her body. My sister's husband will know how. He comes of men who were great doctors in the French court, and healing's a magic in his family these two hundred years, Joanna says . . . whether it's for broken soldiers or barren queens. And Sarah told me that once she can get to her herbs that are stored so deep in the hold, she has a healing potion, too. Didn't you, Sarah?"

Sarah Scriggins, ruddy, square-built, near forty years old, with a

33

bit of a beard, smacked her lips over a strip of rusty bacon she had just fished out of the rank-smelling stewpot.

"I was brought up in the house of Prue Trot—best midwife in Essex. Saw my first birth when I was eight, and swore then that if that was the way it was, for myself I'd have none of it. Nor did I ever, for all my three husbands. Yes, I know a thing or two, though I wasn't with the King's Fleet. I'll fix the lass up and then we'll get her married—awwwwwk!"

She thrust her thick hand into her bosom, pulled out a flea, and cracked it between blackened nails. "Take that, you bloody devil!" she said.

Over their heads the hatch opened to let in a burst of sleet and a tipsy shouting. Then Captain Stephenson scrambled down the ladder, his kind face red and bluff from forty years of facing into the sea wind, salt caked and frozen in his eyebrows.

"Never saw a coast come at you out of the fog like this one does," he said, pleased that the voyage was so near done, with little sickness, only one death, and no harm to any man's goods. "Never sighted the fishing isles, though we're in past them. Yonder's the true coast, and we'll be up the river's mouth within an hour. Anybody want to see it?"

"I do," said Joan.

"I do," said Alice Goble weakly from the arch between the cabins. Everyone turned to look at her, gaunt and swaying, her great eyes agleam.

"Adam, my husband, said it would be a fair land, a green country, and I should grow well there. I shall look at it for him."

"Put blankets round ye then," said Captain Stephenson roughly. "Rain's let up but it's not over, and like to turn to snow 'fore night."

"We three will go," said Catherine Warburton, shaking out a robe from which the vermin dropped and darted. "Joan, you wrap up too. You may be a bride before sunset, and we don't want you sneezing at the altar."

If they have an altar, thought Joan, as she handed Bessie over to Sarah and drew the rough wool shawlwise about herself. Johnny's letter had talked of building "fishing flakes" and "salt pans." It hadn't said anything about churches.

They had not been on deck since the winter storms began on the night December came in, and the salt air tasted fresh and clean to them after the cabin stenches of illness, unwashed flesh, and caged animals. Helping Alice between them, they crawled through the hatchway and tried to get a foothold in the freezing slush that covered the splintery planks. The wet canvas of sails bellied and strained above them and falling sleet stung their faces. Clinging to the side of the ship, they straggled forward, soiled, musty skirts flapping, their hair whipped before their eyes. Shouting sailors ran everywhere at once, and from the roofed pen in the stern came the squawks of hens and the sad roar of the great yellow Danish bull Captain Mason was sending over to serve the cows already stocking his manor. Midway of the *Pied Cow,* and beside a hatch leading down to the hold, stood John Raymond, the purser, his black beard blown out like a pennant, his voice hoarse as he read from the paper in his hands the list of supplies that he was bound to deliver to Captain Neal, and listened for the voice of the sailor below, assuring him that they were there.

"Seven hogsheads of beef . . . eight firkins of butter . . . a box of cheeses—be the cheeses there, Davy?—four flock beds . . . lead and shot . . . cod lines and fish hooks . . . spices and mustard seed . . . twenty-two bushels, three pecks oatmeal—it's a poor country that can't grow its own victuals—four polaines for shallop sails. . . ."

Past John Raymond they edged, and huddled finally in the prow, Joan Sweetapple, workhouse girl, Catherine Warburton, lady, Alice Goble, carpenter's widow, their arms about each other, not only for warmth, because this was a time they wanted to share, even to the touch of the body, this first look at the new country that was to be their home and their children's home so long as the blood lasted.

Stephenson stopped beside them for a moment, pointing.

"Straight ahead," he said. "It'll look out through the fog about there."

The wind quickened, and the mist broke into long, crooked strands that drifted apart from each other till between them you could see the dark gray water before the ship, and straight overhead the white-gray sky with the cold rain coming down. Now you could see more and more gray sea, the fog massing into gray-purple clouds on the right, thinning always on the left. Now a hard, white line sparkled where the fog was thin. The captain passed again and pointed to it.

"That's Rye Sand," he said.

"Rye?"

"After Sussex coast. It's the way to name everything here for something at home."

"Why?"

"You'll come to know," he muttered, his voice harsh with pity.

"But 'Piscataqua'? That's not an English name."

"No. That's Indian tongue. It means 'Rivers Parting.'"

"Oh . . ."

Now straight ahead of them loomed a dark mass like a low hill in the water, turning from black to green as they sailed closer in, and they could see it was an island, covered all down to the sea edge with huge evergreens gnarled like monsters, growing out of slippery slate-colored rock, every twig adrip with sleet, the wynds and lanes between them drifted with snow. Now came a scatter of little islands, all bare, without leaf or stem except a beaten-down, yellow cover that might be sodden grass. There was nothing to say. Nothing. You waited, hoping that something better would lie around the next curve of shore.

And then suddenly they were not in the wide sea any longer, but in a broad stream draining down through wind-lashed forest—and all the world was gray, sucking water, and black trees, and white sky pouring down rain. Not a roof, not a spire, not so much as a cleared field or a shaft of chimneysmoke. A country that God might have made in a bad mood on a winter day, and then left lying here at the end of the world where no one was likely to find it.

"Well," said the captain, "here we are. Not much like Gravesend, is it?"

"But how far is it to the town and the houses?" asked Catherine, her voice sharp with anxiety, "and Captain Mason's manor?"

"That's Mason's manor," said Stephenson bluntly, flicking his thumb toward the wall of spruce and hemlock crowding, implacable, on the western bank. "There's no town yet. Only the stone house at Pannaway, set on the point where gales keep taking the roof off, and a few pole and thatch huts where the men sleep, and the Great House where I'm taking you."

"Is that . . . all?"

"All but the fishing flakes and the salt pans, my lady."

Joan looked down into the stream of liquid gray ice slipping past them into the open sea. She hated the river suddenly, the flow of it, full and malignant as a great serpent, relentless as time, flooding out of unknown darkness, powerful to sweep everything on its bland surface into an unfathomed doom. She was to hate it every day of her life and never to live a day without seeing it, but this curse had not come upon her yet, and she shrugged her shoulders and shivered, and began to watch the beaches of broken rock with eagerness, for Johnny was sure to be somewhere along them. Hadn't he written for her to come?

Catherine's look was one of bleakness and effrontery. She had wanted to come to her sister because she was lonely for someone of her own blood, but why hadn't Joanna written her how it really was? It would have been better to have married the worst of her suitors, bald Sir Roderick, with his Kentish manor and family ghost, and the tumbling, carrot-haired children he had fathered on an Irish house-maid. Almost better . . . she wasn't sure.

But Alice felt her limbs dissolve in the final terror. This was no bountiful, kind country, where a sick woman could grow well, and a baby girl tall and comely. This was a tangle of hard roots, and black, broken crags, washed by bitter salt water, and to take it, a man or a woman would need not only a strong body and fearless heart, but he would need laughter. There was no laughter or fear-lessness left in her. But oh, the long way back—and London without Adam Goble!

"Is this—what it is?" she asked, faltering.

"I—I'm afraid so, lass," muttered Will Stephenson.

Alice looked at the New World silently and well. The sleet nagged at her forehead. She felt the drip of her own warm blood from her unhealing flesh. She shut her mouth tightly, then opened it a last time. "Joan, you look to Bessie," she said. And then she was over the side like a sea trout, caught, but escaping, flashing back from the deck into the misty element that bred it. The sucking tide caught her. The trailing, purple-brown kelp reached up. It was the mortal end of Alice Goble.

And that was how it happened that when John Scarlock carried his bride up the shaly beach at Strawberry Bank, three cold nights be-fore Christmas, in God's year 1631, she had a child in her arms that was no blood of theirs.

Not that they could have been alone then, even without poor Bessie Goble, who lay amiably in her drowned mother's shawl, and smiled, and slept, and bothered nobody much. For the word that a ship was in, a ship from home, had brought men, and women, too, though fewer, scurrying out of the thick trees and down the frozen hillside, like ants that swarm to a dropped cell of honeycomb. They thronged the waterside in the bitter twilight, where great soft snowflakes were falling with a hiss into the black river. Their lanthorns bobbed excitedly about, and their eager voices rose above the low, sucking sound of the swollen current, above the grating of rowlocks that brought the shallops in from the *Pied Cow*. Walter Neal stood in their midst, his velvets tattered, but the fire undimmed behind his dark eyes. His words were all for John Raymond the purser with his list of foodstuffs, but his glances followed Catherine Warburton, as a short, swarthy man with a crooked nose and a furred cloak, her brother-in-law Renald Fernald, the great doctor, stepped out to help her ashore. Just behind him stood a woman, older than Catherine, but with the same blue eyes and calm beauty; and then he came back to the shallop and set Joan ashore too, and Catherine was presenting her to them —"My friend, Joan Sweetapple." (She did not say, "Joan, the bastard barmaid from St. Nicholas' workhouse." She said, "My friend . . .") They could never have been friends at home, but here in the new country—where nobody knew what she was unless she told them herself, where a man could set his own value, and so long as he wore it well it would pass. . . . And then she looked past the Fernalds and saw Johnny.

He strode toward her in the light of the weaving lanthorns, and it was surely he, but it seemed to her as if the eyes and the faded green coat were the only things about him she had ever seen before. His face was sharper and browner, and lines had written what he was all the more plainly upon it. He would never again, she thought, look quite like the other lads leaning against the wall of Jack Gambrell's tavern on a summer night, lads who were like to each other as the blades of grass, or trees in Gamwell Chase, young, smooth trees. He was like the thorny, the writhen tree in the field alone, that faces its own destiny beyond the shelter of its kind. There was a wary quickness about the way he moved, a quickness which she could not know a man must learn if he were to stay alive in the forest and kill before the other. There was love in his face, but there was an unyielding look, too, that was strange to her. He would never again be a laughing boy she could kiss carelessly in the hedgerows. "I am John Scarlock," his look said. "Take me or leave me—this is what I am."

He came up and put his hands on her shoulders, and neither of them said anything.

Oh, Joan, he was thinking. Here in all the hemlock and spruce and pinewood, you are still the holly tree, and that's the strongest tree in England. This country will not take *you*. You will always be home to me. Fast as I clear an acre you will set primrose in with all the pumpkins and Indian corn. Oh, Joan . . .

"You came," he said finally, clearing his throat.

"Yes," said Joan. "I said I would."

And then Catherine and the Fernalds and Walter Neal were all around them, saying they would go to the Great House where there was supper and a fire. Sarah and her husband, as thick and ruddy as she was, their arms around each other's waists, stopped and said it was Joan's turn to take Bessie, and then she had to tell John all about the child and the way of Alice's going.

"So I shall bring her up in our house, John, and she will grow with our children."

John smiled. "When we have a house," he said. "Next summer, maybe. I've cleared land for it. But we'll sleep at Humphrey Chadbourne's this winter. He's built well. Let me carry you. The field's rough."

"What field?" laughed Joan, her voice shaking with delight, feeling herself lifted in his arms. For the hill they were climbing, though bare of trees, was all tough, frozen sod, scattered over with sharp, yellow stumps that thrust out every foot or so.

"Oh, well. It will be a field. Here we are."

Through the darkness Joan could see only that the house was square, with thick board walls and a peaked roof. Oiled paper covered the spaces that were designed to hold swinging casements, and they could hear a great crackle of burning logs and branches the moment Neal opened the rude door. Once inside, John eased her down on a bench covered with a litter of sweet, crisp boughs, and she laid Bessie down at the side and tried to look around her and keep her place in what was going on. But the room was all bright and shadowy with pine torches, and fire roaring up the sallow clay chimney, and there were so many people's names flung at her—Ambrose and Beck Gibbons, and their child, little Beck; Thomas and Ann Warnerton; Francis Williams and Mrs. Helen; Roger Knight, Edward Godfrie, Sampson Lane—too many men to remember—all rough clothes, and kindly faces weathered by cold and wind, a colder wind than ever blew in Nottingham.

Boards on trestles down the middle of the room held a number of smoking clay pots, and Johnny left her to go there and come back with a wooden tray heaped with hot meat and a queer brownish loaf.

He broke the food with his hunting knife, and they dipped their fingers in.

"Hmmm. What's this?"

"That? It's good venison."

"It's not like venison at home."

"Nothing here's like anything at home."

Joan looked at him candidly. "I am," she said.

"Yes," he answered slowly, "yes. I think you are. And so am I— about one thing."

"I hope—"

"I know!"

They ate silently for a few minutes. Everyone knew their relationship and had the homely grace to leave them alone. And there were other reunited couples. Humphrey Chadbourne, who had built the Great House to John Mason's order, scratched his bald head and turned to Neal across a full ale mug.

"Governor," he said, "can we find corners enough for everybody to kiss in?"

"So long as you find a corner for me," retorted Neal, his eyes following pretty Catherine where she spread her skirts to the blue-green-orange flames, "devil take the others!"

"Well, devil won't take them. They'll come to me and ask the score. The sailors are bringing up four flock beds though. That'll help."

"Good. John Scarlock's to have one of them. John's my man out of England and always was."

Chadbourne's brows knit. "Not that I'm a praying man from Massachusetts, but . . . I'm not keeping a Merry Mount either. Is he married to the wench?"

"He will be," said Walter Neal, grinning, "hard and fast before bedtime. I've the Prayer Book in my pocket, and the power to read it over them—or we'll say I have, since no other man has."

His glance roved across the room where Catherine settled herself gracefully in a chair carved in the days of the old Queen, the only decent English chair in the colony, and belonging to Fernald. "Now *that—!*" he said.

"*That,*" said Humphrey Chadbourne, "doesn't kiss in corners."

"Wager it won't?"

"No. Not a ha'penny on any woman's honor. Workhouse gets filled that way. But speaking of Massachusetts, what's to pay upriver?"

Neal's brows drew together, but he made no other sign. "Upriver?

40

We know this: that Massachusetts is scheming to take over all Piscataqua Country and set it praying; that they've sent Tom Wiggin there to stand for certain merchants of Bristol and Shrewsbury who hope to steal from us—John Winthrop's friends."

"Wiggin? Oh yes, I know who you mean. I never heard him called 'Tom' before."

"No, that's the chief trouble with him. Nobody ever called him Tom. Tom's not a stiff-necked name. Church of England and honest fishing and fur trade's not good enough for folk at the Bay, and they don't mean it shall be good enough for us, either."

"We didn't come here to pray. We came here to take up land and get money."

"I know, and we'll fight them. Governor Winthrop loves us like the beaver loves the willow, which is to say he'd eat our flesh. But John Mason can cut his throat at Whitehall, and he knows it, so he won't dare too far. He's a mean devil, for all his psalm-singing."

"Psalm-singing can prove a man's godly. It don't prove you'd do well to trust him."

"No. It's a rare strange thing, but all the good lads I know are better at cursing. Well, don't worry, Humphrey." His fingers moved deliberately along his scabbard.

"Think it might come to that?"

"No. But if it does . . ."

They looked at each other a long moment, with agreement and understanding.

In their corner of boughs with the sleeping child between them, John talked to Joan.

"What's in Nottingham?"

She thought for a long time. "Jack's the same, and Ned. Moll Doubleday's with child by God knows who. They're fixing the cobbles in Narrow March, and there was a fire in the Goose Gate— some tanner's shop, I think. It's been a rainy summer and corn's dear. Nothing much."

"You saw Rob?"

"Yes, of course. When your letter came I was—"

"I know. Let me tell you. You were drawing ale."

"I was. For Jack. We were alone, just at noon. The men were all in the fields—"

"I know. It must have been about gelding time; scrouging out brambles and barberry roots; getting in brake to bed the cattle."

41

"That's out of your book! You're dripping with it still! You haven't forgotten."

"No. You didn't think to bring it, did you, Joan? I came away without it. The weathers here are not Old Tusser's weathers, but still—he's a wise man, any season."

"I did. It's wrapped in my red skirt in a little chest in the *Pied Cow*."

His smile almost dissolved her, made her voice higher and quicker. "When Jack read your letter to me, I put off my apron and walked out of there. I meant to go back and say good-bye and take my wages—but I never did. I started for Old Thorny to get the money to come here, and on the way I met your cousin."

"Where?" He wanted to think of that countryside, to hear its names and description.

"By the sandstone spring under the hazels. First he asked for you and read the letter. Then we started for the house, and as we walked he told me—"

"—how he fought the Spanish bastards?"

"Well, it might have been. It might have been the French. My mind wasn't on him."

"I know what your mind was on. I came ahead of you, remember. You were thinking about the land . . . the trees . . . and the streets in Nottingham; that you were going where you'd never see them again . . . and that you loved them."

"I—I didn't think anything like that. I thought of you and that I loved you."

Speech without words or touch flowed between them for a few moments, saying everything. Then John cleared his throat.

"Women are different, I guess. I've known men come here for many reasons—some, like me, who come without any—but women only seem to come here for one, and that's to be with their men."

"All our lives, cradle to grave, we've never got any other cause to go anywhere for. It's a pity men won't stay at home, where there's good fields, and decent houses, and all the old kin, but if they won't they won't, and there's nothing to do but pack your other dress and start after. Don't you ever think to go home, Johnny?"

"No. No, I won't ever go home."

"Don't you want to?"

"We don't do what we want to in this life. What's more, we don't know why we don't. Tell me the rest about you—after you left Nottingham."

"Oh, I went in the coach to London, straight to the docks just like you told me to, and found the *Pied Cow*. Captain Stephenson took me to Alice Goble's to stay till we sailed. Oh, John! Her ending was so sad!"

"Yes. I know. Did you like London?"

"No. All the red-tiled roofs and the church spires were good to see on the sky, but while you were looking at them, somebody would open a gable and pour the slops over you."

"And the voyage?"

"Oh, we sailed and sailed till we got here."

There are things you do not tell a lover, ever, she thought, and the trials of that voyage would be high among them. You can tell him about the dolphins leaping green and gold in the sunrise, the whales like swimming islands, and how St. Elmo's fire burned over the mast all night. You would not tell him about the sickness and the other women retching all around, and Adam Goble laid on a filthy blanket in one corner, delirious and dying. The rotten food that acted like a poison; the drunken sailor who ripped your bodice while you beat him off with a slipper heel; the fat, white worms that dropped out of the timbers and bit red welts on you; and that storm when the great sea itself came crashing down the hatchway and you thought you'd never need a gravestone . . . those were things he'd not find out from you. But there was one hurt you had to give him.

"Johnny, out at Old Thorny I talked with Bet. . . ."

"How did the land look? Who's helping Rob?"

"It looked the same to me, but I wouldn't know. Kit married Gilly, and they're a really grown pair and seeing well to things. But Bet said to tell you the hog lived but Watch and Warn are dead."

He looked away from her. "They are? How?"

"Watch wouldn't eat after you left."

"Oh! And Warn?"

"With the pups."

A man cannot weep, but he can rage. "Why the devil did Bet let that happen? What was she about? Warn always whelped easy!"

"Don't you blame Bet. Her face ran all tears when she told me. She said, 'I can't help man or beast as don't want to live.'"

Still unappeased he muttered, "I should have thought somebody would have taken care of my dogs for me. Why, Rob brought Watch's great-grandfather home from the Navy. He was one of the fighting dogs that boarded the Armada ships just like the men did."

"The pups thrived, Johnny. Squire's black bitch May suckled them, and they're fine dogs now. Ned says they'll both be bigger than Watch."

"Good. I wish we could get one of them over here."

"Oh, John!" called Walter Neal, striding through the crowded room that was beginning to reek of woodsmoke and malt and sweaty woolen. He had a book in his hand. "Stand up with Miss Joan unless you've changed your mind about her."

Stillness came suddenly into the room like a presence, troubled only by the crackle of fire and the scratch of snowflakes at the paper panes. Piscataqua folk put down their clay mugs, and stopped their gossip, and those who were sweethearts drew closer to each other.

John Scarlock rose up soberly, and Joan sat still for a moment, then scrambled to her feet and stood with her face lifted.

"No," he said. "I haven't changed my mind."

Neal opened the Prayer Book. He looked around him at the yellow pine walls, still oozing amber resin, at the sapling ladder leading up to the dark caves of attic overhead, and the little ridges of snow that had drifted under the door. "Dearly beloved," he intoned piously, and then shot a glance at Catherine Warburton that turned her whiteness ruddy.

"In the time of man's innocency," he read, and Joan remembered a spring night under the hazels, and all the sweet, sweet strangeness of love and the body's hurt that would never come again.

"For such as have not the gift of continency," he read. And what's continency, thought Joan. Something in one of Johnny's books I'd never have much to do with.

"Who giveth this woman to be married to this man?" he read, and there was silence; no male kindred to speak up for nameless Joan in her russet dress.

He fumbled for a moment. "Oh, well—I give her myself."

And at the end they knelt, and the kind, shaggy heads of the people who would be their friends and neighbors for the rest of their lives bowed around them. Joan thought desperately of all the black water from the river's edge to England, of the black woods circling round, and the thick snow dropping down on everything. There was no holly, and no merry bells, and no proper English parson to read the service over them—only a straggling soldier with lust in his eye. For all she knew, no decent bed to go to afterward. But—she was marrying Johnny. She felt her life suddenly flooding out of the narrow bounds of flesh, losing itself in the source and the life that lay beyond, like the full Piscataqua losing itself in the sea. She was no more "Joan." Only a warm mouth and a soft body, turning to him who was turning—oh, wonderful sweet and strange—to her. And when he took her to him this time, it would be in a completeness past the body's love.

And then she realized that Walter Neal was looking in her face, not in Catherine's, and that he saw how it was with her. Perhaps he, too, had lost himself in a far country long ago, as every man and woman must be lost before they can come to live. "Here endeth," he said, so soft that even Johnny could not hear, "the Book of Joan. Mistress Scarlock, kiss your husband. Brethren, let us pray."

In the time of the Great Crossings

THEY went down to London, Southampton, Pymouth, any port a ship could put west out of. Some were heavy-hearted and cursing because the fields they used to plow had been closed to them, or their looms had gone suddenly idle in the cloth towns and England no longer gave them an honest living. Some gathered in little groups on deck for prayer—"Oh follow me no farther than ye have seen me follow Jesus Christ!"—and talked of the kingdom of saints they meant to set up on earth; honest, too, and not knowing they carried the devil with them. And there were merry lads, adventurers from the west country, and prentices from Cheapside, rioting and abandoned, thumbing their noses as the shore dimmed out and shouting the old ballads.

> "And when will you come home again,
>   Oh my son, Geordie Wan?"
> "Oh the sun and moon will dance on the green
>   On the night that I come home."

There were family men from the drowned meadows beside the Wash, with mended coats and anxious faces and children around them; a weaver from Bury St. Edmunds; a younger son of county stock in the Severn valley. Country squires from Essex and Suffolk, whose linen still smelled of lavender, who would dole out burnt wine when the seasickness came on. Devon farmers ruddy as beeves, smugglers wanted on Romney Marsh, and soldiers of fortune with sewn velvet sacks to bring home the precious stones they planned to discover.

Every one of them went for his own reasons, but all of them went because of a wind that blew. Because the spirit of God was moving on the face of the waters again, to make a new man for a new country, and what of the old He wanted, that He took. He stirred the harbors of the gentled English rivers, the river currents of ocean, and the black, brooding streams that drained down through the western forests, and caused them to be all alive with sails that spread for the crossing. And He troubled those deeper rivers that flow in a man's mortal person; the rivers of blood He caused to leap and quicken, and the flow of thoughts across the mind to course where it never had before. He did not explain His ways—any more than He has before or since. He spoke in wind on the water—but He had His will.

For ten years the breath of God blew on England, wafting men out of it, and it was a good land for a man to be up and gone from in that time. For a foolish King kept taking away straw and asking the people for more and more bricks, and in the end he lost, by the people's axe, the head that was of so little use to him—but that was later, after the wars, when the wind had stopped blowing. There was a shadow rode with Charles, and sometimes it wore a Tudor ruff, and sometimes a Norman corselet; it was the shadow of old time, and like Charles, it rode to its fall.

And the men who were blown out of England drove west over the great water, some to the Summer Islands, and some to Virginia, red Connecticut and stony Massachusetts, and up the wide rivers between. Some, who wanted their way in a fuller measure than most, set up in the snowy swamps of Narragansett, and others thought to found a cathedral city on a sluggish tide-wash in Maine. They took England with them, but England never arrived there. Kettles came, a carved chair, a leather book. A gallon of sack and a flitch of bacon could make the journey, but not England.

The branching waters of Piscataqua lay spread out like God's hand upon the countryside: Great Bay for the palm, with four streams run back from it like fingers, and the river itself, a broad thumb pointing down to the sea, and cut seventy feet deep below the rocky, green shores. Around its edges lay a country scourged often with northeast storms of snow, where the frost took hold in November, and at winter's end the cattle were stripped and lean as the wild

47

deer, but stocked with lobsters, fish, beaver, foxes, deer, eagles, grapes, crows, geese, ducks, pumpkins, squashes, corn, marsh grass —and always the trees. Strangers, coming, called it the "home shire" and were homesick to death in it, but their sons saw it a different way, and kept the name.

Four towns grew up there in the years of the great crossings: Exeter, that was for rebels out of Massachusetts; Hampton and Dover for the godly; and Strawberry Bank for men who would love God and honor the King, but first maintain themselves and their own as well as they might. Sometimes they were down to half a barrel of corn and a piece of beef, and once they had only two kegs of beer in twenty-two months. No wonder they wrote home for malt, as well as for children's coats and "maids which are soon gone in this country." They wrote inventories, too, cramped lists of their possessions—so many chamber pots, leather stockings, barrels of pitch, brass ladles, cleaving-wedges, herring nets, blankets, and frying pans. They did not write of the kindnesses of neighbor unto neighbor, at night sometimes, and over freezing water, nor of the courage that made them keep on swinging the axe when the hands were blistered, and go home from the grave of the child buried under snow and deep pine roots, to beget another child who might live to bury them—if he were lucky.

But in guilt they recorded each wickedness. Ruth Gooch stood up in a white sheet before the congregation for adultering with the preacher . . . two nameless sodomists were caught conducting their unholy business in meeting time . . . the devil came in a blast of fire and carried off a man who sat down on a keg of powder and lit his pipe and called on the devil's name . . . two more were drowned rowing to fetch sack on the Lord's Day . . . one was fined for living slothful like swine . . . Dover men split into two armies and marched against each other, carrying a Bible on a halberd for ensign. These were the things they wrote down.

How much they wrote down of the border war they lost to Massachusetts will not be known again, for the books they kept in the year of the taking-over have vanished strangely, but not the word-of-mouth story, not the wry, rebellious echo in every history and memoir. A strong country, burning with a fanatic purpose to make men over, moved in on a small country that had no purpose save the casual good of man. Too common a thing, perhaps—in their time or ours—to need to be written down.

It was a time when the fabulous hopes went glimmering and were given up, for the cleared land took the shape of small farms, not of manors, the gems in the Chrystal Hills turned out to be fit only for penny trinkets, and no one was ever able to find the Laconia Country, with its great sleek beaver—but a time when cornfields, and frame houses, and lusty children came on apace. A time when the country stood by itself, little and alone; a hard time, but a good one. And then the great wind died down. And though men kept on crossing the sea, it was not the same again as it was in those devoted years when they came with the breath of God behind them. England, at home, went on to the wars of ruin, but New Hampshire was well about the business of shaping the new man for the new country.

4. Birth and beginning

〰〰〰〰〰〰〰〰〰〰〰〰〰〰〰〰〰〰〰〰〰〰〰

W HEN I came here," said John Scarlock one spring afternoon
in 1644, setting his mug down hard on the pine table in
George Walford's ordinary, "this was a free country." Older and
leaner than the young man who had come out of England fourteen
years ago, he still looked much the same.

Nobody seemed willing to pick up the argument. Renald Fernald
stroked his beard that had a scatter of gray in it, and looked through
the open door at the new green grass that would be all pricked red
with strawberries, come June. Francis Williams, now governor, looked
even further off . . . at the sails of a fishing boat beating up-river
against the tide. Cod were running well this year, and he had a part
interest in every catch.

Finally Ambrose Gibbons replied cautiously. "Yes. The land was
ours before the Massachusetts meddled with us."

"Aye, it was," said John defiantly, taking a long swallow of cider.

The reason for their silence and caution sat on a bench near the
clay fireplace where only a few banked embers glowed, finishing a
trencher of bacon and boiled pease. Thomas Wiggin, friend of John
Winthrop, agent for the Puritans who had settled the upper river,
turned a bland face with heavy-lidded eyes toward the Strawberry
Bank men.

"That is true. You were a poor country without interest or influ-
ence at home. A group of woeful villages in the outskirts of our
colony; east, like Cain who set up in the east of Eden, and like Cain,
wicked. You scorned the vine and fig tree to nest in the bramble's
shadow. But finally, exhausted with sin and weakness, you signed
yourself away into the protection of Massachusetts, and for that pro-

tection all we ask is that you live godly as we do. A free country! Bah! Who ever promised you such a thing? It would be a crime before the Lord!"

Henry Sherburne came into the low little room that was hardly more than a hut, a young man, moving like a breath of bright air.

"Oh!" he cried. "Welcome, Brother Wiggin. What kind of jackass burden do the holy brethren want us to bear now?"

John brightened at the coming of an ally, but not so Ambrose Gibbons, for Henry was married to his daughter, Beck, and he didn't want to see the lad's tongue get him in trouble.

"But I think I heard you say," went on young Sherburne, who had come as a boy on the *Warwick* in the days of Walter Neal, and helped to take the country when times were hard, but God knows, a good deal more certain than they were now, "that you want us to live godly. Why not let us live honest instead? We're men made out of earth, and wine tastes good to us—when we can get it—and wenches are sweet to lie with, and we pretend no different. Wine and wenches taste just as sweet in Massachusetts, no matter how much they deny it in Meeting. We're as God made us, and so are they, and who's any better?"

Fernald had slipped his hand into a fold of the speaker's deerskin breeches and drew him down on the bench at his own left side.

"Henry's a young man, Mr. Wiggin, and speaks out too bold, but many of us are not happy in the union. Only the Dover men signed it. None of us at the Bank."

"But you had no one to fend for you. Neal, that strumpet soldier, had gone back to England. You had no government, no charter, no goods nor wealth from home. You were as chaff blown through the forest—after John Mason died. He left his servants destitute of means and support."

"Aye, Mason died," muttered John, remembering the plump, benign merchant who had waved at them from the wharves of Portsmouth. "Take this swill away, George, and bring me some good ale. He died, but we did not. We had the ground, and the trees, and the fields we cleared. John Mason died, but that didn't stop the salmon runs, nor the corn from coming up green. The nut trees bore, and the fruit trees thrived, and the deer came down to the salt pans after dark. My right arm did not fail me when John Mason died. I still stood up a man. Destitute servant! In a pig's snout, I was a destitute servant!"

"Talk won't help now, John. We're New Hampshire men, just as we always were." Francis Williams spoke, kindly and troubled. "But New Hampshire's gone under Massachusetts, and Mr. Wiggin is only here to advise us in our ways a little."

"You have brought dangerous ways out of England," went on Wiggin, folding his hands across his gently swelling doublet of stout Yorkshire cloth. "You have a chapel built in the King's faith, and that smacks more of popery every day, and when the wars are over at home may be completely fallen. Soon you must receive a godly minister and I hope you will entertain him well. I understand you are furnished for the sacraments?"

"Yes," replied Fernald, a little uncertainly, for the chapel had been used mostly to store beaver hides in, "there's a great Bible, and a pewter flagon, I think; silver communion ware and two altar cloths. Mason sent them out on one of the early ships, as I remember. We unpacked them and looked them over when we voted the Glebe Land four years ago."

"You'll soon be hearing sermons," said Wiggin comfortably, "and you may as well start to observe the Sabbath. No fishing, bearing burdens, pulling pease, or harrowing the land; no dallying with your wives. And each of you may well begin to read the Bible every day to his household."

"I'll read mine Thomas Tusser," muttered John, "and after that, if I can find my Free School Latin, I'll borrow *Georgius Agricolae* from the Great House and read them that. But I won't read them the Bible."

"Why, John?" asked Ambrose Gibbons very softly at his elbow. "I've found more'n one good tale in it."

"Sure there are," said John. "I've got no quarrel with the Bible. But I'll read it when I want to and not when I'm bid to. Who's Winthrop and Wiggin to tell me what to do? Their fathers whistled to a team of horses the same as mine did."

"I'm afraid," Williams was saying to Thomas Wiggin dubiously, "that the land is still so hungry for our labors here, that we must give even our seventh day to it if we would have more than our families need, so that there may be goods for trade—beaver, and salt cod, and a load of pipe staves now and then."

"Which had you rather set up here—Trade, or the Profession of His Truth?"

"Trade," said all the Strawberry Bank men together.

Wiggin stood up. "Your country," he said, smooth as one of the great eels that whipped its way through channels in the mud when the tide went down, "is still as little as it was in the days of blasphemous Neal; as little, and as full of infamy. But godly settlers are coming here, and they will bring you to the way of Christ, or have your land and send you mouthing into the forest with the other savages!"

"He could have said before," whispered John to Henry, "it was our land he wanted. Walter said twelve years ago it was that; that in his heart he didn't care any more for the way of Christ than we did."

Wiggin heard him and turned about slowly. John set his mug down and stared unfalteringly back.

"You are Goodman Scarlock, are you not?"

"I am John Scarlock of Old Thorny."

Why had he said that? He had only a few fields and cattle and a frame house like the other men had; no wise, settled home with a name. No use to think back to what was oversea.

"And you keep an abomination in your house named Bessie Goble."

John stiffened his shoulders as if to take a blow. He looked down into the flagon of good malt ale George had brought him, and seeing the sloe-brown, frothy circle of it, he thought suddenly that just so his ale had looked when he stared into it that night at Jack Gambrell's years ago, when Walter Neal was first telling him about Piscataqua Country. If one man can love another, John had loved Captain Neal, but when the high adventure of finding the great lakes had failed, when there proved to be beans and corn in the new country rather than gems for the court ladies, Neal had smiled and shrugged, written *"non est inventa provincia"* to John Mason, and gone home to captain the London artillery. And Catherine Warburton, Fernald's sister and Joan's friend, had cried for a week and then taken ship after him. No one had ever known all of what lay between them—but she had another man for her husband now, and lived at court, if the court hadn't fallen. There'd been no news from the wars lately. No doubt Walter was in them, for he often said he hadn't missed a good fight since he was eighteen, and fighting was more to his taste than salting cod fish and cutting marsh hay. But if only he were here, he'd settle this praying bastard.

"Yes," he answered. "Bessie lives in my house."

"Ah! Can your wife sew?"

"Yes . . ."

"Then bid her make a scarlet W for the wench to wear on her gown. I shall expect to see it when I come here to pray for you next

53

week. Good-bye, Governor, and God be with you." He held out his hand to Francis Williams.

Williams bowed low so as not to see the hand. "Good-bye, Mr. Wiggin. We thank you—but we plead to be governed by the known laws of England, and not by the peculiar laws of Massachusetts."

The stout Puritan sniffed, paused a moment as if to answer, then strode down the slope to the little wharf where he had tied up the shallop he used for running all over Great Bay and the river country on the business of God and Governor Winthrop.

Nobody said anything, and Walford brought some more ale from the keg in the corner. Finally Fernald spoke.

"It was wrong for him to speak of Bess. We know what she is, but even the godly must recognize that there will always be some tares in the vineyard."

"We tried to make her a good lass, but she was full of lust from her first days. We had her ever since her mother drowned herself off the *Pied Cow* coming here with Joan."

"I know. You were both good to her and you tried hard, and she fell into evil in spite of you. But I think I know an answer, John."

What answer could there be? thought John, turning his mug round and round, not drinking. Bessie, the orphan girl, hardly fourteen, had eyes like blackberries, an ample smile, and a tangle of light brown hair that flowed to her plump waist. She was no use in the house or the fields, but could often be seen in the lane that led to the huts of the Danish men John Mason had sent over to make potash, or hovering about the waterside in talk with the sailors or hunters just come downriver from the beaver country. Her charm was not that of a beautiful woman, not the frowsy willingness of Moll Doubleday back home, rather that of a friendly animal sidling up to be petted. But she always had shillings and pence in her pocket, which was more than most of the goodwives had.

Once she had let a coin fall on the kitchen floor, and John had picked it up and asked her where it came from.

"Oh, I found it in the lane below the Great House. Some sailor must have dropped it."

"Yes," John had answered slowly, "likely one did."

There could be no answer in the matter of Bessie Goble, but Dr. Fernald was still talking.

"Do you know Daniel Knight? A tall, dark man—has a face like a crag, and the best heart in this country? He owns a house by Hampton Cow Common, and has more in his pocket than any of us."

54

"Brother to Roger Knight who came with us in the *Warwick?*"

"No, but some kin, I think. Owned three farms in Devon, but his wife died there when he was young, and he wanted to get away from everything they'd shared together, so he came here. I've seen him often since the cod started to run, for one of his fishing boats puts out from Spring Hill Wharf, and he's watched Bess and her ways, and talked with me about her."

"What did he say?"

"He says he'll marry her, John, if you and Joan are willing."

"*Marry her?*"

"He thinks she's a good lass at heart, and there are ways, he says, a husband can use to keep her in order which a foster father cannot."

"Yes," said John, still unbelieving, "he's right there."

"He thinks she will settle down and be a good wife to his old age, and he's ready to stand up with her any time. Why don't you ask Joan before Thomas Wiggin sets that letter on the poor girl."

"I will. Can't see she'd have but one answer. It's not good for her to be in the house with our own girls growing."

"No. Isn't Joan's time about here?"

"Any day now." John stood up. Then he smiled. "One thing— I never worry when Joan's with child. She just lies down and calls to them and they come tumbling into the world like kittens."

"I wager she'd not tell it that way."

"Likely not." John turned back from the doorway. "I'll come over tomorrow and tell you what she says about Bess."

"Do. Daniel's gone to the Bay, but he'll be back next week, and wants to go forward with the business. He's a good man, John."

John paid his reckoning, made his farewells, and stepped out on the beaten turf in the warm afternoon. The houses of Strawberry Bank, peaked and timbered like his own, lay along a rough track that followed the river edge, beaches or little wharves in front, gardens and fields spreading up the slope behind them. On the crest of the hill, stretching west and north, certain goodly acres called the Glebe Land had been set apart for the support of John Mason's chapel, but they would be used now for Thomas Wiggin's Puritan minister. John swore softly and lifted the small wooden plow he had left leaning against the clapboarded wall of the ordinary, under the two wolves' heads nailed up for bounty and still reeking of dried blood. He walked along the uneven road past the Great House, noticing that one of the windowpanes was broken, and stopped at Rafe Gee's, for Rafe had a small forge and a knack with ironwork, and he wanted a keener edge put on the plow's metal tip. But Rafe wasn't in, though John called and whistled and all the casements were blowing open. Probably up with the cattle in the town field at the head of the creek. Well, he'd not had his trip to town for nothing; there'd been good talk with the lads in spite of that knave from Dover, and an offer of honest marriage for Bessie Goble. He began to whistle an old sailor's tune Rob had learned in the Navy, as he walked back to where he had tied up his boat just below the town. Most of the men were at work in the fields or woods, but women's voices chimed low from the windows and gardens. Johnny Crowther's wife was setting out some plants in her front yard and called to him.

"How's Joan?"

"Well . . . and waiting."

"When she's up again, I'll give her some of these rosebushes! My sister sent them from England."

"Thank you, Jane," he called back. "That'll please her."

He stopped suddenly, almost jumped backward to keep from running into a tall, bony figure that stood in front of him. It was an Indian, one of the nobler ones, with sharp, bronze-cut features and blue-black hair, no paint or ornaments, or skins, only a rough woolen robe draped over one shoulder and dyed a sort of periwinkle color. Why, he'd seen this fellow before. It was old Passaconaway, the wizard. John had had little to do with the Indians since the first days, except to best one in a trade or tell him to be gone, for the narrow arm of the sea between his farm and the mainland shut him off from many meetings with them which the townsmen had. He wished them no particular harm, but he could not honor them—owning all that good land since the time of God, and what had they done with it! He did not know quite how to greet a wizard. But the man stood there in front of him and would not go. He had to say something.

"Do you want to . . . talk to me?" he asked finally.

"To you—to any man who can help. I am Passaconaway."

"Yes, I know. I saw you once when I went to look for the Chrystal Hills twelve years ago. I saw you at the trading post at Newichwannock once. You can make water burn and trees dance. You can change yourself into a flame, and in winter you can raise up a green leaf from the ashes of a dry one, or a living serpent from one that is dead."

John's speech was all mockery, a mockery that made him feel mean and uneasy. He was treating the Indian just as the other men at

56

Strawberry Bank treated them—he knew no other way—and yet he felt there should have been another way.

The Indian looked back calmly at him out of eyes opaque and muddy as a turtle's.

"Other men say that. I do not say it."

"Then you're not a wizard?"

"Where a wizard has no honor, there his power is gone. Long ago—when the White Men first come—we gather, all of us, to try our magic. I was a young man then. In the twiggy thickets of a great swamp we meet. First, we bid fire go and eat your wigwams, and we blow forth the fire, but it does not obey, and still the wigwams stand. And then we blow forth the sickness that is like winter in a man's throat and chokes him—and many die—but more live, more come. The spirits do not obey, and we are weak without the spirits. Your spirits still obey you, so you take our country."

John shifted a little to one side. Past the scrub oaks to the south, he could hear the voices of men coming home from their day's work on the iron bog. The shadows of the elms were drawing themselves out long on the shingly beach, and he wanted to get to his house and see how Joan was.

"Yes," he said. "We've taken some of it, but there's plenty for you still—more than you'll want to plant this season."

"Trade?" asked Passaconaway, his eyes fixing John like a spear.

"I don't know. What do you want?"

"That. Not yellow beads nor fire water. We must live in your way now, or we die. We must groove our fields—not in the squaw's way, but in yours. We need that—in your hand."

John stroked the small plow he was carrying on his shoulder.

"But you can make one for yourself. See—it's wood. Out of any tree . . ."

"Not that," said Passaconaway, running his hand along the iron edge of the share, "but *this.*"

"What'll you give?"

"Cornfield by Hogstye Cove. Here is a leaf that says I give it. I had it made to carry like wampum." From the fold of his robe he drew a strip of deer hide with rough lettering in red paint. "This man own field by Hogstye Cove. Passaconaway."

The Indian held out the deerskin. "I take your plow," he said simply, "for my people." He reached over and lifted it from John's shoulder.

John let him take it, felt the deed pressed into his limp hand. What

57

good to him was a field by Hogstye Cove over on the Great Bay, away from the Bank and the road to England? Good land, maybe, but Joan would never live there. And everybody knew that an Indian's name to a deed was no better than the scratch of a bear's claw. And there was his plow being carried off into the woods toward Little Harbor! But the man had taken it for his people. "We must learn your ways or die."

John freed his boat suddenly from the overhanging willow he had tied it to and jumped in. Hell, he thought, let the poor devil have it. I've got the bigger one.

When he got to the island and hurried past Fernald's house, he began to feel suddenly anxious about Joan. He went by the round salt pond and grazing cattle, and along the edge of his fields, all plowed and spread with fish carcass, and ready for seed that would be sowed in the Indian fashion with pumpkins, beans, and corn all hilled together. What would Old Tusser say to such a planting, he thought, or to any farm where you couldn't sow till mid-April and there was no winter crop but snow? We have to learn Indian ways, too, he thought, they're not the only ones who must change. And then he was at the house—try as he would, he'd never been able to make it look like Old Thorny, but it had a wide hearth and chimney corners with room for old people and children, and maybe time would do what he hadn't been able to. He went around to the front, crossed the ledge under the open casements, and lifted the wooden latch of the sea-weathered door.

Before Joan Scarlock put herself to bed for her fourth childbirth, she stood in the doorway a long time and looked downriver, at the slate-colored water swirling past the fishermen's huts on Great Island, and the banks of blue-green spruce that curved, and narrowed, and hid the wide sea. Beyond that sea lay England—Nottingham and St. Nicholas' workhouse, Jack Gambrell's and Old Thorny. She had not thought about them so often when she first came here, but now the girls were growing up and liked to hear about "home," for she and Johnny still spoke of it that way. At night after supper was the best time, when they were scouring the pewter and woodenware, for then Johnny would put down his pipe and join in. They'd listen when he told about Watch and Warn, or the ghost of Old Will, but when he tried to tell them about the Armada Fight, they'd get out their corn husk poppets and straggle off, playing. Joan understood; she'd never got straight in her head what it was all about either.

This afternoon, right in the middle of a green and forward April, they were playing down in the rushes at the edge of the salt marsh behind the house, and Joan could hear their laughter, hated to put an end to it, but the faint uneasiness stirring throughout her body told her she should be sending for Joanna Fernald. There wouldn't be time to get Sarah Scriggins from her house on the other side of the Glebe Land, for Joan never spent many hours of her busy, happy life in the woes of childbirth. First there was the discomfort that told you you had better lie down and call some other woman to be there, and then the sudden burst of sickness, frightening the first time, but not again; the short, sharp wrestle with pain, and then the blissful weakness, when you lay, and gave suck, and were glad.

The gulls went over, white and shrill in the spring sunshine, and new grass shoots were coming through the yellow mat of last year's fallen leaves. Even the little, dead-looking trees in the dooryard, dwarfed and gnarled by the sea wind, had covered themselves overnight with hard, orange buds. She did not want to go inside, to the bedchamber, clean, but dark after this moment of blue brightness, and musty from being lived in all winter. She wanted to stay out here on the point where she had made Johnny build their house—because it faced toward England. She wanted to be a girl with her own girls, and run to the spring and gather the tiny violets that were budding where the sweet water overflowed, or down to the little cove beyond the hog pens, to pick up scarlet mussel shells and scale flat stones off the sleek roof of the river.

"But I've cleared land at the head of Sagamore Creek for us, Joan. There're a spring, and a fresh marsh, and an Indian cornfield ready to plow. . . ."

"No," Joan had said, "I want my house where I can stand in the doorway and look to England."

"But you'll have to look at the river you're so afraid of."

"If I'm to turn away from everything that frightens me, you'd best swaddle me in lambswool and lock me in a chest in the chimney cupboard."

"Well," said Johnny, "we'll build it where you want it."

And she had wanted it here, on the crest of a little island, high and craggy where it jutted into the river, sloping back gently into fields and marshes, with Renald Fernald's house on the inner shore, and, across a stone's throw of channel, the town.

With a sigh now, she stepped heavily off the doorstone, went past the open casements of her tidy kitchen, and called down the hill to her daughters. "Kitty! Oh, Kitty, Mary, Alice!"

"What do you want?"

"Is it suppertime?"

"We just found a starfish! He's all wiggly green!"

Three blond heads, set at varying heights, burst out of the rushes, and three little figures, demure in homespun, scrambled across the wet sedge and oozing moss. Pain twisted Joan's comely face for a moment, then her body; she did not want them to come any nearer.

"Go to Aunt Joanna's! Quick!"

"Why? What for? What'll we tell her?"

"She'll know when she sees you. Just go there. Run!"

Away they tore in the direction of a tall chimney and gables that looked out, reassuring, from a covert of elms feathered with new green.

Joan drew a deep breath, straightened herself, and went into the house. She looked around the kitchen and everything seemed to be in order, from the heavy black ironware hung by the fireplace to the shining pewter on the dresser between the windows. She poked the fire and threw in some birch wood Johnny had cut up small so she could handle it. She filled the largest kettle and swung its crane over the fire. Then she went into the buttery at the back of the house, under the stairs. A good thing she'd baked yesterday, and cut up that dried pumpkin this morning, and of course there was the bacon flitch and half a cask of salt cod, and a kettle of pease porridge ready to heat. If her family didn't have any supper tonight it was their own fault.

As she crossed the kitchen again on her way to bed, she had to rest for a few minutes on the settle while a wave of pain swelled and ebbed in her body. At the foot of the narrow stairs that wound themselves around the great brick chimney to the garret where Bessie and the girls slept, she looked upward. She hadn't been able to get up there since February. Bessie said it was clean enough, but Bessie'd say the same of a stable midden. Likely Joanna wouldn't go up there, and she knew what bearing a child was like—but still, a dirty house was a shame to any woman.

Once in the bedroom she strewed white sea sand on the floor that was beginning to splinter along the cracks after twelve years of feet going over it, dressed the bed with clean, worn linen, and pinned back the hangings of pink, painted chintz that were the finest things she owned, except the silver tankard Johnny'd brought home the time he went to the Bay. As she loosened her dress, she turned her eyes to the window for one last look at the spring sunshine, and saw nothing but a great, evil, gray sweep of water rushing by. Then Joan lay down alone with the pain.

In all the whole world there were only the two, the pain and she, but she did not fight it in the terror of a young wife, nor writhe with a novice's abandon. She used it expertly, as a master craftsman uses a tool. Once she thought she saw Joanna go by the bed, but how could she be sure, in a world that held only the pain and she? And then suddenly her enemy dwindled and left her, lying spent but unbroken, and she knew that in a few moments she would be able to lift her head up and rejoice. As the familiar room came back into sight again, she saw that Ann Warnerton from the Great House was there, and that she held a bundle of clean, old shawls, and then Joanna came to the bed with rags and water to cleanse her gently of birth.

Joan spoke first, still a little mazed from her task and its sudden ending. "I think I'll call this child 'Cecily' for John's mother," she said.

"You'll never call *this* child 'Cecily,'" beamed Joanna. "What was his father's name?"

"His father? Why . . . why . . . it was Will. But you . . . you . . . why . . . it's never a boy? After all those girls I thought I could have only the one kind! Dr. Renald said 'twas like I could have only the one kind . . . though he wasn't sure. Oh! Oh, somebody go tell Johnny!"

"'Will' it is," said Ann, holding him up for Joan to see. "Johnny was in the town when I came away." Suddenly she began to weep.

"Poor Ann," sighed Joanna. "Thomas threw a stool at her, so she walked out of his house and rowed herself over the channel to me."

"Why didn't you throw it back, Ann?" asked Joan weakly, reaching up to take her baby.

"I couldn't. It went through the window."

"Ann says he's entertaining lewd company," said Joanna soberly, and then with something that was almost accusal, "She thinks he's been with Bessie Goble."

Joan held her son in her arms and tried to see past the baby softness to the man his father was, the man he would grow into. Why didn't these prattling women go away, and get Johnny, and leave the three of them together? But she remembered Alice Goble's dead face lying on the reef with the kelp streaming over it, and she struggled up in her sick bed to defend Bessie.

"What I hear of your husband, Mistress Ann, he was a wicked man before Bess was born," she said.

"Hush!" broke in Joanna. "Someone's coming. It must be John. Beck Sherburne is at my house, and she said she'd keep the children till we sent for them."

A man's tread, quick and sure, sounded on the ledge that ran under the chamber window. The door swung open and there he stood, against an evening sky the color of the violets by the spring. A draft of sweet air blew in, cooling Joan's forehead. "Look, Johnny," she said, pulling the blankets away, leaving the tiny body bare.

John strode across the room, thinking first of her until he saw what it was she wanted him to see. And then what he thought of was neither woman nor child, but the pit whence he was digged, and the rock he was hewn out of, and his own father in another April twilight, walking across the plowed earth of Old Thorny, head up, whistling to his team of horses.

"See," said Joan. "Will Scarlock."

"Yes," said John, his voice low and shaken. "Yes. I know."

But from every holy moment there must be a descent into hell. Later that night he found himself back in Strawberry Bank, approaching the Great House after a few careful questions had directed him there. A lush, too-warm darkness had settled softly on town and river, and as he turned from the path he could just see that the grape vines covering the low wall had begun to put forth new leaves . . . vines that had been sent over to grace John Mason's manor that never came to be. Halfway up the sloping yard behind the wall he stopped, and what he saw through the broken window kept him from going any further.

Thomas Warnerton, the wicked soldier who had taken the Great House after Mason died and Humphrey Chadbourne moved up-river to the trading post at Newichwannock, was sitting at a table drinking. He wore velvets and a lace collar, and a hat with a feather, pushed back on his dark hair. No one in town could ever keep track of his comings and goings. And beside him sat another man, dressed much the same, but older, with bright, sunken eyes and a sneering mouth. The men were talking in the candlelight that sparkled whenever they lifted their goblets that were finer than any the good folk of Piscataqua had ever been able to purchase by honest means.

"Those were the days, Thomas, and we had a rare good time at it." The stranger was talking. "All those ripe young squaws dressed as English milkmaids, winding their colored ribbons round a lopped spruce for a maypole. God, it was a rare japes till those old drizzle-beards from Plymouth and Naumkeag got there. Old Endicott gaped at the bare bosoms like he'd never seen one, and Captain Shrimp near fell over the sword he had that was bigger than he was. I offered them any shes of the lot, and they never so much as made me a civil answer. We'd have beat the prayers out of them if we hadn't been so drunk."

"Ah, the Bay is lined with rogues that should have their throats cut," growled Warnerton. "Something there is about praying, I've always noticed, takes the manhood out of the body, and leaves but a sack of dry, sharp bones. Neighbor Fernald's a great doctor. Shall we go and ask him why that is so?"

"But it's not always so," leered the stranger. "I've been in gaol with praying men both sides of the water, and they had nothing lacking. Truth, since the old Merry Mount days, I've been in gaol more than out. No town has a welcome for poor Thomas, and that's why I'm here to go with you. Where is it we are to go?"

"Port Royal. When Mason's land and goods were divided up, things fell out willy-nilly, but I kept to myself this house, mostly for what's in the cellar of it."

"What?"

"Powder and ball. I'm taking them to sell to the Tarrantines."

"That's treason. They're like to come right back at this country, blasted out of a musket."

"I know they are, but I won't be here. I'll be in England selling the furs I took for them."

John Scarlock stood in the moist green turf, watching, listening, wondering if there was any way he could keep this evil thing from happening. And then he knew there was not. Whatever lay in the Great House belonged to Warnerton, simply because he had possessed himself of it when honest men did not dare to, and he could ship it downriver with any bland excuse he chose, and no one would move to stop him. Perhaps the law of Massachusetts might not be so bad a thing to have over them, since here there was no law, only the goodness of man, and that did not always hold. And then, into the candlelight beyond the broken panes, stepped Bessie Goble. First he noticed that for skirt she wore a bright, rich thing he had never seen before, and then he noticed that above the skirt she was naked, and her round breasts hung full and heavy, heavier than Joan's, who had nursed three children. She stepped forth thus between the two men, and stood there, her small eyes shining dully, her shoulders moving, almost with a lilt.

"Ah, Bessie, my dear," said Warnerton, drawing her to him. "This is my friend, Thomas Morton, once of Merry Mount, erst of—what English gaol was it, Thomas?"

"None." Morton spat on the floor. "It was a Massachusetts gaol —and filthy."

"Ah well. Little Bessie, my dear Ann is away this evening, but we shall make you good cheer, Thomas and I." He reached out to fondle her. John Scarlock swore and knocked heavily on the front door panel.

He could no longer look through the window, being too close, but he could hear a scuffle inside, then heavy steps, and Warnerton threw the door wide open so that the whole room could be seen. Bessie was gone, but a hanging twitched at the rear. Morton was filling a third goblet from a silver flagon.

"Goodman Scarlock," cried Warnerton smoothly. "What brings you here? Will you share . . . ?"

"I—I—" John could feel his face turning hot and ashamed in the darkness, but he spoke doggedly. "I'm looking for Bessie Goble," he said.

"Ah, Bessie—the little wood dove, the little sea pigeon. She is not here. I have not seen her." The first words were oily, but the last five had the cut of steel.

The two men faced each other. I could go in there, thought John. I could tear the house apart, and beat them both—they're drunk on their feet—but what would be the use? She'd go back there the minute I took my eye off her.

He looked straight at Warnerton and the shame left him. "Well," he said, "my wife needs her. Tell her not to stop anywhere else on the way home."

5. *By one who was there*

≈≈≈≈≈≈≈≈≈≈≈≈≈≈≈≈≈≈≈≈≈≈≈≈≈≈≈≈≈≈≈≈≈≈

LEAVES FROM JOHN SCARLOCK'S
DIARY, 1644–1659

DECEMBER 21, 1644. Cold. Sky thick with snow, but none fell. This day, cutting spruce in the cove beyond the houses the godly have built on the ridge called after them "Christian Shore," Hugh James caught by a falling tree. Carried him home on a board, where he died about noon. None of us had stomach for any more felling, so we did not return to the woods. In the tavern after, we spoke of how a man's time can come on him before he knows or is prepared. Mentioned Thomas Warnerton, slain at Port Royal where he went to betray us to the Tarrantines; his friend Morton, who lived as wickedly, also gone; then good men we had known. Sat with the corpse between eight and nine. Martha, his wife, wept grievously. Said now her son—still in swaddlings—would never know his father. Stopped at Renald's on the way home and bought of him some paper for a diary. 'Twill not be easy to keep, but it may tell my son Will something of what I was, if I live not long enough to show him a better way.

February 1, 1645. A bright day, but cold. Rode through the snow to Hampton to the burying of Daniel Knight, his wife, that was our Bess. Lingered in bed with chills after childbirth and then gave up the Ghost. Times I have cursed her, I am sorry for. Daniel told us they had to thaw the ground with torches before they could dig her grave. Joan brought home the child which is called Nan. Put her in the cradle with Will.

April 11, 1645. My son Will one year old today. Stands alone. Nannie grows apace, too, her hair very golden. Joan says it is not the baby gold that will darken as our girls' already has, but the true gold that will stay till the gray comes through it. Went in town this afternoon to record the Indian deed I had this day last year from old Passaconaway, the wizard. Renald and Henry Sherburne helped me draw it like this:

"Know all men by these presents, that I, John Scarlock, of Old Thorny in Nottingham, sojourning in Piscataqua, have bought of Passaconaway for one wooden plow (with iron-tipped share) the Indian cornfield, now grown up to junipers and birch saplings, above Hogstye Cove on the Great Bay, and that I give it freely to my son Will, on this, the first return of his birth, to be his and his heirs' forever.

John Scarlock."

Met Francis Norton by the iron forge, Mrs. Ann Mason's agent who disposes of such of her husband's property as he can find. Says he will drive the cattle to Boston—near a hundred head—and can sell them there for twenty pounds each, but I doubt she ever sees the money. Talked long with Joan tonight on the doorstone under the warm stars. Thomas Fernald wants to court Kitty, but we think her too young.

December 31, 1646. Bright sun and ice like a skin of glass on everything. This, the worst day of my life. Cracked my axe handle chopping by Little Harbor, and came home early. Joan lying by the spring where she had fallen when she went for water, she bleeding much and had miscarried, alone there in the snow. Will and Nannie wailing in their beds, the girls in town learning the hornbook. Carried her to bed and ran for help. Dr. Fernald and Sarah Scriggins with her all day. Humphrey Chadbourne's maid come to help in the kitchen. Dr. says she will be well but cannot bear again. I do not care. I have my son. Sat with her tonight and said it was my fault for bringing her to this country. She smiled and said she had known such things to happen in Nottingham. Richard Cutt, now at the Great House, heard she was ill and sent wine and wild turkeys. An honest man, for all he holds with the Massachusetts, and of growing power in town. If Joan had died, I should have gone back to England, I think, like a spent fox to its earth. She spared to me, I can do what I must.

June 20, 1648. My daughter Kitty married to John Hall, Thomas Wiggin's nephew, and gone to live with the godly on Christian Shore. May God have mercy on her soul.

April 4, 1649. Life and death spoke to us, this day of spring sunshine. In the morning, about nine, my daughter Kitty delivered of a son, her first child. This afternoon a ship from the Bay brings us the grievous news from England that the people have had the King's head. He was not a good King, but they did ill to take his life, and now they will suffer for it, for they must live under Puritans, and that will be worse. I have lived under both and know. Also Governor Winthrop dead in March, a sounding name to many, but to me the greatest knave that ever came out of England. He said John Mason's early death was God's mercy, and I say the same for his. Also word from Boston that there is to be an ordinance against the wearing of long hair. I have always worn mine short, as it suits better with a yeoman's life, but from today henceforth I shall let it grow. In England I was always willing to follow custom, but in the first free years here when there was no custom at all to mind, I grew used to having my own way and setting my own custom, and I like it too well to change now.

February 19, 1650. My daughter Kitty delivered of a son, her second. Sarah Scriggins not there, for her own husband James breathing his last at the very hour. He much in debt, even to the house they live in, since he adventured all in a fishing boat and lost it at the Isles of Shoals last year in the great fall wind. But Sarah says a midwife will never starve unless the men of Strawberry Bank change their ways, which she doubts they will. A coarse, rough woman, but a brave one. Came in the *Pied Cow* with Joan.

October 25, 1650. All the leaves down, but soft air like May, and with us a grievous time. My son Will chilled by falling into the marsh creek last Sabbath, now so racked with fever and hoarse breathing I have doubted his life. Tonight Dr. Fernald shut me from the room and would have none therein but Joan to fight death with him, I went from the house and walked along the shore, through the thickets to the north. One lone rowan the only tall tree there, the others scrub and briar bushes, and in their midst I sat down on a stone and watched the moonlight on the black river and the marshes half in mist, the cattails swaying. Needed help as a man needs it only when his son is dying, but could no longer call on God after what Massachusetts has made of him. Called on Old Will finally, to help his blood in this, its mortal hour, and looked between the trees on the shore toward Little Harbor to see if he would come striding there. I think if I had been in Sherwood he might have come to me, but here in Piscataqua he did not. And yet . . . when I went back to my house, my son was asleep, breathing easily; Joan, too, in her chair; Dr. Fernald stretched out on the wolfskin by the hearth. When she heard me she opened her eyes. "We will all live, Johnny," she said. "Fix the fire and go to bed." But I could not, being thankful, and not knowing where to carry my gratitude. Sometimes the mystery of man's life is too great for him to bear thinking on.

March 2, 1651. My daughter Kitty delivered of a son, her third.

December 8, 1651. This has been a sad year for us at Strawberry Bank who followed the King and Prayer Book and have not gone with the reformed church. Brian Pendleton, Richard Cutt and John Pickering order most of our affairs, and they are all for the strait ways of Massachusetts and the ministers, but they have been able to get no settled parson to stay here, for which I am grateful. Soberness and prayer go well in a man's life, but they do not make up all of it, and God himself never meant them to. But when new lands are allotted here they go to the godly who sift down on us from Dover Neck and rear themselves up from Boston and the towns between. Many of the old stock who came here with me in the *Warwick* cannot vote in Meeting. Some of us have gathered at night in Abraham Corbett's tavern to bewail these things and study how we may revolt against them, but Governor Endicott, hearing this, summoned Abraham to General Court, where he was admonished and let off. They have made us fine promises, but it all comes to this: that we have little say in our own government. I did not want aught to say in government when I lived at home in England, for King Charles ran the country and I ran Old Thorny, and that was as it was meant, and neither of us was much trouble to the other. But here one man's as good as the next, and no man's father has left him the right to tell me what to do. So much for public affairs.

In our own house we have had little peace since the girls were grown, and of all, Mary is the most troublesome, the most like me. Valentine Hill has on his woodland by the Oyster River a dozen Scottish prisoners caught at the Battle of Worcester Plain and sent to the colonies to fell trees for eight years, after which they may be free to take up land and marry. We of the Bank who are sorry they failed to restore Prince Charles, our rightful King, have opened our houses to these lads, and now Mary has set her heart on one of them, Tam McQuayne, tall, with a red beard, and can sing well, I think, every ballad that was ever made in Scotland. I like him, but eight years waiting is a poor lovegift, and I cannot approve it.

December 12, 1651. Mary came to me tonight between the stalls where I was showing Will and Nannie how to milk old Tawn, the quietest cow. Asked me for a hundred pounds to buy Tam's freedom so that they may wed at once. I told her while she was about it she should ask for a hundred thousand, for 'twould come as easy. Told her to wait for a year and see how the lad carried himself.

December 14, 1651. This day, afternoon, while I was in the shed putting down split cod in brine to ship overseas, Renald looked in and asked me if I knew where Mary was. I saying no, he told me she was working in John Webster's tavern setting out ale for the loggers. Called Joan to see to the fish, and rowed over to town. True it was, and John Webster needing a wench when she approached him, he had hired her for one shilling sixpence a week. She very angry at me for coming there. Said if she could not get a hundred pounds from me she would get it for herself. Said her mother had been a barmaid in her time and she was no better. John told her he was sorry, but since I forbade it, he could not hold to their bargain, and I rowed her home, she very red and not speaking to me.

December 15, 1651. Went to town and bought glass panes for the new gable windows, and sweets for Will and Nan. Took John Webster a sack of dried pease to pay him for two mugs my daughter Mary broke while in his service.

December 16, 1651. Today my daughter Mary came home with one hundred pounds. Joan aghast and angry. Said that was better than

Bessie Goble could do in her time. Mary very saucy. Said there were more men in the Bank now. We questioned her till she finally wept and told us that she had it from Daniel Knight for the asking. Daniel is a rich man through his great fishery at the Shoals and has been our good friend ever since we took Nannie to grow in our house. I know he looks on our children as his, but this I could not allow. Went to the chest in the cellar and took up one hundred pounds, this the last of the money Joan and I brought out of England. Strange it is that money that came from corn grown on Old Thorny should cross the sea to Piscataqua and then go back to England again to buy a Scotch boy's freedom. Tomorrow I will repay Daniel Knight, and we will have Mary's wedding and an end to the matter.

December 17, 1651. Rode to Hampton to pay Daniel Knight the money Mary borrowed. The new highroad across the marshes shortens the journey much over what it was in the old days when Bess died and Joan and I went there to fetch Nan home. Many roads have been run since then, and bridges built, and there are more scattering lights against the dark when we look out of the windows after supper. Now when we cut in the woods, our axes can no longer be heard by the waterside. Daniel gave me dinner— venison with stewed pumpkin and Spanish wine—but he would not take the money. Neither would I keep it. Finally he said let us each pay half, since we both like the lad and approve his fighting for our King. Thus we shook hands. Says Mary's wedding gift shall be lands he owns at Bloody Point where they may live well.

January 12, 1652. My daughter Mary married to Tam McQuayne, but no feast or dancing after as there would have been in England. This country too good for such. My daughter Kitty has a girl, her fourth child.

January 14, 1652. Cold and bitter as always here at this season, the snow drifted deep and the creeks frozen over. In Nottingham we could be getting ready to plow. Both countries despaired of, alas, since the godly men rule them—in Boston Governor Endicott, and in England Cromwell, a rare bastard! God send he choke at the sacrament. All he wants is to hinder other men from their desire. Last night George Walford closed his tavern early, and not a ray of light shone out from it after eight o'clock. But men were there. Renald was, and Henry Sherburne—the others godly. No man knows what they did, but 'tis rumored they altered the Town Book, the sacred record that goes back to our first beginnings, and tore out the words that favored Neal and Mason and the old stock who held with King and Church, leaving only such things as would bind us closer to Massachusetts. I met Henry in the street and asked him, but he said Beck was waiting for him in the Spring Market and hurried off. How his father-in-law, Ambrose Gibbons, has tamed the fiery lad he used to be! I stopped at Renald's as I came home and charged him with it, but he shook his head and said, "John, do not ask me. We live as we must." I know what he means, I think, having left England for that very reason, but it was not good to hear. I had thought Renald Fernald a better man than I, which he is not, and for that I am sorry.

June 17, 1652. Because the Indians in the swamps edges stir and threaten, we are to have a training band and Brian Pendleton, a praying man from Massachusetts, is to lead it. I like him not. Our country is protected from the sea, praise God, against any enemy that may ever come against it, for we have a great gun set up a bow shot from the waterside, just below the town, on the turf mound where the old Indian Fort used to be.

July 22, 1652. One Joseph Mason, a wispy man with a thin, brown beard, has come here to claim our country for the Tufton boys, John Mason's grandsons, under his probate will. I do not know what may come of it, so I will not side for or against him. He has tacked up orders on the Meeting House to keep men from cutting grass or felling timber on ground he says is his, but no one pays him any mind. No one will listen to Mason claims here or at home so long as the Puritans rule, for Captain John—whom I liked—was a good churchman and followed the King.

April 23, 1653. Tonight with the tide went out my daughter, Catherine Hall, after lying four days in labor, the child unborn. Joan sits alone in the dark and will not talk. Sarah Scriggins drunk and maudlin in Corbett's tavern afterward. Said it was a poor world where an old woman must earn her bread by watching young wives die. Anthony Brackett and John Ault carried her home on a board.

Sat long with the widower while he read aloud to himself from the Bible. Later, he gone to see about a coffin, Renald came in, and he and I alone, we read the Prayer Book over her. Hall has done nothing that was not within his right and privilege, but I shall always hate the man. This, the only child we did ever lose; she twenty years old, the first Scarlock to be buried in this country. Kitty was the fairest of all my daughters. I wish she had stayed a maid.

May 27, 1653. John Hall that was Kitty's husband asks to have Alice, but he cannot.

May 30, 1653. Today is the great news here in a ship from Boston that they have favored our petition to be a separate town called Portsmouth, and allowed to have a sawmill, such as even the backwoods at Sagamore Creek and Newichwannock have. The choosing of the name is a jest, smiled at by us of the old stock, but not talked of before the new men, the godly. It was Henry Sherburne put it to them, because, he said, we are no longer Strawberry Bank, for where those wild vines grew, the carts now rumble, and the feet of many men. In front of the Great House is even a strip of cobblestone. But we are still and always will be a harbor town at the river's mouth. "Portsmouth" would be fit. Brian Pendleton and Richard Cutt, the newcomers, approved it, and thus we are, but some of us remember that Portsmouth was John Mason's town in Hampshire, England, and when we say Portsmouth, we flick a finger at each other. We dare not do more. Henceforth I write from Portsmouth.

July 7, 1653. Hot and bright and the marsh hay cut. Near fell afighting with Francis Champernowne in the Spring Market today. He a landowner in Kittery and Greenland north of Hampton edging the Great Bay, kin to Sir Ferdinand Gorges who was an adventurer with John Mason long ago. Stopping me in the common street, he told me he had a mind to my youngest daughter Alice; that he was too old to love a maid, but that he wanted a son and he had seen her and deemed her good for breeding; that he would fetch serving women out of England to wait on her and that she should be his lady. I told him he was too old and the maid had no mind to him. He said it was no matter where the maid's mind was, that his was to her and that he could pay for his fancy. I, almost too angry to talk, used vile language. Told him what to do with his serving women from England, likewise with his money. I would never have talked so to the Squire in Colwick at home. There is something about living in this country that puts an edge to a man's wits that is not exactly bad temper, but causes him to speak out his own mind forthrightly, even when it is not toward.

Tonight at home, I took Alice with me to the hayfield below the cliffs at the south. There I told her that she could have Champernowne money, and asked her what she wished in the matter. She, the sweetest, the brown-eyed one, the one like Joan, said she would tell me her mind honestly since I was her father. And so she did. Told me where her heart was, but said he did not dare to speak to me because he feared Francis Champernowne. I told her if he feared Champernowne he was not the man for her, but that I would do what I could in her affairs.

July 8, 1653. Put out the fire under the salt pans at four o'clock, and rowed across to Kittery, just above Pull-and-be-damned Point where the current is least strong. Went to the tavern, sat down, and sipped sparsely at my ale till the men came in from the fields and woods. Got myself in talk with Digory Frost, he young and light-haired with land at Pipe Stave Landing. Seemed to be more drunk than I was—which was not any—and called for a pox on Francis Champernowne. He asking why, eagerly, I said because he wooed my daughter and I did not like him. Digory then said quick, "Do you like me any better? And what if I should woo your daughter?" Brought him home with me for supper.

August 3, 1653. My daughter Alice married to Digory Frost and gone to live at Pipe Stave Landing. None at home now but Nannie and Will. Today Will asked me what a hedge was, and that makes me sick at heart. If my son should ask me what God was, that would not surprise me, I not knowing either. But not to know a hedge is grievous. He, the first Scarlock since the time of God not to know one.

September 2, 1653. Joan came crying to me in the field where I was plucking corn. At first I thought she had ill news from Mary, who is near her time, but no. Said she had heard the children talking under the kitchen window. Sam Fernald said he was descended from Jean Fernel, first doctor to the King of France. Will, not to be bettered,

73

made boast that he come down from Will Scarlet, the first of Robin Hood's men. Nannie spoke up then, pretty and proud, that she come down from Bessie Goble, and Bess was the first whore in Portsmouth. Joan went out then and asked her who told her that and what was a whore. Nan said she did not know, but it must be a fine thing because her mother was one. She had heard the loggers say so as they came out of the tavern and pointed at her. Joan told her it was nothing to go with her snout in the skies about; came crying to me. Said the child would be taunted all her life with what she could not help. Minded me that she knew what it was herself, being a workhouse girl. I asked her if she had not been happy, and she saying yes, I told her so would Nannie. Walked with her to the haystack beyond the junipers, lay down there and resolved many things. Oh, Joan, my holly tree . . . !

September 23, 1653. Took Joan to Bloody Point, where Walter Neal challenged Thomas Wiggin long ago to a duel they never fought, there to see Mary and her newborn child, a boy. All say he favors me. Joan, as always, so afraid of the water I wished we had gone by the road. Asked her why she fears it, but she cannot tell me. The black mystery of it, or the current welling up from the sunken ledges, or the way it uncoils like a great, full snake in its channel —she does not know. As we came down the Long Reach on the way home, the western sky was misty, with the round sun red in the middle of it. My daughter Kitty who is dead always loved a red sunset. May God damn John Hall.

March 13, 1654. Today as I was digging parsnips out of the black mould in the low field, Abraham Corbett sent a boy to fetch me to his tavern. Seems there was a man from Nottingham there, one Evan Collin whom I did not know, he being born since I came away, but knew his kin. He told me much of home. The Castle was battered fiercely in the wars, but otherwise the town is much the same. Moll Doubleday rotten with the pox, her son a babbling idiot, both in St. Nicholas' workhouse. Ned Trigg can no longer work his forge, and Jack Gambrell keeps him in the tavern for old times' sake. All four Gambrell lads fought for the King; Rafe killed at Naseby, the others home and well. Squire's son lost an arm at the taking of Bristol. Rob, he says, is very old and cannot move about, but Gilly and Kit run the farm wisely, and the land looks well. They still speak of me and believe I will come home. Failing that, they say, I have promised them a son. It was good to see young Collin and to hear his news, but I find I am much troubled thereat and must think on it.

April 11, 1654. My son Will ten years old today. He straight and well made, with hair and eyes like mine, and no part of Joan—except for this, that he is slow to trust anything he cannot hold in his two hands. His muscles good, and he wields an axe or a plow as skillful as I, though not as strong yet. But he has a quicker wit than ever I had. He is quieter, too, than I, and his thoughts go deeper, but there is a kind of gayness, a devil-may-care in him that was not in any of our kin that ever I knew. After supper we sit in the firelight and he reads to me from Old Tusser, for while there is not much in it that holds good here, save the plain wisdom, perhaps he will some day run an English farm and should know the ways of them. All my thoughts nowadays turn on him and what his future will be.

April 19, 1654. After thinking much on it, I told Joan that I thought when Will was grown he should go to Harvard, the Massachusetts college at the Bay. Why, she said, when you hate the Massachusetts so? I said if he learned their ways in their bosom, he would be better armed against them; that they could not make a Massachusetts man of him, it was already too late for that. But he would learn what it was to sharpen his wits against other men's. I know little of books beyond Tusser's *Five Hundred Points,* since I went only to the Free School till I was tall enough to see over a hedge, but if I had gone there longer I would have been the better for it. She still against it. How, she said, can you make a parson out of a lad come down from Will Scarlet? Harvard, I told her, is not only for parsons; that it was too late to make him a parson, I well knew, nor would I want to. But plain men can learn much there that is to their profit, I think. She not convinced. I set out to find a Latin teacher for my son, since few in Portsmouth ever studied the tongue, and they not beyond *amo, amas, amat.*

May 4, 1654. Took Will to Dover for his first Latin lesson with Parson Maud. Nannie wept to go, so we took her. Wind and tide being right, we went in the shallop. Heard Parson school them, he wise and kindly but much weakened with age. Will learned quick, but Nannie, alas, much quicker. He very quiet going home. As we passed downstream through the Horse Races, she moving forward said to me, "Johnny, I have done wrong. But I will not again." Tonight they learned to decline *patria*, native country. Asked what their native country was, and I told them England.

May 11, 1654. Took the children again to Dover for Latin. Will better than last time. Nannie very slow. Parson says he doubts she can learn the tongue.

July 11, 1656. All the town astir these two months because Oliver Trimmings' wife says Thomas Walford's wife is a witch, turns herself into a cat, and caused her body to burn with fire. This may be true but I doubt it. Joan says they are only two hags who have hated each other for years. Court lets Walford off from hanging, which is well, I think. Ambrose Gibbons dead, he wise, cautious, and thrifty always. Came with me in the *Warwick*.

October 8, 1656. Daniel Knight and I in Walford's tavern drinking too much after Renald Fernald's burying, as good a man as this country ever had, but for Walter Neal. When the children came by from school there was much shouting, so we looked out. All were following Nannie with a W cut in red for her to wear, because, they said, her mother was a Whore. Nannie smiled at them, took the letter from Mary Berry who was chasing her with it, and said, "Yes, I know. And I will wear it when you wear this." Picked a red maple leaf from the gutter, tore it into an S which she held to Mary. Everyone quiet, while Mary asked what it was. "An S for you to wear," said Nannie, "because your mother is a Slut. Her face is dirty and her house smells." All the children laugh and shout; choose Nan for follow-the-leader.

Daniel then said we should never fear for her. Said Bess had a bad name, but that he knew Nannie was his. Said she had a softness on her beauty like his first wife, and mother, and all the Devon women had, that he had not found on any maid whose blood was from north of Exmoor or our eastern counties. Having drunk too much, we then drank more, to Renald, a good friend and neighbor. Daniel asked me how I would like it for his Nan to wed with Will when they were grown. Said she would always have money in her

76

pocket, his Hampton land, and the great fishery which covers half of Hog Island. I said I should like it well, but how would they. Asked me if I held back from having my son marry a harlot's daughter. I said no, 'twas like I had married one myself, and had always been much pleased with her. Will to do the same if he likes, but the choice to be his. Drank till all in the house got drunk—save I, who cannot.

August 27, 1657. Cold like fall; goldenrod blooming in the lanes and many crickets in the stubble. The town has voted to build a new meeting house in the crotch of the roads near John Webster's tavern. It to be forty feet long, flat roof with a turret and gallery inside, twelve windows and three doors. It is to be placed there, south of the Glebe, so that men from Great Island which is populous can get easy to service, but the congregation comes as well from Greenland, Bloody Point, and Rye. We will go there since we must, but I do not approve it. These long, overwise sermons that are the fashion now have none of the sweet comfort the old Prayer Book had. It wearied me when I was a boy, but I would be glad for the sound of it in a parson's mouth now. Joan selling herbs from her garden in the Spring Market today and Brian Pendleton admonished her for wearing red slashes in her sleeves. Tam McQuayne stopped by to tell us Mary's child is born—a boy, her second.

November 1, 1658. I, John Scarlock, fifty years old this day, which somehow surprises me. Twenty-nine years ago, it was, about this time of the fall, that I sat in Jack Gambrell's tavern and listened to Walter Neal; first talk I ever heard of this country. When I left there I promised Rob that I would have boys aplenty and send him one to heir Old Thorny, but I have only one boy because Joan fell at the spring. Perhaps he will want to live in England when the time comes to choose, because I have brought him up to think our home is there. I shall make no choices for him. He must follow his destiny as I followed mine. More and more I think on what Daniel Knight said about Will and Nan. Nannie grows up now, she nearly fourteen, slim and pretty, with smooth gold hair, and something about her that puts me in mind of apple blossoms. She has a quick wit; can be either quiet or gay as she chooses, and I never know what she is thinking. She could be to a man what Joan has been to me, I think, and that is beyond most women.

77

February 21, 1659. John Cutt hath this day received the town's liberty to set up mills to saw and grind on the creek that leads to the fresh marsh, and the privilege of cutting oak and pine on the Town Common. The mills will much advance our state. Will starts to read Greek with Mr. Moodey who has come here to preach at the South Meeting House.

August 31, 1659. Misty moonlight over everything tonight, but autumn in the air. The river full and flooding all the little coves and bays as Will and I walked under our apple trees after supper. Tomorrow he and I ride to Cambridge where he will enter the College. I had planned to be alone with him so that I could tell him many things, but once we were alone I was still. Found I had nothing to tell him. Later he and Nannie row to town where the young folk are gathering in the Great House to eat and drink and play games in his honor and bid him farewell. Richard and Eleanor Cutt set a good table, but they keep a sharp eye out lest anyone wax too gay. My daughter Mary McQuayne has promised she will have her husband there to sing his Scottish ballads. My daughter Alice Frost of Pipe Stave Landing cannot come, she being about to bear a child, her first after six years of marriage.

After Will had gone, I walked along the shore alone and looked at all the lights shining out here and there, both sides of the water. Looked back across the fields, the dark shapes of cattle grazing, to my own house tall on the headland facing to sea, where I add an ell or a gable as the mood takes me. Now I know it will never look like Old Thorny. None of Piscataqua and the Great Bay Country looks at all as we planned it should, back in England, before we came here. For we thought to have lordly manors—Walter talked of castles even—but it is all farms and little towns with roads threading between them like a web of bone lace. And we thought to be rich merchants, but we are still yeomen who follow a team of horses . . . not quite the same, but what ways different I cannot tell. The orchards are flourishing, and the tree line goes back farther every year, though we have not worked our way very far up the rivers because they are all barred with falls of broken rock. In the days of Cromwell—bless God for his taking off—the Dutch wars he brought on made such a call for ships as England has never had, and they began cutting masts here. This work goes on apace, and will in time, I think, bring much money home to Portsmouth. Walter told me the last time I ever saw him that the trees were our true gold. And there is hope that good times may come on again, since every ship from England brings word that the people will likely have King Charles home. Henceforth I need write no more in this book. This time tomorrow, my son will be a grown man, gone from home. I have taught him all I can. The rest he must learn for himself.

6. School a plowman

WILL SCARLOCK opened his eyes and looked straight up at the amber thrust of pine beam over his head, still marked with the little planes his father's axe had made on it when it was a living tree. There was enough light to see by, so he knew it couldn't be too early. Outside the gable window lay only gray mist and no world at all, but there was a redness in the middle of it, which meant that the day would be fair after it got around to burn off. He stretched his long length under the homespun blanket and turned his eyes to the green serge coat hanging carefully on a hook near the half-open door, to the small oak chest he had hammered painstakingly together, that was full now with clean linen and two leather-bound books. This would be the last morning he'd see it all this way. Today he was off for the College.

In the next room he could hear his parents astir and talking, Mother's voice so light the words did not carry, his father's heavy, and a little sad. "I got to make a man of him, Joan, and only this last ride to do it in . . . across a fenny country on a foggy day." And Joan was laughing but tender, putting things right, the way she always did. "You've done it already, John. Done it by being a man yourself. Don't worry for the lad."

Will smiled and stretched further down, poking his toes through the carefully mitred sheets at the bottom of the low bed.

They should have seen him kissing Ruth Puddington under the lilacs behind the Great House last night! They'd have known him for a man then. Ruth knew him for a man. What would have happened if he could have taken her home to Christian Shore and hadn't had to look out for Nannie? He didn't know—probably nothing. Ruth would lead you on and then slap you, but she led a little further every time, he'd noticed. Not that he couldn't have been rid of Nan easy enough, for Sam Hall hung to her elbow like he was chained there, but he remembered his sister Kitty had married Sam's brother and died of it, and he wasn't having any of that for Nan.

Father and Mother were downstairs now. First he smelt wood-smoke and then the salty crispness of bacon in the skillet. Why didn't they call him? Whose voice was that by the kitchen door? It sounded like Digory's. Maybe Alice . . . He heaved himself out of bed, got on breeches and a jacket.

"Will! Breakfast!"

"Yes, Mother."

He tumbled down the worn curve of the stairway and into the kitchen, still a little sleepy, trying not to show how excited he was underneath, how eager to be leaving home, for all it was good and he loved it. Digory Frost sat on a stool by the chimney, taking to-bacco with nervous puffs, his eyes following Joan as she moved deftly about getting breakfast.

"How's Alice?" he asked, rubbing the sleep out of his eyes.

"She's in labor. She wants her mother."

"That's no answer," said Joan a bit sharply. "Tell him what you told me. That Sarah Scriggins says all is well and 'twill be an easy birth. One would think to hear you 'twas something hadn't happened before."

"It hasn't . . . to Alice."

Joan went to her son-in-law and ruffled the blond hair over his worried forehead. "I've known Sarah near thirty years and never knew her wrong. I'll go with you in a minute—when the lads are fed." Her smile went from John to Will and back.

Nannie came downstairs then, fresh and sweet, with a white lace kerchief at the neck of her blue gown. Somehow she looked differ-ent to him this last morning, and Will suddenly realized she wasn't his sister, though they had slept in the same cradle and grown up to-gether. Beside her, Ruth Puddington's dark eyes seemed a bit wild, her olive skin a bit sallow. Nannie was clear pink and white and golden. No, by God, Sam Hall shouldn't have her. He'd meet men at the College. He'd make friends there. He'd find a good husband for Nan.

"Your things all together, Will?" asked his father soberly.

"Yes. In the chest. Five minutes will take me out of here."

"After you eat," said Joan. "Pull up the benches now. John, I think Digory needs some brandy."

John lifted the latch of the cellar door. "Come on down, boy. Take what you want. I could do with a drop myself."

"You want some, Will?" asked Joan, putting a trencher in front of him heaped with hot porridge, wheat bread, and bacon.

"Drink? No. I want this." He dug into the food with his wooden spoon. "I suppose they're afraid it might be like with Kitty."

"Hush!" snapped his mother. "Don't talk to them of Kitty. Men! I marvel the things they're brave at, but childbirth's not amongst 'em."

John and his son-in-law came back from the cellar and sat down at the trestle table. Joan had put out mugs of ale, and Digory reached for one, his hand shaking.

"If you drink any more," said John slowly, "I can't let Joan go with you. You won't be fit to handle a boat."

"Tide's coming in and I can row," said Joan coolly. "You better not have any more children, Digory. It goes too hard with you. John . . . Will . . . are you ready to be gone?"

She had her cloak on, a little bag of comforts in her hand. Going to her son, she bent and kissed him. "Good-bye. Learn enough off them to get your money's worth—but don't forget how to handle a plow." She kissed John on the mouth. "Don't stay away long. Come on, Digory."

And then Will and John were alone at the board, sopping up the last of the porridge, except for Nannie at the end, who was beginning to snuffle, tears dripping down each side of her little round nose, that looked as if it intended to turn up but never quite did, with the golden freckle on the end of it.

"Get your things, Will," said John awkwardly, standing up, looking, troubled, at Nan. Will scrambled upstairs, leaving the two of them.

"Don't you cry, Nannie," said John. "He'll be back."

"But . . . not for long . . . and long . . ."

He did not have the heart to answer her. Will came down, proud in the new green coat, carrying the little chest, and John remembered a boy he had seen once in a mirror that hung on a tavern wall in Nottingham. This was—not quite—the same boy.

"Good-bye, Nannie," said Will, smiling. He ought to kiss her, he thought, and then he realized suddenly that he did not know how to kiss Nan. Like she were Mother, or Mary, or Alice—or like she were Ruth Puddington? He stood quite still for a moment and thought about it, knowing that he must decide the matter, but not knowing that he must decide it now for once and all. Then he did by her as he had done by Ruth.

She did not look at him when he let her go and he found himself speaking too quickly, with a roughness and confusion in his voice.

"Good-bye. Don't you marry any of the godly while I'm gone."

"No. No . . . I won't . . . marry."

"Well, don't you. Remember, you're Mistress Nancy Knight, and an heiress who can pick and choose."

"Can I?"

"Listen. You shall have the man you want if I have to break his bones first."

She giggled, a little wildly. "Would that . . . make him love me?"

Will laughed, free and open. "There are better ways," he said, "but you'll know them. Good-bye."

". . . good-bye."

They walked out of the house and down the cornfield edge, where some of the ears were still full and bursting pale gold through the green husks, and pumpkins pricked out orange here and there. They went by the salt pond and up the little neck between the marshes, past Joanna Fernald's house half overrun with grape vines, and into the sedge again. Tide was low, just turning, and they poled the raft across the shallow creek to Strawberry Bank side, and still no word spoken between them. John looked back at the rowan tree he had sat under the night he thought his boy was dying. It was taller now, with more branches, and bright tufts of berry. Will looked straight ahead of him, at the pointed roofs of Portsmouth with the mist thinning round them, and the red glow of morning on everything. In Johnny Crowther's barn their horses were waiting, ready for the journey, where they'd tied them the night before. Johnny was working the iron bog, but Jane came out and stood between her tall rosebushes to say good-bye and offer them bread and beer, which they took but couldn't swallow.

And then they were off down the crooked road, out of the Bank toward Hampton, past brown farms and ruddy flecked orchards, pastures blue with juniper, and wedges of forest set between them. Goldenrod and wild aster colored the ditches, and here and there an untimely frost had crimsoned a leaf of woodbine that crept on a stone wall. Puffs of milkweed down, dried from silk into cotton, drifted before them, wafting the seed to earth. Men were stripping the fields behind the gabled houses as they went by, and axes rang in the purple gloom of the woodland. On the sea side, gulls swooped over the yellow marshes, following the streams that wound there, or lighting on the rounded cocks of salt hay.

Will spoke from his heart. "Couldn't be a better country."

John did not answer him.

They stopped for dinner under the high sun at Daniel Knight's house by the Cow Common. Daniel, they knew, was out on Hog Island where he spent most of his time at the fishery, but his servant fed them well, and then they were off through the Salisbury bogs, past the Bound House set at the edge of Massachusetts. Will had never been this far before, and while they waited by the gray, swirling Merrimack, just above the sand bars, for the ferry to take them deeper into what he had always thought of as enemy country, he began to wish his father would say something—anything— just so he didn't feel he was making the journey alone.

And finally John did. He cleared his throat and spoke, words that must be said, but that did not come easy.

"Don't you believe all they tell you down there. Take it into your mind and think on it. They can teach you Greek and Latin, and there's nothing in that will do you harm, for Troy's past arguing on. But if they try to tell you aught of our time—aught that's between the King and Cromwell, or between New Hampshire and Massachusetts—listen and say, 'Yes, sir,' But remember, they're probably lying."

"Aye."

"And another thing. There's a curse or a blessing goes with all old families, and ours is a curse. That you'll get no good from the grain or the grape, and the more you drink the more dull and sober you grow. 'Tis that way with me, and with you who's been bred in a strange country it hasn't been tried. Perhaps in Ipswich where we stop tonight . . ."

And then the ferry came and they went over into Newbury, and down through the swaying salt grasses to Rowley where the weavers' looms were clacking, and so, just at twilight, into Ipswich. Ipswich was a fair, large town, with shops and a grammar school, and a bell in the top of the Meeting House. There was a rocky brook below the town green, and thick old chestnut trees that dropped their fat nuts on the tavern roof and grooved sand of the roadway. In that tavern, the Scarlocks, father and son, tried out the old curse they had brought in their blood from Nottingham, and they sat and drank all night with the Essex men, and in the raw, cold morning only they were sober.

"Praise God, the curse still holds," said John, as he gave Will a hand up, and together they rode on, through the foggy marshes and crowding towns, nearer and nearer to the Bay.

Once he spoke of Winthrop and Wiggin who had contrived New Hampshire out of the free ways of the first beginnings there, for he could still burn with a sullen anger whenever he remembered it. "Aye," he muttered, "they were bad, sharp men. Call one Wat Tyler and the other Jack Straw."

"Why? Who were they?"

"The greatest knaves that ever were in England."

"What did they do?"

"Tried to upset what was."

"What's wrong with that?"

"If you don't know now there's no sense my telling you."

And Will knew that he had displeased his father, but he did not know why. Hadn't *he* upset what was, when he left Old Thorny and came to Piscataqua? But he was young then, and now he was fifty and saw things a different way. When *I'm* fifty, thought Will, maybe I'll see . . . maybe.

And then there was a mile or two of silence, the houses getting nearer together now, and the roads smoother, and fair bridges over the salt creeks between them. And slowly they came together again in easier talk.

"Parson Reyner's boy, John, from Dover, went down by sea last week. That'll be one lad you'll know."

"Yes," said Will without enthusiasm. Young Reyner was a mild, gentle boy, good at his books and no harm in him, but he couldn't laugh hearty or make a tree fall straight.

"You have to be careful with men if you don't know their folk."

"How about women?" asked Will daringly.

"Women," said John soberly, "they be always a mystery—as you're old enough to know. Of course Joan never knew her father, and sometimes I wonder about Nannie, for Bess hadn't a good name, and there's no look of Daniel Knight about her. And suppose you did know her father and mother—like the palm of your own hand—would you ever quite know where your wife came from or what she was? Women be that strange. Even your mother."

"Mother, strange? Then so's a loaf of bread and the bricks in the chimney. Was *your* mother strange, back in England?"

"No. Nothing was ever so strange in England. Still, a man's mother is never strange . . . but his wife will always be . . . a little."

And on the afternoon of the second day they rode into Cambridge. It was a pretty and compact town with houses set widely back from Braintree Street, and wharves at the edge of a curving river that lay flung down between the reeds, going nowhere, that did not well, and swirl, and eddy, like the Piscataqua at home. They found a tavern and asked there for the president's lodging, and when they came to it, it was a proper house, with a sloping green to the north that held a great wooden hall with a tower, and a smaller, stone hall at the side, and beyond all, the yellowing stalks of a cornfield.

At the front door a little maid met them and took them to the study, a small, square room, far back on the right, facing an apple orchard. President Charles Chauncey sat there among his books, immaculate in a black broadcloth doublet, white collar, and clipped gray hair. He started to rise, but when he saw that his visitors wore thick boots and country clothing, he settled back again.

"Scarlock? Oh, yes. The steward has already received a load of pine boards through the merchant, Daniel Knight, and credited them to you. Does he know the book? Whom has he studied with?"

"With Mr. Maud at Dover. After he died, with Mr. Reyner, who took his place there. Last, with Mr. Moodey."

"All men of parts whom I know well. Let me try the lad."

President Chauncey looked at him and hurled the Latin like a spear.

"Cap this:

" '*Jamque erat in totas . . .*' "

Will heard not one word of it. He heard a little wind go stirring through the apple leaves, and the grinding of wheels in Braintree Street. Then he looked at his father. John leaned back in the wainscot chair, oblivious of his rough clothes and great boots with dung and salt weed still clinging to them. He seemed at ease until you noticed how his hand lay clenched along the coarse cloth that cov-

86

ered his knee, a brown, gnarled hand, no flesh scarcely, only skin, taut bone, and blue vein. Will suddenly knew that he loved that hand more than anything in the world. He knew, too, that he was going to pass the examination. He looked straight back at the long, sleek face with the cold, bright eyes set in it, and weighed his own spear lightly. What had the old gaffer said? Oh, sure . . .

"Yes, sir.

"'. . . *sparsurus fulmina terras;*
    Sed timuit ne forte sacer tot ab ignibus aether.
    Conciperet . . .'"

"Enough," rumbled the president's powerful voice. "English this:
"'Αὐταρ ἐπεὶ δὴ τοῦτο γένος κατὰ γαι'ἑκάλυψε—
    τοὶ μὲν δαίμονες ἁγνοὶ επιχθόνιοι καλέουται
    ἐσθλοί ἁλεξίκακοι, φνλακες θυητῶν ἀυθ ῥώπων.'"

"Yes, sir," said Will.

"'For . . . after the earth has hid . . . a generation . . .
    They are as ghosts . . . but living still, and kindly
    To mortals . . . warding harm . . .'"

And he thought of mode and syntax, but his father was remembering a green ghost in Nottingham that he had never seen, but whose presence had come, with the bit of random Greek, into this alien room.

And so they struck and parried, while shadows drew out long on the trampled grass beyond the window and dusk thickened like smoke in the corners by the bookshelves. But at last there came a stop. Dr. Chauncey waved Will into silence and turned to John, ruffled and perplexed.

"He has a spritely wit—too spritely for a scholar. He knows the lexicons as well as I do. He can learn all we would teach him. But he lacks sober reverence, and he will never follow pure logic for its own sake. He can play the heathen poets like a peal of bells, but he will read the Church Fathers with his tongue in his cheek. You can school a plowman, but he will always love a sown field better than a syllogism."

That might be likely, thought the Scarlock men, neither of them ever having heard of a syllogism.

"You may be wasting your money—if you have the money?"

"I have the money," said John, clearing his throat. "If you will take him. . . ."

"I cannot, in honor, refuse," said the troubled president, "since he answered all that was put to him. But I own I should like to. Before God, Goodman Scarlock, he will never make a scholar."

"I don't care," said John, standing up. "He'll get what I'm paying for."

"And that?"

"I'm . . . not sure . . . I can tell you . . . but he'll be here . . . living with the other boys, reading the books they read."

"Remember, I make you no promises." He took a small, battered scroll from a drawer of his desk and handed it to Will. "These are the College Laws. When you've made yourself a copy, I'll sign it, and that's proof you're of us. I'll have your name put up on the board at the buttery hatch so you can eat in the Hall tonight and meet the tutors and fellows; and remember, we speak only in Latin there. Morning prayers are at six o'clock, with beef and sizings afterward. Then Logic and the Classic Tongues—study in the afternoon. And of an evening any lawful sport—until nine—but beware of riotousness and loss of precious time."

"Yes, sir."

"And now you had better go over to the Indian College and get Sergeant Green to cut your hair."

They trailed through a door at the back of the president's lodging and into the low meadow where the grass was worn by many feet. Once Dr. Chauncey stopped and looked lovingly around him. "If Plato taught in a grove," he mused, aloud, but to himself, "why not we in a cornfield?" The Scarlocks, following humbly, did not answer. Now straight ahead reared up the long hall they had seen from Braintree Street, two storied, with a turret and rows of diamond-paned windows, nobly designed, indifferently built, and not kept up at all, for the clapboards had rotted here and there and the roof sagged. In the wide doorway at the center stood a tall boy, dark, heavy-browed, very handsome, dressed in a gray suit of fine English cloth and cut.

"Oh, Damerill," called the president in the tones of one who sees relief from a disagreeable duty. "This is Freshman Scarlock. Show him where to put his box in the Long Chamber." He turned to John. "If you'll come this way, we'll go to the steward and see how much you owe for his quarter—less the pine boards."

John followed through the door, past the boy called Damerill, and down a passage to the left, where they stopped before the half-open hatch of a room lined with shelves that seemed to hold mostly an array of cups, mugs, and small kegs, with here and there a gallon of sack amongst them. Beyond, to the right, must be the kitchen, for the smell of cooking rose in that direction, and John's nose told him the College would be having stewed beef for supper—old, tough beef, not lately killed, served up with boiled turnip. The floor was uneven and the wall boards crazily matched, he noticed, as he waited while a thin, harassed man in the buttery repeated the name, "Scarlock," and went around shuffling papers, searching through a ledger. Finally he stepped out to join them, speaking an apology to Dr. Chauncey.

"I think we'd better take a look at them again. They're in the Yard with the goods of the other students who paid in kind."

John followed them through a westward door, and the three stepped out of the College and into a turmoil of produce heaped up on the grass, the blood and marrow of New England, offered here to send her sons to school. There were piles of cord wood and pipe staves, apples, corn still in husk, and ground grain; beeves, boxes of candles and bolts of homespun; here a tethered goat. He knew his own white, shaved boards, and went toward them. The steward reckoned in his ledger. John owed him seventeen shillings six pence, he said, and waited. John reached into his pocket and paid it. The president and the steward turned away in the falling dusk.

He looked at the lights coming on in the windows of the town. Then he called after them, "Is that all?"

"All until next quarter," said Dr. Chauncey over his shoulder, "if he stays for it. I tell you, he will never make . . ." Going into the College, he shut the door on his own answer. John stood alone, uncertain, in Harvard Yard.

Meanwhile Will had climbed upstairs after Damerill, into a great yawning room on the second floor lined with trundle beds. Most of them had blankets, but a few were bare, rope-bottomed. "Take any one of them," said Damerill. "Put your box under it."

Will chose one by the window where he could look out into an elm tree, swaying, green. He stowed his oak chest away obediently, then turned to his guide. There seemed nothing immediate that must be done. "Sit down," said the dark boy, now sprawled on an opposite cot. "I know your name's Scarlock, but who's Scarlock, and where do you come from?"

"From Portsmouth in Piscataqua."

Damerill frowned. "I hear they're a nest of savage knaves up

89

there; that it's a small, poor country, but its iniquity is out of all proportion to its size."

"You hear wrong. We're good, decent subjects of the King."

"Haven't you heard the King's in exile?"

"But he's still the King."

"So you're of that persuasion?"

"Aye."

Damerill slipped back a little into the shadows that were falling through the casements where the chill of autumn dark was beginning to replace the warm summer afternoon. "I'm a Cromwell man myself. My father was an Ironside, killed at Naseby when I was a year old. He'd lived here in Boston as two of his brothers still do—came out of Essex in Winthrop's fleet. When the wars began he went back there, hoping to set up the saints at home."

"And what'd he set up? That bastard Cromwell!"

"Cromwell was a great and holy man."

"Can't prove either way now," said Will. "He's dead as a haddock."

His companion stood up, and though Will could measure his own six feet on any wall, he knew this fellow was taller.

"I was baptized," he said slowly, thoughtfully, where Will had expected him to burst out with an angry answer, "in Wyethorne, down in the fens by Boston Stump . . . among my mother's people . . . and the name they gave me was 'Love-the-Truth.' But when I grew to sense, I knew that Truth was greater than Love, so I write myself that way. Truth. I love it, and try to live by it, and when I see another man stand fearless for what he believes it to be, I love him, although I know that his truth is lies."

This was hard for Will to follow, but he caught up with it slowly. Truth Damerill went on talking. "There's few here in the College has any love for the King, and no man else than you would dare to say so if he had. But I warn you to hold your tongue or you'll not be with us long. Don't you know, boy, what it means, to live in Massachusetts?"

"I've heard it's a knave's country."

"No. It's not that, but it's for men whose thoughts bend all one way like a row of poplars bent by the east wind. Mine bend like theirs. That's why my uncles have sent me to school here instead of in England where things have gone all awry and the Stuarts'll soon be home. Your thoughts have a different turn. Your tongue's rude, you're a blasphemer, and your mind is darkened with a great error —yet someways, I know you for the best man I've ever met."

"I think," said Will slowly, "you're likely a better man than I am. You'd spare an enemy. I'm not so sure I would."

Truth's dark face lighted with a wide smile. "The way to best an enemy is to befriend him," he said. "Come on down. It's time for evening bevers."

"What's that?"

"A serving of beer—maybe bread and cheese if you want to pay for it. They deal it out at the buttery hatch twice a day."

"President Chauncey said I was to go to something called the Indian College and get my hair cut."

"Oh! Well, you do look a bit like a court gallant masqued for a shepherd. The Indian College is across the Yard. This is called the Old College, because it was first built, and downstairs is the Hall where we eat and have lectures and recitation. Down on Braintree is Goffe College—some of the upperclassmen sleep there. You'll soon know your way around."

"Where is everybody now?"

"This time of day they'll be in the studies—which are tucked away all over. But there are none for freshmen. We catch the book as we can, mostly in the Hall itself. I'd just stepped out to clear my head."

"Have you been here long?"

"Two weeks."

They went downstairs and across to the Indian College, planned for redskins, Truth told Will, but it was an uncommon hard task to get one to come there, they not being a great people for books. It was built of stone, dark in the upper story, but lighted below, and through the windows, as they approached it, Will could see two men with tousled hair and smudged faces working around a great lever set in a square maze of wooden beams.

"That's the printing press," explained Truth, "where they make books for the Colony. Sergeant Green cuts hair, too, but he's a better printer than a barber. He's good at setting titles in blackletter on an Indian tract or a broadside, but he'll notch your ears if you don't watch him and pull away in time. Especially if he knows your party, for he came with my father under John Winthrop. I . . ."

From the shadows on the path that led westward into Cambridge came a low whistle.

"Oh!" said Will. "I forgot. That's my father. I better go speak to him."

Leaving his new friend, he hastened toward the familiar figure waiting under an elm that dropped down yellow leaves on the dark grass.

"How are you getting on?"

"I? Oh. Good . . . so far. Are you . . . ?"

"I got your bills paid. I better start back. The moon's up, and the horses are rested by now. I have to get home because of Alice."

"Oh . . . I'd forgotten Alice. Send me word how she is. And if it's a boy."

"Yes, I will. Take care of your money and keep your thoughts to yourself."

"I—I'll be careful."

"Let us know if you want anything."

"I will. Good-bye."

"Good-bye, man."

They stood there silent for a moment, under the white moon, at the edge of twilight, while lights kindled in the hall behind them, and the voices of boys released from study beat at the buttery hatch like tide coming in. John stumbled a little as he turned back to the tavern on the Charlestown Road where he had left his horses. Ahead of him lay the darkened farms, and flooding salt rivers of the eastern country, and finally his own house, which would hold now no other man but him. Will looked for a moment at the lights of the town. There must be over a hundred of them, he thought. This was the world, and here he was, right in the middle of it. He stepped eagerly over the stone sill of the Indian College. And that was the last time the two were together, for though they met again, and talked, and shared one roof, it was never quite the same.

7. An English corpse

"SCHOLASTICISM," said Truth Damerill, sitting up straight on the oak stool in his study under the hot eaves of the Old College, and staring into the mild autumn night beyond the open casement, "integrates the universe."

"But who the hell wants to integrate the universe?" asked Will Scarlock, senior sophister, lying on the floor, sprawled over the *Odes of Horace*.

It was half past eight—almost time for quenching the candles—and most of the boys were straggling through the still green Yard, where the frost had not yet come this year, wrestling on the grass, or bursting out with a song now and then, or simply enjoying the starlight and the feel of being young in it. But Truth hated to leave his books even for bevers, and Will, never quite sure whether what lay between them was the deepness of friendship or merely a wrangle that after three years was still a draw, had chosen tonight to stay indoors with him, though he did not always choose that way.

"Why not take the universe as it is . . . take it and enjoy it?"

"And whoever taught you that the chief end of man was to enjoy the universe?"

"I didn't need to be taught; I was born knowing it. Books are good, Truth, and so's piety, but we go too far with both of them here. I'm not going to live and die in Aristotle's works."

"Not Aristotle any more—Ramus is the man now, incomparable Ramus! Besides, you sound like one of those filthy playwrights from the Old Queen's time. You didn't phrase that?"

"No, Kit Marlowe did, but he's not filthy. He's wonderful. And I think maybe Tom Middleton is better. Did you ever read the *Chaste Maid in Cheapside?*"

"No." Truth twisted his handsome features scornfully. "Did you ever read all the way though the *Dialecticae?*"

"God forbid! Listen, Truth, just like Ramus went beyond Aristotle and said he'd naught to do with the way things really were, and that his dichotomies were a perversion—oh, I know the words as well as you do—just so I'd go beyond Ramus, and say his truth has naught to do with the truth of a plowed field."

"You and your plowed fields! That's why Dr. Chauncey keeps you at the bottom of the class list."

"I know. I like him better than he likes me. Old Chaunce! There's a man there, under all the wrappings of Hebrew grammar. He's not so much of a Ramist either."

"He's a scholar. But overcautious with the new."

"I do not put my faith too much in scholars. My mother can't write her name, but she can integrate the universe."

"How?"

"For her, it's my father."

"Will." Truth turned on him in the blowing candlelight, scowling across the pages of blackletter. "To put your faith in Man is to heap up treasures on earth, to forget that the flesh is dust. Ah, the flesh! Our old enemy!"

Will looked up, bewildered, at the raptured face of his friend who did not see him, for Truth Damerill looked on other worlds, and to know him was to know a cold flame burning; to be drawn, and driven back, and then to stumble blindly forward again, shielding your eyes with your hand, for fear of a too-great light that seemed about to break.

"There be white lilies in the world, and there be dung. A man can put his nose to either."

"He's not a man unless he puts his nose to both. Oh, I know Old Chaunce wouldn't hear to it, but I'm ready to preach a sermon. I'd like to stand up in Cambridge Meeting House on the Lord's Day, and scrape my boots, and shift my throat in my collar, and lean out and tell people. I'd tell them this:

" 'Let's leave God alone. There he is, and there's nothing you can do about him. Come out with me now, and I'll take you as near as you'll ever come to him!' Then I'd march them all, the old gaffers in their starched neckbands, and the goodwives in their stuff petticoats, and the maids in white kerchiefs, all saintly faced and just itching to crawl behind the alders with any healthy bullock of a lad—I'd march them down to the reeds by the Charles and stand them up a-line. And then—if we were lucky—we'd see a dragonfly, pink, and purple, and rainbow light along the wings, and a color that's not in earth or heaven, that's nothing you can name. 'That,' I'd tell them, 'is as much of God as you'll ever see.'"

Below in the Yard, boys' voices lifted against the sultry night that closed overhead like a roof.

> *"Come let us scatter them like dust*
> *Upon the wind that flies,*
> *Or beat them down like any dirt*
> *Along the street that lies."*

Will cocked his head to one side, looked at the swinging casement, then at his friend.

"What's that they're singing? It's the words of the eighteenth Psalm, but I never heard it to just that measure before—like a battle cry."

Truth smiled grimly. "That's the way the Ironsides sang it at Naseby. I taught them that."

The song lifted through the whole Yard, and under it you could almost hear the marching of heavy boots, and the clash of swords, and the death cries of men who had killed each other in battle twenty years ago.

"Well, we can't have that!" Will scrambled to his feet, and as the last notes died away triumphant in the darkness, he lifted his own voice, solitary, clear and strong, almost unbearably plaintive, in a cavalier tune that had rung against every hedge in England and somehow crossed the water with the faithful who fled from the reign of Noll.

> *"Oh the man in the moon may wear out his shoon*
> *By running after Charles his wain,*
> *But all to no end, for the times will not mend,*
> *Till the King enjoy his own again."*

"There be gods on our side, too," he observed virtuously, lowering himself to the pages of Horace. "Bards, anyway . . ."

From the Yard came whistles, shouts, a rush for the stairway; from the president's lodging the creak of a casement thrust back and the roar of a powerful voice, "Be still your caterwauling!"

"Why do you want to fight it over, Will?" asked Truth in the brief interval while the crowd stamped from study to study, looking for the damned Royalist who had replied to them. "It's those who lose battles want to fight them over. You've won. Your King's enjoying his own—and everybody else's too."

"Not while New Hampshire's under Massachusetts."

The door was flung back. Red-faced, hot, ardent as any street rabble, the boys poured in.

"Hey! Who sang? Is the bastard in here?"

Truth frowned, said nothing. Will's reply was as bland as a swallow of new milk. "Sang? We're at study. If you can't emulate us, sirs, you may at least leave us in peace."

Quelled, uncertain, muttering a little, the rout withdrew to search the studies on the other side of the Long Chamber. Only one boy, tousled, fair-haired, with a wide, appealing smile, lingered after the others. He ignored Truth. He spoke to Will.

"Say, Will, how about coming over to Vasty's after lights out? There's a couple of dancing girls there, been warned out of Boston. And they're going to . . ."

Will drew himself up and posed nobly with his hand in the front of his jacket. "I vow to you, Thomas Rockwell, sir, so help me God, I shall be there! You know"—his voice dropped, became mockingly confidential—"Old Chaunce had me into his study only yesterday. 'Will Scarlock,' he told me in all soberness, over the Bible and two glasses of beer, 'in the Lord's Name, I appoint you Warden of Dancing Girls for Harvard College.' So you see, Rockwell," he drew his slender shoulders up severely, "'tis my duty to be there. Go thou before and prepare a place for me."

Tom Rockwell from Windsor, who paid his quarter bills in good grain, and came to the College, he said, because it seemed easier to preach sermons for a living than to scrouge up the damn tough grass roots, walked out, laughing. Truth faced Will.

"So you're breaking the College Law! You're going out with Tom Rockwell—'Tom Rakehell,' more like—after dancing girls?"

"Oh, Truth, listen—come on with us! Don't be so damned holy! Don't you know it says in the Word there'll be more rejoicing in heaven over one repentant sinner than over ninety and nine just men? Come on and sin now—good and proper—so heaven can hear a clash of cymbals when you're gathered home!"

"No! You go by yourself. I'll stay awake to let you in."

The bell in the turret over their heads rang portentously. Nine. In the Indian College the candles and rushlights flickered out. Goffe College was already dark. All through the Yard quietness lay like a pall of new-come snow, but there were whispers burrowing underneath it, like moles working a slow course through frozen ground. Truth blew out the candle in the iron socket on his desk. Thin white moonlight streamed through the casement.

Will hesitated a moment. "Truth," he said soberly, "you're my better self. You're what I'd be if I hadn't come from those plowed fields that are such a stench in your nostrils."

The dark, brooding shadow that was his friend spoke to him from the thinner darkness by the window.

"And you are what I would be if I had the courage of sin. . . ."

"Instead of the courage of virtue? Truth, I'd like to see you in twenty years. Find out if you've always been as good as you meant to be."

"And you'll be overjoyed if I haven't."

"No, by God, it'll break my heart."

With no more words Will went downstairs. He knew well just where the creaking boards were and he avoided them. Then he stepped out to become a shadow on the grass, to join other shadows drifting up from here and there. Across Braintree Street, Dame Vashti Bradish kept a respectable house where the boys without too much in pocket could get a comfortable pennyworth of ale and take it in honest fashion. A large, smooth woman, with little, kindly eyes set deep in her face—"Vasty," as they called her—lumbered here and there like a sow with too many piglets. But she was not too busy to greet one of her best customers, the tall, thin, gray-eyed boy from the east country, who could pay cash and drink till cockcrow and be never the worse for aught she served him. "Hey, Will, sit ye there. We have good company tonight."

Goffe College must be cleaned out, he thought, and half the Old College empty, as he watched the tumult of his fellow students milling around him. "Where are the wenches?" he shouted at Tom across the room. "Tom Rakehell, sir, I'm here on an official errand!"

"Pssst, Willie! Here!" It was Vasty at his elbow, and with her she had two maids, one fair, and golden, and overplump, and 'fore God not so pretty as Nannie back home; the other brown-haired, rosy,

97

a bit too thin. They had scarlet and lace about them, and painted mouths, and Brown-Hair wore a small black patch set in the ivory curve of her cheek. "I can love both fair and brown," he quoted to himself, leaning to Brown-Hair. Aloud he said, "If you're a stranger here . . . my lady . . . may I serve you?"

She smiled at him, a smile of promises. "We be rich yeomen's daughters," she babbled, like a grammar school lad mouthing the third declension, "stolen for breeding in Virginia. But we won free . . ."

You be London street girls run away from a house, more like, he thought. He led her to a bench in the corner and she seated herself, but when he sat down beside her she swung over on his knee.

So that was the way she wanted it? Well, he'd not disappoint her. He laid her back on one arm and kissed her. Truth was handsomer than he, Tom Rockwell gayer, more knowing. But a girl would go straight by Truth and Tom, time and again, and come to Will, there being that about him that none of the three could name, nor yet the girl herself. And since it had always been that way, knowing he could pick and choose, just so he never had. When I find what suits me, he thought. But so far he had never found it—not so far, and he was a senior sophister, past eighteen. But as he kissed Brown-Hair, he knew it would not be she.

The night was well begun, he thought, as he stroked the girl's forearm, bare and pliant, and looked about the room. Vasty knew how to save candles. There weren't too many lights going. Gold-Hair was sitting on a beer keg swinging her ankles and talking to Nate Chauncey, the president's son, a good lad who could rhyme Latin like a Roman, but had a hard time getting out at night. Nate put his arm around her. Once he did get out, he knew what to do. Truth would be up in his hot study, trying to liberate the arguments from the categories, but *he* was here—with a full mug in front of him and a girl in his arms. Let Truth keep Burgersdicius and Wendelin and the *Systema Logicae*—those philosophers all caught up in the tangle of their own minds like cod in a great net. "Arms I sing and the man" . . . "We fight by the hollow ships" . . . "As the generations of leaves so are the generations of men. . . ." He'd found fine words in books, thoughts that would keep him warm in the cold years, and that was enough for any man to take home from Harvard College. He kissed Brown-Hair absently. The generations of leaves . . . that phrase made him think of the dream he'd had last night.

He'd fallen asleep over Ovid—the part where Orpheus, bereft, sits down and pipes up all the green trees and they come running. And instead of Ovid's cypress and laurel and ilex, he'd seen the oak and maple, and the great mast pines along the Piscataqua at home. And in his dream the pines had stood there, tall, swaying in a sort of shadowy wind, and then they had left their hillsides and clay banks, and pulled away, and marched down like men on marching feet, between the willows and the alders, right to the shaly edge of the river, and their roots had gone into the swirling, green-gray water. And the minute the water touched them there had been a swift change. Each great tree had become a ship's mast, and the trees marched endlessly down from the hills, and the ships sprung up endless at the waterside and dropped down harbor, out of sight around Great Island, and still more trees kept coming, and more masts crowding to the sea.

"You're not drinking none, Willie," said Vasty Bradish. She poured more ale in his cup. Brown-Hair pouted and he kissed her. The boys around the long board on trestles down the center had begun to sing, keeping time with the beat of earthen mugs on oak. Tom Rockwell had got a chamberpot from somewhere, and he struck it loud with an iron spoon at the end of every measure, throwing his head back to shake the fair hair from his eyes.

> "Oh . . . in Amsterdam there lived a maid,
> Who used to ply a roaring trade!"

Near him John Reyner, from his own country, kept looking down at a scroll of Latin verse he'd been making when the boys called him out—always he would go on a bout but never enjoy himself. "Don't you think, Will," he murmured apprehensively, "with so much noise—the tutors will hear?"

"The tutors? Hell, no. They're lying around the Hall dead drunk on logic."

A girl on his knee, he thought, and plenty of ale at hand; a warm, dim tavern with a white moon looking in through the windows and good fellows singing. And God saw that it was good, he thought—only he wished now that Brown-Hair would find another knee so he could stand up and sing with the boys. He could feel her little sharp bones through her flimsy skirts. And then he lifted his eyes to the doorway and saw Truth Damerill and Daniel Knight, dark as doom and looking for him.

They came forward, cleaving their way through the singers as through a company of ghosts, and he let Brown-Hair slide where she would, ignored her soft, surprised curse, and stood up to them. He saw in Daniel's face that there was trouble, and he knew—almost—what the trouble was.

"Which one . . . is it?" he asked, whitening.

"It's . . . your father."

"Is he . . . ?"

"No." Daniel took off his broad-brimmed hat and mopped his forehead. Truth looked on, sober, suffering for his friend. But Will was not suffering. He was not feeling anything.

"No. Damned if I know what he means, Will, or why I'm here for you. He stands up as well as we, and walks, and eats, and lies down at night—but he says he's dying and he wants his boy."

"Why does he think he's dying?"

"Well, it was like this: you know Tam McQuayne came down to help with harvest?"

"Yes. They planned that before I went back to school."

"And day before yesterday—Sunday—it seems he was rowing Tam back to Bloody Point. He was upset. He and your mother'd been to church that morning, and Parson Moodey gave out an order that any man-jack who was caught sleeping in sermon or taking tobacco on the Lord's Day should be locked up in a wooden cage on the Common.

"That angered John so he couldn't eat when they came home. He kept muttering about Puritan bastards, and that when he came here this was a free country, and he'd shoot red blood out of any man who came to put him in a cage, by God. About dusk he and Tam started upriver, and just north of town a whirlpool opened right under them and down they went. We never found one splinter of the boat. I was up in Richard Cutt's orchard, buying apples off him to feed the men at the fishery, and he and I saw it happen. We put out in his boat as fast as we could, but the current caught us, too, and 'twas all we could do to beat back to shore. They were a-top of the water, swimming, though, and looked all right, but then Tam got a cramp and couldn't move himself, and John had to bring him in. Cold-blue and gasping, they were, laid on the shale, when we got to them. Tam took a cold and he's a-bed now, coughing hoarse, but getting over it. John looks like there's naught wrong with him, but he says he's going to die. Get me an ale, Will."

"Aye. Right now, man. Vasty!" Will could feel his voice tremble. The three of them drank.

Will stood up first. "Good-bye, Truth," he said. "We better not wait. We better start home."

"Yes, we better, Will," said Daniel.

"You tell Old Chaunce and the boys. I'll . . . see you."

"God go with you, Will."

"Thanks for the wish, Truth."

And then he was riding through the sultry starlight, on the horse Daniel had brought for him, east through the swaying marsh grass that edged the Charlestown Road, and neither of them had any words to say.

And next night, just at the fall of dusk, he sat in the kitchen at home, waiting to go in to his father. Joan was in the bedroom, and Sarah, and a young doctor from Dover whom nobody knew very much about. For John did not stand up, and eat, and walk about like other men now. He lay down. From upstairs came the rasping coughs of Tam McQuayne in his sick bed, and the wild sobbing of Mary who knew she could keep her husband—for this time, anyway—but not her father. Nannie was up there trying to comfort her, and Alice, white and spent-looking, with two babies clinging to her skirts. His thoughts went suddenly back to the College. Truth would be putting Ramus aside now and going down with the others into the Hall, to the tutors and fellows gathered around the silver bowl on the high table, with the fragrance of mulled beer coming out of it. Now, he guessed, he would never go back there. He looked out the window at the brown, stripped fields sloping down to the gray river, all patches of shadow under the twilight. They would belong to him now, in a little while—but not so much as he would belong to them. Digory came up from the cellar with a pitcher of ale.

"This is . . . no time . . . to speak such things, Will . . . when your father's dying. But no telling when you'll hear it from some other. And I—I thought you might want to be ready."

"Sure . . . what is it, Digory?"

"Well . . . it's this . . . they say Ruth Puddington's with child."

"That's trouble to none but her."

"But she didn't get it alone, likely. Her family's searching round to have her married. There's been mentioned names . . . and yours. . . ."

Will laughed harshly. "I've not been alone with her in two years, and then I never more than kissed her. Tell them to ask John Hall about it. He's good at getting maids with child."

"But he's . . . her father's age."

"But he took her into the alders by the iron bog last summer. I saw them myself, slipping away there."

"But it's stranger than that, Will. Sarah says she's not with child at all—says 'tis a lie."

"You mean—to get herself a husband?"

"Sarah says the girl's mad."

Will shrugged his shoulders. "I can well believe that," he said. "I thought it two years ago."

And then Joan came out of the bedroom, slim, brown, her great eyes dark with fright, a streak of gray up the front of her hair that had never been there before.

"Oh, Mother . . ."

"Oh, Will! You're here! He wants you . . . !"

"Is he . . . ?"

"He says so. We can't tell. Sarah says he'll go out on this tide."

"How long will it run?"

"Half an hour."

Will walked into the low, square room where Joan had borne him. His father lay in the bed, his eyes sunken, his nose pinched, and the look of death on him. A child would know it, if the young doctor didn't. He walked up and lifted the brown hand that lay outside the blanket.

"How do you . . . feel?"

"Like any . . . dead man."

"Aw . . . it's not that bad."

"Aye it is, lad. I burst my heart bringing Tam in. He's a rare great lump, an' I robbed Joan for Mary. Couldn't do aught else, could I . . . could I?"

"No, Father."

"Listen. There's no time, and there's words to say, so stand in close and we'll get it over."

Will sat down on the edge of the bed.

"All I have's for you, and it's down cellar in the chest. You know it?"

"Aye."

"I'm only a poor yeoman, but I put money in there, time to time, like we always did at Old Thorny. And I never took none out since Mary was married—except for you to go to school. I always made sure there was some cod or pipe staves to sell when the ships came in—but now the money'll be in the mast trade, and you better look to that."

"Yes, Father."

"And sometime—this year, next year, when your heart says it's time—and it will—I want you to go home to Nottingham where we come from; to find out whether Scarlocks belong here or there . . . to see for yourself. Go see the fields, and the house, and talk with Rob if he's still alive, and give Moll Doubleday a shilling if you meet her. I promised them a boy, and I've naught but you—but maybe you'll do better in your time."

"I'll—go."

"Now. There's paper and pen in the cupboard there—you better write my will down while I can put my name to it."

Will moved slowly, woodenly to get out the writing materials. This was the sort of thing that happened in your mind in the dark sleep just before cockcrow when they'd served spoiled beef in the Hall or you'd had too much to drink at Vasty Bradish's. He came back to the bed.

"I'm ready. What do you say?"

"This." John looked up at him from under dark brows that had grown a little heavier every year, the keen, gray light of his eyes beginning to cloud over, and Will knew that those eyes were colored like his own and that his would cloud like this some day, and wondered if there would be a boy sitting by, feeling his heart break as he looked into them.

"They went like this, at home," muttered John. "I remember my father's . . ." Then his voice came out strong.

"Put it down like this, Will. 'I, John Scarlock of Old Thorny in Nottinghamshire, sojourning at Piscataqua in North America, do hereby give up my soul to God, and my body to be buried at the Point of Graves as is here the custom.'"

"You're not a New Hampshire man, Father? Not after thirty years?"

"Not after thirty thousand! I be from Nottingham, and you write it down that way. 'My lands, both sides of the water; my creatures; my clothes and my one book; my house and its fittings—all that I can't take with me' "—he smiled wanly—" 'I leave to my son, Will, out of which he shall provide for his mother and sisters, and all that have honest claim on him. I charge him that he pay no debts, for I leave no debts, and he who says I do is a liar.' "

Will wrote laboriously, while a wet, gray evening mist gathered outside the panes, and the candle flame burned small and steady at his elbow. Joan crept into the room and came to stand at the other side of the bed. And in its broad, rocky channel, the tide kept running down.

"I'll sign it now," said John.

Will, his throat too full to utter any words, pressed the scrawled paper into the groping hand. John held it up and read every word of it, took the pen from his son's limp fingers, and steadfastly wrote his name. He fell back, panting, for a few moments, and then he spoke again.

"Now . . . that's all . . . except this . . . about my burying. I want the Prayer Book read. If Parson Moodey won't read it . . . well, *you* can read. I had you taught how. We read it over Kitty—Renald and I—and nobody ever knew."

"Do you want a sermon, Father? It's the new way in Boston to have one preached in praise—"

"A sermon? A God-damned Puritan sermon? No! I've suffered them while I lived, but death's got privileges, boy. A Massachusetts funeral? No! Mine's an English corpse, and it'll go to its grave English fashion. 'Ashes to ashes and dust to dust,' I want, and plenty of wine for all my good friends to get drunk in memory of him as couldn't."

"Yes, Father."

John had felt a cold heaviness in his hands and feet for the last half hour, and now it was moving up along the veins. Outside the window the fog poured up from the river. He could see the moist grayness of it, waiting for him to arise, and leave his body, and go into it. His thoughts wandered. He could hear his son's voice from a long way off.

"Father . . . if I don't ask you now, I'll never know . . . and I have to! If . . . if you . . . if *we* . . . belong in Nottingham . . . why did you ever come here?"

John twisted on his pillow, trying to throw off the chilly weight that filled more and more of his body, but he knew it was getting the better of him. The fog had got into the room—had somehow got inside his head.

"All I know is . . . there was a wind that blew . . ." he said, fighting to keep his vision clear, to see his son, "a wind that blew . . . over Old Thorny . . . a morning in the fall."

He looked straight at Will, and it was like looking at himself when he was young; the same gray, questioning eyes, thin face, and wispy brown hair. He couldn't die, he thought, while that was alive, and yet, he was dying—the *he* that was more than eyes and hair, that was made out of things he'd lived through, like taking Joan in the hazels and riding out of Nottingham with Walter Neal that rainy day—things that would never fall the same to any man again. And as he looked into his son's face, thinking that, he saw a change come across it that struck him with bewilderment and terror. For he was looking suddenly into the clear eyes of a stranger.

This was a young man, strong, checkered good and bad, quick, learned, not yet wise—but it was not he nor anyone he knew. It was a new man with new thoughts, and he would never follow them. They were parted now, he and this young man with his father's name, parted like the great parting of the rivers by Bloody Point. He remembered that he had heard once it was the fear that their sons would grow up strangers that had driven the Plymouth men out of Amsterdam long ago, but they must have learned, as they died in their bark shelters racked with frost and plague in the terrible winter, as he was learning now, that every man's son will be a stranger to him in the end; that this is the last, most terrible sorrow of life, and that you cannot flee from it by fleeing from Amsterdam or any city under God. Good-bye, my son. Good fortune, stranger.

With a great effort he heaved himself over in the bed and faced Joan. And there she was, still sweet and brown, still his holly tree. He wanted to turn back now to tell Will that you might get sons, but that it would always be a woman—a woman who fed you at her breast before your eyes were open, and a woman who took you back there when the mists drew in dark at the end so that you could not see—and there was nothing worth living for but that. He looked at her, lovely as a young girl in the candlelight, a girl who had given him all she had to give, and come to him alone across the great sea, into a strange, wild country, and loved him there. Now, he thought, he'd never know who her father was. He scanned her face for a look of his old friend, Ned Trigg. He'd always meant to ask Ned outright—only he'd gone away from Nottingham so soon, not meaning to, just the way he was going now from Piscataqua.

"Hold me up, Joan," he pleaded.

Joan bent close to him, her arm under his pillow, lifting him up, for he was gasping. Her eyes shone—love, or tears, or just because she was Joan, and always a shining thing to him. And then suddenly he knew. Every line of her face fell into the lines of a face he'd known when he was a boy—a grave, kindly, troubled face, and not a great nor a noble one, but still—Bennett Traves, thrice alderman of Nottingham.

"Why . . . why . . . I'd never have thought it . . ." he said. And so he died.

Later that night Will was again in the kitchen, sitting across the table from Nannie, who looked at him out of great sorrowful eyes, and had the wits to keep still. Mary's stormy crying went on upstairs, and Tam croaked hoarsely, trying to comfort her. The fog drew all around the house, hiding the river, the town, even the lights in Fernald's windows just across the salt pond. A man could hardly make his way in it, but a soul faring forth would have no trouble. On a hook near the door hung his father's old jacket, earth-stained, the sleeves curving limply down with the curve of the arms they had been wont to cover. He tried to see it full and rounded with the living man, but he could not. That day was over. On the trivet still simmered the thick brew of herbs Sarah had hoped would work a cure. Now it could be thrown away. Joan came quietly in and stood at his elbow, and as he turned and looked into her brown eyes he could see the bitterness slowly dying out. Now she looked no more like a wounded animal. She looked like Mother again. He's not dead while I'm alive, Will thought. She knows he's alive in me, and she's glad.

But Joan was not thinking that. She was reminding herself sharply that she was still a mother if no more a wife; that this was the same little boy who used to cry and climb on her knee when he skinned his knuckles playing on the ledges, and that he needed her comfort now, just as much as ever he had before he learned to talk dark Latin and write himself Gulielmus.

"Poke up the fire, Willie," she said tremulously. "We can't do no more for the dead, and them as be alive'll be wanting their supper. You're the man here now."

"Aye," he said brokenly, looking from Nan's bent gold head to the limp jacket hung by the door. Then he squared his shoulders. "I'll see to it, Mother."

Joan stood silent by the window, looking into the fog. It had begun to lift now, and moonlight struck on a shaft of black tide water flooding in at the edge of the lower field. "I'll never fear it any more," she murmured to herself, staring at the river. "I don't have to fear it any more—now it's had what it wanted of me."

8. To see for myself

〜〜〜〜〜〜〜〜〜〜〜〜〜〜〜〜〜〜〜〜〜〜〜〜〜〜〜

IF EVER the world's at peace, and good for itself and for everybody in it; "integrated"—God pity Truth and all the philosophers—it'll be on a morning like this one, thought Will Scarlock. The river sparkled under the sun, as if a school of fish with golden scales had come up the flood tide on their way to the muddy spawning creeks of Newichwannock, and all the little crooked trees before the house were waving green in the soft air of early June. Back in the fields, the Hall boys—Kitty's sons—were calling to each other as they hoed the weeds away from the young corn and pea plants; big, strong fellows in their teens now, and with Tam and Digory to keep an eye on them, they'd be well able to see to the place while he was away. Below, in the bedroom where his father had died three years ago come fall, he could hear John Hall at the harsh, painful coughing that would take his life any day, likely. In the side yard the hens put up the pleased cackle and thresh of wings that meant Joan was scattering grain for them.

His clothes were packed in the chest—the little battered one he'd made to take to Harvard—and lying on top of it was the new book Truth Damerill had sent him. They had not met since that night in Vasty's house when Daniel Knight came to tell him his father was dying, and they did not write to each other often, for their ways were different. Will had spent most of his time in the woods around Great Bay, or the Fore River, or down Kittery Side, directing the crews of green lads, for nowadays, as soon as a boy had the strength to swing an axe, his father put one in his hands and sent him out to cut masts for the King's ships. Truth had stayed on at the College, reading Master of Arts, and hearing Freshman Greek and Latin, but last week there had been this letter from him, and the book. "It is new," he had written, "just come to us out of England, and I have not the time for its matter, being embarked much on advanced Syriac and Chaldee, but it is all to do with trees, and you tell me they are your life now. Besides, its author, John Evelyn, is as good a Royalist as you are, and you'll give him ear for that if for no other reason. I wish you would come to us this summer for the Commencement, for after that I shall leave the College, being called to a church in the New Haven Colony . . . not sure I shall go there, but somewhere. Cambridge is not such a far journey for you . . ."

Will smiled and let the letter drop on the floor without picking it up. He was going a further journey than Cambridge.

He sat and dreamed in the sunshine. This last day there was little left to do.

Joan had come in now, and he could hear her talking with Sarah Scriggins in the kitchen. He listened idly.

"I got to go, Joan," Sarah was saying in her rough, full voice, for though she was over seventy and her hair like gray iron rusting, she was a spritely old woman and still a good nurse, if you could keep the bottle away from her. "George Puddington's lad's waiting outside, an' I been sent for. He says Ruth's bad again."

"We can spare you, Sarah," his mother answered. "Joannie's sitting with her father now, and Will said he'd be around home most of the day."

"I hate to leave you, though, for it could happen any time. I tell you, the man's chest be like inside a hollow tree. I can tell by the sound of him. He's near ready to go. He's been a great trouble in your house, and you'd no call to be bothered with him. I seen Kitty die."

"So did I," said Joan, no longer bitter for the old grief, having known worse since, "but you've seen death enough to know, Sarah, that it's the living we must think to. John took sick and knew it would be his end, and his children were but half grown, and all his own folk dead. Where else could he come but here? What about Ruth? Is it the madness again?"

Will's thoughts turned from the women downstairs to the feverish dark eyes and seeking mouth of the young girl he had known in his boyhood, the girl who could be yielding and ardent as blown flame, and turn suddenly in your arms into granite, not only denying the wish in you, but making it seem obscene, unnatural. He was sorry for Ruth, but he was glad that he'd not gone beyond a few kisses with her. The Puddingtons had to keep her locked up in the east gable most of the time now. On her better days she walked out with her married sisters, her white, ravaged face drawn far back in her hood, and on her worse ones she screamed and beat her head, and tried to get away down to the docks among the sailors and mast men.

He could hear Sarah chattering to Ruth's little nephew now as they walked together along the edge of the field, headed for town. He picked up the book, letting his hands linger on the sleek, calf covers, examining every scroll of the red and black title page—"A Discourse of Forest Trees." It was a good book and he loved it already. It would be his Bible, he knew, the way Old Tusser had been his father's. He wished while he was in London he'd get a chance to talk to this man, John Evelyn. He'd like to ask him things. There were plenty of men in Portsmouth who knew trees, but in the common way: that all trees have roots, stems, leaves, bark, and branches, and scatter their seeds on the wind in season. They didn't know them like John Evelyn did, and know, too, all the trees of far countries and old time, and what the great authors had said about them.

He tucked it under his arm and started downstairs, wishing General Court would pass a law against making any book too big to go in a man's pocket. As he walked out the front door he had to step around Joan, for she sat on the ledge in the sunshine, kneading a bowl of fragrant red pulp.

"Oh! You're making strawberry bread."

"I thought 'twould be tasty for your last supper with us. You won't find a piece of it in England. Maybe John will try some, though he's swallowed naught but broth for a month now."

"Are you sure you're willing . . . I should go and leave you . . . with him like to die, and only the boys . . . ?"

"Yes, you better go. Your father wanted it. Wanted you to see for yourself. And you're twenty-one and it's time. Where are you going now?"

"The lads are meeting at Corbett's this morning. We find it's safer that way. If we meet at night, the godly are smelling around to see what they can learn of us, but in mid-morning they're too busy about their own affairs. They don't think any man would be big enough fool to leave his plowland or masting when the sun's high for work. Well—what they don't know's no trouble to them. Mother! It's not only for myself I'm going home. You know that, though I haven't told you."

"Oh, I can see light through a glass pane, boy, as well as next. You're going for the country—to get us free from Massachusetts."

He laughed. "Massachusetts! You say the word just the way Father used to. I was ten years old before I knew it wasn't a curse."

The old, merry light flashed in her eyes. "Isn't it?"

He shoved the toe of his boot lightly against her knee. "You could go in the stocks for saying that, woman. If John gets worse and you need me, send Joannie. I won't be long." He swung around the corner of the house and into the fields, whistling, moving fast so his nephews wouldn't catch him for a talk. He was late already.

When he went into Abraham Corbett's tavern, all clean scrubbed boards and the smell of malt, there was nobody there, so he walked straight through to the grass plot at the back. A big, sprawling grape-vine on a trellis overhead and along the wall kept the morning sun from the dozen men gathered there, the oldsters on benches and the lads his age flung down careless on the ground. They wore smocks tucked into their breeches and open at the throat, just as he did, and most of them were taking tobacco.

"Oh, Will! We thought 'twould be better out here—they can't see us from the street."

"'Tis better," he said, easing himself down by a little patch of mint that spread through the lush grass and sorrel, and leaning against one of the uprights of the trellis.

"Have you drawn it yet?"

"A part. I got it here." Abraham Corbett, sharp-faced, dark, with solemn eyes and a lantern jaw, held out a smudged sheet of paper covered with careful writing. Will took it from him and read through it, speaking parts aloud.

"'A Petition to the King's Commissioners, from the Loyal Men of Portsmouth in New Hampshire, so long defrauded of their rights by the Usurpers from Massachusetts . . . who deny us our privileges as Free Men, and keep themselves in power by giving gifts of land . . .'"

"Give me an ale," quavered old Edward Godfrie in his white beard, leaning forward on the edge of a battered armchair placed in the sun.

Will tossed a coin to Corbett. "He wants an ale."

The tavern keeper tossed the coin back and went inside. Will caught the money and reached it up to the old man.

"Thank'ee, Willie," he mumbled, slipping it into his ragged clothes. Old Edward had come with John Scarlock in the *Warwick* and served the colony as a faithful public servant all the years, but he was now flung out to poverty by the new men who ruled in town. "I be not ashamed to have no money," he said, holding his head up. " 'Tis they that should be shamed . . . !"

"You're damned right they should be," said Will, and everybody murmured agreement. "Brian Pendleton would skin a louse for the hide and tallow. I hear he put in a bill to Dover Court to get ten pounds for housing that frozen man who fell in the street last winter. If he'd fallen at my mother's door, she'd have fed him for Christian charity and ten pounds to hell—but then, she's not godly."

Abraham came back with a foaming mug for old Edward, and Will went on reading: " '. . . That we have been much oppressed, our lands taken from us and sold to others, and denied the sacraments according to the Prayer Book!' Oh, I'm glad you put that in! Remember how I stood in the pillory?"

"Yes, you did," rumbled the shaggy giant, Mark Hunking. "Put you in pillory they did, for reading the Prayer Book over your father."

Will laughed. "It seems like a rare japes now. Nannie stood by me all day, and kept the flies off, and the boys from throwing stones, and read aloud out of Virgil. Cutt and Pendleton came and looked and would have liked to drive her off, but they didn't dare."

"No, they wouldn't." Corbett shook his head. "Every man's got his price, even King Brian, an' Dan Knight could ha' met it ten times over. They won't trouble Nannie none. But they do not like you much, Will. You talk too fast for them, and put too much fire in it. And I hear you got a bad name down in Massachusetts."

"Aye. That's for helping the Quakers get away from Dover Neck. I don't hold with their ways of worship, but if any man thinks he's going to cut the ears off any other man with me standing by—well, he's wrong. Or drive women with whips from town to town till the blood drips off them! How anybody can be so God-damned cruel . . . !"

He stopped in angry bewilderment.

"They're doing it for Christ, Will. They say so."

"Christ! I bet He's pleased with them! Well. How soon will the Commissioners be here?"

"Next week, likely. They were supposed to leave Boston today, and stop awhile in Salem and other towns, maybe."

"And what do you think they'll do for us?"

"Much—maybe. King's men have talked all over with Robert Tufton, old John's grandson who took the Mason name, and it's their opinion his claim's good. Soon as Charles came in he started pushing it—to get back his share of the land here. Now King's sending to find out how we feel about it, and how we're affected to him, and whether we want to stay with Massachusetts, or set up for ourselves —maybe under Mason—or what."

"I know all that—what they're here for. But what'll come of it?"

Francis Champernowne, graying, a little heavy, a little more pompous even than in the days when he had wooed Alice Scarlock, answered him.

"They'll talk with us and read our petition, then they'll act— one way or another."

"Well, we're petitioning to be free of Massachusetts and governed by the known laws of England—but we're only a few out of all in town, only we of the old stock. The new men—and there's more of them, and they're richer and stronger—all want things to stay the way they are. How will King's men choose?"

"We don't know, but they haven't been well used in Boston, and King's back in Whitehall now, where Massachusetts has always smelled worse than cod fish. I vow, in God's truth, Will, they'll declare for us."

"I hope so."

"And you'll be in London—talking with Sir William Warren who buys all our masts, to see if you can't get us honest dealings there."

"Aye. And all behind the backs of the godly. How much do they know, do you think?"

Edward West, a quiet farmer from Sagamore Creek, spoke up gloomily. "They know everything. All of what we've planned, and about our petition."

"They do?"

Everybody sat up. Abraham put down the tray of ale mugs he had started to carry round.

"Yes. You know I married amongst them, and my wife's brother rode by our place yesterday, going for Hampton. He said they know, all of them—Mr. Moodey, and the Cutts, and Pendleton, and Stileman—that there's a rebellion afoot against them. He was sent to ride through the towns to tell folk not to sign our paper."

Will spoke first. A somber darkness seemed to have clouded over the bright morning. "Then I guess you lads will have a harder time here than we thought. I wonder how they found out."

"They keep close watch on Abraham. He denounced them once to General Court, you know."

"I should ha' held my tongue then," muttered Abraham. "I should ha' held my tongue. As well denounce the devil in hell as a knave in Massachusetts."

Will stood up. "I'll say good-bye now, boys. Don't anybody come with me to the dock tomorrow. Let them think it's my own way I'm going. And remember what Prince Rupert said—'Three deep and charge with steel!' "

"Aye!"

"Hurrah!" shouted old Edward feebly. "I be glad, Willie, that you be the one to go. I knowed your father all the years, and someways he be a better man than you. But you been to school and can talk better to high folk. You can talk Latin."

Will smiled. "I doubt the lumberyards by Thames'll do much business in Latin."

"But you might go higher. You might even get to see King!"

"Think King would listen to a mast man from Piscataqua?"

"If it's business with King," said Sam Fernald slyly, knocking his pipe against the trunk of the great vine, "we better send Nannie Knight."

Everybody laughed.

"Oh, Nan's pretty enough to please him," agreed Will, "but when he stated his terms, 'tis like she'd slap his face, and how far would that get us? No, I better go."

He picked himself up from the grass, swinging the leather-bound *Silva*, and went out through the taproom, into the street.

It was good to walk, lingering, through the town in the summer morning, with the houses scattered in tumbled disorder all over the hillside above him, and little crooked paths winding between them and along the garden walls. A row of small shops faced the waterside from the Great House through Dock Lane, and you could buy most things you wanted there, from iron nails to spices and an English bonnet. Only the farmers, who rowed their wares downriver, still liked to spread out the corn and roots and apples and smoked meat in the open stalls at the foot of Spring Hill, where the wild strawberries grew everywhere when he was a boy, but were mostly trampled down now by too much coming and going and the earth being eaten away for cellars. He walked slowly past the dock, and as always, there were men pulling on tarred ropes, shouting, and bare muscles straining, and little boats putting in and out. Anthony Brackett had just unloaded a catch of ragged, blue-green lobsters, and a crew of woodsmen and sailors were working together, waist-deep in the brown pulling tide, to get the great hewn pine stems out of the mast pool and loaded into the *London Girl*, the ship that would sail tomorrow for home, taking him as a passenger. He looked out to her now, where she rode just in deep water, out of the current, her sails reefed close, and bare sticks all over. Those sticks had been trees once, green and swinging; perhaps he had helped, himself, to fell them. In any case, tomorrow they would lift white canvas into the wind, to carry him . . . home?

Will turned away from the dock and headed for the Point of Graves just below the town, and he wouldn't have put into words the reason why he was going there, but any man who had ever buried his father and found himself leaving that burial place—perhaps forever—would know without the telling. As he stepped over the low stone wall around the little field, he tried to fix in his mind the curve of every blade of grass there, the height of every tree in the dark fir clump to the west, that the watch had to beat through with a stick every night because the boys and girls would go to make love there. The shining river sucked at the bank on the other side of it, wild roses crept through the grass around the rough, straggling stones, and gulls circled over in the clean, salt air. He had almost reached the spot along the south wall where he had read the Prayer Book over John Scarlock, before he saw Nannie. She sat on the wall a few yards off, but when their glances met she jumped up and waved. He went over to her and they stood together, silent for a few moments, looking down at Daniel Knight's grave. The grass hadn't begun to grow on it yet. He thought back to the way of Daniel's going, and it seemed to him suddenly that it was very like his own father's. First it had been a fall on the slippery rocks at the Shoals that didn't bruise him much but most have caused inner wounds, for from that day his craggy health left him and he sickened slowly. When he realized what was happening to him, he settled his affairs, and then planned to take his daughter and go back to England, so that he would die in Devon and be buried with the Nancy he had loved and married and lost when he was a young man. Their passage was arranged and their chests carried aboard ship, but they had to be carried back again, for Daniel had died on the wharf just as they were ready to put out.

Since then the Scarlocks had seen little of Nan, for she spent all her time in the square stone house at the head of the village on Hog Island, keeping an eye on the turbulent crews at the fishery, and reckoning in its great ledger, as her father had taught her during his last days.

Will spoke first. "Let's sit down and talk, Nannie," he said.

They went back to the stone wall and perched on its rounded boulders.

"I didn't know you'd be in town today. I was thinking we wouldn't get to say good-bye."

"You're going . . . ?"

"Home. To England. Tomorrow, by the mast ship, *London Girl*. She's off the dock now."

"And you're coming back . . . ?"

"I don't know . . . Nannie. You know . . . I have a house and land there."

"But you have land here. All your father had, and that field by Hogstye Cove you're so fond of."

"I know. I'll keep remembering that little field, Nan. It's all tilted and full of bog holes, but I've cleared it and smoothed it—when I could steal time from the masting. I made it myself, really, and I love it for that. You own Hog Island, and I own Hogstye Cove. We could marry and have a coat of arms with a swine rampant. . . ."

She was good to look at, he thought, with a trim, curved figure that would please any man, and smooth gold hair breaking into curls in the back of her neck and spilling down her blue linen bodice. Her eyes—gray-green—he didn't quite know, but there were little brown flecks in them. They were the changing color of the Piscataqua, and about as deep, he guessed. You never quite knew Nannie. He'd known her as a merry child who cried easily, and laughed a minute later the same way, but when he came back from Harvard the child was a poised woman, always gentle and smiling on the surface. What went on underneath, he didn't know, any more than he knew what went on under the sleek top of the river.

Suddenly he realized she hadn't answered him. Maybe she hadn't liked his jest about their marrying. Maybe she didn't care what he did in England or whether he ever came back. She'd have a life of her own, and the money and freedom to make it a good one.

"You're a pretty girl, Nannie," he said. "You'll be marrying somebody while I'm gone."

"No. I'll not marry . . . while you're gone."

"Then you'll have to get out that old rusty sword of Dan's to beat them off. There isn't a single man in town doesn't want to marry you."

"They want to marry my father's fishery . . . and his Hampton land."

"No, it's more than that. Maybe they think of the fishery when they're not with you, but when they are, they want you for a pretty girl."

"Then they want me for a pretty girl who owns a fishery?"

"Well . . . what do you want them to want you for?"

"Because I'm Nan," she said simply.

"I see what you mean," he answered, the smile gone from his face, his eyes clouded and sober. "That's harder to come by. Doesn't happen to you every Sunday morning."

"No. Only once, I guess."

"And it hasn't yet? But it will."

"Perhaps. What will you do in England?"

"First I'll go see Sir William Warren. He makes the contracts for ship timber with the Navy Board, and they'll need more and more, with the new Dutch war coming on. We're pretty well sure in our own minds that he's going to pick a man to be King's purveyor here, and not depend any more on whatever the captains can find in the pools when they make port; a man to run the whole mast trade out of Portsmouth—and we don't want him to pick a Massachusetts man. So we got together—you know who I mean."

"Our fathers' friends—and ours?"

"Of course—and decided who was to go see to it."

"And they chose you."

"Yes, they did," he told her proudly. "My father was one of them, and we've chopped shoulder to shoulder."

"And you'd been to school and seen the world a little."

"That, too, I suppose. We did think of Henry Sherburne—he's able and honest, old stock, too—but Henry trims sails a little too close to the wind from Boston. Old Edward thinks I'm going to take London by storm, and go a progress through the streets, spouting Latin. When I'm through with the business there, I'll go up to Nottingham where my father came from. And after that—I don't know. I just don't know, Nan."

They were silent for a few minutes. Then his eyes brightened. "Oh, and there's one other man I want to talk to. He's written a great book—about trees. Look here!" He spread open the *Silva* on his bent knees, began reading here and there.

" 'Men seldom plant trees until they begin to be wise.' And he says then they do it for their heirs, like the old man in the *Odyssey*— 'I plant against my son, Ulysses, comes home.' "

"*Plant trees?* I never heard of such a thing. A tree's something you have to cut down to get a place to plant corn."

"Yes, that's what I thought till last week—when this book came. Imagine, Nan—trees grow here thicker than the blades of grass— now. But do you suppose we can go on cutting them forever? Maybe *I* can, and my sons, and *their* boys after them, but some day the land'll be bare—nothing but stumps from here to the Western Water. I'd never have thought of it myself, but now that I've read the *Silva*, it's as plain as night and day. All men here know of trees is how to cut them down, with never a care if they'll grow again. The way we've been stripping the woods for masts the last three years, is just like drinking down all-winter's ale to make a roaring Hallowmas. There'll a dry time come. But if we take thought now —to set new trees as we clear—we've a timber country that'll go on forever. Sedge and swamp for the water trees, and hills to grow weathered wood—Agamemnon's spear was made out of weathered wood from the hills, he says."

Agamemnon's spear! The olive groves of Argos sloping down to the wine-dark sea were far away, she thought, and the heroes dead a long time. Beyond the wall they sat on, a salt, gray river, brimming out of the north, tore at the roots under the sweet hay meadows and stunted apples trees. And maybe it was not such a fair country, nor such a great one, but they were alive—alive and together in the summer morning. Oh, Will! Put your book away!

The sea wind ruffled his brown hair, and Nan watched it. She watched the curve of his tanned cheek, and the lean brown curve of his hands grasping the calf cover. She hugged her knees in their blue, looped petticoats, and swayed gently back and forth, the outside Nan, the Nan that everybody knew, listening and attentive while he read. But the inside Nan writhed and twisted and wrung her hands, and fled screaming through a wood of stormy pines that beat at a black sky. He's going away, she thought. Coming back . . . maybe this year, maybe next year . . . maybe never! Maybe I'll never see him again . . . the eyes . . . and the hair . . . and all! *And he talks to me about trees!*

118

He looked up, smiling at her, striking at a black-gold bumblebee that hovered by his shoulder. "That's wonderful stuff, Nan."

"It is, Will. He sounds like a wise man. I hope you can meet him." Then she stood up. "I wish you well in London, and I'm sure we shall be proud of what you do there. I must go up to town now. John Billings and I came in with the small sailboat. He wants to be home before dark, and I have to buy pork and meal and dried pease to feed the men. So . . ."

"Don't you dare go back to the Shoals without seeing Mother."

"No, I won't. I'll go there first. But Jane Crowther'll row me over. You're not ready to leave here yet . . . are you?"

"No . . . not yet."

They looked across the little field to the rounded slate stone that stood up over an English corpse buried English fashion.

"Good-bye, Will," she said. She held out her hand. That meant, he thought, that he was not supposed to kiss her, and it troubled him, though he could not understand why.

"Good-bye, Nan," he said, taking her fingers coolly, letting them drop. She was not of his own blood and family. He had decided that the morning he left for the College. But she had been his play-mate, and he was fond of her, and he didn't feel a good-bye kiss would be out of order—especially when they might never see each other again. But she hadn't wanted it. She hadn't wanted it. Oh, well—women be that strange—just like his father had told him. He watched her going along the field with sure, even steps, holding back her skirts from the rose briars, never once turning her head. If that was the way she felt . . . ! Putting the book under his arm, he walked down to John's grave and stood beside it.

He looked all around him; at the blue air curving over the sweep of hills across in Maine, the white sails beating upriver, and the clustered roofs of Kittery Foreside. He looked down at the springing green grass, and then at the weathered stones scattered through it, and every one of them he could put a name to, the name of a man or woman he had known.

And then he spoke aloud, but softly, knowing no answer would come to him out of anywhere, not sure he was heard, but feeling that was the chance he had to take.

"Father!" he said. "Father! John Scarlock, sir. I'm going home—like you told me to—to see for myself. I thought you'd want to know."

9. A dance on the green

A SULTRY yellow twilight hung over the red-tiled roofs and around the thin, reaching spires, and dun water foamed through the arches of London Bridge behind him, as Will Scarlock stepped out on England, and caught his breath, and tried to consider all the greatness of it. He'd come a long way from Piscataqua last June, for it was mid-September now, and they'd lain over in the Azores with a broken mast and strained seams that needed caulking. But here he was at last, and he'd come by the chalk cliffs his mother had told him to watch for, and up London River that unwound between the yellow-green marshes and drowned banks of mud, just the way she said it would. All afternoon he'd stood on the deck in the hot sun, singing to himself, and watching the thick water, addled sometimes with a rush of snaky brown eels across it. And when he lifted his eyes higher, he could see past the sea walls and miles of shimmering fens to the far line of hills with white towns nestling in the trees there, and once, away off in Essex, a craggy tower. Towns, too, came down to the waterside whenever the ground rose up firm enough to hold them. A sheaf of spires gleaming in the sun past Woolwich Reach caught his eye, and so did the poor pirates' gibbeted corpses chained to the piles off Execution Dock. The river teamed with ships from every country under heaven: barges, and hoys, and flyboats like the *London Girl*, and great sea-goers big as a small hillside, that the sailors told him were the East Indiamen, and little pointed boats called wherries that darted everywhere like vermin. But those who knew said the port was quiet. Seems the town was down with some kind of a sickness, and nobody wanted to land there.

He'd thought to go ashore at Wapping Stairs, for that was where Sir William Warren had his great lumberyard, but when Sir William's clerk came aboard just after they'd anchored in the Pool to find out exactly how many masts and spars they were bringing in, he said his master was down in bed with the ague and seeing nobody. So that would have to wait. Next place he had in mind to visit was Cripplegate—"Cripplegate Without," Joan had called it, but her words meant nothing to him. "Without what?" he'd asked her. "Without the Wall, you dullard," she'd answered tartly. And he'd said that over to the waterman who rowed him up from Wapping, and the man had shaken his head.

"Cripplegate? Be ye sure, lad? There's more lying dead there than in all London."

"Yes, my mother said Cripplegate. It was there she stayed on her way to America. She stayed with folk named Goble who had a house in Fore Street that runs along the Wall. I'd know the house, she said, because there was a fig tree by it—or was, thirty years ago. She said I should go back to her friends and lodge there."

The waterman stood, all shaggy beard and stained clothes, in his pointed boat, holding to a tarred rope that hung from an iron ring at the side of the slimy stones Will had climbed out on.

"This is the way to it, lad. But I don't like it for ye. Ye've the look of the fields, and no call to go in London now. But if ye must— well, walk up these stairs an' ye'll be at the bottom of Fish Street Hill. It's steep an' cobbled, but it's a single way ye can't mistake. Ye'll cross Thames Street first, an' that's one; then a crooked lane. Then comes Eastcheap, an' that's two—be ye counting?"

"I got it all down. It's getting dark." Will looked up at the yellow dusk that thickened around the turrets and gables overhanging the water. "And it's smoky. Must be a fire back in the woods."

"Huh?" said the waterman. "Fire? What woods?"

"I forgot. 'Twould be that at home. Not here."

"You should see Town when there's real smoke hanging on it— dyers' vats, an' soap boilers', an' all the sea coal fires o'winter a-going at once. Air's clear now, for nothing's made or sold. Folk are all either gone out of town, or else they're dying, or caring for sick an' dead. Grass is a-growing up in Whitehall, I hear."

"Can I see my way? Any of the shops sell a cheap torch or lanthorn?"

"No. Shops is all shut, and there'll be no linkboys to light ye neither. Make your way by the fires. Front of every sixth house they're burning sulphur an' herbs an' such, as they hope'll sweeten the air an' kill the pest. Have ye ever seen death, lad?"

"I saw my father die. And once I killed an Indian."

"But ye killed with clean blood dripping off a knife."

"Aye."

"Ye'll see worse, if ye go to Cripplegate."

"Maybe. What do I do after I cross Eastcheap?"

"Oh . . . then ye're in Gracechurch Street, broad an' paved, an' ye go straight on till ye come to London Wall."

"London Wall!" breathed Will, gazing, rapt, into the saffron-colored sunset that burned over the river above the bridge, with a web of spires and towers drawn against it.

"Then ye turn west—left, to a stranger. Ye go past one gate, an' that's Bishopsgate, an' then past Moorgate, that's two, an' the third gate's Cripplegate, an' never mind the posterns between. Old Queen come through it when she took the kingdom, an' it was a proud place once, but most of the high folk live westward now."

"I'm not looking for high folk—for a carpenter's kin."

"Go through the gate then, an' St. Giles'll be to your left, an' Fore Street ye'll be standing on. God help ye, lad."

Will's leather boots slipped a little on the mossy stairs as he stood there by the thrust of the great bridge buttress and looked down into the face of the waterman, shadowed blue now, like the shadowy river behind him. He did not know quite what to say, so he smiled and chose a coin from his pocket, hoping it was worth enough.

"Thank'ee, lad. God ha' mercy!"

Poking his long oar against the stonework of a tall house that seemed to grow straight up from the water, he shoved off. Will turned his back to the river and started gingerly up the stairs. They were slippery, and night had already settled in the alley they led to. As he put his foot down on the top stair, the toe of his boot sank into something soft, inert, barring the way. Looking down, he saw it was the body of a man. A man horribly dead. Of his flesh, only the face lay bare, and that was stained with purplish blotches and clotted blood. Light shone through a dusty window set in the wall over them, and showed Will more than he wanted to see, showed the blood and scraped skin on the lichened stones where the frenzied creature had beat his head, looking for death, not finding it quick enough. And the stench that went up from him set the hair a-rise at the back of

Will's neck and made his stomach turn over, for it was a horrid mixture of cellar mould, old sweat, rancid grease and human excrement, and all of them shut in together for a long, long time.

Stepping over the poor corpse that was past any help he could give it, troubled and wondering, he went out into the streets of London. Underneath him were dusty cobbles, and two rows of shops, all shuttered, ranged up the steep hill the waterman had told him to follow. And every little court or alley that he passed reeked with the same awful stench that had come from the dead man. Here and there a lighted window pricked out, but most of the carved, wooden house fronts were dark. House built close to house, many of them with painted wooden signs swinging over their doors; no bit of garden or green thing anywhere, Will noticed, and he wondered at it, and how did people there get food to eat, and where were the people? He had gone by five more bodies like the first, one of them a woman with long black hair and a dead child at her spotted bosom, before he saw a living man. The man came down the hill toward him, furtive and peering, and bent over a moaning heap in the gutter—not to aid it—only to rifle its pockets. In the middle of his search he saw Will watching him, and hastily slunk into an alley, cursing at the interruption.

The cobbled way was steep and rough, but Will took to his heels and began to run, swift as if he were crossing the Glebe at home, and he wished to God he were. He didn't know whether he'd passed Thames and Eastcheap or not; he only knew he was scrambling across a strange city in a hot, stinking darkness, and there seemed to be no one else alive in it—and then he came to the Wall. It reared up dark on the dark sky where the bright summer stars showed plain because there were so few lighted windows to dim them out. Not as high, somehow, as he'd thought it would be, but even more massive, looking as if God had made it first of all and then created the rest of the world around it. He stopped for a moment to catch his breath, and then he noticed the first plague-sign—a cross chalked in red on the door of a low-eaved house with a weak light in an upper room. There was a fire burning in the open space before the Wall; faggots had been drenched with some potion that gave off acrid smoke and an eerie blue flare. In its light he could see the crosses on many doors. Now and then a deep moan or fading shriek broke the terrible silence that lay everywhere. In a far-off street he could hear the rumble of iron-bound wheels and a confused shouting.

He had always thought that when he came to London Wall, he would go up and lay his hand on the stones and great flints of it, and feel his living blood beat against them in kinship. To touch London Wall, he'd thought, would be part of his ceremony of going home, something he'd do with reverence, like the way he'd heard Papists kissed the cross. But now he didn't feel holy and reverent. He felt damned scared, and a little bit sick, and he wanted to get out of there. He went on looking for the third gate, though, because he didn't know what else to do. Once in a while he saw an old woman with a white wand scuttle in or out of a doorway. Watchmen paced the street before some of the doors marked with crosses, but they gave no challenge and he did not speak to them. He had nothing to say to anybody.

The third gate had a round tower each side of it, round and flattened, the way you fitted a tree you were going to make a mast of. There were windows in the towers, and one wide, lighted window over the gateway. To go through it was like walking through a dry cave.

And then he stood in what must be Fore Street, and almost before he could look for it, he saw the fig tree, incredibly gnarled, spreading its roots through a little patch of grass, its thick, dusty leaves hanging limp in the windless air. And thank God, the broad casement behind it had a light! He strode up to the paneled door in its shadow and knocked loudly. The echo of his knocking died away. Far up a broad street to his right the bluish fires were burning, throwing a weird glow over great houses set with walled gardens and orchard trees. Again came the hollow noise of the cart wheels.

"Dead! Dead! Bring out your dead! Bring 'em out!" somebody kept shouting, hoarse and monotonous, as one might cry fish or lavender.

He rapped again, but no one came. He tried to look through the window, but its thin curtain would not let him. Suddenly he lifted the latch and stepped in. One low room ran across the front of the house, and a fat tallow candle in an iron cresset on the table had almost burned away. The light would not last long. It shouldn't. The sight before him should be put away in darkness forever; the whole house buried in clean earth or scoured with flame. Retching in the foul air, his eyes staring in his head, he stood and looked at it, because he was unable to lower his lids or stir his muscles in flight. Once in the woods, an Indian, angered, had come at him with a drawn knife, and he hadn't been afraid then. His blood had been up and singing, and he had his own knife, too, and went in first with it. And once he'd been cornered on Hampton Cow Common by that mean old devil of a black bull Daniel Knight kept, and watched it come, head down, its right horn straight for his guts—and that time he hadn't been afraid either. He'd gone up the nearest apple tree like a squirrel, and laughed while the mad thing stubbed at the trunk of it. But to be all alone at night in a town full of corpses covered with purple sores was another thing. He was afraid now, sick with fright, and not ashamed of it, and he didn't know what in hell to do, except sit down and wait for the purple sores to kill him, which he hoped would be quick.

He would never lodge with the Gobles. Three people had lived in the pleasant room with the wide hearth and red carpet and carved chairs; at least, three people had died here, miserably, and unable to help each other. An old man—so old he might have remembered a shy, brown-eyed girl from Nottingham who came there years ago —lay naked on the floor, his jaws set in a ghastly grin, his exposed groin a mass of dark corruption already astir with maggots. A plump woman dressed in neat black had toppled in a heap beside him, and lay there, her eyes staring baldly open like blue china beads. There was no mark on her. And on the cushioned sofa stretched a fair young girl, like a child asleep, but with no movement of breath, and dark red blotches, blue-rimmed, on her arms and neck where her silk gown left them bare. A trickle of frothy green bile had dried at one corner of her mouth, and the stains of helpless illness lay on everything. But only a little while ago one of these three must have lived and lit the candle, needing a light against the dark.

Will turned finally, and stumbled, head down, out into Fore Street. His mind came alive again, and he thought he ought to tell somebody to go there and take care of the dead. Why, he didn't know, nor whom to go to. In front of him now loomed up the square church tower, and below it, through the long windows set in stonework, he thought he could see a light burning. Maybe there'd be a parson around there, and they knew what to do about death. Groping his way over the cobbles, he entered the church of St. Giles Cripplegate.

He had never been in such a great room before—it was bigger even than the hall at the College—and the arches came down like tree trunks, as if he were in a stone forest growing underground. He wandered idly about, over pavings and colored tiles, past the pews, and up the black marble steps before the communion table. Two stone fonts with gilded wooden covers, brasses, and pulpit trappings of green and crimson shone in the light of a few dim, hanging lamps, to give the place a rich austerity. But there was nothing there to give help to a man looking for human comfort, so Will started to blunder out again. Near the door he caught his foot on an ill-joined paving stone and came down on his hands and knees. Crouched there, he saw suddenly, from the carved letters under him, that he was on top of an old grave. His father had told him that here at home they buried great folk in the churches sometimes, and he tried to read the stone tablet, but most of the inscription had worn away under the feet of the worshipers. He could only make out "n Frobisher."

"Frobisher?" he muttered, pulling himself to his feet by grasping the back of the rear pew. "Frobisher? Where've I heard that name? I think it was somebody Father used to talk on. I wish my head was clear."

Standing there in the light and remembering his father, he felt his courage come back a little. Now he could hear voices in the yard. He hitched up his belt, sighed, and started out to find who was doing the talking. Beyond the tall, rectangular headstones crowding each other on the greensward to the left, lights veered and bobbed, and men called hoarsely back and forth. He felt his way carefully toward them, stone by stone, but stepping out from the last one into utter dark, his feet sank in a ditch full of stagnant water and refuse that gave off a foul air when he shattered the slimy crust of it. And past the ditch reared up the great black bulk of the Wall. He groped along its rough base, and it led him out of the quagmire to sound turf at the west end of the churchyard. Just ahead were the swaying lights and the grunting of men who toiled heavily, and then he came face to face with a short, stocky figure that swung a lanthorn from side to side and wore its coat collar turned up in spite of the stifling, black heat.

"Be ye kin?" asked the figure gruffly, flashing the horn lamp in Will's face.

"Kin?" he asked stupidly. "Oh! You mean to the Gobles?"

"Gobles? Be they in there? I heard the old man was down, but I talked to Mistress Ann at the window only yesterday. Brought her milk and a penny loaf. But you can't follow them into the plague pit, boy."

"Plague pit?"

The man held the lanthorn closer. "You're not a London lad?"

"No."

"Then why'd ye come here . . . now? And from where?"

"I came from Piscataqua in New England. This afternoon I came."

"The more fool you. But what d'ye want in St. Giles churchyard when we're a-burying—what we be?"

"I—I came for the parson, or the sexton. I found some people dead."

The man slapped his thick leg and roared with laughter. "He's found some people dead, lads!" he shouted. "So help me God, he's found some people dead! Now we never heard of such, did we?"

Curses and laughter came from the murk around the toiling lights.

"That's a rare japes, Doggett, a rare japes! He's found some people dead! Hear! Hear! Oyez, mates!"

"You can't talk with Parson," said Doggett, shifting a wad of tobacco from the front of his mouth, " 'cause Old Prickett's fled to the country to 'scape the pest. Can't talk with Sexton, 'cause we buried him last week, right about where you're standing. But I'm Doggett the Watch, and I'll hear your business."

"I told you. I went to Gobles' house by the fig tree and they're all dead."

"Is that so? We'll send the searcher then and have 'em out for the pit. Too bad. The wench was fair. I'd ha' liked to ha' meddled with her."

"What are the pits?"

"Want to see one?"

"I don't think so."

A group of men in earth-stained clothes came up carrying shovels and lanthorns.

"All under?"

"Aye."

"How many?"

"Davy says one hundred and eight. Which is five too much."

"One hundred and eight, man! You hear that? We dug a great hole in ground and put that a-many human bodies away there. Stacked like faggots 'cause we'd naught else to do with 'em and none to do it. Not a churchyard in city's not rotting, bursting full. And still they die!"

The men filed past, leaving him alone with the grizzled Doggett. In the light of their departing lanthorns, he could see a trampled sweep of grass at the side of the church. He didn't feel so well, and he guessed he'd go sit down there for a little while. He reeled toward it. And then Doggett was gripping the front of his jacket and looking into his face.

"Is it the sickness, boy? Or do you just, by God, need a drink?"

"I—I—a drink . . ." said Will faintly.

"Taverns are all supposed to be shut—but not to Doggett the Watch. Can you make it to the Old Serpent, d'ye think?"

"Far?"

"No. Just up Grub Street. Here we go."

He remembered stumbling over more cobblestones behind Doggett and his light, around corners, and past dark houses that were quiet and lamplit houses with moans coming out of them on the sultry air.

"Here we be, lad," said Doggett, stopping.

Will lifted his eyes and saw a lanthorn hung up over a low door and lighting a carved wooden serpent painted green with innocent blue eyes and a flowing white beard. It had such a ridiculous look that he laughed weakly and leaned against the lath and plaster wall, and leaning there, he looked through the leaded panes of the bow window.

The taproom of the Old Serpent was low, and little, and darkened with the smoke of many fires that had roared up the brick chimney in uncounted wintertimes. The benches and tables had darkened, too, and all their corners worn smooth, and the stone floor mellowed with spilt ale. A badly painted picture of Charles the First, a reedy young man in a ruff, hung on the rear wall, and under it sat a thin wisp of a fellow wearing an apron, an iron-rimmed keg on each side of him, and a hanging shelf of pewter mugs behind. Half a dozen men huddled somberly over their drink, and one old woman sprawled with her head on the table and a white wand leaning against her knee. And perched on a keg near the bare hearth, a girl was singing.

She was a small girl, slim and daintily made, and she wore a scarlet dress cut low over her full bosom and caught up to show her bare ankles. Her dark hair hung loose on her shoulders, and her blue eyes shone with soft merriment. Her voice was clear and low, and she fingered a lute that seemed to be pitched even lower.

> *"Now out alas, I had forgotten to tell ye*
> *That married they were with a ring,*
> *And so must Nan Knight, or be buried a maiden.*
> *And now let us pray for the King!"*

Nan Knight! Nan, clear, and sweet, and golden, and smelling of dried flower petals, that all the girls his mother reared were taught to scatter through their linen. How strange to hear her name here in the filthy, sweltering dark, hundreds of miles away from her! Of course they'd both laughed over that old song with her name in it. Tam McQuayne often sang it when they were children; sang it in honor of Nannie's birthdays. But now it was on the lips of another girl, a girl sitting on a beer keg in a tavern, singing and smiling, and suddenly knocking the fear out of him, making him feel like a man again, making him feel somehow more a man than he'd ever felt in his life. Doggett was talking about her.

"Doll comes down here to sing for the boys every night. She's a good little wench—and not afeerd of death or hell. Says she'll sing as long as there's a man alive to listen to her. Can ye get inside, d'ye think, lad?"

"In a minute. What's her name?"

"Doll. Doll Trasper. Lives at Milady's, which is a whorehouse on London Bridge, but she's not a whore. She's a ballad singer— mostly at Moorfields, when nights is warm and the town's well and can go abroad there. Even Court comes there sometimes. She knows all the old songs and can make new ones when the mood takes her. You know, the King sent for her once and she wouldn't go."

"She wouldn't?"

"No! You know what she said?" Doggett grinned and slapped his thigh. "She said, 'What? Me lie abed with that fat, black Popish sluggard? Not if my name's Doll Trasper!'"

Will smiled and straightened up. "What did the King say?"

"King? Oh, he laughed—what else can a man do when a woman won't have him? You all right? Here we go!"

The first thing Will noticed when they entered the Old Serpent was that Doll stopped singing. She looked at them, first curious, and then with something almost like fright in her blue eyes. And then her head went up at a prouder tilt, and she began to make soft music with her lute. Maybe she had seen plague spot on him. He put up his hand to his face, but it felt smooth and unblemished wherever he touched it. The wispy man put out two mugs of ale. Will and Doggett sat down on a bench that had lost one leg and been propped with three bricks laid on top of each other. Everybody drank, but nobody seemed to have anything to say. Then the old woman stirred and looked up, her face gray and shapeless like a mass of dough, with only the eyes alive in it.

"There was four thousand died last night," she murmured wonderingly, "four thousand . . ." Her head sank again to the table and the white wand fell from her knee.

"That's old Milly," Doggett told Will. "She's not so much drunk as worn, poor soul. This was her day to walk down and give in deaths at the Vintry. She's a searcher—you could tell by her white stick—has to go into shut houses and tally deaths for the parish clerk. Oh, Batt!" he called to the landlord. "This lad's new-come to town. . . ."

"He chose a rare time for it," said Batt, coming to stand by them, his hands in the pockets of his stained apron. "He better leave. Can he get out any ways?"

"I was thinking that. You know, I was thinking if Dr. Hodges comes by here tonight, maybe we could get him to give the lad a pass of health so they'd let him through to the country—as none can go without it. If he stays here—he'll be one more for the parish to bury."

"But I have to stay in London. I have to see Sir William Warren at Wapping Stairs. I came over the sea for that."

Will spoke to the men, but his eyes were on Doll. In all this town of black streets and livid death, she made him remember life and want it, more of it than he'd ever had, and that to last forever. He wanted to go up to her and take her lute and lay it aside. He wanted to touch the scarlet curve of her dress. He wanted . . .

"What's your name? Have ye got kin in England?"

"My name is Will Scarlock—and I own land here. A farm in Nottingham."

"Nottingham?" spoke one of the men. "Then ye better go there. It's healthy yet. The plague's not taken the north."

He twisted around at the table so he could no longer see Doll. That was the only way he could keep his mind on Batt and Doggett who seemed to want to help him.

"So ye be Will Scarlock," said Doggett, wiping the foam from his bearded mouth and taking a stubby pipe from his pocket.

Doll had begun to sing again very softly.

> *"If thou be afear'd, Will Scarlet,*
> *To Robin get thee gone.*

130

Lie safely in the good green wood,
With Tuck and Little John."

Under the voices of the men he could hear every word of it, and he knew she was talking to him, and that no one else in the tavern knew, save the two of them. He could not know how he looked to her: tall, and sunburnt, and wider-eyed than anything you'd see in London outside a cradle, the shapeless homespun coat hanging from his lean shoulders, all the strength and sweetness of a hay meadow on him, and none of the town smartness and cunning. He was like a stranger from some other star.

"Ye be Will Scarlock? Well, we be Batt and Doggett. Yon's Milly the searcher, and Doll the singing girl. There's a butcher from Blowbladder Street, and another from Stinking Lane. Under table's a whore from the Dog Yard."

Will looked down and saw a lean shape in a drab cloak propped under the corner table and against the wall, gentle snores coming from it.

"In t'other corner's Grimkin the weaver, and his sons that be prenticed in Billingsgate; past them, John Trivet, clerk at the Steelyard. And not one of us owns a foot of land anywhere. We be like stones in the streets of London—common and plenty, but a place for each. And we be drinking now, as men past hope, because we've put by all our trades in the face of death—and it's hard to face him sober."

"In New Hampshire," said Will, trying to keep his mind on them, not daring to look at Doll lest all should see his eagerness for her, "when folk get sick we first try to cure them. We don't let them die by themselves and then go putting them in the ground like seed. We have prayers and toll the bell."

"And so do we—other times. But tolling's forbid now, for the bells would be a-go clock round. And who's to pray? Clergy's most all dead, or fled with the rich—save Non-Conformists. You wouldn't want one of them praying over you?"

"No. I'd not want that."

"What do ye do in New Hampshire when there's more lies dead than walks living?"

"I don't know. It's not happened there. Not in my time. How did the sickness come, and when do you think it'll go away?"

131

John Trivet, the Steelyard clerk, answered thoughtfully, cupping his hands round his pewter mug.

"It come in a bale of silk from the East, some say. And some say the drouth raised it up from the old fens London's built on. There was one death o' Christmas. King himself saw a strange bright star, and then old women began wailing they saw coffins in the sky—and that boded ill. All winter was hard, black frost, and all summer clear hot weather, with never a wind nor drop of rain. And every day more died. Court went to Salisbury, and them with money scattered themselves wherever the country'd take them. Great North Road I saw once so full of coaches and drays and hackney hell carts moving out 'twas like a street kennel running full of water in a spring storm. But there's naught stirring there now. Farmers run out with pitchforks to drive off any stranger who might be bringing death. It started west, by St. Giles-in-the-fields, and come down on us through Holborn and Clerkenwell."

Old Milly lifted her head. "There was four thousand died last night," she muttered, and sank back. "Four thousand souls . . ."

"We try cures for it," went on John Trivet. "There's a quack in every cross street selling one—oak galls, and toad's-eye amulets, and such. Some goes to Gutter Lane for a purging, and some fumes their houses the French way with brimstone and amber—and one dies as quick as the other."

The butcher from Blowbladder Street interrupted. "Them as sells tobacco be free of it. An' I hear 'twill not take root in them that has the pox."

"If it's pox ye want," leered the other butcher, red as one of his own dripping beeves, "I know a woman by Bethnal Green . . ."

"Why go to Bethnal Green when there's Liz Harley over the street and two doors down?"

"No thank'ee. I ha' seen Liz Harley. I'll get mine at Bethnal Green."

A tall man strode through the open door now, his head down, deep blue shadows under his sunken eyes. He wore a long coat of fine black broadcloth, knee breeches and a green cravat, and carried a gold-headed cane. He stood leaning on the cane for a moment and looked about him. Will could see the stars through the doorway behind him, burning out clear at the top of the sultry night. He knew that Doll, silent now, was watching him, and he wanted to turn but he could not. Batt hastened forward, dragging a wainscoted chair from the corner, fluffing its stained crimson cushions with the feathers sifting out of a three-sided tear.

"Dr. Hodges! Will it be sack, sir, as usual?"

"Yes, sack," murmured the doctor, sinking into the chair and closing his eyes. "Sack—and pray God it give me one day more."

"He's a great man, Willie," said Doggett, familiar now from having drunk too much ale. "Most doctors has gone with the moneyed folk, but he stays amongst us. He's a great man."

"How goes the sickness, Doctor?" asked Trivet, trying to be cheery.

"Worse—worse it is upon us every sunrise, when we go forth to find we must shut in still more healthy folk for a living death with their sick kin. But what else can we do? We dose with juniper this week, and last week it was pimpernel and ivy, and before that, balm and gentian—and one does as little good as the last."

Batt put a huge glass goblet before him, gleaming clear and golden-brown. The doctor drank thirstily. "They die abed of sores, coughing their souls out," he muttered, and swallowed more sack, "or they run naked, staring-mad in the streets. And the nurses smother the dying to rob them the quicker. It's like a shower of arrows falling. And we've no arms but sack and prayer. The bottle, Batt."

Batt put a green bottle covered with cobwebs in front of the doctor. Just as he tilted it, Doggett chose to speak to him.

"Doctor, you be a great man, as all knows, and my young friend here is asking when it'll stop. Can you tell him?"

Dr. Hodges turned slowly, his eyes even more sunken than when he came in, the lines around his mouth more deeply cut. "Yes, by God. It'll stop when we're all dead, and not before."

Doll was singing again, and the doctor whipped around to look at her, the grimness easing out of his face.

"I never heard that, Doll. Just make it, did you?"

She nodded, not breaking the song.

> "Oh, I'd follow England over,
>   And pawn my shift and shoon,
>   To have you for my lover . . ."

Will got tense all over. She meant him, and she wanted what he wanted . . . but how . . . here in this rotting black town, with men falling down dead all around them . . . to dally with a girl . . .

Doggett, his eyes bleared from drink, drowned out the song, a-bellowing, "Doctor, this lad's a friend of mine. I found him by the pit o' St. Giles, but he come this day from the plantations, clean as a hound's tooth. He wants you to give him a 'pass in plague-time,' an' he's my dearest friend. . . .'"

Dr. Hodges looked sharply at Will.

"You're a country man. I can see that. Is he telling the truth?"

"Yes, sir. I'm from New England—here to do business with Sir William Warren."

"Oh, yes. Timber man for the King's ships. You'll do no business now with Sir William. He's down with ague—we hope it's ague. Will you leave town if I write a pass for you?"

"I—" said Will, swallowing, minding the scarlet dress.

John Trivet gave a little croak and staggered to the door, vomiting blood, to fall in the gutter just beyond the threshold. He wheezed once, and he moaned once, and he shuddered once all over, and then lay still.

Around the Old Serpent the men and women sat dumb and staring, like a group of stone figures carved out to decorate a tomb.

Dr. Hodges was the first to recover. He picked up the bottle in both hands and drained it.

"Don't go to him," he ordered harshly, shaking his head and spraying a mouthful of wine on the paved floor. "He's dead already. They die in seconds when it falls like that." He looked at the tall, wide-eyed lad, who had turned wan under his sunburn and was biting his lower lip. Tearing an envelope from his pocket he scrawled across it—"New-come from the colonies . . . in health and fit to pass . . . Nathaniel Hodges, M.D." Then he thrust it at Will. "Take it, boy, and get out of town! Get out of town before you go out—like that!"

Grimkin the weaver, lean and lank-haired, got back his powers next, and spoke, while Will sat fingering the paper.

"Know what's caused it all?" he asked with a cunning look. "I held with Noll, you know, and his Commonwealth. An' this here is the fault of that knave that's at Whitehall now. Took Noll out of his grave, he did, and put his poor skull on a pole atop Westminster Hall. Well, that poor skull's looking down on London. Out of its eye-holes it's looking down. Looking down and putting the blast on Charlie's wicked kingdom. Purging the town to ready it for the saints again."

"Now you could be right at that," sneered Batt. "We o' the King's

side know 'twould be like your Noll to strike men down this sneak-
ing, bloody way. There was always a queerness there. Roofs an'
steeples blew down the night he died—devil coming to fetch him,
I say. And all that last month he lived and walked in London there
was a waft of death about him."

"What's a waft of death?" asked Will.

"That," said Doggett. He waved to the open door. Will looked into
the dark, crooking web of streets. John Trivet lay stiffening in his
own blood before the tavern. A single light burned weakly yellow in
a far window. And the rest was all close and hot and black, as if a
great foul blanket had been drawn over the city, shutting it in with
its own filth from the sweet airs of the open sky. The blue fires
burned, and east by the Wall came the rattle of death carts and the
cry, "Bring out your dead!" It seemed as if a visible air, not quite
so thick as a shadow, hovered over the roofs and alleys, an evil air
with a gray-white glimmer in it and the odor of old bones laid a long
time underground; an air that stirred, and drifted, and sank into every
crack in wood or stone, every pore of flesh, bringing with it not only
the matter, but the spirit of decay. Suddenly he was more frightened
than he had ever been in his life. Clutching Dr. Hodges' pass, he
started to his feet.

"How—how do I get to Nottingham?"

"Go out through Bishopsgate—by Waltham Cross to the Great
North Road."

Bishopsgate! He knew where that was. Maybe there would be
fields beyond it in the morning light—somewhere the fields of Old
Thorny, if he could get to them, and wasn't stricken down purple in
a ditch on the way. He staggered out of the Old Serpent, stepped
over John Trivet's body, and began to run. Now he was out through
Cripplegate. Now he was running along the roots of London Wall,
running for his life—slipping, falling in a heap of garbage and street-
sweepings, getting up, racing on. How bold and happy he'd been on
the river that afternoon, singing:

> "Oh, the sun and moon will dance on the green,
>   On the night that I come home."

And he was at home, but the sun and moon had gone under, and
what danced on the green was this waft of death, waiting to draw
him into a measure, him and the singing girl in her scarlet dress. It

had used all the sweet temptation of the flesh which he had never known to keep him here in its power. But it had lost. He was going to Old Thorny, and throw himself down on the earth of it, and lie there till they shoveled that home earth over him, and he was back where he rightly came from. And then he stopped thinking, and ran, and ran, and ran.

10. *I seen a ghost*

≈≈≈≈≈≈≈≈≈≈≈≈≈≈≈≈≈≈≈≈≈≈≈≈≈≈≈≈≈≈≈≈≈

IT RAINED in Nottingham the night Will Scarlock got home, just as it had when his father left there, thirty-six years before. While he was fighting his way through the great fens north of London, still mazed and incoherent from his night in the plague-struck city, the summer had broken and the autumn rains swept in from the North Sea. The roads turned swiftly into channels of mud, and drowned meadows sprawled all afloat behind the hedgerows; groves, and thickets, and scattered farms glimmered through the gray drip of the fog; and the towns, strung out like beads on the chain of the Great North Road, were gray and dreary, and their cobbled streets a-slop, their lanes dank ruts of miry clay. Sometimes he stayed at an inn where they eyed him askance and made him show his pass and wash in vinegar to take the smell of London off him, and sometimes he bought a seat in a coach, but the great worn-gilt lumbering thing would only get bogged down at some cross or other, and he'd have to walk after all, head down in the beating rain. Then there'd be another inn with mildew on the plaster walls, and rusty bacon, and weak ale, and a cold welcome—and then he'd be off again, always to the north. Leaves, driven from the trees by the force of the wind that beat them, whipped in his face as he went, and the clouds billowed overhead, breaking sometimes to let through a little weak yellow sunshine that never lasted long. But it was England, in spite of the mean disguise across it. Castles and towers loomed off through the trees here and there—a walled park, a cluster of thatched cottages, a little river winding in a lane of willows, a thriving green grange or half-timbered manor. It was a patterned country where even the woods and wild moors had the look of man's living on them, and nowhere that you stepped could you get the feeling that you were the first man ever to go there, the feeling you had so often whenever you walked into the emptiness of the great forest at home. At home? He meant Piscataqua, of course.

A few differences he noticed. The tree trunks were thicker here, like broad old men set fast in the landscape, while at home they were thin and lithe, swaying out in the wind like young, drunken sailors. And one night when the sky cleared cold for an hour or two and the moon blew across it, that moon was much larger than the one he was used to, mellower, and not half so far off in the air. Cathedrals, walled towns, even the fields at the tag end of harvest and not yet stripped to take the winter wheat—he wished he'd brought Tusser with him—looked as if they'd grown there or had been put up by God in the first week, and were meant to stay a long time. At home—in Piscataqua, of course—a man's duty had been to go out and clear and take; to make fields, farms, and towns where they had never been, and a man was judged as he lifted up his axe upon the tall trees. But here a man's first duty would be to hand on his world when he died, just the way it had come to him when he was a young man. Now he saw what his father meant when he said Wat Tyler and Jack Straw were knaves because they wanted change. If he lived here twenty years, perhaps he'd under- stand his father, but by then some boy would be tightening his mouth and turning away his eyes, and trying to understand him. His son, of course, and when he thought about that, he thought about Doll Trasper in a red dress singing at the Old Serpent. He couldn't see her rocking a cradle or setting a kettle to boil, but then his father had got his mother out of a tavern—maybe it would happen again in his time. Women were strange, you never could tell what they'd say yes or no to. He and Doll had never spoken to each other, but there had been much between them, and the promise of more. He'd never heard her say one word or known one single thought that was in her mind—yes, he had—one. And she must have taken him for a rare figure—a stranger, just off the ship from God-knows-where, tousled, and tumbled, and scared as hell, and too shy to even look at her. And then running away as he had! The farther he got from London, the swifter his fright dwin- dled and the more ashamed he felt. Doll hadn't been afraid. She had sat there, and smiled, and sung, and tried to keep a good heart in everybody. He wondered if he could ever make her believe he was really a man and not a jack rabbit going more or less upright. Anyhow, he knew that he would be back in London before long, and trying to.

And so, after more than a week's wandering, he came to Newark on Trent. The river had overflowed and the streets were all a-wash; mid-afternoon dark gray like evening, and the cold rain still coming down. In an alehouse just off the market square he got in talk with a carrier who offered him a ride into Nottingham, and a little later they were rumbling in a heavy dray over the sallow marshes through the cold wet dusk, marshes that would flower in spring into the crocus meadows his mother had told him of. Below the Castle, he knew, would be Brew House Yard, and the Castle was easy enough to tell, a bulk of black stone gleaming in the mist. His clothes hadn't been quite dry for five days, and his boots for longer, and there was a hoarseness in his throat—all in all, he wasn't the jaunty traveler who'd climbed out on the water stairs by London Bridge that hot, yellow night, but he was still Will Scarlock and looked it. He wouldn't have to prove who he was to any man who remembered his father.

He'd climbed down from the dray in the midst of a winding, paved road that seemed to run athwart everything and follow, half up the hill above it, the course of a dirty, swollen stream flowing in stoned-up channels, that the carrier said was the Leen Ditch. "You'll have no trouble," the man told him, reining up his horses in a little square all set round with lighted shop windows and gabled houses of lath and plaster, very much like the ones he'd seen going up Fish Street Hill in London. "Yard's under Castle, and there's eleven taverns there, all a-row, but the one you want has the bull's head sign—new-painted with brown spots and red in the nostrils."

So he went sloshing his way through water that trickled down the cobbles, with more water from the close-set eaves falling into his collar. Once he paused under the hanging balcony on the front of a half-timbered house, to wipe his face, and clear his throat, and get his bearings a little, and a voice croaked at him, and he saw that another creature had huddled for shelter in the same doorway: a creature who held out her hand as if to beg for alms, and then drew it back and commenced to whine and shudder. It was a hideous old woman with the bridge of her nose caved in and lank hair hanging like wet hay each side of vacant eyes that grew swiftly alive with fright and horror as they peered into his face. They stood there for one moment, and Will, unable to help himself, uttered a weak curse. The hag turned then, with a harsh scream and a whoosh of skirts, and scuttled down the street, rocking crazily round a corner and out of sight. Will uttered a stronger curse and followed slowly over the cobbles in the way she had taken.

The Bull's Head was almost empty that night because of the bad, thick weather. A few lads who lived close by had come in to play shovelboard, but none of the farmers had braved the maze of sodden lanes that covered the countryside. Jack, heavier now, with blue veins spreading around the roots of his nose and his crisp, black hair turned gray, was trying to tell Nelly, the girl he'd hired from the workhouse last week, how to open a bottle of old wine without having it spurt in your eyes and blind you. Ned Trigg, bent and shivering, huddled close to the fire Jack had built to pamper him, and though it was 'way too early in the fall for such, it felt good to everybody, and the lads had stopped their game now and carried their mugs over to the hearth to join him.

"I be going to roast some chestnuts, Jack," said Ned, standing up.

Nelly, pale and scrawny, with no bosom that could be called such, left the taps and scampered about nervously, trimming the wicks and peering out of the black windowpanes with rain running down them.

"Right, man," boomed Jack with all his old vigor. "Roast 'em up now, and what'll you do them snowy nights past Christmas? Thinking back to how good they tasted tonight won't help you then. Summer's scarce over, man, and you'd set us up for Martinmas already. Ah, to be old . . . !"

"Old!" snorted Ned. "I was born same week o' Wednesday that you was born o' Friday. But you wasn't thrown from horse in the stone quarry like I was. 'Course I can't pay, ye knows, an' if ye grudge me . . . !"

"God's sakes, man, you know I never . . . !" cried Jack, hurt.

And then the door flung open. A disheveled old woman with a raddled face and staring eyes bounded into the room and stood panting, her dirty, drab clothes leaking rainwater in the middle of the floor.

"I seen a ghost!" she cried. "So help me God, an' as I'm Moll Doubleday, I seen a ghost, boys!"

"There, there, Molly," said Jack. "Whose ghost was it, lass? Nell, fetch out that Jamaica bottle."

The men at the fire looked up from their pipes and mugs to watch her, and Jack repeated his question, while the candles wavered in the draft her entrance had made, and the burning apple logs on the hearth hissed orange and blue.

"We're getting you drink, Molly. The strongest in the house. 'Fore God, I seen you drunk and I seen you sober, and I seen you in plights a decent woman wouldn't be in. But I never seen you like this before."

"I seen a ghost," she breathed through chattering teeth, sweat mingling with the rain on her sodden features. "I seen John Scarlock, young an' fresh, an' twenty-one years old. I seen him an' he cursed me."

"Molly, you're drunk, and I don't know where you got it. Not off the lads any more, and they don't serve it forth at St. Nicholas workhouse. Johnny went for the colonies before the wars, and we heard of him only the one time when he sent for Joan—never after. If he be twenty-one, then you're eighteen and I'm thirty—and that won't be again. You didn't see Johnny."

"I did. I be no green girl, Jack, but I be not so common as not to know a man I laid with. I tell you, I seen John Scarlock's ghost, coming up from the Narrow March, a-heading this way." She took the glass Nell brought and swallowed thirstily.

The rain came at the windows like a handful of stones hurled against them, and all in a gust of wind, the door swung open again. A young man stood there, drenched, and wearing a shapeless green coat, tall, with a thin face more long than wide, and wisps of brown hair blown above it by the night wind. There were lads all over England looked almost like that—but not quite. Moll reared back and made queer, clucking noises of fright. Ned Trigg had a nut in his mouth to crack its shell, and his broken teeth came sharply together through rind and meat and bit into the soft flesh till blood welled around his old gums, but he did not feel any pain there. Jack turned pale and reached for the fire tongs. To the other men, whose memory of the Bull's Head did not go back past twenty years, this was a stranger looking in for a drink on a wet night, nothing more.

The stranger spoke. "Is Jack Gambrell still host here?"

Jack stood his ground, his hand tight on the iron tongs. "I be Jack Gambrell," he hissed through set jaws, "as well ye know. What do ye want, John Scarlock? We never harmed ye living. We was your friends."

The candles flickered and the back log sank in a moil of blue scattered sparks, and the rain washed down the panes like water through a weir.

"I'm not John. I'm his son, Will. I came home."

Moll put her forearms on the table and her head down on them, and began to cry noisily. Red surged back into Jack's face and he dropped his weapon.

"I should ha' knowed that, lad! I should ha' knowed. But ye're that like him! God, but I'm glad." He waddled forward, both hands extended past the round bulge under his leather apron.

Will smiled a little shyly, and let himself be led to the fire and thrust down on a bench there; took the drink Jack roared for the harassed Nelly to bring him; even sat quiet while, at Jack's order, she tugged his wet boots off.

"She's a good girl, Will," said Jack, watching with approval. "I always hires bastards from St. Nicholas' workhouse, but your mother was the best o' the lot—the best in forty years. Gay and kindly to all, but kept to herself—save for one, an' him she married. By God, Will, she left here so fast she never took her wages, an' I'll pay them to you now." He strode to the till and plucked three shillings from it, which Will gravely accepted.

"I'll keep them for her," he said.

A hand fell on his shoulder, and a gnarled face under silky white hair peered close at him. "I be Ned Trigg, Willie. Ever hear of me?"

"Of course I have. Ned Trigg, sir! My father always wanted to ask if you were my grandfather, but some ways I'm bolder than he and I'll do it. Are you?"

Sadness went over the old face like cloud shadows over an autumn field. "No. No. I wasn't Joan's father," he said, thinking back to a lost spring all white hawthorn, and boys and girls who had companioned him there, and few of them left living any more. "But every time I mind her mother's pretty face, I wish to God I had been. How's Johnny, lad?"

Will saw that Jack and Moll were listening for his answer, but he had no easy words to put it in.

"He's dead. He died three years ago."

Moll's grief turned noisier. The men had resumed their own broken talk now. Jack and Ned waited for him to go on. So he did, slowly, sipping his ale, and eating the beef pasty Nelly brought him; told them about his father's death, and Joan and his sisters, and the house in Portsmouth and their way of life there. They listened, and nodded, and then they were all silent together, until finally Jack spoke.

"So he sent you home. He promised he'd have boys a-plenty, and one would be for Old Thorny. And you're here now, and Rob can go out in peace like he's been wanting to."

"Tell me about Rob."

"Hasn't left his bed for three year. Lies, and mostly sleeps the clock around, and wakes to eat a little now and then. God, he's old, lad. He fought the Armada in the Old Queen's time—I dunno how many year ago, 'fore I was born, sure, an' I was sixty-six last Michaelmas. But he says he won't die till there's an heir for Old Thorny, so there he lays. You'll look good to him, what little he can see."

"And Bet?"

"Bet's old too, but strong and spry, and takes most care of him while Gilly runs the kitchen. Kit and Gill Harroday had a flock of lads, but they're all grown and gone now, except Hal and Colin who helps Kit with the farm. Kit's a good farmer, and I've never seen the land look better. Some would have tried to steal it from you, but he's honest. Says he hopes it'll be his home while he lives, but he's worked for Scarlocks, man and boy, since he left his father's roof when he was twelve years old, and he knows he's but keeping the place for John. Ye'll see for yourself tomorrow."

"I'll see tonight," said Will, shoving the dishes one side and reaching for his wet boots.

"No! Not tonight, Willie!" cried Ned. "It's dark an' raining, an' ye don't know the way."

"I've not seen much but dark and rain since I got to England, and I'm used to them. And I heard my father tell the way so often I could tread it blind."

And he really believed that when he walked out of the Bull's Head, with Jack and Ned protesting behind him, but as he got off the cobbles of Nottingham and into the soaked fields stretching eastward, he felt less sure of himself with every step he took. Here, the houses should stop; and there, should be a rick; and there, an oast house —but there was only drenched fog, lifting to show a maze of lanes, and as much reason to follow one as another. The clouds overhead had thinned a little, and the rain turned soft and clung to the skin instead of needling it with a hard drip. Now the moon struggled through, and in the thin light of it he could make out the long sweep of shadow on his left that would be Sherwood Forest, and the break in the land on his right that would be the edge of Trent valley. He stumbled on, between drowned hedges. Now and then he passed a stone cottage with a thatched roof, most of them showing no light, for it was getting late. And then, suddenly, there seemed to be no place to go at all. The lane he had been following ended in a farm-yard, and he could hear the stamping and rummaging of cattle in the barns, and smell the mixture of dung and chaff and chimney-smoke that seemed to belong with the farms about here. He hoped for a minute that the sleeping house beyond might be Old Thorny, but then he knew that it was not, because it was built of timber and clapboard, and his house was red stone with a curved roof. And so he blundered over a stile and out into the open fields in the watery moonlight, and finally stopped, not even sure of his direction any more.

Then he saw a man coming toward him, over the dark, water-sodden land. The man was tall and walked with an easy stride in spite of the treacherous clay that slid away under the bootsoles and the thicket of little thorny trees that reached out their twigs to snag his coat. He had a small lanthorn and he turned it on Will as he greeted him, leaving his own face in the shadow.

"Lost your way?" he asked casually, his voice low and deep.

"Yes. I'm looking for a farm called Old Thorny. It's hereabout somewhere, isn't it?"

"Over there. Up nearer Sherwood. I'm going that way myself. Come along with me."

They stepped off together, the lanthorn lighting up the wet earth and floating grasses underfoot, the moon overhead weaving in and out of the cloudbanks, and a fresh wind rustling the dank leaves of the hazels scattered here and there. The man beside him went with long deliberate steps, not offering talk, but whistling softly to him-self, an air that Will did not know. After a little while they turned sharply and clambered over a crooked wall of flints and mortar, and Will noticed as the lanthorn tilted upward that the sleeve of his guide's coat was the same worn green as his own.

"I see you wear a green coat too," he said uncertainly. Looking close at the stranger in what little light there was between the lant-horn and the moon, Will could see that he was a man neither young nor old, with strong, blunt features, his eyes far back in the shadow.

"Yes. Green's a common color here."

"You live hereabout?"

"Hereabout."

They plodded on. Finally his companion stopped and swung the light. And just ahead of them Will saw the red sandstone house with thatch curved down all over, the squat chimney in the center of it, and the square windows framed with oak. The crab orchard sloped away to Gamwell Chase, and the fields circled round three sides, and everything looked just the way his father had said it would. He stood still, staring at it, taking it into his heart forever, but as he did so he found to his surprise that there was another house there already—a peaked house with gables set by a salt marsh river far away; but that there was room in his heart for both. Wondering and shaken, he turned to thank the man who had brought him there, only to find that he stood alone. Then he saw the lithe figure striding off toward Sherwood Forest, swinging his lanthorn, not looking back. He had not said, "Here you are," or "No trouble," or even, "Goodbye." Will looked after him, uneasy and bewildered for a moment, and then suddenly everything seemed right, and the way it should be. It was only fitting that he should enter this holy ground alone.

One of the square windows that seemed to be hardly more than a few inches off the turf had a light burning behind it, and he crossed the farmyard and went up to the timbered door and knocked. He could hear a little stir inside. Then a stalwart, gray-haired man opened up for him, holding a candle to see who it was. He peered out and slow terror came across his face.

"Don't be frightened. I'm Will Scarlock, John's boy—coming home."

The man drew a long breath and lowered the candle.

"Well then, praise God. I thought you were a ghost. But I should ha' knowed you was kin, when Watch didn't bark. Come in, sir. I be Kit Harroday, as farms the place for your father. Is he well?"

"He's dead, Kit," said Will, stepping into the low room that seemed to fill the whole inside of the house, and large as it was, looked crowded; a great trestle table, carved chairs, benches and chests, a spinning wheel; blue tapestry on one wall, herbs and cured meats hanging from the blackened rafters overhead; on a hook a rusty suit of armor. A huge tawny dog lay flat on the hearth between the andirons, reaching almost the length of it, his head down on his great paws, his wide, amber eyes open. Will walked up to him and scratched the top of his head. "Remember me, Argus?" he said. It was an old dog, he saw, and it dropped one eyelid wisely and wrinkled its muzzle.

"So John's dead. I was afeared he might be. It's been so long since we heard. The dog's named 'Watch'—not what you said—great-grandson to one your father owned. I'll call Gilly and Bet."

"No—not if they've gone to bed."

"Oh, they're not abed yet. They're making the old man easy. He always has a milk posset late, and my boys be in town courting. I like to stay up and keep a light till everyone's got home."

"I heard at Jack Gambrell's you're a rare good farmer, Kit, with an army of sons who take after you."

"They be good boys—Will, is it?"

"Aye. Will."

"I got a lad named that. Prenticed to a baker in Newark. Three has tenant farms, an' Colin an' Hal I keeps here. Old Thorny'd feed that many more. I put away owner's share in the chest every year, Will."

"You can keep right on, Kit. Everything here looks too good to change."

"You've not seen all—except by dark. Tomorrow I'll show you. Be you coming back to be heir?"

"I don't know, Kit."

"Old man'll be pleased he can die now. He's been waiting for it ten year, but he said he wouldn't go till that boy o' John's come. Have trouble finding your way?"

"Well . . . yes . . . I did . . . a little, after I left Nottingham. But one of your neighbors came by with a light. Tall, in a green coat. Do you know who it would be?"

"No, lad. It could be one of half a dozen. He didn't tell you?"

"No. He didn't ask me who, nor where, nor make any talk at all. He just brought me home and then made off for Sherwood."

"That's strange. That's not like anybody I knows on Colwick Farms. They're all friendly men as talk easy and ask questions. That's not common at all."

"So I thought."

And then two women came down a stairway at the far end of the great room. Gilly's hair was white but sleekly combed, and her face still smooth and ruddy, and Will thought that she was probably still a pleasure to her man. Bet must be the little old creature with her, brown and shriveled as a dried butternut. He was glad that Kit warned them before they could look close at him and take fright.

"Gilly and Bet! You know who I got here with me? I got the heir to Old Thorny we been waiting for. I got John Scarlock's boy Will, come home from the colonies. Come see him."

Gilly smiled and stepped placidly forward. Old Bet drew a sharp breath and scurried past her to thrust a seamed face into his, very close, and peer and peer.

"Yes," she said finally. "It's Johnny's boy. I couldn't mistake. He's here, and Rob can go. But we won't wake him up for it this night."

"Is he hungry, Kit?" asked Gilly. "Are you hungry, Will Scarlock?"

"No. Jack Gambrell fed me."

"Then you're tired?"

Suddenly he knew that he was terribly tired. His night in London, his journey up the country in the cold, wet autumn, and then all that had happened in his heart to trouble and disturb him weighted his flesh as if he were trying to move inside the case of old armor that hung beside the bench he had sunk down on.

"I am tired," he said. "We can talk tomorrow. If there's a bed . . ."

"There's your father's bed," answered Gilly, turning to the stairs, "stripped and aired, and no one in it since he went away. I'll go make it up clean. Kit, get out the ale and apple tart and tonight's cream. I don't trust to a man saying he's not hungry."

And later, much later, it seemed, he lay in well-lavendered sheets on a narrow flock bed under the eaves, with the cloying taste of apple tart in his mouth, and all his limbs so heavy with exhaustion that it was like a sickness on him. To lie still and warm and dry, stretched out full length, seemed the sweetest thing in the world. Downstairs he could hear the smothered laughter and jests of the boys back from their courting in Nottingham, having their turn at the ale and pastry. Here he was, in his father's house, in his father's bed, and tomorrow he could pick up old time where his father had laid it down, and go on to work this land, and marry, and raise up boys like Hal and Colin, and in a few generations nobody would remember that the Scarlocks had ever gone away from Nottingham. He could feel a need to do this, a need as deep as the hunger for breath or food, and yet somehow, the little, sharp, prodding doubt that he would ever be able to. For no good reason. And then he thought of the tall man in the green coat whom Kit Harroday did not know, the man who had brought him here and left him, and turned back to Sherwood Forest. "I wonder if *I* seen a ghost," he murmured to himself, settling deeper in the goosefeather pillow, smiling as he remembered Moll's terror. "Could have been the ghost of Old Will seeing I made it home."

Then sleep flooded over him like the tide flooding up Piscataqua, and the last thing he thought of was not Old Thorny, nor the lad who had slept in this bed before him, nor green ghosts slipping out of Sherwood to aid their generations lost in rain. He thought about a girl in a scarlet dress swinging her ankles, and he heard her singing, "Oh, I'd follow England over . . ." "She won't have to," he muttered, letting his head sink on the fragrant linen, "she won't have to. Only . . . next time . . . I hope I'll be more a man." And then for a few sweet hours he forgot everything, even Doll Trasper.

11. Goose Fair marriage

WHEN WILL SCARLOCK left Old Thorny and walked up to Nottingham to the Goose Fair that mild, sad autumn morning, he had it in mind to bring home a wench, and he did it sure enough, but not in the way he thought to. He had been at home for a week, and he'd gone fishing in Trent and ranged through Sherwood after dark, looking for Old Will. He'd beat the briar patches below Gamwell Chase, trying to find the little field that had been there forty years ago, and he'd sat long hours by old Rob's bedside, gazing into the sunken eyes where no light woke to answer him.

"Sometimes he lays weeks this way—not knowing," Bet had told him. "But he'll rise out of it one day and greet you, and see he's got leave to go. You wait for that."

So he was waiting for that. He'd see the old man through—if the old man wanted it. That was his duty as his father's son, as he claimed manhood in his own name. And afterward, plague or no plague, he was going back to London, and not to see Sir William Warren. Oh, that in its time, of course—but first he was going to the Old Serpent, maybe to the house on London Bridge. He was going to find Doll Trasper. And he did not think beyond that. Beyond that would be the great question of his life to answer, and he hoped he'd have the wits for it when the time came, but 'fore God, he hadn't now. He felt better if he didn't let his thoughts run out too far in any direction, but put all the life in him into the play of his muscles while he worked about the fields and barns and orchards, helping Kit and the boys do all the things Old Tusser had said should be done in September.

They plowed for winter wheat, and mended the quickset and holly hedges; they gelded the rams and a young bullock. One afternoon he helped Gilly set out strawberry plants and strip the herb garden. Once he even went gathering mast for the hogs because it took him among the great oaks up the Chase, and he was more at home in the woods than out on the plowed land.

And then one warm, cloudy morning, when the air was heavy with the scent of apples picked and lying on the grass in piles and ready to barrel for winter, he stood in the kitchen window while the others sat at breakfast, and heard the sweet bells of St. Mary's tower ringing faintly over westward in the town. Gilly stepped smartly past him with a big bowl of frumenty—a fragrant stew of boiled wheat, milk, currants and spices, much favored hereabout. His eyes turned to follow her, and he noticed that Hal and Colin had their best coats on, and had cleaned the dung and straw from their boots, and their faces shone ruddy from scouring. He went to the table's head and sat down.

"You ought to go along with the boys, Will. It's the last day of Goose Fair. Johnny told you about it, didn't he?"

"Goose Fair? Yes, I remember. Didn't he serve as some sort of steward or warden for it?"

"Lord of the Taps, he was!" cried Kit, a look of happy remembrance coming into his eyes. "Lord of the Taps from the time he was fifteen. I used to make his rounds with him. Always said he needed my help."

"Aye, that was it. But what does it mean? What's 'Lord of the Taps'?"

"Ever been to a fair?"

"No."

"Well, you go today. You'll find the Market lined with booths that'll sell everything in the world a man'll give money for. And along the wall down the middle'll be Ale House Row. That's where you buy what's-to-drink—ale, beer, cider, French and Spanish wine, bottles of fiery stuff from the western islands. And it's custom to have a Lord of the Taps go to each of the stalls there and taste what it's selling, to be sure it won't rot our Nottingham gullets as it goes down. Mayor'd always appoint a Scarlock to that office when he could, because they had an uncommon head for the creature, and while 'tis a work all men would like, 'tis not one all men be equal good at. I've seen some lords fall headfirst in the street before they was through."

"Well, I'll go then, and see if it's being done as my father'd want it. Can't you and Gilly come?"

"Oh, Kit—you said you'd help me with the cheeses!" Gilly cried plaintively. "We can't go gadding abroad."

Kit wavered. Will turned thoughtful. Then he said, "Gilly, why don't you have a dairymaid? I'm one more to cook and wash for, and it's not sure I'll be going soon—and there's Rob's broths and possets and linens—and Bet"—he looked around to make sure she was not in the room—"can't see, and drops things, and forgets."

Gilly beamed like a round, sweet moon. "Oh, 'twould be such a fine thing! There's not been one here since I came for the work when I was a young girl. But her wages—can we?" She looked appealingly at Kit.

"How about it, Kit? Isn't there aught between me and St. Nicholas' workhouse but a dairymaid's wages?"

"I guess Old Thorny wouldn't fail for it, Will."

"Gilly, you shall have a dairymaid."

But Gilly's practical mind was already at work. "Then if 'tis agreed, perhaps you can bring one home from the Goose Fair."

"So they have booths that sell dairymaids?"

"Almost. 'Tis a famous hiring fair. And the men and maids that wants places go, likewise farmers who has need for such, and they come together and drive bargains."

"I'll drive one for us then. I'll get you a dairymaid."

And a few minutes later he was striding through the plowed fields between Hal and Colin, thinking that if the Fair was as well stocked as they said, there'd be a bookseller somewhere about and he'd be able to get a new *Silva*, for his own was back in the chest on the *London Girl* down by Wapping, and he wanted one by him now, to read in the long, soft twilights when the boys were courting and Kit and Gilly dozed in their chairs, and thoughts he didn't want to think kept coming into his head, and all the low stone farmhouse teased him with memories that wouldn't quite come clear. Once they got upon the cobblestones, he asked the boys if they wouldn't stop by Jack Gambrell's and have a drink with him before they went on to the Fair, but it seemed their sweethearts were waiting in the Market, so he parted from them and headed alone for the double stone squares of Nottingham Castle. He had never been there in the daytime, and it seemed to him as if the whole town was cut out of red sandstone, all a-row and cluster with half-timbered houses, and here and there a great house of stone. Shade trees grew in some of the streets, and many of the houses had gardens. St. Mary's stood up, and St. Peter's stood up, but St. Nicholas' had been pulled down during the wars and they hadn't restored it. He found his way back to Brew House Yard without any trouble, and into the Bull's Head, empty but for Ned and Jack, with everyone else gone to the Fair.

"Glad to see you again, Will. And what do you make of Old Thorny? Think you'll like it?"

"A man would be a fool not to," said Will gloomily, partly because of the soft gloom of the sunless morning, and the slight chill of sadness that lingers in every town when the year turns down for fall. They drank together.

"Going to the Fair?"

"Aye. To get Gilly a dairymaid."

"Ah . . . watch out for the dairymaids! Don't you get caught in no Goose Fair marriage, boy."

"What's a Goose Fair marriage?"

Ned explained to him. "The particulars of a Goose Fair marriage be these: that 'tis quick and easy and does not endure. It be held in a hedge, and blessed by the rooks cawing over, and lasts, most times, the one night only."

"I see. No, I'll not likely make any Goose Fair marriage."

A tow-headed boy, lean, and weedy, and draped in a red coat with blue cuffs and tarnished silver lace that had never been made for him, thrust himself through the doorway and stalked up to the bar, addressing Jack.

"I be the mayor's messenger, and he sends his greetings to Jack Gambrell, and says he hears John Scarlock's boy's about, and is it so?"

"You take my greetings back to Will Jackson—as drew ale for me when he was a lad and I've borne good love to ever since—and tell him John Scarlock's boy's sitting in my tavern, and what does he want done about it?"

"He wants him for Lord of the Taps today."

"What's wrong with Dick Pogg as was Lord all week?"

The boy made a downward gesture like a flail falling. "Abed. And cannot be seen. His wife says that if he hears the word 'ale,' he holds his head in his hands and howls like a dog."

The men laughed. Will stood up. "All right, lad. I'm Will Scarlock, and I'm ready. Bring it on!"

"Got to go to the hall over Shambles and be proclaimed and get the coat," said the boy. "I'll show you."

They went up the pavement and along the greensward at the back of the Castle, the messenger calling out the way importantly, eager to impress the stranger. "This be Castle Gate," he cried, and then they went down a narrow close, "and this be Jew Lane." Jew Lane led into Hounds Gate, and Samuel Row took them from that to Moot Hall Gate, and from that, just beyond the house of the White Friars, the Market opened out.

Nottingham Market spread before him, six acres of such surge, and color, and life that he stood still and held his breath while his guide with swift tumbling speech put names to everything for him.

"Well, here 'tis. Folk comes here from all over England. That's the Horse Market on your left there . . ." The Horse Market was an unpaved, sandy strip where stallions, mares, and colts were tethered closely; sorrel, dappled, black, brown, and bay; some stamped and whinnied, but the great-hocked plow horses waited patient and docile. "There'll be racing on the course this afternoon. T'other side, 's Timber Hill."

On his right Will could see the familiar sight of white heaped boards, deals, planks, laths, shingles, clapboards, and wainscoting—every sort of wood fitting—but except for the oak timbers they looked sparse and meager beside the woodyards of Piscataqua. A wall, breast high, went down the middle of the market place, with frequent openings in it for men to pass back and forth, and against it stood canvas shelters on pole frames where ale was dispensed, but their front curtains were all drawn now, and their proprietors pacing back and forth on the cobbles before them, waiting for the Lord of the Taps to give them clearance. But other booths and stalls burst open everywhere like gaudy flowers, and the mayor's messenger was naming them over.

"North by the Long Row," he droned, "you can buy corn, meal, chinaware, salt, millinery, men's coats, hardware an' bakers' goods, collars an' garden shrubs. South, 'tween the old wall an' the hanging bank, ye can buy spices, teak-weed, an' silver 'broidery out of Cyprus. West of the Horse Market be the Beast Market, where ye go for sheep an' swine. East by Cuckstool Row be the Shambles an' the butchers, an' over them be mayor, waiting to open the Fair. At the west end be the Malt Cross where brewers trade an' wars be proclaimed—we be a great malt county an' supplies all o' Cheshire,

Lancashire, Shropshire, Stafford, an' Derby Peak. East be the Butter Cross—under yon tiled roof—where you can buy bacon, eggs, an' dairyings."

Will's eyes followed the pointing finger of his guide, and he tried to take it all in. Beyond the Butter Cross, the lush purple and red and orange-tawny viands of the Fruit Market cast their heavy sweetness on the air. Here was a stall full of bright ribbons, and another for nosegays and field flowers, and another for march-pane—pewterware; twiggy baskets; fustians and kerseys and druggets from the great cloth shires; smoked salmon and pink, curling sea shrimp; fresh, white-bellied tench from the Leen; herrings, Kentish hops, birdlime, cowhides, coal for smithies, bundles of faggots, barrels of rosin, pitch and tar—he couldn't think for the minute of any trade on earth that wasn't a-plying there, except the bookseller's!

And over the sand and cobbles thronged a company of men and women, most of them looking very much like the Harrodays: some sharp, some smiling, some old and gnarled, some fresh and rosy; and all their colored garments moving, red, and gray, and green, and brown, and blue; and voices lifted up, and coins tinkling together; barkers shouting, and far off to the northeast a lilt of music. Here and there rode out a fine-cloaked figure on horseback.

"Today be the day the gentry comes in," said his guide reverently, calling off names. "Pigot of Trumpington; Mansfield of West Leak; Pierrepont, and Sir Scroop How, knight o' shire; Hacker of Colston-Basset . . . !" He started off now, past the Butter Cross, and up a wooden stair at the left of the Shambles where fresh-killed beeves were dripping down blood, and Will followed him into a high, plastered room that smelled of spices and had but three walls, the fourth side being a great open window that faced the Market. In the center of the window stood two men, dressed in flying cloaks of gold and scarlet, the one much finer than the other, and to one side waited other men, in violet silk mantles with fur collars and cropped sleeves.

"That be mayor and sheriff, and these be the aldermen," whispered the boy.

The mayor stood forth now in the window, lifted a horn and blew it thrice.

"Oyez, oyez, oyez!" shouted the sheriff.

"I proclaim the Goose Fair open—it's last day, and trade in wisdom," called out Mayor Jackson, lowering the horn.

Cheers rose up from the Market, and the din came on again, louder than before. The mayor turned back into the spice chamber and saw Will standing at the head of the stairs. The boy messenger threw back his head and closed his eyes. "Will Scarlock," he droned, "I hereby present to my Lord Mayor of Nottingham."

Will bowed, never having met a mayor before, but somehow feeling he should bow.

The mayor was a slight, pleasant-faced man; his mouth curved up sweetly now, and his eyes twinkled.

"Welcome, Will Scarlock. Does the curse of your family abide upon you? Is it visited unto your generation?"

"It is."

"And the drunker you get the soberer you grow?"

"I do."

"Then you can serve us well here in Nottingham this morning. Have you been instructed how?"

"I have."

"Will you accept the charge?"

"I will."

"Then I pronounce you Lord of the Taps. Taswell!"

An aide in the town livery stepped forward then with a worn crimson coat and held it for Will to slip into. It hung limply on him, having been made for a round-bellied man.

The mayor shook his head. "It's an ill fit! You were never made for a Nottingham toss-pot. Taswell!"

Taswell now lifted up a light chain hung with small carved wooden spigots, and put it around Will's neck.

"And now," said Mayor Jackson, "be off to your duties, my lord."

Will bowed again and put his hand to the crazy wooden stair rail. Just then an old man tottered out from among the aldermen and fastened a gaunt claw into his crimson sleeve.

"I be Bennett Traves," he piped in a reedy voice that suited ill with the weathered-oak look that the rest of him had, the look of an oak gone woolly at the heart and about to fall; suited ill with the purple silk cloak and gold-knobbed cane. "Bennett Traves, alderman in your father's time, and a-many times after—if you be John Scarlock's boy—?"

"Yes, I be he."

"Joan Sweetapple's boy. Be ye Joan's boy?"

"Yes, I be Joan's boy, too."

"And how did ye leave her?"

"Widowed, but well—with her girls and her grandsons around her."

"Provided for?"

"Provided for."

"Why then, praise God!" quavered the old alderman. He started to say more, and then he dropped his hand, and hung his head, and drew back among his fellows, tears of weakness running from his faded eyes.

Will looked at him in bewilderment. Never know, he thought, what queer things the old will do. I hope I never live to get that way. I better get back to what I know about.

He stepped quickly downstairs and shouldered his way through the crowd, heading for Ale House Row. And once there he had a fine time of it. To swing over the cobblestones from one canvas stall to another, greeted everywhere by cheers and cries: "They got a Scarlock again!" "I knowed your father, boy!" To have his hand seized and wrung by old men, and feel young maids trying to catch his eyes; to mix with all the brightness and crude, lusty gaiety around him, tempered with the soberer, gray-clad men who were trying to drive bargains—all of it worked more strongly on him than ale out of any spigot ever twisted. He finished his rounds in good season, and just about the time the sun would have been straight overhead, if the sun had been out, he was coming away from a hopper-cake booth brushing the crumbs off his borrowed coat, when he met Hal and Colin with two pretty, black-haired sisters. He treated them all to glasses of sack, and asked them where he should go for a dairy-maid, but they wouldn't tell him.

"Oh," said Colin, "they hire near the Malt Cross somewhere, but don't go there now. Come on over to St. Mary Gate with us. There's wrestlers, and tumblers, and a sword-swallower, and a rope-dancer, and a singing girl—and a strolling troop is going to play *Nineveh Town*. And after that'll be the horse races. Then you can look for a dairymaid." And the pretty sisters caught his arms, and the boys caught their arms, and off they went down Cuckstool Row, past the fishmongers, and into the wide, paved space before the square-towered church, where chestnut trees had rooted themselves in the rim of grass beyond the gutters. The crowd had drawn back under the trees, leaving the middle pavement bare, and two thick-chested wrestlers strained and vied in front of an empty wooden platform with a canopy over it. Clowns and jesters ambled here and there, jabbering, followed by titters and guffaws. But it was quieter here than in the Market, and Hal's sweetheart whispered that the players would be mounting the stage any minute now. Will waited with the others under the chestnut trees. The warm, gray sky looked as if it would let down rain any minute, and a warm wind lifted a wisp of hair on his forehead; a dried yellow leaf fell silently past him and lay on the rounded cobbles close to the toe of his boot. The hush deepened, and the sense of waiting deepened, and he stirred nervously and leaned his shoulders against the smooth bark of the tree he stood under. He picked up a prickled burr from the gutter and began to pull the tiny thorns out of it.

And then, across the pavement in front of the stage, tripped a girl in a scarlet dress, picking a lute and singing:

> *"Oh, I'd follow England over,*
> *Seeking what is mine,*
> *From Land's End to Dover,*
> *From Thames mouth to Tyne;*
> *A green-coated lover . . ."*

Will Scarlock pulled off the brave crimson he had worn as Lord of the Taps and threw it down on the sprawling roots of the chestnut tree, baring his own green jacket. He stalked through the crowd, straight up to the edge of the open street, and stood staring at her till she saw him. Her song stopped then in the middle, and she ran forward, her little slippers hardly touching the cobblestones, and held out both her hands to him.

He took them in his. "So you followed England over . . ." he said, his eyes lighting with eager wonder, and none of the shyness and shame he had felt in London.

"Yes, I did, Will Scarlock. I told you I would. In my song I told you."

"Do you . . . shall we?" He fumbled for words happily.

She tucked her hand under his arm. "Take me down to the Market to see the geese. I heard all the way coming here that it was a rare sight."

"We'll find out," he said. "I haven't seen it either."

While they walked along she chattered as merrily as if they were old friends, back together again after a brief and unaccustomed parting. She'd left London the day after he did, with a pass of health she'd coaxed Dr. Hodges to give her, and walked to Waltham Cross, where the coaches left from, now that London was closed in with its sickness. From there she'd gone swaying north, mile after mile, in those dank, lumbering wheeled boxes, wedged into a corner, and with raindrops beating down on the roof overhead. Sometimes she had stopped off at an inn for a day or two, singing always to pay for her food and fare to the next town. He learned, as they walked, that she had no money, that she never kept money by her. She took no pay for her singing, save her supper, unless her rent was due or she needed a new red dress or strings for her lute. Then she would spread out her cloak or her kerchief beside her when she sang, and all London knew what that meant and would throw coins into it. She would buy with them what she needed and the rest she gave away. She had never been off the stones of London before, and felt more lost in the middle of her own country than he, the stranger from oversea.

When they came out into the Market this time, Will thought for a moment they were at another fair in another town—the real Goose Fair he'd been hearing about—for all the people were gathered back into the doorways and balconies of the half-timbered houses that circled round, and the open reach was full of geese. Geese—gray, white, blue, mouse-color, black-banded; Gray Lag geese that swam half wild in the fens; bean geese, stubble geese, Christmas geese, green geese; orange, pink, black, and livid bills, lifted and hissing and honking; webbed yellow feet, plump breasts, crooked necks, and flapping wings—geese—six acres of them. He stood still in the gutter, with Doll in front of him and his hands on her shoulders, and looked at geese.

"It's the Lincoln men got here finally," he heard one man telling another beside him. "There was goose herds in Lincoln a-fore there was Nottingham, and that was nine hundred and eighty years a-fore Christ. They be known all over. Didn't get in till today, and we thought they weren't coming this year. They been bound in by the flooded fens after the long rain."

Suddenly Doll ran from under his fingers, straight to the edge of the great, heaving flock, and knelt down, and put her arms around a huge snowy gander, burying her face in the rich down at the side of his snaky neck. Will was after her quick as her own shadow, and caught her up before the bird could turn to strike, frightened to the point of scolding her.

"He . . . he could pick your eyes out . . . they're mean devils . . . they . . ." But his muttering died away futilely, for the gander was uttering soft croaks and bending its narrow head to rub her arm.

"Oh," she cried, "he won't hurt me. They looked so fat, and soft, and rounded I wanted to touch them."

"Come touch them another way," he said to her, a little gruff still from the incident, and they walked to a booth he had noticed that morning, with stools to sit on, and a turning spit that roasted the spicy, larded slices of breast meat while you watched it, and together they ate roast goose and drank a queer black brew called "coffee" that Will had never seen before, but Doll said some people were beginning to set great store by in London.

By the time they had finished off with a fruit tart, the geese had been herded into the fields, and everyone was off for the race course, so Will and Doll went too, their arms around each other's waists, always learning a little more about each other. He was carrying her lute now, and she was wearing, about her pretty throat and falling into her bosom, the chain with the dangling spigots that had marked him as Lord of the Taps. They went by Piepowder Court where all disputes of the Fair were heard and settled, and by an old church pulpit with the paint peeling off, where Parson Aystorpe from St. Peter's was preaching a sermon to those who would listen, and Will found out by asking that there was always a minister appointed to bring God's Word to those at the Fair who wanted it, few though they might be. Mr. Aystorpe had a bald head and looked jolly— as if he could chew down his share of roast goose and spell Will off with the tapsters, should need arise.

After the races, the thick, bluish dusk was falling, and no moon coming out, and they were hungry again, so he took her back through the straggling crowd to the best inn he could find, and there they sat at a little table in a dark, wainscoted corner, with one smoky candle lit in the sconce over them, and a white table cloth, and silver, and they ate goose livers baked with apples and sherry, and drank spiced wine served with honey cake.

By and by, when it was quite dark outside, he leaned back, and lit his pipe, and looked across the table at her. And she looked straight back at him. One thing he liked. She hadn't pretended and told a fine story. She hadn't said she came to the Goose Fair in Nottingham because it was a likely place for a singing girl to get coins flung in her kerchief this time of year. She'd come here to be with him, and she'd said so—in her song she'd said so. He watched her through the smoky air of the inn. This day would end —it must end—all days did. But he didn't want it to—he wanted to catch it and hold to it forever. Wasn't there a place in the Bible where the sun stood still? Truth would know, if he were here. And then he smiled as he tried to imagine Truth, Harvard-bred and godly, sitting in a tavern with Doll Trasper who'd grown up amongst harlots and player folk. Her father had been a merry andrew and her mother an Irish gypsy, she said, and she was born backstage at the Cockpit theatre during a raid by Cromwell's soldiers, who'd carried her father off to prison for a common rogue. Her childhood under the Commonwealth had been a time of lean bellies and frequent alarms for all actors and entertainers, and once when those evil days had flung them into the London street, Milady, the fallen court beauty who sold lodgings and other conveniences on London Bridge, had taken them in. There her mother had died. From there her father had been carted away again, to die of disease and bad food in the Old Bailey. And Milady's girls had petted her and decked her with ribbons, sometimes slapped and cursed her, and taught her the sharp ways of the street. How different his life had been, among the green trees and bare salt marshes of Piscataqua, growing in the shadow of John's strength, nourished by Joan's sweetness and love.

"Do you want any more wine or cake?" he asked her.

"No. No more, Will Scarlock." She slipped out of her chair and stood up. "Are you going back to your Old Thorny now?"

He stood up too, looking at her thoughtfully. "Would you . . . like to come with me . . . there?" he asked her.

"Is it all yours, and there is no one who will care? No godly women?"

"Oh, no! There's Gilly and Bet who keep the kitchen—but they'll make you as welcome as I will. My house has no mistress—yet. If you mind the walk I can probably hire a horse."

"Oh, I'll not mind it. Let's go now."

He paid the reckoning and they stepped into the Market and went eastward out of town. They crossed the fields, arm-in-arm in the thick, warm dusk, with a sad little wind rustling in the dry leaves of the hazel thickets, the air sweet with the scent of clover stubble, and heavy with rain that did not fall. And under a sprawling beech tree that reared up white in the darkness, he stood still suddenly and took her in his arms. They were moving now in the dark realm of an old knowledge, the knowledge of a shared need, that can bring strangers closer in a few sharp moments than blood kin can come in all the generations. He kissed her forehead, and he kissed her mouth, long and deeply; and then he brushed aside the thin silk over her bosom and kissed the softness there; and she was all yield and answer. She belonged to him, and they both knew it, and there was nothing now to keep him from laying her gently down on the drifted beech leaves and doing what he wanted to with her, what she wanted him to do.

But as he bent forward to that end, a cold wind came blowing through his mind and brought a picture with it—the look of the Bank in winter, with snow all over, and the Piscataqua flowing black at the center, frozen round the reeds at the edge, and in the gray sky overhead, the thin, sharp, decorous sound of church bells ringing. The chill went out of his mind and into the blood that had been beating upward through his body. He had made his boasts at Vasty Bradish's table, and swapped vile jests in the Yard and the Long Chamber, but he knew in his heart that when you took a girl, there was only one way to do it. He held Doll out at arm's length and looked into her startled blue eyes.

"Doll! Do you want me?"

"I've said it, and I've sung it, and I've looked it at you—and still you don't know?"

"Will you marry me—honest and forever—up there by the Goose Fair pulpit?"

She looked down at the stubble underfoot, and put her hand to her cheek, stroking it thoughtfully for a moment. Then she looked up. "If you want it that way."

"We'll go back then."

Slowly, without any words, they toiled back through the thickening night and fog drifting over Trent valley. The Market was still gay with many lights, though nearly everybody had gone home, and sweating, shouting men had begun to fold away the canvases and take down the pole frames, while street sweeps plied their brooms busily to clear up refuse and broken feathers and goose dung. They found a goldsmith packing his wares away, and Will bought a ring, and put it in his pocket. Workmen toiled all about the pulpit, lashing it to iron rollers so it could be wheeled off and stored for Easter Fair time, but Mr. Aystorpe still lingered, sitting on a bench and balancing a plate of roast goose on his knee. The swinging lanthorns overhead lighted his merry face, with the jowls all goose grease, and he smiled broadly as he saw them coming.

"I want to get married," said Will gruffly, walking up to the vicar, holding Doll tightly by the hand.

Mr. Aystorpe put down a nicely browned goose wing and licked his mouth.

"Does *she* want to get married, too?"

Will did not answer, but he turned and looked at her.

"Yes—yes," said Doll. "Yes, I do."

"But I want it to be honest before all men," said Will. "Is it? Out in the open street like this? And the three weeks' banns . . . ?"

He hadn't thought about banns before. There had to be banns. That ended it. He wasn't going to wait three weeks to have what was under the scarlet dress . . . he'd take her back to the beech tree . . . he'd . . .

Mr. Aystorpe smiled and put his supper one side. "I be vicar of St. Peter's, Nottingham—an honest cleric who knows his trade, and whatever I do will stand in the sight of man and God and go fast in the parish register tomorrow morning, so do not worry, lad. Not any other time of year could it be so, but of late we've made it Goose Fair custom to marry out of hand and on the spot all that asks for it."

"Why do you do that?"

The parson stood up and he had a book open. "Because it makes for fewer bastards upon the parish. Oh, lads! Here a moment!"

Two of the sweeps put down their brooms and came over, and there in their sight, under the hanging lights in the deserted market, at the tag end of Goose Fair, Will Scarlock and Doll Trasper swore all the hard, old vows so that they could lie down together in sweet love.

Once more they started for Old Thorny, and this time they did not stop for the beech tree. There were no caresses now, and no tender chatter—only haste that all else would wait upon. One candle burned in the kitchen when they opened the farmhouse door, and Gilly stood there in her nightgown, feeding Watch.

"Oh, Will! You're back! Watch was out so long, when I heard him scratch I got up and came down. Oh, you brought the dairymaid! But, Will—she's so slim and little—kneading a cheese will break her in two!"

"I forgot your dairymaid, Gilly," he said soberly. "This is Doll, my wife."

Gilly sat down weakly, the dish of beef marrow still in her hands, Watch staring at it, aloof and patient.

"Oh . . . I didn't know . . . you had . . . a girl."

"I know. I should have told you. But she came in from London today—and we were married by Goose Fair pulpit."

Gilly was recovering. Doll stood there at his side, smiling, waiting for her welcome.

"We don't want anything—to eat or drink—we'll just go upstairs now. You can get acquainted tomorrow."

"Oh, but Will. Kit and I have the only wide bed. You let me get him out of it, and I'll put on clean linen for you and your bride." She smiled at Doll. "I can sleep in your old room, and Kit with the boys in the loft . . . for tonight . . . and . . ."

"No," he said, turning away, leading Doll gently to the timber stairs, "we'll go to mine. It'll be wide enough."

1 2. Heartbreak Hill

~~~~~~

THEY HAD to get a dairymaid for Old Thorny after all, for the new mistress smiled willingly at Gilly and Bet, and tried hard to do things the way they showed her, but her work went always wrong. What she baked she burned, and when she pared apples she made crisscross cuts on her rosy knuckles, and when she washed the linen it never came quite clean. Jack Gambrell was glad to let them have workhouse Nelly, for he said God might have a place for a meek wench but the Bull's Head didn't, and the bargain pleased everybody well enough and Nelly and Doll extremely. Winter came on in Nottingham the way it always did, but not the way it came upon Piscataqua, Will learned, as he toiled through the mild, gray days, shoulder to shoulder with the Harroday men. In November they butchered, and sowed pease and garlic. Next month they cut logs, spread straw over the gillyflowers and rosemary, and set out fruit trees in the open weather before Christmas. And then they stubbed up roots of meadow alder, coaxing willows to grow instead, and thickened the box and hawthorn hedges. Came Candlemas, and spring was on already, time to dung the barley, sow lentils, and mustard seed, and vetch, and sit up all night in the fold where the ewes were lambing. Here you could sow something in every month of the year. It would be a fine crop you'd be sowing in New Hampshire now, in iron-hard ground, under two feet of snow!

England was a gentler, more ordered country; it never set a man's veins afire and drained out of him all the strength he had. At the end of the day's work there was always something left, hungry, and restless, and incomplete. And that something he took to Doll in the narrow flock bed under the eaves. She responded sweetly to him there, and what was between them leaped up like live fire whenever they touched each other. But sometimes when he let her alone at last, she would be asleep in the gray light, breathing softly, nestled against his shoulder, and he would be lying cold awake, with his eyelids smarting, and his throat dry, and his heart heavy with confusion and disappointment. Not with her—God knew he wasn't disappointed with *her*. It eased his work in the fields all day to know she was waiting for him back in the house, napping like a kitten, or making new songs for her lute. And after supper they'd go in town to Jack Gambrell's, and Doll would sing there just as she had at the Old Serpent, just as she loved to do, and he could be proud to watch her and hear Jack gloat over the business she brought him—biggest ever in the forty years he'd owned the Bull's Head, he boasted gleefully. Then they would walk home together through the dark to love, and in that she never failed him. No, he wasn't disappointed with Doll.

But he remembered his friends at home in New Hampshire—Abraham Corbett, old Edward Godfrie, and all the others who had expected him to do fine things for them in England, talking Sir William Warren over to their side. And he had done nothing for them! And for that reason he sent no word home—not even to his mother—at least, he told himself it was for that reason.

The plague was languishing, dying out with the colder weather, and all the merchants, and rich men, and King's Court had come crowding back into London. He'd learned that by asking the carriers. It was time now that he took himself back there, too, to the timber-yard by Wapping, to plead the cause of the mast men who would be gone into the deep woods raked with icy wind blown straight from Canada, plunging to their thighs in the drifted snow, lifting up their axes upon the white pines that could tower into the bitter, blue air for two hundred and twenty feet. The time to be gone, and yet the time still on him during which he must stay, for Rob came to himself often now, and whenever he did so, his hands groped for Will's hands, for the hands of Johnny's boy who had come back to heir Old Thorny, who would not go away again. And he knew that while Rob lived he could not go.

Just after supper on Twelfth Night, Doll was waiting for him to start for town where everything would still be gay with candles and Christmas holly, and in every street or by-lane a merry-making, but he lingered beside Rob, for it seemed as if his old cousin might be stirring a little from the sleep he'd lain in the last three days. He stared down at the hairless, gray skull with blue veins pulsing across it, the papery lids, the hands lying like a dead bird's claws on the counterpane, and he remembered how his father had looked in his coffin, strong shoulders and brown hair, almost a boy's mouth—and he was glad that it had been that way.

Then an eyelid stirred, and the old man began to murmur thinly.

"Queen had a navy o' oak an' a willow admiral. But she had Drake an' Frobisher—Red Marty o' the *Triumph*—an' I was there an' seen."

That's where I must have heard of Frobisher, thought Will, remembering how he had felt when he came on the grave in St. Giles Cripplegate—my father telling Rob's stories over when I was a little boy.

The old man rambled. "I seen 'em come up the channel in a great half moon—like floating cathedrals they come on. An' there was we, afloat in cockleshells, an' a black wind blowing up from the Narrow Seas. . . ."

Will reached out and lifted a thin claw.

"Got caught off Portland Bill, we did, by four galleasses—an' I come down on the deck—all red. They painted them that way then so the blood wouldn't show an' scare the men in mid-fight. Oh! Boy! Where be ye? Be ye still here? John's boy as come home!"

"I'm here, Rob."

And then they talked for a while—first of America—while Doll came to the door and stood tapping her foot and smiling, and then made up a face and went downstairs again.

"Ever see aught of Scrooby people there?" asked Rob. "Scrooby in the north? Some of their folk went godly and left here—first for Holland, then over the sea like Johnny. Will Brewster's boy went, I mind. . . ."

"No. They'd be Plymouth Colony. I knew some Plymouth men at Harvard, but no Brewster."

And then they talked of England and Old Thorny, and Will told him about the stranger who had guided him home that first night and asked him lightly did he think it could be the ghost of Old Will. But Rob did not take it lightly. He moved his head from side to side in disdain, as if he, though spent and broken and moulded away, was the better Scarlock of the two.

"That wasn't Old Will you saw. I seen both and know. I been

166

near fooled by the same man too. He's a poacher—Tom Flear of Gedling—an' he lives in a hut up Gamwell Chase an' east by the cleft beech. You go an' see him there by daylight. Then you'll know. You've not seen Old Will. Times is changing, lad—in the wars I seen it—old time's coming down, an' things are not what they were. I doubt he's ever seen again. Lads be too wise nowadays."

And Will had gone with his wife into Nottingham and tried to sing, and drink, and dance, and be as merry as she was, but Rob's words stuck so in his mind that he could not put his thoughts to anything else. Next day, when Kit and his sons stopped work at noon to share ale and barley bread where a rick would keep the wind off them, he walked into the woods and met the poacher face to face in the pathway—and it was just as Rob had said. The man who had led him home was not any ghost at all, but a piece of good Nottingham flesh and blood, silent and surly because it was out stealing rabbits.

That was another thing he thought about when he lay awake at night. If old time went, with it might go the old ways he had come home to. To see the ghost of Will Scarlet—or to believe that you saw it—was part of the heritage of Old Thorny. And he did not see, and he did not believe. Rob said that lads were too wise nowadays. Probably they were, but were they any better off for being so? He'd rather trust, he thought, to his own old kin, watching over the land they had loved, and grown from, and gone into, watching over their heirs upon it, than to that stern piece of old righteousness back of the jasper ramparts that Mr. Moodey preached about. But he did not trust much in either. From boyhood he had only believed in what he could see with his eyes, in what he could put his fingers on. He had thought for a while that he could be all over again the man his father was, and now he knew that he could not—but he did not know whether to be glad or sorry for it, and that deepened his confusion.

He had found a bookstall in Nottingham, in Bright Moor Street, just below the Middle Pavement, and got him another *Silva*, and he tried to share it with Doll, but she took no delight in words that did not rhyme. Sometimes when he could not sleep he'd light the candle and read out of it: how the oaks grew tall at Troy when Hector walked there; how Plato wrote his laws on cypress, and Semiramis bridged the Euphrates with it. He smiled when he read: "Cedar grows even in the cold bogs of North America; it seems no place will afright it." And he turned sober when he read: "We believe nothing impossible except what our grandfathers taught us." And then he would turn to Doll again, and take all the sweet comfort a woman's body can give a man—and still it would not be enough.

As spring mellowed on Old Thorny, the winter tightened on New Hampshire. Snow piled to the eaves, all the swamps and the black river froze at the edges. Every able man and boy went into the woods with axes, for the best timber comes from trees felled in the hard cold when the sap is down. The women shivered and dragged logs into the great fireplaces; fed the children and taught them the hornbook; heard Mr. Moodey's sermons in the frigid meeting house on Sunday, and told each other that spring had always come before and would again, likely.

The King's Commissioners had come and gone, and the four towns been all a-flurry since early summer. There was much galloping haste-post-haste over foggy roads at night, and letters flew back and forth between the Select Men and General Court at Boston, thicker than wild geese over Great Bay in the fall. But as everyone expected, the King's Commissioners found for those who were loyal to the King, and upbraided Massachusetts vigorously.

"Your ways are darkened with ambition and covetousness. You pretend to be the best sort of Christians, but by striving to grasp too much you make to have but little. Even Rhode Island, long known as a filthy sink of iniquity, is better than you be. Take care lest you lose your Charter. . . ." So pronounced Carr and Cartwright and Maverick, and it sounded fine enough, but in the end they sailed away and left things as they found them, saying they would air the matter in England—sometime. The rebellion dwindled down. Abraham Corbett lay in Boston gaol. Mr. Moodey preached a sermon of thanksgiving, and announced a fine of five pounds would be levied on anyone caught keeping Christmas.

Nan Knight spent much of that winter in the house by Portsmouth Harbor where she had grown up, for no fish ran in the bitter seas for her men to be out netting, and ice and frozen spray so covered Hog Island that the few who stayed there did not dare to go abroad unless they had need for bread or firewood. And Joan was lonely without Will, sad and worried at having no news from him. John Hall rotted piecemeal but hung on till Christmas, and after his death and burying, Mary McQuayne had twins and sent for her mother. So it happened that one frosty evening just after the turn of the year, Nan was alone in the kitchen with little Joan Hall, whose brothers, down from the woods for a few days, had left them after supper to row over to the Bank for a mug of ale and a peep at whatever might be going on there.

Nan stood by the window, looking out at the great bright stars hung over the river, and the heavy shadow of the wooded island across the mouth of it. The road to England . . . so far, so far it was . . . and *he* was there . . . and they had had no word. Behind her, little Joan sat demurely, hemming a kerchief with the fine, neat stitches her grandmother had taught her. And then outside came a crunch of boots on the snow, and a movement of shadows across the dark, and then a knock on the door panel. Joan looked at Nan, who turned from the window. Everybody at the Bank knew everybody else. Neither of the girls thought to be afraid. Nan went to the door and opened it. Three men stamped in from the cold, their cheeks and noses gleaming red, pulling off their bearskin mittens, blowing on their hands, opening their greatcoats: Richard Cutt, the portly Select Man; Brian Pendleton, who swayed and ordered all affairs, both civil and military, at his pleasure; Mr. Moodey, the youngish parson, whose sermons were mouthings and frothings beside the lovely words of the old Prayer Book, but mouthings the law said she must listen to. Nan, startled but not frightened, stood facing them. Joan quietly folded up her sewing.

"Will you sit down near the fire?" Nan motioned to the settle and a pair of low benches. "Joan Scarlock is at her daughter's by Bloody Point, if you want her. The Hall boys . . ."

"It is you we came to talk with, Mistress Knight," said Pendleton, clearing his throat. None of them moved to sit down. "And send the child away, I pray you. What we have to say is not for her ears."

Nan hesitated. Joan ran up and kissed her, lit a candle at the fire, and climbed to bed. The men watched Nan. She saw that their eyes were cold, colder than the night air. She stepped back and put her hand on the corner of the oak dresser that held Joan Scarlock's few pieces of silver.

"You are acquainted with the ways of our town, Mistress Knight?"

"I should be. I never lived anywhere else."

"Then you know that a woman's duty is to her husband. That women are so made of God as to require a man's hand strong upon them in husbandly guidance, lest they commit folly."

"I know you think they are."

"You were always a saucy wench, Miss Nan," cried Richard Cutt, still puffing from his pull through the drifts and across the channel, "but 'twill do you no good now."

"We mean, my child," said Mr. Moodey, looking piously down his long nose, "that we deem it seemly that you should take a husband to protect your interests and cherish your goodly estate."

"But suppose," said Nan bluntly, "that I don't want to take a husband?"

"That will make no difference," said Brian Pendleton, sucking his long upper lip. "I hear your mother stood up to be married with the sign of the harlot sewn on her bosom. You will be worse thought of —if we give it so abroad."

"Say I am a harlot if you want to—run up and down Dock Lane and blow it on a horn! That does not make me one."

"It might be," said Brian Pendleton again, "that if you rebel against our authority—for no good reason—General Court will see fit to take Hog Island from you for the good of the Colony; to tear down the fishery and mount guns and palisadoes to defend our coast. It can —if you defy us."

Nan stood before them, rosy and smiling, not one sleek, gold hair out of place, but inside her heart a cornered wildcat turned and waited.

"I see. Whom do I have to marry?"

"We understand that three men of suitable age, upright character, and sufficient estate—all of them confirmed in the New England way of worship, the stern hard way, yet the most pleasing to God—have wooed you to no end. Thomas Peverly, Francis Odihorne, and Ichabod Davis. They are still at your disposal."

"But I've disposed of them."

"Perhaps, my child, you will wish to reconsider in the light of what we have said tonight. We shall give you a week's time."

They fastened their coats. Nan bowed her head.

"I shall let you know," she said. But all the time they took to get through the doorway, she could hardly keep her eyes from lighting up, or hold back the laughter in her throat. The idea had come like the first firefly dancing over the meadow grass on a June night. A merry japes, and if God let her live to row over the channel to Sarah Scriggins, she'd play it on them! She'd show them whether they'd take Hog Island away from her or not! They didn't want to pull down the fishery! They wanted to turn it over to one of their own party! "For no good reason," Brian Pendleton had said. Well, she'd give them a good reason. Hardly had their footsteps gone still outside before she was calling up the stairway.

"Joannie! Are you afraid to stay alone? I have to go over to town for half an hour."

"No. You go on, Nan," murmured a sleepy voice above.

When she got to the waterside, her visitors were still in midchannel, and she had to wait till they had tied their shallop to the wharf above John Crowther's beach before she could follow them. Broken snow-crust crackled under the little boat as she shoved it into the icy, salt stream flowing around the black rocks and swaying the half frozen seaweed that clung there. And the stars were so thick and bright overhead that the whole sky looked like a lighted city on the crest of a purple-dark hill. Perhaps the lights of London looked like that, and somewhere under them Will Scarlock walked the streets, or sat in a tavern, or read his *Silva* by candlelight. And they thought she'd marry Thomas Peverly or Francis Odihorne or Ichabod Davis! She'd see them laid at the Point of Graves first!

Half laughing, half angry, she rowed quickly over the arm of tide and dragged the boat up the beach without bothering to moor it. Pulling her fur cloak tight around her and drawing back into her hood, she stepped quickly along the lane to Tom Everie's house. Tom was cutting masts up Oyster River, but his wife lay sick in their chamber, with Sarah the midwife to care for her. Nan ran under the wooden arbor in the side yard, with tendrils of dead vine serpenting over it, and tapped at the back door. Sarah came to let her in, wiping the ale froth from her mouth, but still sober, Nan assured herself gratefully.

"Come in, Nannie! Good God, girl, what ye doing out in the cold tonight? Some of your folk sick? Mary had a bad turn?"

"No." Nan sat down at the table and flung back her hood and cloak. Sarah followed, and eased her squat bulk down on a broad stool. "No. Sarah, I'm in trouble."

The logs crackled on the hearth and an iron pot hung over them with gentle steam creeping under its lid. Nan could smell bay and marjoram and squirrel—no, rabbit—rabbit stew.

"You mean you be . . . ?"

"Oh, no! Not that! It's the Select Men and Mr. Moodey. They say I have to get married."

"Ah? Well, ye know, Nannie, the godly do not like to have single maids and bachelors about—they say it makes for sin and is against God's design. An' I think the godly be right, for once. A husband's not so ill to have."

"But I'll have him when I'm a-mind to, and he's a-mind to me—not to please the Select Men. I won't do it and they can't make me."

"They be powerful, Nannie, and ye be one lone maid."

"A lone maid? Yes. But I have from my father what will stop them."

"You mean his courage? Of that he had a-plenty. I mind . . ."

"No, I do not mean his courage."

"You mean his quick wits, then?"

"No, I do not mean his wits."

"You mean . . . ?"

"I mean his money," said Nan levelly. "Listen, Sarah, I heard Joan Scarlock say once that in the tavern where she worked when she was a girl in England, there used to be a tale going about of a great queen who never married, who was a virgin all her life—because, they said, she was incapable of man."

"I have heard of such things. I mind Prue Trot in Essex told me of a woman once—but I have not seen it."

"And you—the midwife, whom none will question—are to tell Mr. Moodey, and Cutt, and Pendleton, that I am incapable of man, and hence I cannot marry as they would have me."

"Oh, no, Nan! Never I!"

"I'll buy you that little house at the edge of the Glebe Land that Anthony Brackett wants to sell, and you shall have it all for yours."

"They might find I lied."

"You shall have corn whenever I harvest."

"Nannie, I love you. Your grandmother come with me in the Pied Cow—but I cannot."

"You shall have leave to take your pitcher among my cider barrels whenever you will."

Sarah was still for a long time. Then she wagged her hairy chin and slapped her bulging thigh.

"Nannie, I'll do it! 'Fore God, you shall die a maid!"

"I hope not," muttered Nan, slipping on her cloak. She never knew just what Sarah told the Select Men and the minister, but they did not speak to her of marriage again, nor did her erstwhile suitors call. Now and then some woman would give her a pitying glance in the Spring Market, and once she heard a whisper behind a hand, "I wouldn't be her for all her money."

Joan Scarlock was aghast when she came home the next week and heard of it, more aghast when Mr. Moodey called one afternoon, his cheeks flushed dull red and his eyes shifty, to say that he had come to pray with Nancy in her affliction. Nan hid her face modestly in her apron, and Joan put an arm around her and listened humbly while the minister declared he was sure that God would still find virtuous tasks in this life for women whom he had not appointed wives and mothers. When he finished talking, Joan served him with cakes and mulled ale, and Nan handed over ten pounds for the church. And after that the Select Men gave up trying to get Hog Island, not so much from pity for her—but they could not think of any other way within the law, and they worked always within that.

Ice drifted downriver, and after it came the logs that the Portsmouth men had been making in the woods all winter—great white and amber floes of them, lashed together and choking the Pool, and waiting their turn at the mast pond. The country opened up now, and the fields lay wet and bare, first brown-yellow, then turning green in the warm sun. The redbud maples crimsoned everywhere, and the children went into the woods to look for arbutus after school. A few of the mast men—mostly those who were landless and unmarried—returned to the forest beyond the riverheads, from Lamper-eel to Quamphegan, but the husbands and fathers settled into the life of their stout houses now, hung up their axes and took plows and harrows. So spring went. The apple trees blossomed and dropped their petals on the soft grass; the June pease ripened, and the summer moon looked out of a warm sky. Will Scarlock had been gone a year, and sent no word, and not come home.

One hot night, Joan and Nan were sitting on the high ledge that reared up before the house, watching the last patch of sunset color die from the swelling river. They had been talking of the trip to Boston that Nan planned to take the following week about the business of the fishery, and somehow a silence fell between them, troubled only by the sucking of the tide and the shouts of men working late in the mast pond.

"Joan," said Nan finally, pulling a fern leaf apart and twisting its separate fronds in her fingers, "what would you say if I should not come back from Boston, if I should take a ship there and go—to England?"

"I should say it was high time. I wonder why you haven't gone before."

Thus the two women understood each other, and leagued themselves together for all time. There was nothing left for further speech except such matters as Nan's clothing—should she buy a new dress in Boston or wait till she got to London and saw what they were wearing there; should she take her thin cloak or her heavy one? And would the fishery be safe in the hands of John Billings, coarse and cursing, but a master of his trade?

One hot, red sunset at the end of June, 1666, Nan Knight found herself sailing out of Boston Harbor, and northeast by the marshes of Lynn and Swampscott. She was going home—she supposed— back to London where the Gobles had come from; the young carpenter dying early, and his frail wife who could not face Piscataqua alone. But she was going where Will Scarlock was, and that was what mattered. She sat on a heap of wheat sacks in the stern, provisions for their voyage which had not yet been stowed in the galley, and felt her heart singing in time to the beat of the little waves against the side of the ship. She watched the coast towns as they passed, and the rise of darkening hills behind them, and thought of all the things that might happen to her before she saw this country again, and they were all happy things she thought of.

"I delight in the company of wise and virtuous women, and you seem to be both. May I . . . ?"

Nan turned quickly about and opened her eyes very wide. A young man stood on the deck before her, the handsomest man, she thought, she had ever seen in her life. Dark, heavy-browed, very tall, with a full, sweet mouth, and eyes the color of a river at night. He wore a suit of mouse-colored velvet, sleekly cut, and carried a tall-crowned hat in his hand, the salt wind blowing through his crisp, black hair. Nan caught her breath and considered him. His words had been most strange. Men at Piscataqua did not talk that way, but then, you never met strangers in Piscataqua. What an odd way to tell her he thought she had a pretty face, for that was what he meant, of course.

"I'm surely not wise, sir, nor virtuous, past most. May you what?"

"May I walk with you about the deck and make your acquaintance? England is six weeks off, and it is a sad thing to be lonely at sea."

He took her arm without waiting for an answer, and they moved halfway down the deck and then stood still, pressed against the side, watching the dim, twilit shore.

"You have made the voyage before?" she asked him.

"Yes. In the other direction. I was born in England and my mother still lives there. My name is Truth Damerill. Will you tell me yours?"

"Nancy Knight."

"A strange one to me. You do not come from Boston?"

"No. From Portsmouth in Piscataqua."

He frowned. "I never know—with a Portsmouth man or woman. For they are not all of Christ's church there, as we in Massachusetts are."

Nan did not answer him. The wind blew fresh in the night, and she pulled her blue cloak round her. He went on speaking.

"But I had a friend once who came from there—who was with me for a time at the College. Do you know Will Scarlock?"

She felt her heart stir and quicken. This was his friend! Truth Damerill! Of course. She should have remembered when she first heard the name; Will had talked of him often.

"Yes, I know Will Scarlock," she said, looking down, trying to hide how much it meant to her.

"Then perhaps we'll all meet in England. I wrote him that I was coming, and Will is not much given to letters, but he answered me, and I shall see him as soon as I get to London. Do you go to visit friends—or family?"

"I'm going first to Lady Catherine Audley who lives at Whitehall. I do not know her, and she does not know me, but she came to this country years ago with my grandmother in the *Pied Cow*, and there is a great kindness for each other among those who came in that poor little ship, in the old, hard days. I think she will be glad to see me."

His face clouded over. "Whitehall is one with Sodom and Gomorrah. It is no place for an honest maiden. You would do better to come with me when we land, and I will take you straight to Will Scarlock and his wife."

"His—wife—?" faltered Nan.

"Yes. I know naught of her, except that her name is Doll, and

175

they are but lately married—but I am sure she would welcome you and help you find decent lodging. Look, Mistress Nancy, the dark is coming down, and this is the last town we shall see in America. Ipswich—I can tell it by the long, reedy sand bar at the river's mouth."

Nan held to the wall of the ship to keep her body upright. She could feel herself slowly dissolving into particles like the sand slipping through an hourglass, particles that would never again come together to be Nannie Knight, that would always be little bits of her, blown hither and thither on the wind. Truth Damerill went on talking, not knowing that he stood alone.

"That tall hill sweeping back from the sea . . . I don't know which it is . . . I don't know the land too well about here. But it's either Town Hill or Heartbreak. . . ."

"I think it must be Heartbreak," said the girl in the blue cloak.

13. *Lovers' meeting*

≈≈≈≈≈≈≈≈≈≈≈≈≈≈≈≈≈≈≈≈≈≈≈≈≈≈≈≈≈≈≈≈≈≈≈≈

THEY WERE holding hands coming down Fish Street Hill. Will had on a new suit of green camlet with gold ribbon facings, bought at Bennett's in Paternoster Row and fitted by Mr. Penny over against St. Dunstan's, so that he should appear as well as the men he had to do business with at the timberyards and the Navy Office. He had a periwig, too, but now that it was evening and nobody by he had to impress, he wore it back on his head like a cap and rakishly, with his own brown wisps showing at the front. Doll was singing, a song she'd made up as they lay late abed that morning at Milady's, listening to the rush of water under the Bridge, three stories down.

> *"Oh, Venus was caught in an iron net*
> *With only Mars to shame her by!*
> *Venus must take what she can get;*
> *She is not so lucky as I."*

"Where'd you hear about Venus, Doll?" asked Will, looking around him happily, at the red-tiled roofs and white spires, and crook-gable houses crowding down to the muddy wash of the river that was the city's one good street. He wondered if Portsmouth would ever crowd house on house to Piscataqua like that. He thought he didn't mind if it did. London had been uncommon kind to a man who could speak for a whole masting country and promise ship timber to the harassed Navy Board scrambling round desperately for supplies to patch up the hulks that reeled upriver from sea fights out past the

Nore. All last week the guns had been a-going, hot and heavy and heard way to Whitehall, but today men talked in the streets of a great victory—a hundred and sixty Dutchmen sunk, and houses burnt in Schelling and the Vlie. And now, in the cool, cloudy dusk that smelled of rain, triumph bonfires crackled and stank the length of Cheapside, and the cannon roared from Tower Hill.

"Tell me, Doll," he said, looking down at her, forgetting the Dutch war.

"Oh," she answered lightly, "I knew a clerk from Oxford once. He told me all about Mars and Venus and the old gods, and a merry lot I thought them—better than our dreary virgin brought to bed in hay. If I wanted anything very much, I should never go asking God for it. I should pray to Venus, and I think she would be kind to me."

Will smiled and put his arm around her, half lifting her from the egg-shaped cobbles. "Yes, you could do worse. She's one of the gods who live forever, and you don't have to go to church to find her. She's back of every pretty face." He wondered idly about the Oxford clerk. He did not ask about him.

They went down the steep pitch of the hill and crossed Thames Street where the warehouses overflowed with naval stores . . . hemp and tallow, oil, turpentine, spirits, fitted yards and spars. Somebody was cursing behind the open windows of the Old Swan, and carts rumbled by, full of beer kegs and manure; full of timber and coal for the wharves of Billingsgate and Queenhithe; cables, and ropes, and wheat and rye for the ships loading at the Steelyard. Men and women took the air in doorways under the swinging, painted signs, in the bow windows, on the leads at the housetops. Everywhere were lighted panes, and hawkers up the hillside crying fish and lavender and what-d'ye-lack; the hum of voices, and the smell of breathing flesh and chimneysmoke and herrings and cloistered gardens and street refuse—and no waft of death walked in the city now. Great Paul's loomed oblong, blue-gray and unlit, to the westward; and to the east, beyond the almshouses and apple trees, rose the four onion-shaped turrets of steel-gray stone and whitewash that made London Tower. The Bridge stretched ahead of them, a low street of houses built on stone archways and rubble starlings; the fantastic, gold-veined cupolas of Nonesuch House rising empty near the center, its casements flapping, and its green paint peeling off, and its great days over. People were going to vespers at St. Magnus' by the

Bridge Head, and they could hear the groan and whir of the works near by that pumped river water into the city, that could throw a thin stream over the church steeple.

"What did you do in Moorfields all day?" he asked her, for they had met by plan at the Old Serpent, and were on their way back to Milady's.

"I sang. In the little pavilion at the end of the lime tree walk—away from the booths and jugglers and peepshows—out where the maids used to dry their linen on the grass before so many folk took to going there. Ladies from the Court, I sang to. The Queen's in silver tissue again, after mourning for her mother. Castlemaine, I'd not seen since she lay in last winter. Her waist is thicker. What did you do?"

"Went to a bear-baiting over in Southwark with Sir William Warren."

"I thought you didn't like bear-baitings."

"I don't. I hate them. The damn bear got hold of a good mastiff marked like Watch and ripped him so I doubt he's alive now. We shoot bears, where I come from, and use their hides to keep us warm in winter. But Sir William expects me to go, and cheer, and wager —so I will. Till I've got what I want from him."

"And then?"

"Why then—we'll go home."

"Where's that?"

Will stopped suddenly at the gate of London Bridge and looked down the dark tunnel of it, all the lighted gables and shops hanging across and peering into each other, all loud with roaring water underneath.

"I don't know," he said slowly. "I don't know."

Candlelight from the windows of the Bear Tavern fell on her face, and she was not smiling.

"My home is here," she said. "If you want to go away we will . . . but if you don't like London . . . well . . . you may like Paradise, but nothing will please you this side." And then her voice softened, and she lowered her lashes and tightened her fingers around his, aware that her sharpness might have hurt him, which it had. You did not look for sharpness in Doll, but sometimes you came on it.

"What did you do after the bear-baiting?"

"Came back to the Dolphin in Tower Street. Sir William thought to meet John Evelyn there, and I'd go without my supper any night for a chance to hear him talk about that great book he wrote. But he'd left word that it looked like a wet evening after the long drouth, and he was going down to Sayes Court to pick snails off his fruit trees. So then we went around by Seething Lane—a fine street it is, all brick houses, every few doors a porch of carved oak, and the Navy Office, shaped just like the Old College where I went to school. Sir William stopped to call on Mr. Pepys—he's Clerk of the Acts, and a man of great power making the mast contracts and in all the Navy does, for he knows all. If you want to buy a poop lantern or find out what milord keeps his hand in the Chatham Chest for Sick Seamen, you go to Mr. Pepys. He and Sir William settle many Portsmouth matters walking in that close garden of his, and 'twould be to our gain if I could walk there too. We could hear him up on the leads playing his flageolet, and he has a twelve-foot optic glass I want to look at Jupiter through . . . some night . . . but tonight . . . you were waiting . . ."

They were out on the Bridge now, the houses that walled the narrow way and overhung the water on great wooden struts, swallowing up their light in their own shadow; here a draper's, there a mercer's, a chemist's, a milliner's. For the moment there was nobody coming by except a prentice trundling a barrow of cockles. Will put his face down in her neck.

"Oh, Doll," he said, "I love you."

In the pause before she answered him, he could hear the turmoil of the water pouring through the stone arches, the evensong from St. Magnus', and a burst of ribald laughter from a dicing house ahead. A white shaft moved weirdly across the darkness behind a paled gap where no houses stood, and at first he started, and then he knew it for the mast of a tall ship tacking in for Billingsgate.

"And I love you," she said, stopping suddenly and pressing her body to his, till he felt the quick, sure beating of her heart.

He kissed her deeply. "When we get home . . ."

"When we get home there'll be a dish of prawns and cheese for supper."

Pulling out of his grasp, she began to run, down the dark thoroughfare of the Bridge like a light wind. He swore, and laughed, and went running after. Breathless, they stumbled into the taproom and sank down on a bench near an open window that looked over the foaming sweep of black water below.

Milady's had a wooden sign swung outside, like most of the other houses, the likeness of a girl with ebony hair and a full, pink skirt. Its proprietress, raddled and toothless now, with blue veins at the roots of her fine nose, badly dyed red hair, and a bulbous stomach, had still the remains of a great beauty on her that no decay could hide. Her name was lost somewhere, but everyone knew that she had been a Lady of the Bedchamber to Queen Henrietta, and run away from her husband with a court gallant, and fallen from that into sin and disease. Her friends could have lightly forgiven the loss of her virtue, but never the loss of her looks, so here she was, an old procuress, but prosperous and kind, and loved the whole length of London Bridge. She and her girls lived on the upper floors of their timbered house built out over the river, and Thomas Tacke rented the street floor of her and sold dressed meats and strong water. The place was listed as a lodging house, and true enough, you could hire a bed to yourself there, if you were so strange you liked to sleep that way. Or you could bring your own girl, or if you hadn't thought to, you could be supplied. It was a careless, easy house, and Doll had grown up there, and she loved it. When old Rob died just before midsummer and left Will free to go about his business, she had insisted that they should stay here when they came to London.

"You mean I should take my bride to a bawdy house?" he'd asked her, running his hand through his tousled hair as they lay in bed that last night at Old Thorny, with the summer moon shining in the windows and the scent of new-cut meadows drifting everywhere.

"Why not? If that's her home . . . ?"

And so they had come here, and Doll had slipped back into her old happy life of singing and applause, and Will had been shapin. affairs for the New Hampshire mast men, in Wapping, and Deptford, and Seething Lane.

Now a little maid brought them the steaming dish Doll had said would be ready, all yellow and pinky white with a baked crust, and mugs of frothing, brown ale, and they began to eat. The tavern was only half full, and none of Milady's girls had come down yet. You could hear the sharpness of their voices in the rooms overhead, where they were putting on their sooty patches, and painting their lips, and moistening their laces and bosoms with East India scent. Milady's voice rose deep and musical over all the rest—a voice trained for singing to the palace virginals, while her household had been mostly brought up to cry fish in Thames Street—assuring Poll that the redness she suffered from was only heat rash and not the pox, calling one Sir Gilbert an unmentionable name and promising Lucy they'd not serve him if he came there, that she herself would beat his shoulders with a broom first. Doll lifted up her head and smiled, loving it all, being at home. They ate silently.

"You want to go upstairs?" he asked, leaning to her.

"No. I want to sing."

The summer night deepened over the river, and a few sweet drops of rain blew through the dusty town, spattered the window sills. The maid put more candles in the sconces, and more men drifted in from the Bridgeway. The girls swept downstairs, one after the other, laughing, dressed in flame color, purple, and violent pink, blazing with glass jewels, and Milady moved among them in a yellow satin gown big enough to have covered a flower stall, ponderous and slow, like a tower lurching along. She came to their corner and stopped, smiled toothlessly, and struck off Will's periwig.

"Take that off, Willie! Looks like a chamberpot with hair! You're handsomer without it. Doll, is your lute broke that we've no music a-going here? And Tom! Give us ales around, or I'll raise your rent!"

Will smiled. He agreed with Milady about the periwig, and he did not pick it up from the floor. He settled back in the angle where the beams were pegged together, lighted his pipe, drew on it a few times, and let it go out. Doll perched on the table's edge and tuned her lute strings.

He watched the gay scene before him, all white arms and bosoms, flashing eyes and swaying curls, the men avid and merry, now and then a couple slipping up the crooked stairs at the rear; and Milady leaned against the door frame, where she could take the air and watch the street. He thought of the fragrant twilight that would be falling through the hazels at Old Thorny now, of the mastiff pup he'd wanted to bring with him, but couldn't because it wasn't weaned yet, and of Rob lying in the yew tree close by the tiny red sandstone church. It was done for Rob. The Spanish bastards could run all over, and he'd not know nor care. But for him it was not done. There was a square, low house with gables, on a granite headland looking seaward through the salt marshes, and his mother was in it, and his sister's sons. Two houses called him master and waited for him to come home. He heard the water foaming under the floor, and he knew that he heard in it the voice of a mighty river alive with ships from every nation under heaven, that it was the greatest highway of the world. But he thought of another river, black and salt, and full of floating logs, amber and ivory, full of lopped green boughs; a five-pronged river, spread out like God's great hand upon the countryside. And all the waters of the earth might come together and go back into chaos, he thought, but those two rivers would never meet. He tangled with his thoughts for a while, but they only wound and snarled themselves the tighter, so he stopped thinking, swallowed his ale down fast, and called to his wife, loud and falsely gay to hide his trouble.

"Come on, Doll! Sing us 'Dice, strong waters, and a whore'!"

She turned, her blue eyes laughing into his. Couples were twined drunkenly together on the benches back in the shadow, and the unpaired men had drawn around a great cask under the stairs.

"No," said Doll, brushing her lips across his forehead, "not now. Not till everyone's drunker. I'm going to sing 'Kissing goes by favor.' "

She laughed and bent her body forward till he could see into the little hollow between her breasts, and shook back her dark, loose hair.

" 'Kissing goes by favor,' and when we come to the chorus, you don't sing it, you kiss it—if you've anyone to do it with."

Will put his arm around her waist where it would not hamper the lute, and Doll sang, and all of Milady's sang with her.

> *"Oh, Adam first kissed Eve,*
> *And so begot a son;*
> *'Twas above five thousand years ago*
> *That kissing first begun!"*

Will looked at Milady who lounged in the doorway, at her great dugs straining in their tight yellow satin, and thought that even she had been kissed long ago, and if she had, why it wasn't likely there was anyone who hadn't. The fields, and the rivers, and the old kin's houses were close to a man . . . one way . . . but kissing was even closer . . . or was it? Yes, it was, he thought, feeling Doll's nipples through her thin, red bodice . . . or again . . . was it? Would he ever be sure?

> *"And ever since that time,*
> *The trade came on amain . . ."*

Doll's voice was light and the other girls' drunken, but the men sang heavily and beat their empty mugs on the table, while Tom Tacke moved here and there refilling them.

> *"And she who has been kissed once,*
> *Must needs be kissed again."*

He leaned to Doll and swayed his body with the music as she swayed hers. He was Will Scarlock, son of John Scarlock of Old Thorny sojourning in Piscataqua, Will Scarlock who had gone to Harvard College and come out of it no more a scholar than when he went in, the yeoman from Gamwell Chase, the mast man from Portsmouth, standing up to sing with his wife in a house on London Bridge—and why the hell not, if he wanted to? Only he didn't want to.

And then there was a stir at the door, and he could hear Milady's voice, fawning and eager, and another voice, cool, and gentle, and familiar as his own mother's. He looked up and his heart turned over.

> *"Oh, kissing's Hampshire honey . . ."*

sang Doll.

> *" 'Tis wondros rare and sweet . . ."*

bellowed the drunken men by the keg at the staircase. He dropped his arm from around her and reached for his ale mug, only to knock it over and look heedlessly down at the brown tide creeping across the table top and dripping froth on his new green breeches.

When Nan Knight got out of the hackney coach at the gate of London Bridge, she thought first that she was back on Hog Island, the tilted square smelled so of fish—scales, oil, wet, sleek sides and bubbling gills. Men were pouring out of a towered hall built close to the water on the left, with a little rock terrace in front of it, and the smell came and passed with them. A fat man squatted like a great frog in the door of the Bridge House, and when she stopped to ask him if she must pay toll to go part way across, he told her there'd been a meeting at Fish Mongers' Hall, and the break-up of it was what she saw and smelled. She wrinkled her nose a little, and he reproved her.

" 'Tis an old guild, lass, and a high one. It's a proud thing to cry fish in London; better than to be an ale-seller or a goldsmith, but not so fine as to be a draper or a mercer."

"It's not so much at home," said Nan. "I do it myself there." But when she told him she wanted to go to Milady's he looked at her shrewdly and asked her what for.

"Oh . . . to see a friend there," she told him, trying to make it sound as if it didn't matter much whether she went or not. And he finally let her through with a headshake, saying if she didn't come back in half an hour he'd call the watch. Nan did not understand, but she gave him a few coins and started across the arches. She had had six weeks to plan her life over—nights awake in the foul, heaving cabin under the ship's deck, and days of walking that deck with the handsome young Puritan, Truth Damerill.

I shall go on, she thought. I shall die—some day—but not now, nor of this. I shall live years, and my cheeks will wrinkle like russet apples, and my hair be drifted over white, like snow come down on the yellow grass in the fall. But I shall not go by myself all the years between . . . except that in my heart I must always go by myself now. I shall marry and bear sons and daughters, for that is what a woman lives by, and I shall have my life in my time, in spite of all—as much of it as I can get. They will not have Will Scarlock's eyes and hair, my children, and I shall not love them for their father's sake, but for themselves I shall love them, and perhaps that will be better in the end. And in the end will be the dark, and it can matter to none of us there, who loved whom or how we married. But all the years till then—with a man I do not love— he not to blame either. And he will grow as sad and wistful as I, when the fog drifts over the low fields and through the twisted trees at night. We shall both be sad, and think back to the days when we were young and loved, and felt so sure of everything—and wonder why it all turned out the way it did, and begin to hope that we may live again, and that next time things will fall out more as they should. No, I shall not die now. I shall go on to that.

She thought that she could face Will Scarlock, and give him a sister's kiss, and praise the beauty of his young wife. She thought she could. But the need to try this bitter strength had driven her down from Whitehall through the city night that surely held stenches, and thick, choking dust, and riotousness, and was said to hold pickpockets and worse. In the river gardens Truth and Lady

Catherine would be searching for her now, but she did not care. She thought she was strong but she had to know.

Her blue cloak streamed backward in the rainy wind as she picked her way down the lane between the shop fronts, unlit now, save for a candle burning here and there in a sheath of horn. "Milady's," Truth had said was the name of the house Will lived in, and here it was, the word scrolled in black across the flowing skirt of a pink wooden doll. The great river poured beneath, and the noisy, lighted town sprawled up the hillside behind her, and Nan thought of the fireflies weaving over the hayfield at home, the clustered chimneys of Portsmouth standing up beyond Sam Fernald's house, and starlight through the elm trees branching everywhere. She felt the tears pricking at her eyelids, but somehow she held them back. In the door under the sign stood a fat hag swathed in satin, her old face a ruined canvas of paint and sweat.

"What d'ye lack, dear?" she said easily, leaning her steamy bulk toward the cool pink and whiteness of Nan.

"This is—Milady's?"

"It is, and I be she. What'll you have?"

She hated to say, "I'm looking for Will Scarlock, the married man." She could not say it. She fixed her sober, gray eyes on a candle in a sconce behind the window.

"I think—I may have friends here. May I go in?"

"Why, that you may, and we'd be glad, pretty." The woman leaned forward. There was garlic and pepper on her breath, and something fouler.

"Where did you hear of the place, dear?"

"Oh . . . everyone knows Milady's."

"Ah!" The wise old eyes like amber stones grew narrow and long behind their beaded lashes. This girl had come here knowing what she was about. Met with ill luck, and not caring how she mended it. Her clothes had good cloth in them, but no air or style. From the country, likely, with all the country sweetness on her.

"You've come at the right time, my pretty. Only last week I lost my little sister Liza. She married a rich goldsmith from Cheapside west—whom she met here. You could have her room and her friends—"

Nan looked bewildered. "I didn't mean . . . to stay . . ."

"Oh, but you'll like it here. We do as we please, and that's a better shift than you'll get in heaven."

Milady looked over her shoulder. Drunks and blowzy boughten

women they were in there, but this girl was fresh lavender and hawthorn—the men would come like rutting stags for a new thing. She'd
be worth a thousand pounds. Better speak plain, though, and not
have her take fright later and run shrieking for the watch.

"Have you ever known man, dear?"

"Known man . . . ?"

She looked past Milady, into the dim room strewn with its ribald
company—and then she knew. Knew what the phrase meant, and
what this house was—the house where Will Scarlock had got his
wife. Nan drew herself up coldly, sick with the terrible hurt of it.

"No," she said, "and I don't think I ever want to." She stepped
around the yellow satin mass and into the tavern, hearing only one
voice lifted above all the others.

> *"Oh, kissing's Hampshire honey,*
> *'Tis wondros rare and sweet . . ."*

She stood still and looked straight at Will, and he looked at her,
and took his hand out of his wife's bosom, and spilled his ale, and
there they stood, face to face, not saying anything at all.

Then she walked proudly across the room, her head high, holding
up her skirts a little.

"Will. I came here. And I wanted to see you."

Doll stopped singing and looked her up and down. Her smile
stiffened like water when the frost moves over it. Will could not
speak because his throat swelled and tightened. He could not think
at all, but he did not even know that he could not think. He only
stared. Finally Doll shrugged her shoulders, got down from the
table, and stepped forward.

"My lad's lost his tongue," she said. "What is it he ought to be
saying?"

Nan smiled back as frostily. "He ought to be saying that he's glad
to see his sister—for I'm almost that. We slept in the same cradle
and the same woman nursed us. You must be the wife I heard he'd
taken."

"Yes," said Doll slowly, her great eyes widening at the center.
"I'm his wife. I'm glad to see his *sister*. Will . . ." She turned.

He stepped forward then. Oh, Nannie, he was thinking . . .
Nannie Knight . . . in a bawdy house on London Bridge . . . after

187

me! He felt as if he were walking down Lombard Street in a busy noon without any clothes on.

"I—I—how did you get here, Nan?"

"I came," she said guardedly, "about my father's affairs. And I went to Lady Catherine Audley—you know—Joanna Fernald's sister."

"Yes. She came in the *Pied Cow* with our people. Remember how Mother used to tell it over? Those three girls in the winter rain . . . ? And Alice drowned herself, and Catherine came away soon. But wasn't there something between her and Captain Neal?"

"I don't know. She's a rich widow now with rooms over the river at Whitehall, and she made me very welcome. But she is in some trouble, I think, that she will not tell me of."

"How long is it since you came?"

"A week—about."

"And at home? My mother?"

"Your mother misses you. She's well otherwise. John Hall died at Christmas, and Mary has twin sons. The boys got in a good harvest, and Tam and Digory see well to everything."

"The Commissioners? Did we get free of Massachusetts?"

"The Commissioners came and went and did no good. We're as we were—only Abraham Corbett—and he's in gaol."

"By God, there's always liars and swearers enough to beat the honest men and hang them up! What do they say of me?"

"They trust you, Will—but they're waiting."

She became aware suddenly that Will was staring at the open door behind her back. Doll lifted one dainty, arched eyebrow. She turned around. Truth Damerill stood there, dark and threatening as a storm about to break.

"Nancy! Why did you come here alone? I would have brought you—in due course." His glance went, cold and appraising, about the room. "If I deemed it fit—which it does not seem to be."

Will spoke then, his words coming out with the crack of a whip-lash.

"What the hell is it to you, Truth Damerill, where she goes? Or how? Or why?"

"It is everything," said Truth simply, his displeasure suddenly gone, and his smile lighting up with something of the white glory of a holy candle. "She has promised to be my wife."

"I don't believe it! Nan . . . ?"

She smiled thinly. "It's true, Will. You set me the example, you know."

They stared unhappily at each other, the four lovers, and outside Milady's a sobbing wind broke about the eaves, and a swift rain began to fall on the tiled roofs and dusty streets, and the black, shifting surface of London River. Up in Seething Lane, Mr. Pepys put away his flageolet and scurried indoors, and down at Sayes Court, John Evelyn heard the shower on the sad leaves and rejoiced at it. London men went on about their own affairs, and the sand ran down a thousand hourglasses, bringing the world that much closer to the blessed time when it would not matter who loved whom or how they married.

14. The hour of my death

~~~~~~~~~~~~~~~~~~~~~~~~~~~~~~~~~~~~~

THEY HAD been out in the town all afternoon, that hot Saturday, the first of September, but now, by ten o'clock at night, it was dark, and a little cooler, and they sat together in Thomas Tacke's alehouse under Milady's, trying to drink their boyhood back—but there was not enough liquor in all England to do that for them.

Will had his periwig off and his green jacket flung wide open, but Truth sat across the table from him, his white collar and gray stuff suit immaculate, only the little beads of sweat above his full upper lip showing that he felt the close, thick heat. Milady sat with them, fanning herself and sweating openly, her silk dress the color of a dish of June pease falling off one plump white shoulder that could still make a man want to stroke it—if his glance stopped there and didn't go to the face above. It was a quiet night for them. Some of the girls were upstairs, and a few had gone into the town or rowing on the river with their favorite customers. Saturday nights were never busy in summer. The hot weather put the men in mind of ale by midafternoon, about the time they got their wages, so that by this late they were apt to be lying drunk somewhere and need no further attention. Phillis, never christened that, and Temperance, who had run away from an east country parsonage when her blood got too hot for it, were not working, and they sat at a little table where the coolness of the river came in, and Doll was with them, showing the cloth for a new dress she'd bought in Paul's Walk that day. Will listened to them, turning his head a little. His wife held out a bolt of scarlet goods striped with gold for the other girls to touch and value.

"Ummmm! That's rare stuff, Doll," said Temperance. "Good enough for Castlemaine herself. What'd that fair girl buy? She went with you, didn't she?"

"Miss Nan?" said Doll slowly. "She bought an India muslin—all pale like dead violets, with pink-white flowers on it. It cost more than mine, but I did not think it was very pretty. 'Twould never take a man's eye."

Milady heard her. "That girl doesn't need red satin to take a man's eye, Miss Doll! You watch your step there. And watch that lad of yours. She'd play goose to his gander any day."

"I know she would," said Doll lightly, "but she'll not get the chance."

The men flushed and stared at the wall. Truth opened his mouth to reprove them, to say that Nan was his promised wife, and then he closed it again. Why stoop to quarrel with such creatures? Will tried miserably to remember what he and his friend had just been talking about, so that he could start the conversation again before the women said some worse thing. They had been arguing—he was certain of that—all day long they had been arguing, mostly in terms of their fathers' politics, neither of them willing to admit that it was some closer cause that kept them hostile and apart. He couldn't remember, but one thing would do as well as another.

"How'd you happen to come to London just now, Truth? You had a church in New Haven Colony, and you can't preach here, for the King has silenced all you parsons. It's Prayer Book country now, like it always was, Non-Conformists thrown out of their livings everywhere. Hadn't you heard the weather set that way?"

"Yes, I had heard, and that is why I came. I feel that I am chosen of God, Will." Truth spoke soberly, his fine, dark eyes fixed on the starry night sky beyond the open casements. "And when you feel that a great strength comes upon you. I am to wage His battles, and the fight is hottest here. When my father was a young man, God called him to go oversea to claim the wilderness for Christ, and he went. Then the wars came on here, and God called him home to fight in them, and he followed the call and died of it. And I hope to live as righteously as he did, and die in as good a cause."

"How will you go about it?"

"I shall go down to my home country, to Wyethorne in the fens, where my mother writes me that there are many men and women of godly persuasion, lost, and groping, and needing a leader. I think we may have to fight much as you Royalists did in Great Cromwell's time, secretly, with comings and goings in the night, and prayers in hidden holes in the chimney. And because God is with us, I think we shall win. The ill-got passion of these days shall make way for a manly purity. We shall yet have our country of saints."

"I think I'd clear out of a country of saints quicker than my father cleared out of England. Old Noll's head was sure a fine sight this afternoon."

They had been to Westminster and seen Cromwell's head on a pole there, where Charles had had it put soon after his coronation, the lean skull long picked bare by rot and the brown city ravens. And Truth had looked at it reverently and uttered a blessing, and Will had lit his pipe.

"I was thinking," he went on, "if New Hampshire could take over Massachusetts, we could have Governor Winthrop up the same way, and stick his head on a pole above Boston Common. Our men would wear a good smooth road across Essex County, coming down to look at it."

"Cromwell," said Truth slowly, "was a fen man like my father and like me. He was a great and holy man. He would have preferred to stay with the flocks under his woodland."

"Then why didn't he?"

"Because he was called to save his country."

"Again—why didn't he?"

"He was cut down."

"The Lord giveth and the Lord taketh away," observed Will piously, "blessed is the name of the Lord. I'll pay for this round, Truth."

Milady, always a kingswoman, had been silent as long as she could.

"Ah, that for old Oliver!" she said, and spat on the floor, and took a swig of Madeira, her favorite drink. "If you ask me, he was no better than a stable boy. Threw sack-posset on his daughter's wedding gown and thought people would laugh! Filled our town full of sour-mouthed men in black hats, and took the scarlet coats off the palace guard. Let his wife, Old Joan, build a secret stair in Whitehall to spy on the servants, and plastered dung on the royal statues. I wouldn't have *his* statue put up in my privy. Well, I've seen kings come and go, but it does not matter to London, so long as they leave the river behind them, for 'tis that we live by."

She sank her nose in her glass. "First one side rises and then the other, and 'tis all alike at Milady's, for our craft does not change—'tis always the same whoever's in power, and we need no guild to guard it. Come, Doll! Give us 'Hey boys, up go we!'"

Doll took her lute obediently, and smiled, and played over the old, boisterous tune softly, putting a minor wail in it.

Will and Truth smiled at each other behind their hostess' back.

"I wish I could *believe*, the way you do," said Will, "feel God and the church—any church—was worth standing out in front of and fighting for with my two fists. But I haven't the faith. How do you *know* the Bible's true any more than the Iliad is? One sounds as good to me as the other. All my life I'd swear to only this much and no more: to what I can see with my eyes and reach out and put my fingers on. And beyond that's mystery. And you know no more about it than I do, Love-the-Truth."

"I know this," said Truth, "that there is a mighty struggle going on between good and evil throughout the universe, but chiefly in the soul of man, and that I must fight forever on the side of good, as God in my own heart directs me how."

Milady, who could not contain liquor well, was leaning forward on her elbows, her eyes grown enormous and round, but wearing a veiled look.

"Stop prating of God, boy! When I was a girl I could talk Latin a little, and I learned to say a fine thing in it. I learned to say, '*Rex est lex.*' Do you dare deny it? Do you know a prettier word, old holy-bones?" She looked at Truth.

"Yes," he said, "yes, Milady. I know this: '*Deus est rex et lex.*' Does your Latin take you that far?"

She swallowed more Madeira, and while she was drinking, Will threw back his head and laughed. "I'll cap all you scholars. I know a better thing. '*Vir est lex, est rex, est deus!*' 'Man is law, is king, is God.' Man beats you all in the end."

"That's blasphemy," said Truth quietly.

"Blasphemy? Why sure it is. Have a glass to blasphemy, Truth! Here I stand with Truth and drink to Blasphemy! If I'd stayed at Harvard College a month longer, I'd be able to whip up an allegory out of that. Praise God, I came away in time."

Truth frowned, and Milady took another drink and giggled a little, not following the talk at all, and Doll came over and stood with her hand on her husband's shoulder. Her touch was light, but strong enough to start the old fire leaping between them. If she would go up to their bed in the gable with him now, he thought, he would take her as he never had before, and he would end forever all this doubt and question, all the seeking and unhappiness. She would be utterly and forever his, and having her he would need nothing more. But before he could tell her what he wanted, quick steps came running over the threshold and along the uneven floor.

"Oh, Truth! I was so afraid you wouldn't be here. I need you to help me so!"

Will had his head down, his cheek on the back of Doll's hand, but now he snapped upright. Nan Knight stood there, talking fast and eager to Truth, and paying him no attention. She wore a filmy pink dress he had never seen before, looped up with black velvet the way the Court ladies wore theirs, and a mist of lace under her chin, a dress that Joan could never have made for her by any New Hampshire pattern. Her curls were tumbled a little, but her smooth gold hair all sleek on top and the trim curve of her head—it was a sight that could bring any man out of chaos—or thrust him further in.

"Truth," she was saying, "we've got to help Lady Catherine get a man out of the Tower. All her servants are afraid to go, but I said I'd be back in five minutes with a man who wasn't afraid of anything."

She looked at him proudly. He turned his glass round and round in his fingers.

"First, Nancy, I told you never to go abroad in London at night. Secondly, that you must never come to this house—for reasons I gave you when we spoke privately."

Privately, thought Will. He saw them in his mind, sitting under the almond trees in the palace gardens. He saw Truth kissing her, Truth's hand stealing under the lace and filmy pink, which it had every right to do.

"You have disobeyed me, but you say you have need. Why is this man in the Tower, and why does Lady Catherine want to free him, and why does she not speak to the King, who owed great kindness to her dead husband?"

"Oh, Truth! Come on! Don't ask me to tell you all that now! If the tide turns—and it will any minute—it'll be that much harder to shoot the Bridge. He's in gaol because they thought he took his ship out of a sea fight to help the Dutch, and was a traitor, and I think

Catherine loved him a long time ago when she was a girl at Piscataqua, and I think she does now, and we've got to get him free. I said I knew a *man*. . . ."

She looked fixedly at him.

He shook his head. "Nancy, a gaol break is against law and order. Where is Lady Catherine?"

"She's in the boat at the Old Swan Stairs—all alone—her servants took fright and walked home through the city. I said I'd come back with you."

He stood up. "I shall go and talk with her and discourage this mad prank—and then take you both home."

"But, Truth—she loves him!"

"Then she will try to save him in some honest way. Come . . ."

He put his hand on her waist but she struck it off.

"All right. Go be honest! Sing psalms till you choke to death! I said I knew a man, and I meant you, but maybe I know another. Will . . ." She turned away from Truth, tossing her head, and came toward him. "You heard. Will you help me? You're from New Hampshire like I am, and at home we don't sit around waiting for God when it's something we can do for ourselves."

"What do you want me to do, Nan?" he said to gain time, feeling Doll's fingernails biting through the shoulder of his jacket.

"I'll say it over slow in little words for you. There is a man Lady Catherine loves, and he is in the Tower—and we have to get him out. We have to shoot the Bridge, and go in and carry him—for he cannot walk—and take him up the river to hide him at her manor in Oxfordshire. Will you help us do it?"

Truth stood black and silent, saying no word. Doll answered before Will had a chance to.

"Miss Nan," she said, "I don't wish you any harm, nor your Lady Catherine either. But my Will's not going. My father went into a prison in London, and he never came to us again. His bones were put away in lime, they told us, but we never knew. I'm not going to have my husband go from me the same way."

Will said nothing. A flicker of triumph went over Truth's face. "Nancy," he said, "I'll take you home."

"Will . . ." said Nan.

Doll's hand upon his shoulder pressed closer, closer, stirring all the fire that was between them, a fire great enough to burn all London down.

"I—I'd like to help you, Nan," he said.

She sensed his refusal. Her gray eyes were black now, and to look into them was like looking into the bottom of a well.

"I know you would, Will," she said sweetly, "and I know you have a wife and must do what she tells you—"

Doll's blue eyes clouded with pure hate.

"—and I'm going now, if I have to shoot the Bridge and carry him out myself. But before I do it, I'll tell you who he is, though I swore I never would. He's Walter Neal, the man your father followed out of Nottingham."

The fire might still be flowing through Doll's fingers, but it no longer reached into his body. Her touch did not have any more power over him. He forgot her. He leaped to his feet.

"Why didn't you say so? Walter Neal in trouble and needs a man?"

"Yes," said Nannie, "that."

"Well, we'll help him—help him at anything, any time at all. I might have to face my father some day—can't be sure I won't—and I couldn't do that if I'd failed Walter Neal. Come on, Damerill-good-at-the-warcry!"

"I don't suppose I can stop you from going," said Truth slowly. "I don't suppose I can stop Nancy, since she is only betrothed to me, not yet married. I suppose you will think I am a coward. But it is only this. You are doing a wrong deed when you try to save a guilty man from the consequence of sin."

"How do you know he's guilty? Seems to me I've heard there's a few Puritan parsons in gaol roundabout."

"That is not the same. That is in the name of God. You are going to steal away an old wornout rakehell—oh, I heard about Walter Neal back in Cambridge from godly Thomas Wiggin, whose arch-enemy he was—save him from the just fate his country has apportioned him. No. You must shift for yourself with Satan's help if you can obtain it, but you shall not have mine."

"Thank you, Love-the-Truth. We don't need it. Doll, I'll be back. Come on, Nan."

They walked out of Thomas Tacke's alehouse, a good two feet between them. They walked along the Bridgeway and headed for Old Swan Stairs.

"Nan, what about this? Can you tell me any more?"

"I only heard about it this afternoon. I'd been shopping with Doll in Paul's Walk and the Exchange. Then she went out to Moorfields where they're playing *Polichinelly*, and she had to sing between acts, and I went back to Whitehall."

"Yes, I know."

"And when I got there, Catherine was all tense and crying, and finally she told me. It seems she knew this Walter back at Piscataqua in our mother's time—before we were born. And something went all wrong between them, and she married at Court, and it went like that—all the years. But this summer, after a great sea fight with the Dutch, she heard he'd been in it, and failed some way, and been put in the Tower for treason, so she began to try to get him out. She went to the King, but the King looked at her and laughed, and said thirty years ago, maybe, but not now."

"Then the King's a bastard."

"Anyway, he's still the King, and he wouldn't help. So she tried other ways, and tonight it was to be—the servants bribed and the warders drunk. I said I would go with her, and she let me. We left Whitehall with a whole boatful of men, but when we stopped to meet another who'd been to see all was ready at the Tower, he told us that something was wrong with Captain Neal, that he couldn't walk out himself—that somebody would have to go way in there to the deepest dungeon to get him—and they were all afraid to go. So they talked, and they argued, and they swore, and then they all left us. Will, I do not understand these men. They are not like our men at home."

"Well, no, they're not. How do they look to you? What's the difference?"

"They go all a-row, like children holding hands. Tom says, 'I'm a-feerd!' and Jack says, 'Well, now that you speak of it, so be I.' And Bob says, 'I am, too!' And away they go! No man says, 'What the hell, I'll stand to this and see it through and great Christ can't stop me,' the way I've heard men say at home when there was anything hard to be done."

"They've only known this kind country, Nan. They haven't known New Hampshire, where many times a man's got to fight it out on his own or go underground for it; kill his own Indians, and put his own corn away against the winter. Here, if you can't stand up like a man, you can always call for the watch or go on the parish. It's not that easy where we come from. You mustn't blame them too much. So they all left you, did they?"

"Yes. She's trying to hold the boat close to the stones, but her fingers were starting to bleed when I came away."

"We better hurry then."

They walked off the Bridge and turned left past Fish Mongers' Hall.

When Will looked at Lady Catherine Audley, he knew that he saw the most beautiful woman he would see in his time, though she was old as his mother now, and finer worn. She sat all alone in a deep, hollow boat, and held fast to a tarred cable that dangled from the piling. A severe, black cloak covered her to her white throat, in spite of the hot night.

"Lady Catherine," said Nan gently, "you remember Joan Sweetapple who was with you in the *Pied Cow* and married John Scarlock?"

"Ah, Joan—who could forget Joan—the sweetness, and the love, and the courage! And we three girls holding hands, on deck, in the winter rain."

"This is her son, Catherine—Will Scarlock. And he says he will help us. Truth says we are wicked and he will have no part of it."

"I am sorry for Truth," said Lady Catherine. "You must forgive him and be kind to him, Nan. He will have to suffer so very much before he will be wise. But we could have no better help than John Scarlock's son."

He choked in his throat, knowing this was not praise for himself, but for a dead man. Then he smiled at her. "My mother said you were fair, Lady Catherine, but she didn't tell me how fair."

"Ah! There's a gallantry come into the stock since John's time. But, Will, I can't rightly let you go with us till you know the danger."

"It's for Walter Neal, isn't it?"

"Yes."

"My father would have me fried in hell if I didn't help his old captain when he needed it. Nan's told me a little. You want me to row down to the Tower?"

"Yes. Do you think you can get the boat through the arches?"

"Why not?" said Will, jumping in beside Lady Catherine, and reaching up to lift Nan down.

"The water foams so swift through the narrow way."

"No worse than when the tide's turning off Bloody Point at home, is it, Nannie?"

"No worse than that."

Will shoved off from Old Swan Stairs and rowed upriver a little, then out toward the middle of the stream. He took his bearings: Southwark lights strung out in a line on his right, and London's hundred steeples rose up white in the darkness on his left, and across his way stretched the long, lamp-jeweled bar of the Bridge. He feathered his oars and headed straight for it.

When Will and Nan walked out of the alehouse and their footsteps died away in the cobbled lane, Truth sat still for a few minutes, staring into his half-empty glass, and then he rose and followed them a way, but instead of turning back to the river, he went on up Fish Street Hill and into the city. He would go to his lodgings in Friday Street, he thought, and pray, and take counsel with himself, and lay plans for tomorrow. Already he knew what those plans would be. He would get himself out of London before daylight, go to his mother in Lincolnshire, and bid her prepare for his marriage. Then he would come back to Whitehall and tell Nancy that it was time they were married and settled in the work of God that awaited them. She had promised to forget the Prayer Book and all the old Popish customs that went with it, and pray God to fill her heart with His glory after the New England way. He was not sure she meant it, but she said she did, and he intended to have her, finding her in every way admirable and all that a woman should be. He would not examine her too closely for heresy now, nor chide her much for tonight's willfulness—not while she was still Nan Knight who could flick her finger and bid him be gone if she wanted to. Mistress Damerill would be another thing. Mistress Damerill. He thought of all that would mean and smiled gently to himself as he passed Bow Street Church with the glass lanthorn burning away at the top of it, and ran up the steps of the tall, narrow house he'd taken a room in. Her beauty troubled his body but fouled him with no mean lust, for he had allowed himself scarcely more than their betrothal kiss, on the ship's deck, in plain sight of crew and passengers, and when he assuaged that trouble, it would be in the honorable bed of marriage, with the getting of children. Once in his sweltering hot room under the eaves, he lighted a candle, flung himself down on the bulging straw mattress, and took a Bible from under his pillow. He thought to read the Sermon on the Mount, but turned instead to the Songs of Solomon.

When Truth walked out of Thomas Tacke's alehouse without saying goodnight, Milady shrugged her shoulders and joined the girls, taking a pack of cards out of her dress and saying she'd tell fortunes now, and good ones. Phillis and Temperance sat by and humored her, but Doll took her lute and climbed alone to the top of the house. Out on the leads she climbed, and sat there, playing softly, "The world turned upside down," peering over into the black river that ran far below and up at the stars overhead, lonely, and troubled, and not understanding, and wondering what would come of it all. After a while she heard voices downstairs and Milady shouting.

"Oh, Doll! Dolly, come down! They want you to sing at the Star."

"Not now—it's past midnight—there'll be nobody there."

"Oh, yes there will. Landlord's boy's just come home from the Dutch war. His ship was missing and they thought he'd sunk with her, but tonight she made into Wapping, and he's home! There's free beer and a tub of sprats open, and they say half the street's gone crazy. They want you to sing."

"Then I'll go," said Doll.

She went downstairs, out of the house and along the Bridge, shaking back the loose hair that hung too warm in her neck, plucking her lute dispiritedly. She went up Fish Street Hill into London.

"It's a great feat to shoot the Bridge against the tide. Even skillful watermen drown at it sometimes, but I have never seen it done better."

Lady Catherine brushed the spray from her cheeks and forehead, and settled back in the boat while Will guided it into the smooth reach below the bubbling, rushing turmoil of water that half filled the stone arch they had just fought their way through. He rowed steadily forward, making to the shore now, toward the broad, shelving steps below the Tower.

"It's worse off Pull-and-be-Damned Point," said Nan; "less froth and more whirlpools, but worse all in all, I think."

"Hush," said Catherine, lowering her voice. "See there, Will, that open square to the left?"

They were under the walls now, where the black water lapped at the slimy ledges, the old walls of soft gray stone, built on oak pile set over living oak roots, mortared, 'twas said, with the blood of wild creatures killed in old time. "That's the Traitor's Gate. We'll hold the boat here, and you must go in."

"Straight ahead—and where?"

"Have you ever been on Tower Hill—from the street—by the apple trees—where the soldiers train?"

"I went there once with Doll to see the animals in their cages. Monkeys, and some kind of foreign bobcat—and an elephant."

"You don't go that far. Go straight through the stone lattice and then you'll come out on a grass plot by the little garden Sir Walter Raleigh made when he was shut up there. It's all a maze of towers. The Bell Tower is on your left, and Wakefield and Lanthorn on your right. Straight ahead is the Bloody Tower, and 'tis there you must go."

"And inside?"

"Two flights of steps, then turn toward the river. 'Tis a little terraced room all barred."

"I could find it in my sleep now. How did you learn all that?"

"With money. But in the end, money fails, and it takes courage and loyalty. It takes a man."

"You can't beat man," muttered Will. He climbed swiftly out on the stones and slipped into the shadows of the archway, leaving the women to hold the boat fast against the pull of the river.

There were gardens on Tower Hill, and orchard trees, and he could smell the fragrance of them, smell the strong odor from the animal cages at the left, and hear the grunts and stirrings of the creatures there, restless and eager to be ranging abroad in the night. White-mottled sycamores hid the low house where the lieutenant lived, and he had no light in his window. No need for him to stay awake, when he could hire forty yeomen warders to keep guard for him, and he did not know that certain of them were down in the Ram's Head getting drunk now, at the expense of two discreet gentlemen, amiable, with full purses, and showing an uncommon love for yeomen warders.

Will found the Bloody Tower and walked in. Dim lanthorns behind horn shields burned in the stone corridors, and he slipped up the low, stone stairs as silently as he could, meeting no one. He went peering from room to room, but there was no light in any of them. Back and forth he went, listening for the sound of a drawn breath or movement, not daring to call, hearing nothing.

"Walter," he whispered finally. "Walter Neal!"

He stopped, stood still, and listened, with his hand pressed to the cool, musty stone blocks of the thick wall.

"Ho!" came a faint answer from a near-by doorway, a wooden door, studded with nails and ajar. He pushed it wide and went in. At the far end of the small, arched room, a frame pallet stood under the window and a huddled mass lay upon it. He walked toward that mass, guided by the light coming in from the dim passage. He stopped and bent down.

"Walter Neal?"

" 'Fore God," croaked a faint voice from the tumbled blankets. " 'Fore God, there's something about you of a man I used to know."

"You mean John Scarlock, and I'm his son Will, and I've come to take you out of here."

"I'm leaving here anyway, boy, and no trouble to you. I'm dying."

A little wind stirred in the corridor and swung the door wider open. The light shone on the prisoner's face, and Will could see that he spoke the truth. The blanched hair, the livid skin, the sallow lips seemed to be dead already—all but the bright, dark eyes, and they were so strongly alive Will wondered if even six feet of earth would quite put them out.

"Well, you don't want to die here." He bent lower and put both his arms under the body of what had once been a man and had a man's stature, but was wasted now to the bulk of a little child.

"We've a boat at the Traitor's Gate, and Lady Catherine is waiting."

"Who? Who is Lady Catherine?"

"You'd know Catherine Warburton, wouldn't you?"

"I would—indeed—" he murmured weakly. Will straightened up and started out of the dungeon. He could understand why they hadn't chained the man or locked him in, for he was a dead weight, utterly helpless. He made his way downstairs awkwardly, easing his burden where the walls curved, silently and in haste. Just as he stepped out on the grass, a drunken figure reeled up the path toward him.

"Hey! Gaol break! Help! Wardersh!"

"For thee, thou Dogface," quoted Will, and lifted his foot because his hands were not free, and gave the man a kick that tumbled him headlong into a bed of thorny vines. There he lay, roaring like a bullock and unable to pick himself up. Will ran heavily, bent almost double.

"Go on a' God's name," muttered Walter Neal, his shattered fingers clutching his rescuer's collar.

Will pounded across the damp pave of the Traitor's Gate and tumbled down the water stairs into the boat between the women. Nan already had an oar and was shoving off. Shouts and moving lights broke out on Tower Hill and somebody shot off a musket. He saw the flash of it under the sycamores. He rowed furiously out to midstream and headed upriver. He shot the Bridge again, but this time with the tide, and it was only like being thrown forward on a great wave crest, not the furious thrust against all the force of a black, beating current that it had been before. He didn't quite know where they were going, and he couldn't waste breath to ask, but Nan had said something about Oxfordshire, and that would be upriver. Besides, any pursuers would expect him to be going down. He was past the Steelyard and the Vintry, and pulling even with the great river palaces of the rich milords before he could take his attention from the oars and sense what was going on in the boat.

Then he looked into Nan's face, for she sat very close to him, and she seemed sadder and older than he had ever known her to be, but somehow more beautiful. Behind her, Walter Neal was talking to Catherine, his head lying in her lap.

"You were angry at me that time in the spring under the yellow willows, Kate. Do you remember how they hung all feathery gold there at the edge of the old cornfield up the Fore River where the brook came down? How they fringed all the coves by Newichwannock when I took you rowing that afternoon?"

"Yes. I remember."

Nan's fingers touched Will's arm, and there was no fire in their touch as there was in Doll's, but it went as surely to his heart.

"They're still that way there in the spring, aren't they? We've seen them in our time just as they did."

"Yes. We've seen them."

"You were angry, Kate." He was oblivious to everything but her. "You wanted me to love you—then and there on the new green grass with violets scattered through it. And I would not. I told you I was a soldier of fortune and not for marrying, but you said you did not care. I told you I had taken many girls, but I would not take you—because you were too good to be used so—and I knew it. And I went away from you. And you married. Are you still angry at me, Kate?"

"Not at you now, Walter. But I am still angry at the man you were then. I have never wanted anything so much as I wanted what he would not give me."

He stirred restlessly, and she tried to make him easier.

"That should be cold comfort to me now, but it is not; it is good to hear."

He turned suddenly from her and looked at Will Scarlock, his head dark on the dark sky and thrown back, his hair ruffled in the wind, his strong, slim shoulders swinging to and fro as he rowed.

"You're a good man to row upriver, just as your father was. But there's a difference on you. You're a better man than he was, I think."

"Not in a thousand years."

"Yes, 'fore God, you are. He'd have gone in there tonight and got me out just as you did, but he'd have gone with a sober eye, jaw set like a mastiff, and you come with an air, and a smile, and a curse out of the Iliad. I do not know just how those fierce winters and sour clam flats have changed the blood, but they have, and they've bettered it. John was my man always, and a good one—he still alive?"

"No."

"I was going to send him a message by you; instead I'll take it myself. I . . ." He began to gasp.

"What did they do to you? What did they do, my dear?" asked Catherine, holding him up. His voice lifted again, this time so weak they could hardly hear it.

"They put me in the Scavenger's Daughter—a vicious wench made out of iron, that doubles and folds a man together till he bleeds everywhere. And for what? Yes, it's true. I did take a ship out of battle. I took it out because the great compass piece was cracked, and I knew there was not a knee of timber in all the yards of England to mend it if it foundered worse. We lose a compass piece, and then we lose a ship. Lose enough ships and the fleet's down, and if the fleet's down, we'll have the Dutch bastards running all over and their flag up in Westminster. I took my ship to port to save it for England—to save England"—he was gasping—"and they killed me for a traitor—because they could not see." He turned his dimming eyes toward Will. "Scarlock—what of those woods of yours back home? I tell you, our forests are done. Come five years, the way our ships are taking it, and England won't have boards to shingle a privy. But you could save us—with your trees."

"I'm here about that business now—dealing with Sir William Warren."

"He's sharp at all points. But you can have your way with him if you threaten to take your masts to Pieter Vroot, the Dutch purveyor who hides in Hangman's Gains."

His crushed chest heaved painfully. Will forgot to row.

"Will . . . Will Scarlet . . . the Merry Man . . ." He was whispering now, far back in his throat. "When I took your father out of England, I thought I did him a wrong. Now that I ha' seen you, I am not so sure. But when I did it, I said, 'Hail, Mary, forgive me, now and at the hour of my death.' And that hour's now. And it's well enough. Soldiers of fortune are not the fashion any more. Men's all turned merchants and shopkeepers! Kate!"

His head lolled back and she steadied it. "Kate . . . the yellow willows . . . and you were right, I think . . . and I was wrong."

And all of a sudden Will Scarlock realized that he was rowing aimlessly up London River in the night, in a boat with a dead man in it, and two stark-silent women, and that somewhere over by Whitehall Stairs the watch was crying over the water, "Two o' the clock, an' all's well!" Perhaps it was—at Whitehall.

15. *London's burning!*

THEY PUT into Whitehall Stairs, all in the dark and nobody speaking, but a low hail greeted them, and the blunt prow of a river boat veered gently at its moorings there—the boat from Catherine's country manor that would have taken the poor, worn captain to sanctuary—if he could have waited for it. Will helped her ashore, and she talked with the boatmen for a few minutes, and then they reached down and he passed up to them the wasted figure of the dead man wrapped in Catherine's cloak.

"I shall go on the journey just as I planned it," she said, smiling wanly down at Will and Nan, "only we shall not talk, as I had thought we would. He was always a wanderer, but he shall have rest at last—in a spot I know by a little stream, low-lying, where there are willow trees."

"I'll go with you, Catherine," said Nan, pressing her fingers into Will's arm in farewell and standing up in the boat, but Catherine waved her back.

"Nan, my dear, do not be hurt, but this I must do alone. If you have ever loved, you will know."

"Yes," said Nan, holding back the tears, "I do know."

She and Will watched Catherine climb into the other boat, watched it edge away from the stairs and plow outward, breasting the current of the river, headed for the willows of Oxfordshire.

He looked into her face, white and blurred in the darkness. He said slowly, "What do you want to do?"

"Oh, Will! I couldn't go in there—to her rooms, crystal and velvet—all alone. Take me back with you, and I'll sit up in the tavern for what's left of the night and talk with Milady. She's coarse, and crude, and ribald, and I know her house and her business—but she's alive and gay—and I need that now."

"I need it too," he said.

He shoved off from Whitehall Stairs and rowed downriver.

The heat had dwindled and a strong east wind began to blow, flecking the Thames with white all over and whipping the branches of the lime and almond trees that fringed the great river palaces below the Strand. They moved steadily downward toward the city, in a world quiet, and cool, and waiting for dawn. Lights flickered here and there on the Lambeth Marshes, and when they passed the mouth of the Fleet Ditch they could smell all the rich filth of it, where the street kennels and houses of office drained down. Far below them the thread of lights that was London Bridge crossed over into Southwark. On the left rose up the white spires and black wooden gables of London City, that would never look just that way again.

"It's not like coming down Piscataqua from Dover Point, is it, Nan?" he asked her, resting on his oars.

"No. Nothing here's like anything at home. I think—I wish I were back there."

"But you're not going back. You're going to marry Truth Damerill, and go and sing psalms in Lincolnshire."

"Yes, I guess I am. Nothing seems to come out the way I always thought it would. But he is a good man, and when you listen to him you can believe as he believes—almost. What are you and Doll going to do?"

"I don't know. There's Old Thorny, and there's Piscataqua Country. One's a good, rich farm, and the other's just about to start on the biggest timber trade since old Hiram in Lebanon rafted the cedars down."

"How did you feel about Old Thorny while you were there? As if you belonged to it?"

"Not while I was there, I didn't, but after I came away I was not so sure. Meeting Walter Neal tonight, and hearing him talk about my father—and seeing him die—it all ties me closer to old time than anything has before. I don't think I belong anywhere. I wonder if I'll ever feel I'm home."

He let the river carry them, he did not row.

"Look, Nannie, what's that light just left of the Bridge? Dawn won't break over that way." He knew where London dawns broke, because he had often been awake in them—awake with Doll. "Looks like there's something afire."

"Yes, it does. Something on Fish Street Hill."

They passed Queenhithe and the Steelyard, and edged into the stairs below the Old Swan. Mean shacks and warehouses and tenements crowded down to the water's edge; on the right, toward the Bridge, rose the tower of Fish Mongers' Hall, and beyond it a great flame billowed into the sky. They heard the crackle and roar of it, and the shouting of men under the pall of smoke. Will helped Nan out of the boat, and they hurried up Thames Street, straight for the flare and noise.

"It's in Pudding Lane!"

"No! It's the Star in Fish Street!"

"No, it's both!"

There seemed to be two lines of blazing houses, one in the little dark lane to the east, the other in the main throughfare leading up from the Bridge into London. Three houses close by were well aflame, and the roofs of five others smoking. A crowd had gathered and stood about as if they were watching a peepshow at Moorfields, nobody trying to help save anything. Will and Nan came up to the edge of it and stood, watching the Star Tavern burn, the flames wreathing its galleries and porches, thriving lustily on its stable well full of hay. London houses were always catching fire, they stood so close together, and they were made of old, dried wood, and the chimneys wry and cracked.

"Remember home, Nan, on the cold days in winter when people drive their fires so hard the thatch and shingles are always catching —and we men be running all over town in the snow all day with leather buckets?"

Nan drew her brows together. "Yes—I know. But at home there are free fields and spaces for the fire to burn out in. Here—where there's not an inch between—where one house's wall is the wall of another's—I'm frightened. I wish they'd try harder to put it out."

But nobody was trying very hard to put it out, beyond each man saving what he could of his own goods when the flames attacked him. Up in London nobody was even awake yet. The city slept, after a hot, boisterous, hard-working, hard-drinking Saturday. Next to Will stood a man and a woman, she with a child in her arms.

"Where'd it start?" he asked them.

"Farynor's—in Pudding Lane—you know, he's the King's baker. His man woke up choking about two and the house was full of smoke. He and his wife crawled out the garret window and over the roofs, but the cookmaid was afraid to, and they think she's burnt."

"What'd he do? Drop a candle?"

"He says he put his bake fire out, and that somebody must have set it, but I been there myself and know he keeps flitches of bacon hung all over and kindling wood piled against the chimney. Likely a spark snapped. The Star's about gone now."

Just then the roof of the Star fell in, filling the street with a whirl of sparks and smoke. Will lifted his head, and the strong east wind tousled his brown hair.

"Nan," he said, "I don't like this. There's another house catching. Let's go round into Pudding Lane and see how it looks from there."

They walked back into Thames Street that ran parallel with the water and just above it, and turned east into Pudding Lane. Ten houses up the hill lay a pile of smoking rubble that had been the shop of Farynor, the baker, flames still playing about it. Further up the hill two more roofs had caught, but nobody seemed to be watching from this side. They were all alone in the thick air, half white mist off the river, half yellow, acrid smoke from the burning houses. They stood there and looked at the fire for a few moments, and then they turned to each other. Each of them was about to speak, neither knowing what they would say, but just at that minute a flake of fire sailed down between them in a long arc and lighted on Nan's skirt. The filmy pink muslin blazed up like tinder, and Will stood by in horror for a moment, unable to think or act. She felt the heat of it biting through her petticoat, the hard light blazing past her eyes, and her first thought was that she could put it out in the river, so she turned and ran that way. And her running fanned the flames till they played all about her as she fled down the tilted pavement toward the Thames. Will recovered himself and ran after her, trying to tear his jacket off, but it stuck at the elbows and he could not get out of it. He caught her in front of St. Magnus' Church before she could get to the water stairs, and threw her down in the street, stretching his body on hers, beating madly at the flaming stuff of her dress, bruising her against the cobblestones, blistering his own face and arms as he crouched above her, trying to smother the fire.

And he succeeded. Suddenly the scalding pain eased on his flesh and the tiny whisper of flames died away under him. He dragged her to her feet and stood looking down at her, both of them black-ened, and blistered, and hurting all over, their clothing a mass of charred rags.

"Nan!" he said. "Oh, Nan!"

"My dear," she said, and he took her in his arms, took her and held her, oblivious of the fire and the river, and the thick, smoking sky, and all the pains of the flesh—knowing only that he held her, and that in holding her he was complete and whole, and nothing in this world lacking to him, and that he would never let her go.

"Oh, Nan, Nan, Nan!" he said, still holding her, while the banners of smoke blew out above them and the flames crept on and on, and further up the hill another house fell in and another roof caught. Finally he loosened their embrace a little and looked down at her.

"Oh, Nannie—I love you—and I want you, and you're all my life, and you've always been—and I didn't know. What'll we do?"

Thick orange light played on all the old gables, on the old stone streets, and up the hill another roof fell in and another house caught.

"I don't know, Will. What do you want . . . ?"

Suddenly he thrust away from her and stood out alone, all in the flickering light of burning London.

"I want to have you with me—always and forever, and every min-ute of the day and night so long as I'm alive."

"But Doll . . . ?"

"Doll's a good, sweet girl, and she gave me all she had to give and I'm grateful for it. But it wasn't enough. It never was enough."

"Do you think I could give you more?"

"Oh, Nan!" He cried out in pain that did not come from his burned flesh, and took her to him again.

"All my life, Nan," he said. "We slept in the same cradle, and we'll sleep sometime in the same graveyard—but all the years between —do you think I'll let us go apart?"

"But, Doll?"

He smiled proudly. "Don't you worry about Doll. She's a great girl, Nan, not little or mean. I'll go to her now and tell her I love you, and ask her what we can do about it. She'll see. She won't want to keep me, knowing how I feel."

"Won't she?"

"Never. Come." He put his arm around her half-bare shoulders, and they limped down the Bridgeway together, but the fire came up close behind them, growing every minute.

Will looked back over his shoulder as they crossed the Bridge. "Nan! This damn fire! It's all about St. Magnus' and must be worse up the hill, for the wind's that way. If it comes out here . . . these houses are all tinder and they'll go like that." He snapped his fingers. "Milady might have to move her goods out."

They dropped their arms from about each other and walked into Milady's, ragged, but in all decency.

"Where's Doll?" asked Will, a little self-conscious, hating himself for what he had to do.

Temperance and Phillis had their heads out of a window watching the fire. Helen and Flora had come in and were tippling at the bar. Milady bustled forward, her painted face all runneled with sweat, her voice quick and excited.

"Will! How's the fire going? Where's it burnt to now? Get those rags off. There's a suit of Tom's in the back, and Miss Nan can have one of Audrey's dresses. Have you seen Doll? She went to sing at the Star."

"The Star . . . ?" he faltered. "The Star's . . . all done. It burnt down. I saw the roof fall in."

"Well, that's one place you won't have to look then. Doll Trasper's not the girl to let a house fall down on top of her. Probably she's somewhere in the crowd, looking on. I been over, but I thought I'd better come back and see to things. If we have to move out . . ."

"I don't think you will," he said slowly. "The wind's the other way, coming strong off the water and blowing up into town. I wish Doll would come home—though you're probably right about her."

"Oh, she'll be safe. Change out of those clothes and come up on the roof and watch the fire."

So Milady and her girls and Will and Nan climbed the stairs and out on the leads where Doll had sung to herself earlier that night. A little thrill of fear went through him when he saw how fast the fire had grown since he had come away from it. The low, square belfry of St. Magnus' Church was all wrapped in flame now, and St. Margaret's up the hill had begun to burn. The wind whipped his hair and whistled through his borrowed jacket, tumbled Nan's curls and flicked one of them across his face. He stared down into her eyes and saw a stricken look there.

"Will. I'm frightened for Doll," she whispered. "We don't want her to . . . *burn*."

"No," he said, "we don't want that."

They stood looking at each other. Are we honest? she was thinking. Do we really care—if she does? Perhaps we want her to. It would be so easy for us then. Oh, we must be very wicked, she thought, suddenly turning her face away. We must go and try to save her—now. Will was thinking, too. Suppose Doll had been under that roof when they saw it fall—of course she wasn't. I wouldn't have to hurt her then, he thought. I could have Nannie without that. He hated himself more every minute.

Daylight whitened the sky down the river when he looked that way. Upriver the fire had got into the warehouses and tenements and cellars of the poor stevedores and wherrymen, a close, stinking rookery that stretched all along, from the Bridge to Queenhithe Dock.

He moved for the narrow stair. "I'm going in town," he said. "I'll find Doll and bring her back."

Nan ran after him, holding up the brocade skirt that belonged to Audrey the red-haired whore. "I'm going with you."

He did not ask her not to. It would be better to have her with him when he met Doll, for he did not mean to hide the thing that had happened to him, to pretend and lie. He had loved Nannie always, but he had just found it out. That was the truth, and he would stand to it. What had been between him and Doll was fire, pure fire, as irresistible as that hot, red tide now flooding over the London waterfront. But now he was done with all that, for he had touched Nan. Touching Nan did not make his blood whirl and his muscles tighten. But it was as if he had touched a part of himself that he had never known before, and that in touching it he was made whole, and utter, and complete; to lose it would leave him broken and maimed and half a man. Doll was a pretty girl whom he had known as intimately as he knew the coat he wore, but Nan was the flesh upon his bones.

They had trouble getting off the Bridge, the way was so choked with people running hither and thither and shouting—a single, sweaty workman carrying away the great hidebound register from St. Magnus' where the roof was about to fall in, the clerk wailing because he could not get to the plate that lay buried in the vaults below. Two lines of fire went up the hill, through Fish Street and Pudding Lane, lines that seemed to grow longer every minute. Thames Street was all afire to the left and flames glared red against the square, Norman tower of the Bridge House. Three new houses that stood beside it had fallen, part into the river and part into the street. Up in London sounded the dreary wailing of bells pealed backward, the sign of general alarm. Already a little fleet of boats had collected at the back doors of houses that opened straight on the water, taking out families and goods. Will hesitated. Just then a dirty, babbling stevedore, his face all tears and sweat and his front hair burned off, caught him by the arm and began to plead for help in tumbled words that came too fast to make out. Nan caught the man's story first, and it was this: that his wife lay in childbed in a threatened house below Fish Mongers' Hall, with four small children around her, and the watermen wanted ten pounds to take her out . . . which he did not have. Will remembered then that he had a boat tied up below the Old Swan.

"Nannie," he said, "you better go back to Milady's. I'll help this man get his wife out, and then . . ."

"No, Will. You help him, and I'll go look for Doll."

"If you want to—but, for God's sake, keep yourself safe."

"I will. And you."

"When you find her go to the Old Serpent and wait there for me. That's away off in Cripplegate and as safe as heaven. Good-bye." He kissed her gently on the forehead.

"Good-bye, my dear."

They did not meet again till past eight o'clock that night, and by then it seemed as if the whole world might go down in horrid, bloody flame. Will toiled all day at the oars, ferrying the scorched and home-less and their goods over to St. George's Fields in Southwark, and Nan ranged the town wherever the fire would let her, looking for Doll. The fire moved out on the Bridge early in the forenoon, but the wind drove it back before it got to Milady's house, and Will watched that house, standing up safe and unthreatened, as he plied back and forth in the grim heat that deepened as the destruction spread. He saw little figures on the rooftop watching, and three of them wore red dresses, but that was the favorite color with London women, and he could not tell whether or no one of them might be his wife.

All that day the flames, driven by a hard wind under the clear bright sun, swept westward along the riverside. They flowed like a torrent down the channels of the narrow lanes and alleys that led to the wharves. Fish Mongers' Hall burned early, the tower standing up, but the inside gutted and the wings gone. The seared machinery would no longer turn at the waterworks, and they stopped pumping up Thames water that might have saved all. By late afternoon when

213

Will looked up into town, he saw a great bow of fire burning steadily up the hill into the very heart of the city. The Watermen's Hall went, almost undefended, because they were out saving other men's goods—at prices that ranged higher every hour. Before suppertime it had crept through Duck's Foot Lane and the Merchant Taylors lost their grammar school. Goods were swimming in the river all around the rescue boats: spinets and cradles, loaves of bread, a cask, a pair of stays, a flaming timber—all afloat in the brown river like beans in porridge. Showers of fire flakes, an evil crackling sound, and whirls of thick, oily yellow smoke drifted everywhere. By moonrise he pulled in below the Three Cranes in the Vintry, now all afire, and let his oars drop from hands that were too weary to ply them any more. He'd walk to the Old Serpent and see the girls, and have a drink and a dish of meat and go to sleep. He wouldn't tell Doll tonight. Nan would have found her by now, he felt sure.

At first Nan found nobody much worried, people going to church as usual, though more than three hundred houses had gone, and there was talk of pulling down other houses to check the flames, but when they began this work near noontime it was of little use because they began too near the fire, and the sparks leaped over and kept on. By afternoon, though, everybody was up on the housetops watching, and mutters began to go around that Dutch ships had come up the river and set it, to pay England for burning Schelling and the Vlie. Others said it was a Papist plot, and here and there a mob gathered itself and swept through the streets, pommeling every unlucky Frenchman it could come on. The Papists were throwing red-hot balls of fire into the houses, somebody cried, and then a man long known for unsound wits came riding through the narrow, hot, windy lanes shouting, "Arm! Arm!" But no visible enemy appeared anywhere, and still the rookery of squalid shacks covered with pitch and leatherboard went on burning along the Thames, and the fire spread out, west of it and north. By afternoon crews of men started working with leather buckets and axes and ladders and iron hooks, pulled out of storage in the church towers and the halls of the livery companies, but more men kept watch with staves and muskets for the Dutch, or harried any foreigner they could lay hands on. They cut the hollow elm pipes to get a quick water supply, and so wasted much of the New River water brought down from the hills round Islington, for it flowed away on the pavements and down the kennels. They trundled up portable cisterns, small kegs on iron wheels, and worked urgently with brass hand squirts, but these took three men to throw out a gallon, and were soon left lying useless in the gutters. Here and there a pigeon with scorched wings tumbled into the street. Sick men were carried past on litters, and coaches and hackney hell-carts lumbered post haste through the crooked ways, whipping for the country with the rich men's chattels. The poor choked every lane and street, pushing carts and barrows, carrying their children. And everywhere Nan wandered she asked for Will's wife, for Doll the singing girl from the house on London Bridge, and nobody had seen her.

Finally, about dark, she went to the Old Serpent, and told Batt and Doggett her trouble, and they tried to reassure her, but they looked at each other behind her back, and she caught the look and did not like it. Then Will came, hot and dirty and aching all over, just as she was hot and dirty and aching, but neither of them had ever seen anything so beautiful as the other.

Batt got him a cold ham pie and a bottle of brandy, and Doggett rubbed butter on his blisters. But first Will asked for his wife.

"I couldn't find her, Will," Nan told him, trying to make light of it, "but I don't wonder. There are so many people running all about everywhere to see it—and the trained bands hunting for Dutch and Papists. They say it's the worst fire ever in London, and all who can are leaving. The goldsmiths have sent their wares to the Tower, and you can't hire a cart for less than thirty pounds. I haven't seen Truth anywhere either. I wonder where he is."

"Oh, God," muttered Will, "I forgot all about Truth. That'll be another thing . . ."

"That," said Nan, "I'll handle."

"How far had it got when you came in, Will?" asked Doggett.

"It's catching the Steelyard, and you know what that'll be—all the Navy hemp and oils and timber. The Rhenish winehouse there is gone." His throat was rough and scratched from breathing smoke, and his back hurt him, but tired as he was he couldn't sit still. Oh, where the hell was Doll? And did he really want to find her? *How* did he want to find her? Dead? "It's burning up Dowgate. Looks like Tallow Chandlers and Skinners'll lose their halls—they've taken the plate out. The bells have fallen down in St. Lawrence Poultney."

"An' them bells was new! What'll stop it, Will?"

"Nothing, while this wind keeps up," he said. He put his head down on the table and went to sleep.

Monday was the day that burnt Lombard Street, all the shops and the merchants' tall, rich houses. Lord Mayor Bludworth, frightened out of his spent wits, roamed the streets alone, wringing his hands and crying, "Lord, what can I do? The people will not obey me! We pull down houses and more houses, and still the fire goes on!" The Duke of York came down from Whitehall with the King's Life Guard, and the sailors came up from Woolwich and Deptford, and fought a good fight. But still the fire kept on. Sheets of flame swept over the golden grasshopper on top of the Royal Exchange, and the kings' statues there fell down on their faces. All the silks and carvings and baubles and fine Eastern merchandise from the booths in the Pawn went, and the air about was full of the unearthly savor of spices and pepper burning. And still the wind beat up from the river, and the yellow smoke hid the blue sky overhead, letting now and then a ray of bloody sunlight through, and showers of fire drops seemed to fall out of it.

The drug shops burnt like stinking rainbows in Bucklersbury, the taverns burned in the Poultry, and the flower gardens in St. Swithin's Lane. Timbers crashed and flames crackled, and everywhere the panic grew. The rich fled and the poor pilfered, and the best thing a man could have was a stout back and a two-wheeled cart to get his goods away. By Monday night one half the city had come down, steeples flamed everywhere like beacons posted in a pit of fire, and the noise of the burning was like the roar of a thousand iron-wheeled chariots on the cobblestones. The great stone blocks of Baynard's Castle crumbled like paper, and the bow of fire burnt from Blackfriars to Leadenhall Street. Pools of blazing oil and tallow floated down the Thames, and the flames were leaping round London Wall. Now and then a drifting ember came down on the low roof of the Old Serpent, but Batt ran up a ladder and beat them out so quickly that they came to naught. Most of the people had fled by now into the cleared spaces of Moorfields, and Finsbury, Soho, and St. Giles, and Highgate, and Nan plodded among them, from group to miserable group. She went to Friday Street just before it started to burn and learned there that Truth was safe away in Lincoln. Will worked all that day pulling down houses. They met at the Old Serpent that night, and there was still no word of Doll.

Tuesday was worse. It burnt the goldsmiths' shops in Cheapside, with all their swinging, wooden signs of gilt and red and blue. It burnt the Guildhall and the Customs House, and the Mermaid and the Dolphin. Tuesday's fire was triple Monday's fire, and ten times that of Sunday night. You could stand in Cheapside and look straight to the Thames with not a house between, where houses had stood thicker than anywhere in the world—now only a waste of black ashes, calcined stone, and fallen beams beginning to cool. Will was staggering out of the Mermaid with an oak chest on his shoulder that the landlord had wept tears over, the old inn smoking behind him, when a dark, jovial man with heavy jowls, his rich coat spattered and awry, strode across his path handing out guineas among the firefighters. Will didn't want guineas. He wanted the shortest course through the rubble and streaming smoke to the safety of a far street.

"Get to hell out of my way," he growled, elbowing the largess giver.

For a moment the man looked startled. Then he tossed his head in its curling periwig and laughed.

"By God, nobody's talked that way to me since I was made King o' England."

"No," jeered Will, "and I've not talked that way to anybody since I was made Pope o' Rome." He staggered down the street.

It was not till that night when he got back to the Old Serpent that he heard King Charles had really been abroad in the city with a bag of gold to hearten the toiling men, but he was too tired and distraught then to care whether the guard came to take him to the Tower for his offense or not. He had been at the Tower that afternoon anyway—where nobody, he had noted, seemed to be taking much account of the escape of Walter Neal. For Sir William Warren had found Will after the Mermaid went, and got him to steer one of the boats taking Navy gunpowder out of the Tower and up to the safety of Whitehall. Enough explosive was there to scoop the whole city out of the earth, and rend the Bridge, and make a waterspout of London River . . . if the fire got to it . . . and they must see it didn't. So all afternoon Will ferried gunpowder upriver through a burning city, and then he went back to the Old Serpent, and Nan was there, dead asleep in a corner, and she hadn't found Doll.

He went to sleep too, but then she waked him up to say St. Paul's was burning.

"You mean," he said, "you want me to go and look at something *burn?*"

"Yes. It's great Paul's, Will, and there was nothing like it in all the world, and maybe there won't be again. And besides, if Doll's alive, she'll be there. No one in London would stay away."

So they walked through the city, ablaze from Newgate to the Tower, as near as they could to the cathedral, in time to see the dry timber roof sink through the stone arches and the nave become a seething cauldron of fire. Noll had stabled his horses here, and King Harry had lost away its bells in a dicing game, but the people of London loved it all its days; slept, and ate, and traded in it, and met their friends there. It was more to them than a matter of prayers and Sunday pride. Melted lead dripped down in great, blistering silver drops, and flakes of stone scaled off and crashed into the street. The rose window bloomed for a moment, a crimson flower outlined on the yellow, sulphurous rainbow of the night, and then the glass shattered and rained down on the crowd below, where they clustered among the broken and trampled graves in the yard, heaped and rounded high with the store of corpses from last summer's plague.

Will lifted his head, suddenly alert. "Nannie," he said, "the wind! It isn't blowing any more! That means—it'll start dying out. Let's go home."

They walked back to the Old Serpent. Doll had not been at the burning of Paul's. Doggett waited soberly under the faded picture of old King Charles.

"You been to see Paul's go?"

"Yes."

"I haven't. I went down to the Bridge, Will. Ashes and cobbles be cool enough to walk on now."

"I suppose so. The fire was dead down there by yesterday morning."

"I went to the Star."

"Yes . . . ?" He could feel Nan stiffen against his side.

Doggett began to blubber. "I—I be sorry, Will." He held out a shattered gilt frame with strings dripping down from it, and a scorched kid shoe. "I found 'em there—in the rubble and live coal. Both together—and they be hers."

"Yes," said Will. "They be hers." He stood there, saying no more words, holding the little slipper and the broken lute.

16. Their proper scorpions

S HE'S DEAD," said Will. "She wouldn't have been parted from her lute any other way."

It was Friday morning, a cool, gray day with mist clinging above the river, and the sky overcast, and the black, calcined ruins of London still smoking. He and Nan sat together at a table in Thomas Tacke's alehouse, not eating or drinking, not talking very much, just sitting there. Milady stood in the doorway with her hands on her hips, her eyes still reddened by tears, but a determined smile turned on the passing gentlemen. Nan had spent the last two nights here, sleeping alone in Audrey's bed, for the red-haired beauty had gone down the waterfront on adventures of her own, as she did every so often. Milady kept threatening to get a new girl in her place who would be more reliable, but she never did. It would have upset too many of her best customers; besides, she liked Audrey.

"I—I'm afraid she is, Will," said Nan very low.

"It wasn't my fault," he muttered, looking intently at the graining of the oak table top. "But I feel as if it were—as if I'd killed her. Killed her by wishing. I didn't want her. And just as I didn't want her, she died."

"I know. I feel the same. We've done a wicked thing."

"I *didn't* want her to die. God knows I didn't want that. I didn't wish her any harm. I wanted to be free of her so I could have you, but I wanted her to go on as she had before—alive and gay here in London she loved so much, playing, and singing, and taking another husband."

"She was young and lovely and sweet, and she sang so well. It's sad to think that she . . . that she isn't . . . any more."

"Nan," he said bitterly, "that's true, but that's not what makes me feel like I ought to be beaten with rods or put in the Scavenger's Daughter. It's this: that I'm sorry Doll Trasper's dead, but I'm not sorry I lost my wife. Can you still love a man who's that vile?"

"Of course I can—I do. I'm just as vile. I'm not sorry either."

After a long time he spoke again and the suffering in his voice tore her heart. "At least, we're honest, Nan. I can't pretend I'm heart-broken to lose her. Her death's our gain. But it'll be a long time before we can be happy. There's a line somewhere in Evelyn—'Leave the guilty to their proper scorpions.' We've been left to ours, I think, and they're biting hard."

She did not try to answer because sobs came choking in her throat.

"But afterward—when it's all a little older, and further back in the past—what's between us will save us from any scorpions, Nan."

"Oh, it will!"

"There's nothing more I can do for her. I've been up to the Star— to where it was. Doggett helped me rake all the hot ashes away and lift the beams. But we never found anything more of her. She must have been all burnt. Tomorrow I'm going down to Wapping and speak my mind to Sir William and get him to speak his. And then —if he says what I think he's going to—I'll have to go back to Portsmouth, or else make up my mind I'll never go there to live again."

"You haven't made it up . . . yet?"

"No," he said miserably. "I still don't know where I belong. Hell, likely, from the way I feel right now."

"What do you want me to do?"

"Just stay where I am," he said. "Just don't go away from me . . . till . . . till I feel I'm fit to touch you again . . . till we can be . . ."

They became aware suddenly that Milady was talking to somebody in the street, loud and fast, and beginning to weep all over again. They turned their heads that way just as Truth Damerill strode into the room. He looked at Nan and the moment he saw her his eyes lighted, but he went straight to Will and put out both his hands.

"Will. I'm sorry. About your wife. It's grievous news. May God help you to bear it."

Will looked down. He could not meet the honest eyes of his friend. "Thank you, Truth," he mumbled. He knew then that Truth had turned to Nan though he was not watching them.

"Nancy, I came back from London the moment I heard of the fire. Ashes fell into all the counties round, and the smoke drifted over half of Essex. I was afraid for you, but they kept telling me all the way that Whitehall was safe, and I thought you would be there— at Lady Catherine's." There was a faint edge of accusal in his voice.

Explaining would be a long, long story, and she felt suddenly too tired to rehearse it for him.

"Were you here all the time?" He looked disapprovingly·at Audrey's flamboyant dress. "And have you seen London? I came in at the west end, and there's about thirty houses standing in Fleet Street, and from there to the Tower scarce another roof that's whole. Some of the steeples are left, but the churches under them are gutted away —and all around, from the Wall to the river, nothing but fallen beams, and rubble and ashes. The stones are still hot under foot, and smoke everywhere. But already they've put up wooden stalls to sell ale to the men who are trying to clear all away. It looks like Doomsday'd come and gone."

"It has," said Will slowly. "You don't need to tell us what London looks like, Truth. We saw it go. House by house and stone by stone."

"Do you know how it started? I heard all sorts of tales as I came through. Some blame the Papists, and they're still hunting for Dutch fireboats along the river. One old man stood up on a broken stone telling all who would listen that he knew London was burnt by Government to get rid of the plague seeds. And there's half a million people lying out in the fields around, with no roofs over them, and nothing to eat but what the farmers bring in carts. I do not think any city has ever been worse punished for its wickedness. It is an inspiration to me."

"Is wickedness always punished?"

"I believe so. I hope so."

"And how about mercy?"

"For our souls' good, God is sparing with his mercy. Nancy." He sat down beside Nan and put his arm about her. "I was gone into Lincoln when the fire came, because I wanted to prepare my mother for our marriage. She is ready to welcome you. I met with members of the church I will serve, secretly, of course, because I shall not take the King's oath and give up our purer ways. And I have told them that I shall return with a good and beautiful woman—with my wife." He kissed her full on the lips.

Around his bent head, just as his mouth came down, Nan caught a glimpse of Will's face, bleak as a winter sky. She suffered the caress but did not respond to it. Instead she drew herself back from Truth and turned her head away.

"What is wrong, Nancy?"

Oh, God, thought Will, she's going to tell him, she's going to tell him now. Should I go or stay? He got up and went to the open window and stood there, looking down at the river flooding through the arches underneath. Charred timbers drifted on top of it, here a crate of peeping chickens, there a scorched periwig. None of the ruin showed from here, only the long curve of the Pool with ships anchored all over it, the red roofs on Tower Hill, and the teeming waterfront below. He tried to listen to Milady's banter in the street door, to the cries of the silver-gray gulls flying close to the water looking for little fish. But he could still hear Nan so plain. He could hear only Nan.

"I am sorry, Truth. But I will not lie to you, not even for one minute, though it might be easier. I cannot go to Lincoln and I cannot marry you."

"Why not?"

"Because I love another man."

"But you have given me your word. Why . . . ?"

"Must you be so much like God, Truth? So hard in judgment, and so sparing with your mercy? I have always loved this man, but when I promised you I did not think that he loved me. I thought I must live all my life without him. And I honored you because you were so good, and your faith in God was not a whited sepulchre and a clash of cymbals—it was alive and pure—as a flame burning. A cold flame."

His soul was looking at her out of his dark eyes. "Go on," he said grimly.

"This man I loved had a wife . . . then . . . when I promised you. But now . . . he does not have a wife . . . and he loves me."

"Who is this man who can put off a wife like an old cloak?"

She faltered. Will came forward then. "I am," he said.

"You . . . Will? My friend . . . ?"

For a few moments nobody said anything at all. Nan watched the two men anxiously, but they did not move or speak. They stood there looking like statues of themselves. Out on the Bridge a hawker was crying new-caught eels, and Milady came in and took her purse out of a drawer, and went to buy some.

222

"Truth," she said finally, "you think we're vile and wicked, and we are. Nothing I can say will make you understand sin and weakness, and love that's not for God, that's between man and woman. It was when the fire first came and he had to save me from it that he knew he loved me, and as soon as we knew that, we knew we had to tell Doll—and you. But when we went to look for Doll we could not find her. All through the fire we looked for her. And then, when we found she was dead . . ."

"You were probably glad. That made everything easy for you."

"Easy? Oh God!" croaked Will.

"Oh, Truth!" she cried, "don't be angry—don't!"

"I am not angry," he said proudly. His soul was no longer in his eyes, and she knew that he would not show it to her again. "But God is angry, and he will punish you worse than ever I can."

They bowed their heads. "I believe you," said Will.

"So you are going to marry him, Nancy, instead of me?"

"Yes—if he wants me."

"I have no choice. I was born married to her, only it took me so long before I knew."

"Can you be happy—either of you—knowing what you are?"

Will looked up soberly. He could feel the first strength of returning pride and manhood beginning to rise in him. "Yes," he said, "I think we can. I think we love each other enough for that."

He looked at Nan and her eyes were shining.

And then outside they heard a swift commotion, and the glad cries of Milady. Truth and Nan turned quickly, Will more slow, because he hated to take his eyes from Nan's face. But he was in time to see his wife Doll as she tripped through the doorway. She was barefooted and her red dress hung in tatters; she had a streak of soot across her nose, and one eyebrow quite burned away. But she was alive and laughing. Doll Trasper was not the one to let a house fall down on her. She ran straight to Will and threw her arms around his neck.

"Oh, Will!" she cried. "Oh, Will, I thought I'd never, never get me out of that place! Oh, I'm so glad to be back to you! Oh, I love you so much!"

He held her in his arms woodenly, trying to collect his wits, but it was like trying to gather dead leaves awhirl in a swift wind.

He heard Truth gasp. He did not look at Nan, but he knew that she had sunk down on the bench nearest her.

"Where were you?" he finally managed to make himself say. "We thought you were dead. We found your lute."

"Oh, my poor lute! Is it burnt? And where can I get another with all the shops gone?"

"I—I'll get you another. There'll be shops in Southwark . . ." he said.

Milady had followed Doll into the tavern, and she could hold back her questions no longer.

"Doll, I know you're glad to see your man, but will you take your mouth off his long enough to tell us where you were that you didn't come home before? I was about to have prayers said for your soul—if I could find a whole church to do it in. Tell us now."

Doll pushed Will to a bench and sat down on his knee. He kept his arm around her but he did not feel the soft curves of her body. He might have been a wooden poppet clasping a poppet of rag.

"Well, I will tell you. And it was my lute that caused it all. When the Star caught from the hay in the stable it burned so fast and we all ran into the street so fast, I left my lute behind me. So I had to go back."

She waited for them to chide her but they did not. They knew as well as she that she had to go.

"And then the smoke hurt my eyes so—no flame, only smoke—that I groped to a door, and there were steps, and I fell down. Then I picked myself up in the cellar, and the stones turning hot all around, and I could not get out, and there was no light."

Will watched her bright, eager face as she told her story in words that tumbled over themselves. "I went from that cellar into another where the air was cooler, and then—well, you know how London houses were along the river there—all a web of cellars, and cellars under cellars—and then when the heat and smoke grew bad in the one I was in, I'd feel my way into another."

And there she had stayed, in the cool, stone water vaults, while London burned to death over her head. She had finally come to a deep-set chamber with an open window on the river, and she had put her head out that window and breathed the sharp, salt air. When she got hungry she opened a tub of pickled herrings she found, and when she thirsted, she broke the top off a bottle of old French wine and drank that. She had thought to crawl out the window and jump into the Thames and try to swim, but could never quite make up her mind to do it. And finally, as the stones cooled, she had worked her way above ground, and out through a network of fallen beams, and so come home.

"And the worst of it," she sighed finally, putting her arms around Will's neck, "was the way I got tired of pickled herrings—that and missing you."

"I—I'm glad, Doll—you didn't die," he said.

She pulled away from him, a little startled. "Well! I should hope you are!"

And then she jumped to her feet and caught his hand, looking down at him, her blue eyes alight with eager love.

"Oh, Will," she cried, "come up to our bed with me—and I'll tell you all—how I missed you every minute I was gone—and then we'll make love and go to sleep! I could sleep forever, I think—in a bed— after those cellar stones!"

Will bit his lip. "Doll . . ." he said.

"Come on!"

He got to his feet uncertainly. Doll had started up the stairs. He looked at Nan.

"Go with her, Will," she whispered. "It's our proper scorpions. You to go—and me to sit here."

Without a word he turned after his wife.

Milady had missed all of this, being in talk with a man at the doorway, and now she came back, smiling broadly under her rouge.

"Aye, it's just as I was saying to Sir Gilbert now. London was not a splendid city—it was a dirty, narrow, huddled, roaring, stinking town—but we loved it and we'll never have it back again, the way it was. Thank God, Dolly come home." She sprawled on the settle, kicking off her tight slippers. "It gave me a turn to see her. That's the fifth man I've had to send away this morning, Nan. They come and ask for you, and I can't seem to get it into their thick heads that you don't work here, that you're a guest. If you ever change your mind, you can have Audrey's bed."

"I may come to it at that," said Nan, smiling sadly. "I do not seem to be very happy in an honest life, and I've often been told my mother was the first whore in Portsmouth, the town I came from."

"There's worse things than being a whore," answered Milady placidly.

Truth came forward then and put his hand on Nan's shoulder. "O Christ Jesus, lead our hearts to wisdom," he said.

17. "Turn again, traveler!"

〰〰〰〰〰〰〰〰〰〰〰〰〰〰〰〰〰〰

"YOU NEW ENGLAND lads," said Sir William Warren, looking Will
Scarlock straight in the eyes as they stood together on the slimy
timbers of Wapping Stairs in the thin autumn rain, "have been here
before, and most times you come with a Bible in one hand and a
broadaxe in the other. But you've brought a broadaxe in both. I'd
welcome the change—if I wasn't like to lose money by it."

"You mean Massachusetts men. We don't carry Bibles much in
Portsmouth. Axes we have."

"I speak in parables, lad. What I mean is this: I gave you my
terms and you did not like them. You said you'd take your masts to
Pieter Vroot, that rascal Dutchman who hides in Hangman's Gains,
and sell them to the foes of your country—to make ships to fight
against England. If that's not wielding a broadaxe, what is it?"

Nan and Doll waited just behind him, sitting on the chest that
held all Nannie's clothes and her London purchases, the chest John
Scarlock had made for her when she was a little girl and taken to
Rafe Gee's forge for iron bindings. In a few minutes the three would
board one of Sir William's ships to sail to Boston in the fen country, to take Nan to Truth Damerill and their wedding, that was to
be now, after all. At Nan's feet rolled a great lumbering mastiff
puppy from Old Thorny that Sir William had just handed over to
them, Kit Harroday having sent it to Will in his care. Will knew
both girls were watching him and listening, but he looked only at
the bluff, ruddy face and thin, fair hair of the man he spoke with.

"I'll give you a parable back, Sir William. Where were you born?"

"What? I was born in Devon. In Islington by Hay Tor, where they cut the stone for London Bridge. But what the . . .?"

"Then tell me this, Sir William: comes great death, or plague, or battle—any doom—and on your one hand's the men of Islington by Hay Tor, and on the other the rest of England—and you could save but one. Quick and honest, which would it be?"

"Islington."

"And I was born in Portsmouth, and I'll put Portsmouth men and what's good for them first before all the world."

Sir William looked past Will at the brown, slipping river, alive with ships as big as country houses, at the roofs and steeples over in Rotherhithe.

"You have me at the wall," he said finally, "the last wall where all men turn honest. Do you know, Will Scarlock, that all who have aught to do with the Navy or knowledge of its plight are quaking in their shoes? The Dutch are coming on; Spain's great days over, but France beginning to rise a little. We're like to have foreign admirals sweeping the channel with a broom at the masthead again, the way they did in Cromwell's time; like to have them swarm up the Medway and run all over—and naught's to stop it but the fleet, and the fleet takes wood. England's forests are down the wind: a few oaks in the Andred Weald, and Scotch fir that'll do for yards and spars—but the great compass timbers and mast trees, where are they? They're oversea in the new countries, and we haven't got the money to bring them home."

"We still fight by the hollow ships," murmured Will. "Who says old time's coming down?"

"What's that?"

"Nothing. Mr. Pepys said the same as you and urged me to take what you offered."

"He ought to. I've given him enough plate, and white silk gloves for Mrs. Pepys. Gave you a sharp talk, did he? He's a fool for a wench, but wise at other points. Many a time the fleet's asked for bread and he's sent 'em back an invoice; cleverly writ, 'tis true, but you cannot feed hungry men with it. Listen, lad, it costs twenty thousand pounds a week to keep the ships afloat . . . bare afloat. I've offered you two pounds six a load, and a hundred pounds apiece for your tallest pines. For oak . . ."

"I wouldn't sell you our oak. 'Tis from too far north and the weather changes make it spongy as turnip. We don't use it ourselves

—to build ships with. We send to the Carolinas—theirs are dark brown horny wood and worth your money. But spruce, fir, pine—the mast trees—*And it's not so much what you pay for them . . .*"

"Ah! So now we come to it! I'm to hear your price at last?"

"Yes," said Will. "I have my price—like any other man." He felt the thin rain misting down on him and watched the fog close around the dreary houses and taverns and fish stalls crowding the river. A faint, charred smell still lingered in the air. "I want the mast trade out of Portsmouth to be for the men who rightly own the trees that'll be coming from there. We were taken over, sir, the way the Normans took over England and the Dutch would like to —we—"

Sir William dashed the rain from his eyes with an impatient hand. "I'll mix in no woodcutters' quarrel," he growled. "I want the masts. If you'll start rafting them down and shipping them over, so they come up Thames sound and dry and into my mast ponds there"—he shrugged his shoulder toward his great timberyards below the dock— "I don't care if they were cut by devils in hell. I . . ."

Will's eyes gleamed and he tossed his bare, brown head. "If *I'll* start rafting them down . . . ?"

"Who else? I can't call a man's name from Virginia to Newfoundland and say I know him—except yours."

"You mean I can . . . ?"

"I mean I have the King's paper in my pocket, appointing his purveyor of masts for the Royal Navy, from Portsmouth in Piscataqua, to come through Sir William Warren at Wapping Stairs. 'Tis blank. I can put any name to it."

"Put mine, and you'll get your trees."

"At my price?"

"At your price. I've already inquired about, and it's a fair one."

"Done. There's a scrivener up the street who'll have ink and quills. How long before . . . ?"

Will turned to the girls. "I'll be back," he said, looking at them, not smiling.

Doll made a face. "Hurry," she said. "It's raining down my neck, and I'm afraid the damp'll slacken my lute strings."

Under her cloak she carried the new lute he had bought for her in those strange, nightmare days after the fire a month ago, while London went on smoking, and he went doggedly about the mast business; while Truth announced that he would go down into Lin-

228

coln, that Nannie had promised she would come there and marry him; while Nannie said no word at all, just as she was saying none now.

"Yes," he answered, "I'll hurry." He followed Sir William across the cobbled square.

A sharp east wind that raked and whistled in from the North Sea drove them scudding across the Wash and up the reedy Witham almost a day earlier than they had planned, so Truth was not on the sagging wharf below Boston Stump to greet them when Will helped Doll and Nan ashore there in the thick, gray rain. They straggled past the cathedral with its flying buttresses of carved stone and great square tower that could be seen for twenty miles across the water-meadows, and got themselves into the Green Hound, west of the marketplace, between the corn stalls and the pillory pit. Over hot mulled ale and a cockle pie, when the generous inn fire had dried their clothes a little, Will asked Nan what she wanted to do. Doll had picked up her lute already and started to sing, very low, but loudly enough so that the men at the bar and tables turned her way and stopped drinking to listen. She finished one song, and they cheered, and she began another. The firelight flickering through the old, beamed room, where the ill weather had brought in dusk at noonday, lighted her rosy, young face, her dark hair tossed back in gay abandon. Will broke off his talk suddenly and sat watching his wife.

"She doesn't care that I'm with you, Nan. She doesn't know I'm with you. When she's singing she knows nothing else. She loves me best of all men, I think, but not so much as she loves a gilt frame and a set of strings."

Nan smiled sorrowfully. "And I'm to go to Truth—who loves God. He says he loves me, too, in spite of our wickedness together, and that his love may guide me to salvation. He says that he is loath to believe that I am doomed forever, and not like him, an anointed one, touched with God's grace."

"I know that talk. I heard it at Harvard College. Don't you believe in it, Nannie. It's all in the thoughts of men, and they're like the shadows of clouds blown across a field on a windy day. They come and go, and they're naught, but the field's still there. It's the field that matters, and the trees, and the men—the things you can reach out and touch."

And they looked desperately at each other, thinking of all the things they could not reach out and touch—not ever.

"Nan," he said, "the rain's let up. If—you—if you don't mind, I think I'll get a boat and ask the way, and take you down to him now—and leave you there."

"And not stay to see me married?"

"No. I—I want to get it over."

"Whatever you want, Will."

When they stepped into the flooded streets half an hour later, Doll stopped her music long enough to listen to their reasons and watch them go. As she stood facing them, the young mastiff, Watch, threw himself, heavily playful, against her, slobbering on her skirt, his head lifted for caresses. Doll frowned and drew back. His rough eagerness frightened her.

"Oh, Will!" she cried impatiently. "I'm all black and blue with that great thing thumping me! If he's to live with us, I'll get that suit of armor down from Old Thorny and crawl inside it, I swear I will."

Will looked crestfallen. "I wanted to take him home," he said. "He comes of good fighting stock—and of stock like mine—grown from the same land. I thought to start the strain in America. But if you don't like him . . ."

Nan stood still, waiting to be gone. Then impulsively she put her hand on the sleek, brindle head. "Let me have him, Will. I'll—I'll—" She could not finish. Doll looked at her with serpent's eyes, but she did not look at Doll.

"If you want him . . ." Will agreed wearily, turning to the door.

"Good-bye, Miss Nan," said Doll sweetly. "Your man's handsome, handsomer than mine—though it's mine I'd rather have. I wish you joy in his bed, and a long life, and many fine children." Then she turned. "You'll come back to me soon, Will?" She laid her mouth on his and kept it there. He bent his arms around her, then pulled away.

"Yes. I won't stop. I'll row down there and straight back."

Doll stood in the diamond-paned window for a few moments after they had gone, and watched them, two bent figures plodding through the old town in a gray-white mist under a gray-black sky—he carrying the oak chest, she holding her skirt from the floating weeds that grew where the street stones met, the dog ambling after. She frowned for a moment, and her delicate fingernails gripped the lute frame till tiny dents came in the gilt of it. "I don't know what's between them," she said to herself. "Maybe much. But I know that things have never been quite, quite right for us, and now they are all awry and wrong. All I can do is sing and love him—and somehow that is not enough. It was folly to scold about the dog—but when I am unhappy I want to scold, and now it seems I am never happy at all." Suddenly her brow cleared. "But he's leaving her now, and she'll be married—and then we shall be together again—as we were before she came." Boston men were calling her. She turned back to them, smiling. She began to sing.

None of Boston spread very far from the river, and they were soon in the boat Will had hired, pointing up the sluggish channel choked with water weeds, driving ahead on long, sure strokes for the open country.

"They told me to go up the river to Dogdyke Ferry, which I'm to know by the great thicket of pollard willows there, and then down a crooked waterway that winds south into Holland Fen. Nothing but marsh and sedge we're to see all the way, save a village here and there built out of the muck on piles. God, Nan, if you can stand the man you'll never stand the country! Come on home!"

Behind them in the sleepy little seaport town, fallen into decay in the time of Elizabeth, when the wine and wool trade dwindled because its waterways silted up and grew shallow, the great, famous swaying bells of Boston tossed themselves and rang out over the miles of drowned farmland linked by the threading streets of water. "Turn again, traveler, turn again to Boston Town!" Yes, she would turn there again, and again, and again, all the days of her life, thought Nan. She would come there with Truth when he met with his brother parsons, and she would come there for Saturday Market, to sell wool and goose eggs, and buy hornbooks and children's shoes. She would go fleeing in on hasty oars with half the countryside when the spring tides rose, driving the farmers round to take refuge in the nave under the great Stump. Will would come there only once again—to take his wife and go away—and then he would turn to Boston Town no more.

"I can't go home," she said gently. "You know why I can't go home to Portsmouth—and live in the same town with you and Doll all the years, and watch your children grow. You do mean Portsmouth, don't you? You are going there?"

"Yes. I'm going there. I've got in my pocket the thing our people sent me after. I'll be calling the tunes there now, and they won't be hymns, Nannie. What'll you do with the fishery?"

231

"Let it go on—just as if—I were coming back. John Billings runs it well, I know, and there's a good tenant on the Hampton land. You look to it for me."

"If you want. I know how you feel. I wouldn't sell Old Thorny either. Let Kit keep on with it. I'll see nobody cheats you."

"One thing, Will. I heard you say when we left Wapping—that about the masts. You wouldn't really have sold them to the Dutch, would you? To harm England?"

He smiled wryly, bending with the pull of the oars. "Never! I'm not a knave, but Sir William took it for granted I was, because he deals with little else. It was a trick to force him, and praise God, it served us well. Walter Neal told me how—that night in the boat. My father picked a man worth following. And I'll have to follow them both—out of England."

Behind them Boston bells quieted down. Because of the early dark, the sexton had kindled the beacon at the top of the high stone Stump, and its light gleamed on the slowly moving water all about, on the sleek, wet grasses, and banks of sedge plants dipping shoreless into the stream. Now and then a huge pike darted through the cloudy, brown water, or a welter of eels writhed and tangled away from the prow. Nan's thoughts went restlessly to the stories Truth had told her of his country, that would be her country now, the old Puritan shire that had bred the great gospel leaders for the new Boston in the new England—old country tales of how the ancient fenmen herded their cattle on stilts, and paid their taxes in mussel shells in a hard year. Nowhere stood up a hill or forest—only channeled fields and dikes, black windmills with silver sails hanging motionless, and here and there a lifting church tower. The gray sky grew darker and lower every minute, a sad wind mourned through the stunted aspens and alders they passed by, and coveys of wet geese and herons huddled on the tufts of plashy roots.

"Out of England," repeated Will. "England isn't my home, Nan. I've found that out. But neither is Portsmouth—not the way Old Thorny was home to my father. It's as if in leaving there he did a strange, cursed thing. It was more than a man's getting in a ship and crossing a sea, and building a new house in a new country—more than that, he did. It was like selling a birthright. Not like plucking out his own eye and leaving it at that, but like plucking it out a way so that his sons and his sons' sons would be one-eyed forever after. Does that sound like Tom Bedlam talking?"

"No. I can follow it with my mind, but not quite with my heart, for it could not be that way with me. Men have to have a country, and land, and a house; a father, and sons, and seasons coming by the way they always came. But women do not have to have all that. They only have to have the one thing."

He rested on his oars, looking at her. Wreaths of fog drifted over the bramble banks on either side of them, and sharp raindrops fell through the dark gray air, splashing in the dark brown water.

"I loved Portsmouth, and I loved my father," she went on, "but it's not his name I'll give my children. All women have to 'go out of England' when they marry, and always have, and what's back in the old blood doesn't matter to them. They haven't any home, and they haven't any country. What would be the use, when they'd keep it such a little while? I can be where I belong if I'm back in the willows by Newichwannock, or coming down London Strand in a satin dress. Just so long as you are there. That's what matters to me. That's all that matters to a woman."

"Then—Nan—just so long as we live—you and I will never be at home, never be where we belong?"

"No."

He bent toward her. "Nan. What shall we do? What do you want me to do?"

She lifted her face, white in the darkness, and they stared at each other. For a moment a light shone in her eyes, and then it went out. "There is only one thing we can do," she said, in tones as level as the fen country she would be spending her life in. "There is never any choice, Will. We think there is, but there is not—not ever. You will take me to Truth and leave me, and you will go back to your wife. You and she will sail for Portsmouth, and you will have a good life there, and stand up a strong man who will save his friends from their enemies. Because we are made the way we are, there is nothing else we can do."

He bowed his head and began to row again, with long, deep strokes. They turned at the pollard trees and drove forward through a forest of tall, drowned grasses, shimmering purple-gray in the light of the iron lanthorn fastened to the prow of their boat.

"No," he said, so low she could hardly hear him. "No. You are right, Nannie. We have no choice. No other way."

Ahead of them now, lights woke in the dripping mist, and a dike set with low trees stood up on their left.

"I—I think we're coming there, Will. I can see windows shining back from the water. It looks like a lath and plaster house with a tiled roof, and Truth said Wyethorne was like that. The trees lift and spread like elms, too, and he said there were elms."

The boat edged gently along a sturdy wooden landing stage built out on piles in the stagnant water. The rain had stopped.

"Good-bye, Nan," said Will. He bent forward and kissed her on the forehead, not as a man kisses a woman, but the way a pilgrim kisses a holy relic.

"Good-bye, my dear. We shall remember this—all the years—take strength from it."

He choked and muttered. A rush of tears washed suddenly over her face and she put her head down in her two hands.

"Oh, Nannie! Nannie! Nannie! To hell with what we are! There'll never be another time!"

And then they heard Truth's voice calling from the dike above.

"Will! Nancy! I heard the geese cackle and I came out to see why—and it is you! I was coming to Boston tomorrow. I hadn't thought you'd get here before that . . . !"

Nan dried her eyes and Will stood up and tossed a rope to Truth as he leaned over the narrow wharf above them. Sure enough, geese were cackling—about fifty thousand, one would think from the uproar—and along the riverside under the sallow trees a whole village of wicker nests rose up, tier upon tier in wooden frames, each nest full of feathers and beak and noise.

"My mother was a Cubbledyck from Frampton—all famous goose-farmers—and she can't get along without the creatures. You'll come up to the house now. Supper's hot and Will must stay the night. Nancy, I thought you would keep your word, but I do feel better now that I see you."

"No," said Will. The three of them stood on the landing now. Beyond the goose nests he could dimly make out fields and gardens, tidied after harvest, with the tall white house all alight in the middle of them. It was here that Nannie would live and lie down beside her husband, and grow old beside him. "No. We got here early because of the fresh wind. I left Doll in Boston, and I must go back to her—tonight."

"But you'll bring her out here tomorrow? And stay for our wedding? I want you to see the fens with the sunlight on them, Will. It's a fair country, better than your north, all sand and briars, better than the stone crags and great forests of America. You know they say the fens'll never change, so long as the grass grows up and the rain falls down, and sometimes it is good for a man to have that under him that does not change. It's an eerie landscape, I own, on a wet fall night, but in blue spring when the corn is waving—I want Nancy to love her home here."

He stood with his hand on Nan's shoulder, tall and lithe as a corn-stalk; a good man, and a manly man, and a proud one, generously forgiving them, wanting to be friends. To Will he seemed at that moment to be the arch-enemy, the fiend from hell, but Nan sud-denly felt her heart almost burst with pity for him. He was called Truth, but he would not face the truth—the truth that she would never be his, not if she slept in his bed for fifty years, and bore him sons, and got buried in these reeking bogs of his after it. She loved Will Scarlock, and she would never belong to any other man. Truth would have nothing, nothing all his life . . . but men are that strange perhaps he would never know it. Suddenly she realized they were talking without her.

"History's hare and hounds," said Will, "and what's hound today is hare tomorrow. You Puritans did your share of hunting under Cromwell—God knows you're still doing it at home. But here all's against you, and you're the quarry, gone to den in a swamphole. What'll you preach to? Ducks?" He was standing now in the boat below them, looking up at Truth, his gray eyes bright, and bitter, and mocking.

Truth laughed. He could. It was his arm that closed round Nannie Knight. "No, to men, Will—and good ones—sick of Popery and hungry for the Word. They flock along the dikes, and their boats thrust out of every water alley, quiet in the evening, when the word goes out we're to meet. Wet won't keep the fenmen home when they've aught to go abroad for. We're all born webfooted. This week we have been building our church—with bricks we floated in by barge, and a poor thatch roof, the better to hide it among the cottage thatches. I shall soon be interpreting the will of God there. I believe that His great days are about to come on—now little groups like us arise all over England."

Will picked up his oars. He did not look at Nan. I shall never look at Nan again, he thought. He lifted his gaze only as far as the wooden floor where young Watch sat, his amber eyes glowing, his thick tail thumping the deals. All about went up the hiss and babble from the geese in their wicker nests, disturbed by the voices and lanthorns, and he remembered there had been great flocks of Lin-

235

coln geese about on the day of his Goose Fair marriage that seemed a hundred years old to him now.

He looked at Truth, then motioned toward Watch.

"You're getting a good dog there. Got him on Old Thorny—one of the Lyme Hall strain from Cheshire, 'way back. Take care of him," he said gruffly. He could say take care of my dog. He could not say take care of my girl, my Nan. But Truth caught his meaning. For the first time his proud shoulders drooped, doubt and fear and pain came in his dark eyes as he stood alone there under the dark—his arm round Nan, but still alone.

"I'll do that," he muttered.

They said no more. No "Joy of your wedding," no "Good voyage home." Blindly Will shoved the boat into midstream. He did not want to look back where the two would be turning toward the lighted house under the dripping, swaying trees. And he did not feel the rain, nor the dank wind that blew across the fens that autumn night. He was not aware of the pollard trees by Dogdyke Ferry, but he must have passed them, must have rowed and steered, for the next thing he knew the lights of Boston thickened and brightened ahead, and he heard the great bells of Boston Stump booming down the air:

"Turn again, traveler, turn again to Boston Town!"

And then he thought suddenly of all those men who had sailed out of Boston in his father's day, just as his father had gone from Nottingham. They had all gone oversea, these men here, for different reasons, and taken new country, and put the curse of homelessness on their sons. Massachusetts, Virginia, Piscataqua Country—saints and sinners, godly and ungodly, friends and enemies, fishers, preachers, fellers of trees. Some felt their doom more than others, but none could quite escape it. "In three generations they return again," he knew for an old saying, but he knew that these men would not return. He had tried it in his own time, with his own blood and heart and body, tried it hard and failed, and his sons would be further away, and like to do worse instead of better. And then his own sorrow, that he had found for himself, that did not come down to him from his father, welled up like the welling river, and he wondered if any of all the travelers, outbound from Boston never to return there, had left behind them with their pulpits and thatched houses anything they loved as much as he loved Nan Knight. And he did not think they had.

236

All the years

THE years of the Great Crossings were over now, and to sail from London to Piscataqua was no longer a dream and an adventure, but a common thing. More ships traveled the sea roads, carrying salt and spices, and wine and oil, masts, and fish, and Yorkshire woolens, and beaver hides, and Virginia tobacco, and Jamaica rum, and Bibles printed in Paternoster Row. But not so many men went nowadays. The prentices, who had sailed off thumbing their noses, had turned into grandfathers, portly, and falling asleep to snore after supper, right in the middle of their praises of old time. The householders had cleared the fields along the coast, and their children had cleared the fields beyond the first row of hills, and felt comfortably certain their children would go on beyond that. And the soldiers of fortune had simply gone out of fashion, like coats of mail and the ruffs of Drake and Raleigh. Massachusetts had set up the Profession of His Truth, and the other colonies had set up Trade, and Massachusetts had not scorned that either. The new man had grown with the new country, but no man could say, in Will Scarlock's time, just how much of England he had in him—in truth, no man has ever said —but it was not enough to make him go back there and put his roots down. In Will's time, the breath of God did not blow strong upon a man, driving him willy-nilly, as it had in those blessed early days. No spirit of the time walked abroad, by wind, or land, or water, to guide him, and no pillar of fire moved before. He had to choose his own way, and make it himself, once it was chosen.

The way Will chose took him back to Portsmouth with his wife Doll, and he came there with the first snows of winter and went into the woods, the Mast Master, who must give up all his time to the trees. And there it was that he learned, in the midst of icy drifts, and frostbite, and great pines crashing down, that time does not move in ordered squares in an almanac; that years can go over a man between two sunsets, when he stands alone under the dark, and takes his life out of his mind and looks at it, and faces what it must be.

All the years would be like this one now, and he lived them all in the one. There would be the seasons' changes coming across the landscape, the iron of autumn striking to root and bone, and winter wearing out through endless Marches, and each of them bringing a change to the tasks in hand. There would be the things he could touch, food and clothes, and the shoulders of friends gathered for good talk in the tavern after supper, and the body of his wife Doll in the bed at night. There would be the thoughts he must think: counting house thoughts, worked with a quill and ledger, having to do with so many feet of pine for so many shillings, or how to make a tree fall the way it should—and he would grieve himself with no other thoughts but these. And hardest of all, he could not wander empty in time, like the gray, robed ghost of himself that he felt he was. He must be Will Scarlock, and stand up, a man with other men, and give and take, and walk alive in the streets of Portsmouth, and have a strong arm for his mother, a wise word for his sister's sons, and a tender kiss for his wife. All the years would be like this, and they would not be empty, there would be much in them—too much—but there would never be Nan Knight. For Nan would be married now—looking for a child, maybe—gathering goose eggs, and riding to market over the flooded rivers, seeing the light shine out from Boston Stump when she blew out her candle at night and went into the bed of his old friend, Truth Damerill. This whole countryside spoke to him of Nannie, for she had always been with him here, but she would not come to him here again.

He remembered the days when they were little in old Strawberry Bank before it got its English name, children playing in the sedge and disagreeing over the hornbook—once an idea's written down in words, it's something that everyone will disagree over, even a male child and a female child in dame school. Better not to write them down in words. Better to keep them in your own mind, like the waters of a frozen brook. He had a faded diary of his father's that he had found hidden away under the attic eaves, and in these last few months he had read it over and over, and found more wisdom and comfort there than in all John Evelyn or Thomas Tusser, or the Bible, or the Iliad. But he would never leave a book like it for his sons to find after he was dead. His thoughts were nothing he'd want to pass on to them.

Once when he was going home in a spring twilight, he saw Sam Fernald standing with his new wife at the edge of the salt marsh, half hid by cat o' nine tails, and they were laughing the way he and Doll used to laugh. He saw the two sharp-cut figures through the shimmering of the reeds, saw Sam put his hand to her bosom. O Christ, he thought—not Christ like the men swear by at the mast pond, but Jesus Christ like they call on in the churches—what shall I do? How can I stand this all the years?

18. No need for a gypsy

"Ho, WILL, they want the mast master!"

"Who?"

"Richard Cutt and Brian Pendleton."

"I thought they would," said Will Scarlock.

He stood in water to the knee, at the edge of Johnny Crowther's beach, a great drift of logs crowding the little cove there, his head bare and his brown hair blowing in the soft May wind. His eyes smiled but his mouth set in a hard line.

"You can tell them where to find me."

The embarrassed logger moved away toward the road where Will could see from the corner of his eye the two plump figures in scarlet and gold lace which they were sanctioned to wear because their estates would warrant it. He looked out over the blue river into Kittery, and then back at the town, its low roofs half hid in a burst of apple blossoms, and then even his mouth smiled. There was little enough of joy in this life, but, by God, he was going to like the next ten minutes of it.

He clambered out on the shale and stood, leaning on the long pole with the iron hook at its bottom that he had used to herd the timber sticks in from the current like so many stray sheep. All around the banks of Piscataqua the mast men were toiling, wading, lifting, shouting at each other, trying to load the winter's cutting into the fleet that had made port yesterday to carry the precious masts back to Sir William Warren at Wapping Stairs. Wapping Stairs, thought Will. It seemed like something in a dream or a book he'd read once

—Priam's city or the cave of Dido—nothing a man could sail to in six weeks' time, which it was.

"Goodman Scarlock!" There was less of rage than of outrage in the tones of Brian Pendleton's pompous crying. Will turned, his hands in the pockets of his leather breeches, to face the rich merchants who ordered all affairs in Portsmouth—who *had* ordered them.

"Yes, sir."

"What is this we hear? That you have the King's papers on you?"

"They're not on me. They're at my father's house on the old Doctor's Island. I'll show them to you there, if you want."

"We went," said Richard Cutt grimly, "as we always have, to the fleet captain to sell our masts. And he said he could buy and transport no cuttings that were not stamped, approved, and recommended by his Majesty's Mast Master, Will Scarlock."

"He's right. He can't."

"We've had no word of this from the General Court of Massachusetts."

"It so happens," said Will, "that his Majesty, King Charles by the Grace of God, can get up and lie down, and make known his own pleasure without consulting the General Court of Massachusetts. And that he's done."

"You've come on mightily in pride for a lad whose father whistled to a team of horses, but you needn't think to best us because you were bred in the College. What hell broth did you brew in London?"

"No hell broth. I made a contract to get masts out of our Piscataqua Country for the Royal Navy, and I'm doing it—look there!"

Five great ships rode in the seething blue stream, and alongside every one of them the men toiled with ropes and pulleys to lift the long, lopped pine stems aboard.

"It just happens," said Will, smiling, "that this spring I was able to fulfill his Majesty's requirements without your help. Maybe in three or four years we might take a pine or so from your uplands, but don't count on it."

"Will Scarlock, we inquired along the dock before we came here, and we know what you have done. Without a word to the Select Men or the elders at the Meeting House, you have bought the trees your friends had to sell—your friends, the churchmen, the iniquitous, those who call themselves 'the old stock' and boast that they or their fathers came in the *Warwick* with the villain Neal; who rebel as hard as they dare against the righteous law and custom we brought here from Massachusetts. You have bought their trees and paid the King's good gold to them—and the rest of us—our timber lies rotting in the mast ponds. 'Twill be quite destroyed before the fleet returns again."

"Yes, it will. You better cut it up for pipe staves and sell it in Barbados. You won't get half the mast price, but a little's better than naught."

"Is this honest dealing?"

"Yes, I believe so. I deal honest with all men—but I deal with honest men first. The others must wait. Ten, twenty, thirty years, maybe by then there'll be a shortage of timber among the honest men and I'll have to buy from rogues—but not now lads, not now, and by the way our woods look, not for a good long time. You can burn your trees to keep your houses warm. I don't want them."

Brian Pendleton's throat swelled like the wattles of a cross goose.

"Do you mean this is going on?" he fumed. "That you're the ruler of all the mast trade, and that you refuse to deal with those you disapprove of?"

"Yes. That is what I mean. 'Tis a way I learned from watching the General Court at Boston."

"We'll petition the King—"

"You better save your quills and paper. He'll turn to his own Commissioners and ask about you, and you know what they had to say when they were here. They'll say you belong to the party that killed his father. They'll say you're at one with Massachusetts, and when you name that colony to him, he holds his nose. You won't petition the King."

Will spoke easily, lifting his eyes from the hot, indignant faces of the merchants to the sea gulls going over in the bright air, almost disappearing as their whiteness crossed below a fleece of white cloud. He did not need to look at Richard Cutt to know that his small eyes had grown smaller; the tone of the question told him.

"Well—what do you want? How many pounds?"

"You mean to let you go on having your way in Portsmouth as you've done ever since you got rich?"

Cutt and Pendleton looked down at the spring dust blown through the tough green witch grass underfoot, and up the winding river street, to their houses flanked with fields and orchards, wharves and warehouses, the windmill, the cornmill, the sawmill, the tannery. They had all these, and these were worth money. But the future was all in the mast trade and they knew it—and they meant to share.

"We mean we want to sell timber trees," said Brian Pendleton finally. "And we can pay for the right—if we have to."

"Not my price, I'll wager. I'm to be bought, but you won't buy me."

"Why not? Who can pay more?"

"Sirs, it's only this—but I know you won't give it to me. We're four little towns on the edge of a great wild country, but a rich one. We're not safe or strong. Our men are valiant to stand alone, but they cannot always. The Indians are quiet just now, but they do not love us—they will be our enemies till they or we are dead. Wolves carry off our sheep in the night, sometimes our children. Cold, and hunger, and disease are never very far. Oversea the old, sharp countries are all set about to take what they can of our goods and give us naught for it. We should stand together like a house of brothers—but each brother to be free, as we were here in the first days, none to tell the other what to do, so long as he wreaks no harm on man or property. I'll buy your masts, and gladly. You shall have your share of the King's gold, and I'll only ask but this—that you take down the stocks and the whipping post; that you who want to be godly stay godly, and let the rest of us run as we will. That you leave to us who want them our Prayer Book, and our old ways, and the land our fathers came here and cleared for us. We shall not meddle with you. We don't care how you spend the Sabbath—you can listen to sermons, and we'll play football on the Town Common. And we'll get to heaven as soon as you will, but we'll each go there the way of his own choosing. Let every man look to his own plate and leave his brother alone—except to help him. We can all share in the goods and the gold that'll come of this country. That's my price, gentlemen. Do you have masts to sell?"

Richard Cutt and Brian Pendleton looked at each other for a long moment, and Will Scarlock looked at both of them. He looked at the sunny river, alive with shouting men and great ships, wallowing logs, and little darting boats. He looked downstream to where the chimney of his house rose through the feathery green elm boughs —where Doll would be sitting with Joan, silent and spiritless in the long, mild afternoon. All the hot pleasure of triumph went out of him, and he could feel the hard, proud, laughing lines of his face sag like an old man's.

"No," said Brian Pendleton coldly. "At that price—we have no masts to sell."

They turned and left him, pompous anger bursting from every line of their well-fed, well-clad bodies. A wind-wracked elm grew there, just at the sea's edge, its twined roots helping to hold the bank together, and he put his hand out and laid his palm flat against the shaggy bark of it.

"Oh, the hell with them," he muttered. "They'd rather lose money than lose their grip on people's throats. Why's it so fair a thing to be able to tell other men what to do? I don't think I'd ever find it so." He turned his face toward the Point of Graves, all green and smooth around the quiet stones of the dead. "Father," he whispered, "Father." Nobody answered him from anywhere. And then he said, even more bitterly, "Nannie . . ."

White sails were blowing upriver, around the end of Great Island, not big enough for a mast ship—maybe a ketch from the Barbados or no further off than Newburyport—nothing he'd have to be at the dock to meet. He flung down his wood hook and started home.

Joan Scarlock moved about her clean-swept kitchen, quiet, and unobtrusive, watching her daughter-in-law. She's unhappy, she thought; homesick for England, maybe—maybe sad some other way. I wish I knew, so I could tell her nothing's ever so bad as it seems when you're young. Nannie loved him, and I'd hoped he'd marry her, but he didn't, he married this one. And we two—there's something we share that Nannie can never understand because she's always had money in her pocket. We're just dust blown down the common street, this Doll and I. I was born in St. Nicholas' workhouse, and she grew up in a house on London Bridge, and we both earned our bread in taverns. I—I must be good to her. I mustn't always be wishing he'd married Nan, just because her people came with me in the *Pied Cow*. . . . She crossed to the fireplace, lifted the lid of the kettle swung on the iron crane, and peered at the bubbling stew.

"I hope this will be done by the time Will gets home. Did he tell you when to look for him?"

Doll glanced up from the table where she sat bending over scribbled sheets of paper. Will had been teaching her to write, so that she could put her songs down, and she had clapped her hands and laughed at the idea. She seldom laughed now. She had never thought to come to a country that had a law against singing girls in taverns. She had never thought there was such a country. Nor a country that would not let her wear a scarlet dress because she did not own enough houses and land. Will had promised her that next year they would have enough for that. In the meantime Joan had sewed her a gown of plain russet, for Doll could not sew. She could not cook, or clean well, or make a bed so anybody would want to sleep in it. And after a while Joan gave up trying to teach her.

Today she had put a sprig of apple blossoms in her hair, the pinkest ones she could find, and the full blown petals had come off here and there and clung to her dark locks and white neck.

"He said he'd come by five," she answered listlessly.

"Well, it's that now." Joan went to the window that faced toward town. She looked out at the green land sloping down to the salt marsh, past the spring where she had fallen that day in winter long ago. Yes, she could see him striding across the furrows, his head flung back and his hair blowing. Oh, she thought, he looks so much like Johnny! She turned to meet him at the door.

He came in soberly, smiled at her, and put his hand on Doll's shoulder, bending to look at her wild, painful script.

"You're doing better," he said, smiling down on her uptilted face, "but you're not quite ready for Harvard College. What are we eating, Mother?"

"Stewed beef and dried apple pudding. You'll have to wait about twenty minutes though. Are the boys going to be here?"

"No. They're with Ralph Twamlin's crew, still loading masts, and they said not to wait for them, they'd eat at Webster's tavern on the way home. Where's Joannie?"

"Over at Martha Everie's helping with the baby. You'll have to go fetch her home before bedtime."

He gazed around the orderly kitchen, all savory now with the smell of boiling meat. It had looked the same way the first time he could ever remember it, when he was a little boy. None of the house had changed at all. But the trees in the yard were taller and there was more gray in his mother's hair.

"I'll go over about dark then. Don't you want to come, Doll, and see what's going on at the Bank?"

"I don't care," she said. "It doesn't matter what they do. I'll go if you want me to."

"We could row downriver if you'd rather. The moon's about full, and we could go ashore on Great Island and see all the new houses there. Or maybe down as far as the Fort. The fleet brought a great stock of arms for it, arquebuses that cock with a wheel and can carry a three-ounce ball, and sakers and murtherers, besides small arms. I hear the great guns will be set up by tonight and they may shoot them off to try them. If you want to . . ."

He had his back to the door, facing Doll and his mother, and he heard nothing behind him, but he saw their faces change sharply. Into Doll's blue eyes came a look of woe, but Joan drew back in something that he read for fear. He turned around, and just as he did, the whole room sounded with the deep, gruff baying of a great dog. There on the threshold stood the young mastiff, Watch, seeming almost double the size he had been when Will had shoved him ashore on the wooden landing at Wyethorne in the Holland Fen.

"She's back," whispered Doll. "I knew that she would come."

"Will!" Joan's fingers caught his arm. "That dog! Where'd it come from? I could swear 'tis the one your father left in England near forty years ago."

He did not answer either of them. He waited. But all inside of him he felt the way a brook must feel when the ice of winter breaks and thaws and leaves it, to live and move again under the sun. He knew now that the quick steps would come running across the ledge under the apple trees, and he waited for that. And they did come, and Nan stood in the doorway, all the spring twilight of blossom, and green, and ruddy water spread out behind her, and she more lovely than any of it.

Joan was the first to move, and she went quickly forward and put her arms around Nan and kissed her.

"Oh, Nannie," she cried, "I thought you'd never come to us again. I thought you were married in England. . . ."

Will did not speak, nor Doll.

"No," said Nan, smiling at Joan, "I didn't marry in England. I found I couldn't after all. And I wanted to come home."

Then she looked at Will without seeing him at all.

He went forward carefully, holding out his hand. "Nan," he said as well as he could, "you know we're glad to see you—we—"

And then Doll rose, and tossed her dark head, and came up to them, smiling.

"Sit down and have supper with us," she said, "and tell us why you didn't marry that handsome man of yours." She twined her arm through Will's.

And they did sit down, around the worn, old trestle table, but they forgot about the stew boiling away to nothing on the fire, forgot that most people light candles when twilight comes on. They sat long in the growing dusk, Doll very close to her husband, and Nan told how it happened that she had come home.

"We had to wait three weeks, you know, for the banns," she began soberly. "Truth's mother was kind to me, a thin gray woman, like a piece of linen that's faded with too many washings. And two Sundays we went after dark to his little half-built church set on a dike where three crooked rivers come together and dwindle away in reeds. And it was the third Sunday, and the day after, we would be married. I woke up very early in the morning and went to the window. November it was, and the light all cold and white and clear over the gray and russet grasses, and the low, black trees, and the winding, brown water. And I looked at it, and I thought: tomorrow when I marry him, I shall marry this, too, and I shall have to stay with both of them all the days of my life. I have given my word, and I have to do it. And then a wicked voice spoke in me and said, 'Why do I have to?' and then it said, 'I do not have to at all.'

"And do you know what I did then? I put on my cloak and slipped out of the house with Watch, and took a boat of theirs and rowed to Boston. From there I went to London and back to Lady Catherine, and I lay three weeks in her house, sick with cold, and a fever, and the trouble of it all. But I grew better after a while, and I stayed with her through the winter. And then—and then—I came home."

Her voice dropped and died away.

Will cleared his throat. "Didn't Truth come after you and try to get you back? He must have known where you'd go."

"No, he never did. Perhaps he was too hurt and angry. Perhaps he never really wanted me."

He laughed harshly. Joan could sense agony all around her, but she could not quite tell which of the three was suffering, or whether they all were, or why. She got up and walked a little uncertainly to the door, and stood there, her hand on the dog's blunt head, her cheek pressed against the oak frame her Johnny had hewn from a living tree long ago.

She wants to talk to him alone, thought Doll. I must let her talk to him alone; say it, get it over, whatever it is. She jumped up suddenly and went to Joan in the doorway.

Then, for the first time, Nan and Will looked at each other deeply, looked into each other's eyes, each of them seeing only the soul and not the flesh at all.

"I had to come, Will," she whispered. "I couldn't stay away from —from where you are. Catherine said to come—not to let anything else matter. She spoke of herself and Walter—how they had lost—all the years."

"I—I'm glad, Nan," he said very low. And then they sat silent, not looking at each other, having no more words.

Leaning in the doorway, Joan spoke under her breath. "Trouble . . ." she breathed. "There'll be trouble . . . I can see."

Then she realized Doll stood beside her, still smiling faintly, still holding up her head. "What do you mean, Mother Joan? Can you tell fortunes? Do you have gypsy blood like my mother had?"

"No," said Joan ruefully, looking out at the moonlit river below the dark trees on the headland, "no, I'm no gypsy." And in her heart she added, "But it doesn't take a gypsy to see trouble when it's this plain."

19. My sins and go to hell

H<small>IGH</small> <small>SUMMER</small> burned itself out in shimmering blue haze above
Piscataqua Country. Green corn stood higher than a man's
head, tasseling into golden silk as the ripe ears burst open. The hay
was cut and stacked, the pea crop past and gathered, and the root
crop heaving and cracking the ground open as it swelled into white
and purple and amber fullness that would taste sweet in the stew pot
all winter long. For winter would come, and the mast men go into the
deep woods again, and Will Scarlock had spent half the hot summer days there preparing for it. He had gone up all the rivers
round, Sturgeon Creek, Salmon Falls, and Spruce; Newichwannock,
Cocheco, Oyster, Swampscot, and Lamper-eel; even the grass-choked
brooks wandering through the low alder thickets toward Hampton
and Greenland. He had gone to choose the great pines for his Majesty's mast fleet, and cut the Broad-Arrow mark of the British Ordinance in the sleek bark of those he wanted. Nothing that did not
measure twenty-four inches through by the time it had risen three
feet from the ground would do for him, and he did not visit the
woodlots held by the Halls, the Wiggins, and others of the Puritan
party. He could find more than enough that suited him without.
Along the Cocheco they were laying out another townland above
Dover Bounds, and northwest of Exeter, still another town beyond
the head waters of the Lamper-eel.

England would not get masts from here forever, he thought. The
trees would go; not only the tall white pines, but the birches and
butternut, the oak, the ash, the spruce, the beech, chestnut, maple,
mountain laurel, hemlock. Farms and towns would lie all around

Great Bay and run up into the land beyond; New Hampshire would be all as green and smooth as England, he thought. But not in his time. He remembered the fine ideas he'd had when he read the *Silva* first, ideas of cutting sparsely and seeding over, and keeping the forest as it was here, so that it could furnish wood to England forever. But now his thoughts no longer ran that way. Why should New Hampshire exist only as a timberyard for the sake of England? Why shouldn't it be a country in its own right, with its own cities as well as forest, and its own fleet to cut masts for? It would be, maybe. He couldn't tell. He only knew that his work was to get the trees down, but he went at it now with the urgency of a double reason.

After he had surveyed and planned the winter's cutting, he stayed at Hogstye Cove for a while, and got his brothers-in-law to help him, and the three of them built a small, tight house there on the land his father had given him with the old Indian deed, signed by the wizard Passaconaway. One hot day in August when the house was all done but setting a few more bricks in the chimney, he coaxed Doll and Nan into the big shallop with the sail in the middle, and took them upriver to look at it.

They moved swiftly upstream in the bright morning, the flood tide and what little wind there was carrying them along. Doll sat on a keg of nails in the stern and played on her lute and sang to them, seeming happier than she had for a long time. Will held to the tiller, and Nan trailed her hand over the side in the blue, salt water. They met and hailed other boats like theirs, farmers going to trade at the Bank, or headed for the open sea and a day of inshore fishing, some of them loaded with ears of green corn and baskets of blackberries, others with the brine-crusted slat cages that could be baited, lowered overside, and drawn in full of lobsters. At the top of the Long Reach, Digory Frost called to them from a large, flat, shallow boat full of sweet hay from his uplands that he was taking across to Tam McQuayne, whose grass was mostly salt.

Then they came to where the rivers parted: where Dover Point ran down from the north, a long sliver of hill with a town and a church and a growth of pine wood on top of it; where the green, stone-walled farms on Bloody Point reached up from the south. To the east ran the Fore River, straight into the sandy pineland and old fur country of Newichwannock. To the west, the Back River turned sharply, flooding along the broad, sedgy reaches of Great Bay. And between the Points, where the Piscataqua split itself in two, the water foamed and boiled, and shifted in great heaving circles that could drag down a live ox, or a struggling man, or a good-sized boat, and spew forth no traces, save maybe a splintered plank or a broken body drifting into Kittery Foreside in a week or ten days' time.

"I said this was worse than shooting London Bridge," said Will to Nan, "and now that I've done both, I say it again. Look, Doll, this is where our country gets its name from; this is where the rivers part."

Doll had had her eyes closed for the last five minutes, trying to pretend that the water dancing under them was the Thames—say in front of the Three Cranes in the Vintry, the way it used to be before the fire, and that she could go ashore if she wanted to, and out to Moorfields, to play, and be loved, and clapped, and listened to. "Here's Doll!" "Here's Doll Trasper!" "She's going to sing, 'Kissing goes by favor!'" "She's going to sing, 'Cuckholds all a-row'!" "She's going to sing, 'Oh, the green leaves they grow rarely'!" She opened her eyes, but she did not see the Vintry. She saw a field of Indian corn with pumpkins yellowing at the foot of the tall stalks, a small frame house here and there, and a thick tangle of trees coming down to the water ledges.

"What did you say to me?"

"I said this is the rivers' parting."

"Oh, it's all such a sad, lone country. I . . ."

She was going to say, "I want to go home," but then she thought better of it. Suppose they met her words with a silence that said, "Well, if you want to, we won't stop you." She picked up her lute and tossed back her soft, curling hair. "I'm going to sing, anyway," she said, and she did sing, a sad old Scottish ballad of maids betrayed by daemon lovers.

Nan felt as if she had just seen a thing she should not see, a passage between the other two that should have happened only in their chamber at night, and not before a third, and she did not know why she felt that way. Their words had been common enough. She stared unhappily at the slate-colored depths of tide as Will took to the oars to force them evenly through the dangerous water race, keeping close to the south shore.

There's another curse on our Goose Fair marriage, he was thinking somberly. It isn't enough that I don't love Doll—she and I can't even live in the same country and be happy. She belongs in London, and

I belong here—more than anywhere else. He looked at Nan for comfort, but Nan was still gazing into the water.

Hogstye Cove on the Great Bay had a beach of broken rock fringed with rank, yellow grass, and a sweep of old field where the Indian squaws hoed corn before this country had ever seen a white sail from England. South of the field rose a thick oak grove where the men from Exeter used to pasture their swine in the old days, giving the place its name. Will's new house stood half up the slope, small and square, with a glass-paned window in each wall, a chimney up the middle, and room in the slanting roof for dormers, if he wanted them later on. The cleared land all about was a riot of tangled grass, herbs, and weeds, for he had not plowed it yet, and behind, a thicket of blackberry vines sprawled to the circling pine wood heavy with lush, purple fruit that sweetened all the summer air. A brook flowed out of the black pools of bog just under the wood, and willow and alder shoots followed its crooked course downward to the Bay. Silvery green weeds grew half in the water, too, and sharp, scarlet flowers on slender stems that Doll ran to gather with cries of delight.

They had walked about the house now, inside and out, and praised it. Nan had said he was a good builder, and Doll had promised she would try to learn to cook and keep it for him. They had eaten the cold ham pie and pease pudding Joan had made them take along, and the sun had just one minute past moved over the noon line into the west.

"When Doll has enough flowers, we could pick some blackberries," said Nan. "I know you want to work."

"Yes." He stood in the doorway and looked up at the low eaves sloping almost to his head. "The chimney's tall enough, but it needs a coping. There's a clay bank where the oaks run down, and I made and burnt the other bricks there. It just means making a few more, and I'd like to get it done this afternoon."

They smiled at each other as deeply as they dared, and went to where Doll stood, half in the brook, plucking her red flowers. She twisted her slight body away from the clinging alders and came to meet them, her arms full of green fronds and scarlet petals. Her eyes sparkled and she put a finger to her lips.

"Hush!" she whispered. "Don't you tell the Select Men, don't you tell the minister, and those hard, cold, grim, dull, gray folk at the Bank—don't you tell them there's something scarlet here that pays no

252

taxes in the Meeting House! They'd come with hooks and hoes to root them up and burn them out with fire."

"They're your color, Doll," he said. "You look more like yourself when there's something red about you. I'm going to burn bricks."

"I thought we could pick blackberries, Doll," said Nan. "You've never tasted one of Joan's blackberry pies, served up hot with clotted cream."

Doll put her arms around Will's neck and kissed him. "Go burn bricks if you want to," she said. "We'll work, too. We'll pick berries."

Without a word he went down the field into the oakwood, and Doll and Nan climbed the hill to the blackberry brambles. They dropped the fruit into the baskets Joan had packed their dinner in, and they ate more than they picked, and they talked together.

An uneasy friendship had grown up between them, cherished on Doll's side because she had no one else who would know what she meant when she talked about shopping in Paul's Walk, and singing at the Old Serpent and the Star. Will's sisters were kind to her, but puzzled and forgiving rather than understanding, and they lived away on their farms with their husbands and children and she did not see them often. And in the rest of town whispers had gone their way. "What do you think of the wife Will Scarlock brought home?" "They say he found her in a house on London Bridge." "They say she can't stir the porridge without burning it." "They say all she can do is play the lute." "They say . . ." "They say . . ." She had not looked for friends in a town that forbade "rude music in alehouses," and she had not found any—and besides, when she was with Nannie she knew what Nannie was doing, knew she wasn't kissing in corners with Will. No woman ever really trusts any other woman. And Nan, for her part, understood Doll's unhappiness better than Doll did herself, and pitied it —except in those bitter moments when she had to watch the girl caressing Will. She remembered, too, those guilty days after the Fire when they had been glad—and she was very gentle with Doll.

"That looks like a myrtle," said Doll, pointing to a low, gnarled tree just beyond the brambles. "Do you think it is, Nan?"

"I don't know. I don't even know if myrtle grows here. Do you like it?"

"It's sacred to my goddess—myrtles are, and sparrows. I do not pray to Christ, you know. I pray to Venus."

Nan was shocked in spite of herself.

"Why?"

"Because she can give love and beauty, and I do not want anything else."

"Oh, you do too, Doll! You want sons—some day—don't you?"

"I don't know—But then, she must be able to give sons, too, for how are we to get sons without love and beauty? Perhaps you women in this cold country have a different way, but I doubt 'twill ever be much in favor."

Nan was silent. Then she said, "You want another thing, Doll. You want another thing more than you want love and beauty. You want to make songs, and sing them, and have people listen to you."

They looked at each other across a thorny bough heavy with blackberries.

"Yes," said Doll slowly, wonderingly, "I think . . . I do . . ."

And then they heard him calling below the oakwood, and he was calling for his wife. "Oh, Doll! Doll! Come here to me!"

Doll turned slowly away and set her basket down and walked across the field, her slim shoulders drooping. Nan stood all alone in the brambles, the hot tears stinging her eyes. You could never take a man away from a girl who prayed to Venus.

Will was packing clay in the molds lined with flat stone under the rough oven he had built, when he heard the hail at the waterside. He turned around and looked up. Two men were there in a small sailboat, one getting ashore, the other shoving off. He recognized Blake Cotterill's boat—Blake in it, of course. The other man? The man coming toward him, tall, young, his shoulders bent a little, his dark hair blowing under his high-crowned hat, now his dark eyes, his well-known face . . . it was . . . it was . . . Truth Damerill. And then somehow he knew that it meant nothing to him at all. Truth was no longer his enemy. Truth could not take Nan away. He knew that now. He need not be afraid any more. He could only be sorry for the man who had been his friend, the man who had communed with God and studied Ramus while he went out in Cambridge breaking windows with the other lads.

"Truth," he said, stepping forward. "Will you believe—I'm glad to see you?"

It was Truth, but somehow not the Truth he had known. The face was paler and a little sallow, the eyes darker, if possible, and the man was thin . . . his well-cut clothes hung about him. "Truth . . ." he said again, faltering.

"Yes, Will. You're wondering what happened to me. I've been in gaol. You've seen Nancy, so you know she left me."

"Yes. I—I'm sorry about everything."

"I know. All of us are, I think. Will it ever be mended?"

"No."

"While I was in gaol," said Truth gravely, "I learned many things —I—but I won't talk of that to you. They took me the day she left, before I scarce realized she was gone."

"Was it for preaching outside the Church?"

"Yes. They pulled down our new Meeting House with iron hooks, and put me in Boston Gaol. And as soon as I got out, I went to look for her—to London, and then over the sea. I came to Portsmouth this morning, to your mother's. She said Nan was here—I didn't want to wait. At the town dock I found a farmer coming home this way."

"She's up the hill with Doll, picking blackberries."

"I'll go there—in a minute. Will, while I was in gaol I thought of what you said to me once—that history's hare and hounds, and what's hound today is hare tomorrow—and that it's a pity. And instead of thinking about God's word while I lay there in Little Ease, the chamber all the old Plymouth pilgrims lay in when they first tried to flee from there, I kept thinking about what you said—that and another thing."

"I? There's no wisdom in me."

"No, I wouldn't have said once that there was, but now I am not so sure. I'm not sure at all—not even that my soul's to be eternally saved—and I was always sure of that."

"Oh, you were, Truth! So damn sure! I know it's cruel, but it does my heart good to see you troubled a little. We other men—whose souls aren't saved—are always troubled so much."

"I thought about you, and about history, and our fathers, and the way we were brought up to think. Do you still believe in everything your father stood for?"

"No," said Will, "I can't. A lot of it's gone and won't come back." He looked about the sweep of land John Scarlock had bought for him in exchange for one wooden plow with an iron tip on the day he was a year old. "But he was a great man for the old, free ways, and I like them, too."

"I guess you do. You were the talk of London for a while—for being the only man in all the world who'd told the King of England to go to hell."

"How'd they find out 'twas I?"

"The King remembered your face, and caught you once with Sir William Warren afterward and asked who you were. You were lucky. He chose to make a jest of it. But while I was in gaol I kept wondering why they couldn't live side by side in a country as great as this—your ways and mine."

"Why, Truth! I believe that! I believe that, stronger than anything my father taught me! I tried to tell that to the Select Men, but they wouldn't listen."

"Do you think they'd listen to me in Boston—Boston in Massachusetts—if I went and suggested it there?"

"No. I think you'd be back in gaol again."

"I suppose I would," said Truth, bowing his head, his shoulders sagging wearily. "And maybe I'd belong there. I'm not even sure it is right, rather than the old way—that we should carry the Church of Christ before us like a banner wherever we go. I only know that I am not sure."

"I am. It's only a thought in the mind, but I'm as sure of it as if I could pick it up in my hand. Are you going to stay in New England?"

"Yes. I shall live with my uncles in Boston and give lectures at the College till there's a pulpit for me. And now—where is *she?*"

"Up there." Will pointed to the field beyond the oak trees. "I'll call Doll so she won't be in your way." He lifted his voice in a shout.

"Nancy!"

There was a tremor in the voice that had always been so steady and controlled, the voice that she had not thought to hear again. Nan looked up from the brambles and saw Truth Damerill. And now, she thought, I've got to do it all over.

"Oh, Truth! Why did you follow me here? Didn't it tell you

how I felt—my leaving you that way?" And then she looked at him more closely. "What is the matter? You've been ill!"

"I've been in gaol, Nancy. For my work in Christ. They took me the day you left."

"I'm sorry for that."

"I went proudly, Nancy. Did you ever hear of John Bunyan, our great martyr, who lies even now in gaol in Bedford?"

"No."

"He has suffered sad years of prison for preaching in the faith, and he has written wisely about it. He says the gaols are Christ's schools, and that shut away from the vain delights of the world, we are all the more free to study God, but for me it was not that way. In prison we are to meditate, he says, on the emptiness of this world and the glory of that other, and that we will be carried as on eagles' wings beyond carnality. But alas, I found I only sank the deeper in."

"What do you mean?"

"I mean that I should have thought of God and how to make my soul more pleasing to Him, since it was a soul that He had saved. But now I doubt that He has really saved me, that I am one of His elect—because while I lay there and tried to think of Him, I could only think of you—of your smooth gold hair, and your deep eyes, and your white flesh, Nancy."

"You must forget me."

"Why do you say that? I shall never forget you, and I have come to make sure of you this time. You do not belong to any other man."

There was just enough of the old taunt stirring in his voice to quiet her pity and stiffen her pride in the course she had to take.

"Oh, but I do," she said, "and you know it. I belong to Will Scarlock. You could say that no man belongs to me, and you would be right in that."

"But he chose another and he will never marry you. What do you think to do? Stay a maid?"

"It is good to stay a maid. Your Bible says so. I cannot live with him, or lie in his bed, or keep his house; I can hardly walk with him in the common street. But I can love him all the same, and live by myself and wait, and maybe sometime there will be some little thing I can do for him that will make him happy for a moment or two. And that is worth being born for, and growing up and

257

suffering, and lying down to die. That is more than being the cherished bride of any other man."

Truth shook his head. "It's good to be a maid, but the Bible says, too, that it's better to marry than to burn. Oh, I know you are good, and he is good. And you have sworn, both of you, to put this thing away. But there will come a warm night and a moon —and Doll will be somewhere singing—you know that, don't you?"

"Yes. I suppose I do."

"And afterward? How will you feel?"

"How can I tell you—now?"

"You mean that you are not certain you will feel lost and damned?"

"Yes, I shall feel that. But probably I shall feel glorified and holy, too, and visited by a god."

"Then it comes to this, and you admit it: that to stay here in the same town with him is to face the almost certain chance of losing your soul forever—while to come with me, my wife, into the way of the faith, is to present yourself pure before God and worthy of His eternal salvation. You must make the old choice, Nancy, that is laid upon all men. Will you leave your sins and go to heaven, or have your sins and go to hell?"

She looked straight at him. She did not stop for one moment's thought.

"I'll have my sins and go to hell," she said.

"Nancy!" He stared at her across the brambles, sharp hurt and bewilderment and a depth of eternal sorrow in his eyes. "I shall never understand you!"

"No. Probably not. But don't worry too much about it, Truth. There will be other girls you can understand, girls who will be glad to leave their sins for you—and you will not have to deal any more with me. Perhaps I am God's instrument to remind you of the earth you come from."

"You are God's instrument," he said, drawing himself proudly together, "to remind me that when I thought upon my given name, I chose Truth as greater than Love. And it was a wise choice. I shall not waver from it again."

He turned from her and walked down the hill toward the water, not looking back. She could not know that he was fighting unmanly tears and muttering half aloud, "But where is a man to look for Truth? Christ Jesus, tell me where!"

20. The foolish girl

≈≈≈≈≈≈≈≈≈≈≈≈≈≈≈≈≈≈≈≈≈≈≈≈≈≈

SHE HADN'T meant to do it when she left the house that afternoon: the forbidden thing, the thing that would get them all in trouble. She only thought she would walk out a little way in the thin, chilly sunshine, maybe pick some red maple leaves along the edge of the swamp, or a spray of bittersweet up on the rocky knolls where the cows were still at pasture. She took her lute with her, of course, but then she often wandered around the island, playing it softly to herself. Nan was far in the sea at her fishery, with the great autumn cod catch to be salted down for shipping, and Will spent all his days in the woods now, where the men were bedding down the Broad-Arrow trees with heaps of broken brush and small timber underneath, so that they could be felled later without shattering themselves to pieces. And Doll was lonely.

She walked across the brown furrows and between the dead cornstalks tied together in bunches at the top in the shape of Indian wigwams. Here was a heap of yellow pumpkins the boys hadn't brought into the cellar yet, and there a few clusters of black, frost-bitten grapes, straggling across the stone wall. She scuffed a little in the harsh fallen leaves and dead grasses, and wondered where she was going to, and looked at the empty blue of the sky and the full blue of the river, speckled with little white-sailed boats threading up and down.

She went by Sam Fernald's house, and he and his wife were just coming out, bent sideways under the weight of big, covered baskets leaking salt water.

Sam, dark, and heavy, and merry-faced, called a greeting to her. "Going to the Bank, Doll? There's room in our boat."

"I—I—I wasn't. Yes, I think I will," said Doll.

He went on, talking easily as they walked together, but his wife kept silent. Doll looked sideways at her once and then shrugged her shoulders. Yes, she thought, I *was* brought up in a bawdy house, and you needn't talk to me if you don't want to. I never worked in it, but I'd rather do that than be all unkind and sour-faced the way you are.

"Keep back from the baskets, Doll," said Sam, as he helped her into the boat. "They're dripping full of oysters. I want to trade them in the Spring Market for wild duck if any of the Great Bay men are down."

She smiled at him uncertainly. "I think you can. Will brings home duck every night. It has a strange wild taste—not like in London."

"You must miss the goings-on there. Here . . ."

"Sam," said his wife, and her words fell like drops of acid, "you're heading for Great Island. The Bank's the other way."

He flushed and drove his oars deep into the water, changing their course, and did not speak to Doll again.

She climbed ashore without any help on Johnny Crowther's beach, thanked Sam, and left them piling out the oyster baskets. She walked up through town. Women leaned from the low casements, calling to each other across the dirt road and dead marigold hedges, but none of them greeted her. She passed the Point of Graves, lying serene between the dark hemlocks and the river, and shuddered a little. Children ran hither and thither among the old, crooked stones, playing a game of their own, and she watched them for a while, wondering if they would like to have her sing to them. It seemed to her that the little boys had wide, friendly eyes, but that the girls had thin, tight mouths; so she kept on walking. She passed the dock and looked wistfully at the bare-armed, lusty, shouting men, busy about the two fishing boats tied up there. They wouldn't want to listen either. She crossed the timber foot-bridge over the little creek, and came to the tavern just below the Great House where Richard Cutt lived.

A path of sea-washed pebbles went up the grassy bank to the tavern door which stood invitingly open. Inside she could see a few men sprawled leisurely on stools and benches, see the mugs passing round.

She took a step up the pebbles. "No," she said. "I mustn't do it." She ran lightly on, past Richard Cutt's.

Spring Hill was the place where the strawberries used to grow so thick they gave the town its first name, but now it was all houses and kitchen gardens, with open stalls near the water where the farmers brought their harvest in—eggs, and poultry, and dairyings; in this season, the wild game—to trade them with the Portsmouth men for fish and lobsters and English wares from oversea. Quite a little crowd walked among the stalls, for the ferry boat from Kittery had just pulled in there, but Doll passed by, a stone's throw above, and down the narrow lane at the back of John Cutt's warehouses between the stalks of dead goldenrod.

To her left, and running up the hill, the great Cutt orchard covered the whole slope above the North Mill Pond. An apple orchard it was, and most of the boughs had been stripped now, and their fruit carried to the cider presses at the head of a little cove facing Christian Shore. Doll left the lane and climbed between the twisted trees, and wandered there for a while. She pulled one sleek red apple from a drooping branch that the men had overlooked, and ate a little of its tart, white flesh, and threw it away; and then she rambled down the north ridge and along the reedy shore, making up a song. She passed the cider mill, silent and empty now, its season's work over, a tall mound of yellow-brown fruit pulp heaped against the ramshackle gray boards at its rear, and the thick, sweet cider tang clotting the air, stifling the smell of salt and shellfish that clung about the cove. She followed the winding shore line of the millpond till she came to the riverside again, and turned back toward town. A little, low house of brown deals rose half out of the water ahead of her, just before the row of warehouses began, and its door stood open, voices spilling through it. She took a look inside, and saw men seated on log benches drinking—and in she went.

It was hardly more than a hut, with dusty windowpanes and a smoking driftwood fire on its hearth, and no tables at all, save one for service. It smelled of fish and cider and a rank wolf's hide nailed on one wall, but somehow it was friendly. Coming out of the sharp sunshine, it took Doll a moment or two before she could see it plain, and by that time everyone was looking at her. A dozen rough men in coarse wool jerkins and leather breeches lolled around the close little room drinking—and in one corner sprawled a thick-bodied old woman with rusty hair and bleared eyes that seemed to be looking in opposite directions. Doll had never seen any of the men before—loggers, fishermen, apple-pickers John Cutt had just paid off—but she knew the woman. It was Sarah Scriggins the midwife, and Sarah spoke first.

"Come here to me, Goody Scarlock," she said, patting the bench beside her. "I've heard it whispered that singing in a tavern's the thing you do best. Are you going to prove it for me and the lads now?"

Doll looked around. "It—it's against the law, isn't it?"

One of the men guffawed and climbed to his feet. He stood so tall that he had to bend his neck under the low ceiling, and the hand he held his mug in bulged like a bear's paw, but he was young, with kind, blue eyes in a ruddy, wind-burnt face.

"That'll make it all the sweeter, Goody," he said. "I've never heard a woman sing, except for hymns on the Sabbath."

Doll stood still, poised on the threshold like a butterfly, uncertain what to do, wanting terribly to take up the invitation, her fingers picking soundless at her lute.

"That's not singing," she said. "That's the noise my husband's dog makes to the full moon."

The men were all looking at her now, and they were smiling.

"Then show us something better."

"Do you want me to?"

"If you can."

Suddenly her whole face lighted with a smile, and she tripped forward and turned to stand, facing them, her back against the warm, soot-stained chimney. And she lifted her lute and sang. She sang timidly at first, because it had been such a very long time since she had stood up like this, and never before in America. And it took the men a few songs before they could be easy and understand that this was a good thing, common as ale and to be enjoyed so, not an uncouth wonder, like a two-headed calf or a comet streaking across the sky.

The tall, blue-eyed man, who said he was John Billings and had come in to buy cider for Nan's men at the fishery, shared his mug with her, and told her the names of all the other men. And then she sang again, and this time they laughed and clapped as if they had been listening to singing girls all their lives, and when she chose a song they knew and came to the chorus, they sang with her. Long shadows fell through the apple orchard, and a sharp wind blew in

262

at the doorway. The sun was going down in purple behind the chimneys and gables on Christian Shore. The host, Ben Leighton, a round old man with solemn eyes, stirred up the fire and took away from Sarah the candle her weaving fingers could not light, and lit it himself. I'll go, thought Doll—after one more song.

John Billings looked out the window at the apple trees.

"Give us a cider song, Goody Scarlock. Do you know any cider songs?"

"I—I know an apple song. I made one up this afternoon. I've never sung it before."

"Then now's the time."

"I'll beat the measure," said John.

He picked up a small, stone bottle from a cobwebbed shelf, and held it by the neck, poised above the edge of the bench beside him, and Doll sang sweetly, gaily, there in the small, squalid, shadowy room, while the old midwife struggled to hold her head upright, and the master fisherman kept time.

> "Oh, russet, amber, tawny, red,
>   The sweet fruit weights the stem
> Whose roots upon your fathers fed,
>   Stand up and drink to them . . ."

She held out her hand and cupped it upward in a gay little gesture, and the men stood up and drank, and Doll sang on, thinking she had never been so happy.

> "The men who brought our world to pass,
>   Tavern and spired town.
> But pledge we, too, the foolish lass
>   Who pulled the apple down."

She played over a few bars between verses, and a tousled boy named Hal, with a blithe, freckled face, leaned toward her calling, "Ha! I'd like to pick apples with you, Goody Scarlock!"

Doll swayed away from him, laughing sweetly, fending him off with her lute. To parry such jests was her stock in trade.

"And you shall!" she promised, nodding her head. "When they grow on plum trees!"

The men shouted with laughter, Hal as loud as any of them. She went on, in a lower key.

> "The daughters of the foolish girl
>   Betray themselves to pain,
>   But the torn flesh heals, the child grows tall . . .
>   And the boughs bend again!"

John Billings beat sober time.

> "And the white arms reach up again,
>   To pull the sweet fruit low.
>   Your girls will have a strength, my son,
>   Your boys will never know."

"It's true!" gabbled old Sarah, her mouth hanging loosely open. "It's true, an' I seen it. You can preach better'n Parson Moodey, Doll Scarlock. You know more o' truth than he."

Now her face lighted up, and all her music swelled strong, like a great organ a-going.

> "Now last year's apples brim the cup,
>   So pledge we with a will,
>   The men who ran the steeples up
>   And raised the cider mill!"

The men knew their part in the rote song now, and they stood up heartily to the toast.

> "But which of them has built so tall
>   His name will last in town,
>   Unless he loved a foolish girl
>   Who pulled the apple down?"

And then she tumbled on a bench, breathless and laughing, and called across to Sarah, "See! They think it's their world, but once in a while we have to show them the truth of it!"

Hobnails grated on the crazy sill, and a thin, taut voice cut like a whiplash through the smoky dusk.

"Is Sarah Scriggins here? Is she fit to be seen?"

It was a young man who spoke, a tall, gangling young man, with bleak gray eyes, a sharp jaw, and a hooked nose, and the lines of his sallow face curved down.

Sarah tried twice to stand up and failed. "What you want—Anthony Wiggin?" she asked him, bewildered, and pitiful, and all addled with drink.

He shrugged his shoulders. "One of you put her head in a pail of water. They need her at the Great House. Ruth Puddington's edging on a fit again."

"What's she doing at the Great House? I thought they never let her out," spoke John Billings.

"Her folk are from home and Eleanor Cutt said she'd mind her. They've got her locked in the back chamber there." He was eying Doll and her lute. "Were you playing that here?"

She did not answer.

"You were, and you were singing. I heard you from the lane. Don't you know there's a law against making rude music in taverns? But I suppose—coming from a whore house . . ."

"Yes, I know," said Doll faintly.

"You'll be hearing from Mr. Moodey and the Select Men about this." He turned, sneering. "Get the old hag sober. They say only she can handle Ruth." He turned on his heel and walked into the sharp dusk.

"Sweet-tempered lad, he be," muttered old Ben, gathering up the mugs the men were leaving as they drifted out, the holiday spirit gone from them. "Thomas Wiggin's kin, an' a damn pry-all."

"Give me some more cider," said John Billings, sitting down. "I'm not going yet."

Doll stood, trailing her lute down, knowing her great moment was over, and that she had been very wicked and would probably bring disgrace on Will before the whole town. She could not bear to walk home past all the lighted windows—just yet. She watched Ben putting cold clouts on Sarah's head and holding a thick slice of raw onion under her nose.

"Who's Ruth Puddington?" she said. "And what are her fits?"

John's heavy brows drew down. "If you ask me," he said, "and you did, didn't you, I'd say she was a poor, unlucky lass raised by fools—but most in town would tell you she's mad. Used to be an old sweetheart of your husband's before he went to the College— nothing but boy-and-girl."

"Was she mad then?"

"No. While he was away it came on her. Oh, it had nothing to do with *him,* more than with any other lad. 'Twas just that she had hotter blood than most around here, and her mother and father told her that to have hot blood was a sin that damned you to hell, and she believed them, and it shook her wits—so they locked her up."

"Locked her up!"

"Aye. She knows what she needs, and if she was free she'd go and get it."

"But—but—what does she need?"

"Only to be loved—like any other woman."

"But, before she went mad, didn't she court like other girls—to marry?"

"She was just coming to the age for it, but her folk preached at her so when they found she liked kissing, that by and by she thought she saw hell-gate opening up for her, red and blazing, every time she lay down in the night—least, I heard her cry that once when she took a fit in the street. And if you look close at her—under her sick color—you can see she's still a pretty girl." John hugged his glass in his great hands, his blue eyes clouded and somber.

"They were wicked—to make her frightened—to keep her from love."

"They were," said John Billings bleakly, "an' if there be a hell, they'll fry there. But that won't help Ruth none." And he swore one of the great oaths he was famous for from York to Newburyport.

Doll sighed. A round, yellow moon rode high in the sharp autumn night outside the little alehouse. Joan would be worried, and Will would be out searching for her. She must go home and confess to them what she had done. Sarah lay with her head on the table, snoring, and Ben had given up trying to wake her. John Billings brooded over his cider. She stepped into the lane without saying goodnight.

When she got to the Great House, she stopped in the shadow of the grape trellis beside it, and looked through the kitchen window. Eleanor Cutt, a serene woman with a colorless gown and smooth hair, moved unhurriedly about, getting supper. She seemed to be all alone in the house. Doll slipped suddenly under the trellis and into the back yard. She picked her way across the frosty grass and dead flower stalks, and stopped under the unlit windows well away from the kitchen. Then she looked up, wondering which chamber

266

Ruth was in. As she stood there, a white face peered out, looking down at her, and then drew sharply back. Doll felt along the clapboard wall till she found a door, lifted the iron latch and slipped through it, and then—oh, lucky, lucky, those who pray to Venus —she stumbled over something and it was a bottom stair. In the kitchen she could hear Eleanor Cutt singing.

> "Let me walk holy in Thy sight,
> And spread Thy Grace afar.
> I thank Thee that I am a-right,
> Not as the Wicked are."

She smiled gently to herself. Eleanor Cutt was singing through her nose and not in tune. She crept up the crooked little stair, feeling her way with her hands stretched before her, and stopped at the top. Not one ray of light came from anywhere, but her searching fingers ran their way along the edge of what was surely a door, a door with a heavy wooden bar across it. Doll drew the bar back, and the door swung open. A gasp came from inside, and the moonlight pouring through the diamond panes of the half-open casement showed a tall, gracefully made figure drawing itself back, its hand half to its bosom. Now the head jerked sharply to one side, and the figure retreated and gasped again. Doll could see that the moonlight shone into two deeply beautiful dark eyes set in a face like paper.

"Ruth," she said very softly, "Ruth. Don't be frightened. I want to tell you something."

Another gasp answered her, but this time there was not so much fright in it.

"Ruth, they lied to you. It isn't wicked to love—to love with the body. It can be very beautiful—and holy. It's better to love with the heart, too. But it's worse not to love at all. That's the real sin —not ever to love any man. God won't forgive you that."

"Who are—you?"

"I've brought you a message from God, Ruth. He says He knows how He made you, and He doesn't expect you to be any better than that. Go out now! Before it's too late and your beauty's gone."

She stood aside, leaving the door unblocked and open; stood and waited, there in the musty dark at the top of Richard Cutt's back stairs, where the crisp, salt smell of eels in butter wafted upward from Eleanor's frying pan.

"It's—it's too late now. Nobody wants a mad girl—and I've been wicked, too."

"Oh, you're not mad, and I don't think you're wicked. I think you'd be surprised. Just you go down by Ben Leighton's tavern . . ."

Ruth gave a little sigh, and took a step forward—and then, suddenly, she ran by Doll like a dark wind, downstairs and out into the night.

But when Doll tried to creep after her, she was met at the bottom step by Eleanor Cutt, holding up a candle, first in fright, and then in understanding and rage. Eleanor sank her long, supple fingers in Doll's shoulder and began to scream for Richard, and Doll knew that the dance was over now, and the piper coming for his pay.

21. Things of no matter

THEY LET him take her home that night, but only because they
hadn't liked the set of his jaw and the way he balanced the new
musket he'd bought in London—the stout, heavy-barreled one,
like the King's Life Guard carried. Sam Fernald brought him word
that half the town had her in the Meeting House, questioning and
railing at her, and the other half was scouring the river bank and the
woods beyond the Glebe Land, trying to find Ruth Puddington.
And he'd run out in the sharp night just the way he was, bareheaded
and without his jacket—but he hadn't forgotten his gun.

Now they sat in the boat going home, for a few hours, he sworn
and bound to deliver her at eight o'clock to the Select Men, who
had the power of magistrate under an act of General Court; she
bound to be there. She crouched in the stern, and he fixed his eyes
grimly on hers and paid no heed to where he was rowing.

"Oh, Doll—I can understand your singing in the tavern—I
knew you were going to do it some day. But why did you let Ruth
out? Why did you? The girl's got no wits in her head, and she'll let
any man have her. Didn't you know? What did you do it for?"

"Yes, I knew," she said, lifting her chin proudly in the starlight.
"I had to do it, and I'm glad I did."

"Doll. I won't scold you. I'll do everything I can to get you out of
this. Only please tell me why you did it. Cutt and Pendleton'll ask
me tomorrow—they'll ask you. What will we say?"

"Oh, Will . . ." She twisted her hands together in her lap. "I
know so well, and yet I can't put it in words at all. She wanted to

be loved—and they'd kept her from it and frightened her—and it wasn't right."

"Well, yes, that's true. But when you let her out she wasn't going to find *love*. If any decent man found her he'd have brought her home. The other kind would—well—they wouldn't *love* her, Doll. The loggers just down from the woods, and some of the fishermen—they'd just have their way and leave her. You should have known that."

"I did know it. But suppose she found somebody who did love her—somebody she could love?"

"Is that likely?"

"I thought so—I still think so."

"Then you know something I don't."

"I think I do. Won't you trust me?"

"I suppose I'll have to," he sighed, beaching the boat and lifting her ashore. "What will we tell Mother?"

"I'll tell her," said Doll, holding herself stiff in his arms. And when they got to the house she did tell Joan, just the bare words of it, and Joan accepted it and did not question her at all, which puzzled Will and made him feel like a flesh-and-blood man shut up with a couple of witches. What was it his father had said once? "A man's mother is never strange, but his wife will always be—a little." Now Mother was turned strange, too—so were all women, except maybe Nannie. He took a last look down the black river past the lights on Great Island, and thought of that other island, nine miles in the sea, where she would be lying asleep by now, innocent and away from all this maze of trouble looming.

And it seemed only a few moments after that he was turning and waking in the bed beside Doll, hearing heavy raps on this same door, and coming down in the cold gray of daybreak, thrust only into his boots and breeches. He took the bar down to let Henry Sherburne in, Henry who had been a young man when his father was a young man, and whose face looked frightened, and troubled, and still boyish, in spite of deep-cut lines, and sagging jowls, and thick gray hair above it.

"Come in, Henry. I'll poke the fire. Been a frost, I guess. It's damn cold, anyway."

Yes, there had been a frost. Little white flakes of it were clinging to Henry's boots, and his breath hung white before him in the air.

270

He stepped into the still, dark kitchen, and Will lit a candle, and went to beat life into the banked fire behind the hearthstone.

"Will. I—They say I run with the hare an' hunt with the hounds, an' trim, an' play both ends against the middle. But you know—when it means blood an' breath—I'm with those of the old stock. You know . . ."

Will turned around and dropped the poker. He could see sweat on Henry's brow in spite of the cold.

"What in the devil ails you, man?"

"Will. I was drinking with your father the day you was born."

"Good. I'll bet he needed a drink. Needed a good friend beside him, drinking too. But you've had time to get over that. What's the trouble, Henry?"

"Will. They been up all night, trying to decide what to do with her."

"They have? Did they find Ruth?"

"No—not yet. For the singing, they're going to fine you thirty shillings."

"Well—that's not what's making you sweat, Henry?"

"No. They been going over an' over the Body of Liberties all night, an' they can't find no place at all that says what to do with one as lets a mad girl out of keeping. They've talked of the ducking stool, and they've talked of lashes. When I come away, they was trying to make what they could of the twelfth law."

"What's that?"

"It's the one that says whosoever ravishes a woman shall be put to death."

"But *she's* not ravished anybody."

"Not she, but they claim—it's sure to have happened to Ruth by now, she being as she was. And that your wife's guilty as being the cause of it."

"You mean . . . ? You're not telling me, Henry, they think to . . . ?"

"Yes," he said. "I'm telling you that."

Will sat down on the bench and looked straight at the older man, without saying anything at all, but Henry's words came out in a rush then.

"We're with you, Will. There was others—of our party— slipped out of the Meeting House then, just as I did. And we met outside. Every man's gone home for his gun, Will. We talked it over, and none of us knows your wife well, but we don't care if you did get her where you did. She was what you wanted— And if they try to harm her—there'll be a fight in Portsmouth today, an' to hell with the General Court of Massachusetts. The lads have been spoiling for it—and it looks like the time's here. We petitioned the King, and the King's men came and said we were right, and then went home and forgot us. All the good we've had comes not from the King—it comes from you, Will. You went to England for us, and whether you did it by talking sharp or sly, we don't know and it doesn't matter. You got us the mast trade. You got the money coming into the right pockets—not just into your own—and it's the power of money that will give New Hampshire back to New Hampshire men. So now—when you're in trouble—there's not one of us won't stand up and fight for you as long as he can hold a musket."

"Thanks, Henry. I did what I could. It was little enough."

Will sat and played with the poker. Overhead, he could hear Joan and Doll talking in low tones, so as not to awaken the Hall children. He knew they would be coming down.

"But, don't you think it might be better—just to slip out and row her downriver. We could go to Hog Island, to Nan Knight—and get her on a ship."

"They thought of that, Will. They're waiting for you at the Narrows."

"And of course the roads out of town?"

"Everything."

"Then—I guess we'll have that fight, Henry. But it seems there ought to be a smarter way."

"Well—you think of one. You'll have plenty of help—and you know who to call on."

"Yes, I know. Thanks, Henry."

And Henry trailed away over the frosty furrows, toward Sam Fernald's house, looming gray through the bare elm trees around it.

Doll crept down, and Will noticed that she was wearing her scarlet dress that had been folded away ever since they came from London. He did not chide her. She might never wear another dress, he thought. He wondered what he should tell her. But she came straight to him, and reached her hands to his shoulders, and looked into his eyes.

"Will. Somebody came here—and he brought you bad news."

"Yes. He did."

"They—they—? What do they think to do with me?"

"We're going to fight them, Doll."

Her hands dropped. "I see," she said.

But when he stood up with her in the Meeting House, on the hill just below the South Mill Pond, it wasn't that way at all. There was something else in their faces, something crafty, and sly, and exulting—and he looked them square in the eye for a few moments, and then he knew what they were after. It wasn't Doll, the singing girl in the red dress. It was he whom they wanted. The King's Mast Master, who would have no dealings with them, who was bringing money into the Churchmen and making their party grow stronger all the time, stronger and richer than the entrenched Puritans, till that day might break over Piscataqua Country when those who wished could say as Henry Sherburne had said, "To hell with the General Court of Massachusetts."

He stood in front of the pulpit with his hand on Doll's shoulder, and he looked up at Brian Pendleton, and Richard Cutt, and Elias Stileman; and Richard Walderne from Dover was there, too, the Indian fighter, tough as a broadaxe, now speaker of the Boston Assembly. He stood, and looked, and waited.

"Goodman Scarlock." Pendleton cleared his throat and adjusted his periwig—it was a second-rate one, Will noticed, threadbare, and would have been a laughing stock in London, but here it passed for fine. "We charge your wife with the known crime of making rude music in the alehouse, and we fine her thirty shillings."

Will said no word but reached into his pocket. He had been to the chest in the cellar and brought a hundred with him, in case he needed it. He counted the coins out and handed them over. Men and women crowded the benches behind him, but he paid no attention to them, and neither did Doll as she stood there, looking up, her face pale, but her eyes intensely bright and blue. Pendleton counted the money twice, and passed it to Mr. Moodey. Walderne and Cutt joined him, and the four whispered together.

"Will Scarlock," resumed Brian Pendleton, "your wife has given a poor, crazed girl over to ravishment, and we have talked of requiting her justly with death."

He could feel a tremor go through Doll, but her face did not change.

"But we have not chosen that way."

A sigh went over the benches and rude galleries of the Meeting

House. He could not tell whether Portsmouth was glad or sorry. He didn't give a damn. He knew they were going to serve him with some kind of sharp trick, and he tried to gird his wits to meet it.

"Will Scarlock, we have been merciful and decided thus. Your wife is to stand in the pillory all day, and then be released with six lashes."

He looked at Doll, and he could see her sag, limp and crying in the cruel wooden frame, see red welts raised across the soft flesh he used to love so.

He smiled at them, and licked his lips, and ran his hand along the barrel of his musket.

"Unless . . ." Pendleton leaned over, and spoke clearly; soft, but not so soft the gallery could not hear. "Unless you should decide to reverse your policy 'bout face; buy masts only from those who are just and godly, and prohibit the wicked, the old stock, the Churchmen, from any share in the King's gold. In that case—we feel— it would be just to fine her five shillings. After all, she is a stranger to our ways here."

So now it was out. He had heard, and Doll had heard, and all the Meeting House—half his friends and half Pendleton's friends —had heard, and the air grew tight and hot with pent-up battle about to break.

"Isn't there . . . isn't there . . . any other way?" he said.

"Yes, there is one. We can deliver you up to Boston Gaol, to see what they will do with you there."

"Deliver *you*," they had said to him, not Doll. They didn't care about punishing Doll. They were just using her poor, pretty foolishness as a way to get at him. And by God, they had.

"Then you best do that," he said. "You shan't hurt my wife, and you shan't have the trade. I'll go to Boston with you."

And then Doll spoke. She stood away from him and she smiled, just the way she did when she was going to sing, the kind of smile that brought men around her like bees to the honeycomb, and she cried out sweetly, "Oh, but, sirs! It wasn't my husband sang in the alehouse and let Ruth Puddington go free. It was I."

Richard Cutt's jaw dropped. Brian Pendleton adjusted his periwig and leaned forward.

"I am guilty," she said demurely, "and any just court of law would see that I should pay. You have said the pillory and six lashes. Take me, sirs, to the pillory."

"Doll!" he cried. "You shan't!"

She turned toward him. "I shall," she answered, "and you can't stop me!" And then softly under her breath, "Will . . . it's only a little pain . . . only for today. And the thing you are trying to do . . . for your friends and your country . . . is great, and is the whole world . . . and is forever."

"Doll. I can't let you."

Then she looked at him, and he felt her look cutting through to the flesh upon his bones.

"You would let Nan Knight," she said. "You would let her stand in the pillory for you . . . if it meant . . . so much. Wouldn't you? Be honest."

"But Nan . . . Nan's different . . . not like you, all little, and soft, and gay, like a child."

"I am your wife," said Doll proudly. "And I ask to be allowed to do . . . what . . . what you would let *her* do."

"Oh, Doll, don't. I can't," he breathed miserably.

She brushed past him and walked straight up to the pulpit.

"I have committed a crime, and I plead guilty, and I have been duly sentenced," she said. "I demand now that it be served on me and the business ended."

So they had no choice, and they led her to the pillory on the Common. She was not tall enough to fit in it, so they had to get a milking stool for her to stand on. They put her head through the great hole, and her fine wrists through the little ones, and they fastened her there. And Henry Sherburne held Will on one side, and Sam Fernald held him on the other. A dozen of his friends had gathered and stood all about him, gripping their muskets and fowling pieces. "It's better this way, Will," they told him, all of them cheering and agreeing together. "It's better this way. It'll hurt her, but it won't kill her, and when it's over we can trade with the masts again the way we please. She's a rare, brave girl, and she can be the Queen of Portsmouth, if we have the say in it."

He could see their way of thinking, but he strained against them for a while, not knowing what he would do if they let him go, but still feeling like a sort of cuckhold, to let his wife be taken away from him and used so. And meanwhile Doll stood propped in the pillory and sang the most ribald songs she knew. She sang "Cuckholds all a-row," and she sang, "Dice, strong waters, and a whore." She sang some verses Will had never heard before, about the unspeakable adventures a Puritan parson had when he met the Maid of Amsterdam, and finally, she started to make up a new one:

> "Oh there were three knaves in Portsmouth,
>   Moodey, Pendleton, and Cutt,
>   Moodey, Pendleton, and Cutt . . ."

But she could not finish it, for Mr. Moodey went to her quickly and tied his heavy cotton handkerchief across her mouth. Will stiffened, but Sam Fernald held him hard. So she hung there silent, and the sun went past noonday, and the day waned.

All in the autumn dusk, when the moon shone white on the corn stalks, and the flood tide poured up the black river groove, they took her out and bound her to a stripling beech tree on a little hill, just off the footpath that went over John Pickering's dam, and the outlet of the South Mill Pond. Then Brian Pendleton went here and there with the long lash made out of strips of raveled leather, trying to find some one of the faithful who would give her the six lashes, but nobody wanted to very much. This man had to go home to supper, and that man had sprained his arm casting a net, and the third one had a moth's wing in his eye and wouldn't be able to see straight. And so it went.

Will stood, his musket hanging down from his tired shoulder, and he looked at Doll, and Doll smiled, tired almost to the point of lying down to die, but still brave, still determined that he shouldn't sell his friends because of her.

Finally Pendleton lost his temper. "Very well," he cried, shifting the lash in his hand for a better grip. "I'm not afraid to beat a wanton to the glory of God. There's nothing wrong with my arm and my eye. Doll Scarlock"—he stepped toward the girl, tied to the beech tree in the cold twilight, with all the town circling about her and murmuring, for one side or the other—"you are to receive six lashes on your bare flesh for the ravishment of Ruth Puddington."

He came closer and tore the scarlet silk from her slim shoulders. Sam Fernald and Abraham Corbett, who had been guarding Will, stood away from him. Tam, who had fought at Worcester Plain, was the first after Will to lift his gun. Others followed him, but they did not fire.

"And can you prove Ruth Puddington was ravished?" asked a cool voice in the shadowy roadway that led up from the river.

276

Everybody turned, and everybody saw the same thing. It was Nan Knight who had spoken, her blue cloak streaming back in the salt wind, and she came forward, and behind her came John Billings and Ruth Puddington herself, and they were holding hands. She walked up to Brian Pendleton, and she looked down on him as if he were a body louse, or some other creature too mean to crawl.

"Ruth Puddington is as whole as ever she was. Get Sarah Scriggins to examine her if you doubt me. My man, John Billings, brought her home. He found her hid in his boat, just as he was dropping out past Whaleback. Wind and tide were against him, so he could not return her here, and he brought her to Hog Island—to me. She lay in my bed all night beside me, and she has not been harmed. Will you untie Mistress Scarlock now! She is guilty of no crime."

Brian Pendleton looked at her, and remembered just in time that the faithful subjects of Christ do not curse; barely saved himself from it. He knew that he was bested, for he did not see, when he looked at Nan, a proud girl with golden hair and grave eyes. He saw a thousand fishermen hauling in nets that were full of guineas rather than cod and herring, and he saw her credit with the Boston merchants and the London goldsmiths, and he knew that money is power. He flung the lash down on the chilly, gray grass, and turned away. Richard Cutt was there suddenly, and his thin-shanked Eleanor, and Moodey, and Stileman, and Major Walderne, and they were all sputtering like candles ready to go out.

"And furthermore," went on Nan, "John Billings has taken a great liking to her, and asks to have their banns put up on the Sabbath. I do not think her people will have to lock her away any more. Will someone please see to Mistress Scarlock."

They were untying Doll now, reluctantly, and Will could linger only for a moment by Nan.

"Nannie. Were you telling the truth now? Did she really stay with you?"

"Does it matter?"

"I just wondered."

"What do you think?"

He looked at Ruth. A soft bloom had come over her sallow features. Her drawn mouth relaxed softly, and her fingers lay, light and possessive, on the fisherman's sleeve.

And then he turned to Doll. Nan looked down, tried to hold back the tears creeping under her eyelids, saw him embrace his wife.

Everyone had a sweetheart now, even poor, mad Ruth Puddington. But she must go always alone, autumn and winter out, and forever into spring.

Will stared at Doll as he helped unwind the ropes around her, looked at her as if he had never seen her before, and shame and horror swelled up in his heart and nearly overcame him. Doll was not a merry child, as he had thought her. She was a woman—who had done a fine, brave thing because she loved him, but all her courage and spirit was like Ruth Puddington's virginity—a thing of no matter. He loved Nan, and he didn't love Doll, and never would —no matter how fine and brave she was—and he looked deep into her eyes, and both of them knew it.

22. The manner of all the earth

〰〰〰〰〰〰〰〰〰〰〰〰〰〰〰〰〰〰〰〰

THE WIND blew west southwest when the world was made, so an old squaw had once told Nan Knight, and Nan remembered it that mild November afternoon, warm enough for summer, when she walked out of her square stone house at the top of Hog Island, and down through Appledore Township in the pale yellow sunshine—for the wind set in that quarter now. The little fishing village her father had named for the North Devon town he came from spread over the southward slope of the island, above the cove and the flakes and stages where men were curing the last run of dun fish, drying and sweating it again and again. Snowy owls had been seen, flying about the crags of soft gray rock, or perched on the bushes among the dead bayberries and ruined rose haws, and that meant early snow. It meant the fishermen would no longer spread out their great seines at night under the moon for the mackerel to dart into like silver and dark blue arrows; that every cranny must be stuffed with straw and dried weed to tighten the houses against the bitter season, when there was nothing to do but mend nets and drink rumbullion, keep the fires going and wait for spring.

Nan walked among the low, thatched houses that stood scattered all about, not following any line of street. She passed the alehouse, and the small brick church, and the bowling alley, and the school, and walked out beyond them, through the sparse grass clinging to the ledges and the stunted cedar trees that grew no taller than her shoulder. She looked toward Duck Island, with its jutting fangs of rock, a terror to small boats; and she looked at Smutty-Nose, where the best fields were, and away to the mainland, all hidden from her in a soft, tawny haze. Under her feet the tangled thistles and spicy shrubs ran out into a mass of purple rock with colored quartz veins cutting through it. The Isles of Shoals lay there, in the middle of the dull, quiet, waveless water, like a heap of stones, too rough for the builder to use, flung down, and drifting miraculously on the autumn sea. Nan had always loved it here, where the flowers took on brighter hues than the same flowers did ashore, where spring came more softly, and stormier blasts brought the winter in. London was in the world, and Portsmouth was, and Boston in Lincoln, and all the towns of man save this one. There was in the universe, she thought, earth, and heaven, and hell—and then there was Hog Island, a misty realm in the sea, affected by none of the hard old laws that held good in those other places; where you could walk with a dream and hold it to you, and be satisfied and complete; where trouble was at least nine miles off.

"Nannie! Be you sleepwalking? I've bespoken you twice, and you paid no more mind than you would to a curlew flapping over."

John Billings came out of a sumach grove toward her, headed for town. He had been, she supposed, to the little cottage he was building with his own hands for his bride, Ruth. She smiled up at him.

"I'm sorry, John. I'll walk back with you. I was just wandering around."

"Good. I wanted to tell you the *Rose o' Rye* put in this morning."

"I could see from my kitchen window. I thought 'twas she."

"Well—she's brought Tortuga salt again."

"Oh no, John! You didn't accept it, did you? It spots the fish so!"

He shook his head and swore. "I did not. We can make better ourselves out of sea water."

They were threading among the bleached wooden frames now, where the fish were spread to be salted and dried: the leaden gray haddock with dark, striped sides, the yellow-brown ling, the great, mouldy black catfish, the grinning hake, the rockling, all red fins and indigo eyes. Fifteen hundred men fished out of these islands—with nets, and seines, and ketches, and pinnaces—and a thousand of them worked for Nan Knight . . . and all of them called her Nannie. They were running here and there in their scarlet shirts, lifting their gruff voices, splitting and salting and grading and putting down in brine: the great three-foot cod and all the best catches for Malaga and the Canaries, the second quality to the Portugal islands, and the leavings to feed the Guinea slaves in the Barbados. The ships would go out laden with these, and come back bringing fruit and oil and wine, soap and cotton and wool and sugar, and, of course, the precious salt.

Nan and John stood in the midst of them, looking on for a few minutes. Then they heard a hail from the head of the cove and turned that way. A man was bending over the single-sailed boat he had just drawn up on the limpet-covered rocks, past the waterline marked with snaky brown kelp, and sea wrack, and mussel shells. He straightened himself now, and Nan caught her breath, for it was Will Scarlock. He came toward them slowly, his head back, and his hair blown about by the fresh wind. When he drew closer she could see a disturbed, bewildered look in his eyes. He came straight to her, not noticing John at all.

"Oh, Will!" she cried. "I'm glad you came out. What . . . ?" Under his straight look her gay pose left her. "Will! Is something the matter?"

"I—I had to ask you, Nan. About something I heard last night." He touched her ever so lightly on the arm, and she felt a tremor go all over her as if her heart had stopped stone-dead in its beat, and then started again, trying to overtake itself. "Nothing that's any of my business, of course." They had stepped aside from the reek of the fishing flakes, into a tiny valley between two hummocks in the uneven land, where a few crimson leaves still clung to the creeping woodbine and a faint color to the spikes of tarnished goldenrod.

"What is it, Will?" she asked, looking straight up at him.

He did not look at her when he answered. He looked at the gray, lapping water on the rocks, and into the tawny haze thickening around Hog Island as the sunset came on.

"They were talking about you in the tavern, Nannie."

"Well. They talked there about my mother before me, but I'll wager they weren't saying the same thing. What did they say of me?"

"They said . . . they said Richard Cutt has in his keeping the affidavit of Sarah Scriggins, signed with her mark."

"Has he?"

"Yes. It says you are . . . it says . . ."

"It says I am incapable of man, doesn't it?"

"It . . . it says so."

"You didn't . . . *believe* it?" Horror and amusement struggled for rule in her gray eyes.

"Oh, Nannie . . . Nannie . . . how could I? After I've held you in my arms . . . and felt you . . . ? But it was sworn! It had the seal of Massachusetts!"

"And since when, poor lad, have you been believing all that comes out of Massachusetts? Listen! I'll tell you how it was." She put both her hands on his shoulders. To touch him was a privilege she rarely allowed herself, but this was one time she was going to, she made up her mind. "You were away, and I was all alone, and Cutt came to me, and Pendleton, and Mr. Moodey. They had a fine scheme to get the fishery for one of their side. They were going to marry the fishery. But of course they needed me for that. They said I had to choose a husband in a week—one who met with their favor. Or show good reasons for not doing so. I tried, and I tried, and I could think of only the one reason that would seem good to them."

"Damn them to hell for that! But how did you get—Sarah?"

Nan sighed. "I offered her her price and she agreed, and I'm still paying it. I do not mind the shillings it costs me, but it has been bad for her. She chooses, she tells me, to stay drunk all the rest of her days—sober of mornings only till she can get to the bottle again. But if that is what she wants, I must put her in the way of it. I gave her my word."

"So that's how you were so sure she would make them the right answer about Ruth Puddington."

"Oh, Sarah swears as I wink my eye. But are you easier now?"

"Oh, Nan! You're right and sound! I knew you would be. But if you hadn't been . . . I'd . . . I'd rather spend all my days with you than with any other woman."

"I know you would, sweetheart."

She looked straight at him, with all her heart in it, with nothing veiled and cautious. And she could. They were on Hog Island, out of the universe, and none of the hard old laws applied here.

"Nannie . . . ?" He gave her her look back with a question in it. She dropped her hands from his shoulders.

"Come now," she said lightly. "We'll go down to the tavern and get you an ale and some supper."

They skirted the edge of the cove, their feet crunching on the beach of wave-ground shells, all rosy indigo, sea-green, mother-of-pearl; they walked up the turf path winding around the houses, and came to the small stone tavern. Lights and a kind of crude, swift-moving music poured through its open door and windows into the dusk, and laughter, and the sound of heavy boots thumping rhythmically on the floor.

"It's Scozway," said Nan, "the Indian fiddler. This is the third night he's been here."

She and Will elbowed through a little group of fishermen blocking the doorway, and stood just inside the low room lined all round with smoke-stained, sea-stained timbers that had been carried there from broken ships. Tables and benches were stacked in a corner, and all the floor swept bare for the dancers, the men who left Appledore only to go fishing, and the women who never left it at all. Not all of them were young, for among the fair faces and sunburnt lads moved their fathers and mothers, and here and there stood up an elderly couple, with gnarled muscles and skin the color of dried haddock. They were loud, and boisterous, and gay, and they had been drinking rum . . . not too much, but enough to loosen their tongues and set their feet rocking, as they tried to fit the sailors' jigs and English country dances their parents had taught them when they were children to the weird, wailing airs of the Indian Scozway. He stood in front of the yawning chimney place, his brown face a-gleam in the candlelight, his long head thrown back, and his eyes closed, as he fiddled nimbly away.

"Let's go round to the kitchen," said Nan. "I—I thought we'd better not go to my house."

"No," he agreed hastily. "No. I'll eat—and I guess I better sleep here. The mist is too thick to go home in."

She looked out of the window they were passing on their journey round the edge of the dance floor, and true enough, the fog had drawn in and was floating in long skeins through the village. There was a full moon though, shining somewhere behind it, so that all the twisted trees and low, stone houses seemed to be drifting just below the surface of a river of golden water. It was so beautiful that she caught her breath.

The kitchen, hardly bigger than one of Joan's cupboards back in Portsmouth, was so crowded they had to stand up, but they got themselves ale and lobster, and drained their mugs and cracked and emptied the scarlet claws, and then they went back to dance.

At first they danced together, and he held her close in his arms, for they were on Hog Island, and there was nobody here to care or question. True, Massachusetts had sent out a Puritan parson, but he had gone to Salem to keep a synod with the Essex ministers. So Appledore was free to rejoice that the harvest of the sea was reaped for another season, and it chose to rejoice by dancing and drinking, and slipping out under the foggy cedars to make love—strange ways, maybe, but the ways that men and women have chosen ever since the world began. Then a giant fisherman, with salt stuck in his black beard, held out his arms to Nan and cried, "Hey, Nannie!" And she went to him and he whirled her away. And a laughing girl hardly past fourteen caught hold of Will and swept him into the dance with her, and Scozway's brown fingers raked the bow through the fiddle strings ever more hard and strong.

The candles burned down, and the thin gold air flowed past the windows, and rum and ale and cider flowed in the kitchen, and so the evening went. It was past ten o'clock when Will found himself alone near the door, and he stood watching Nan dance with John Billings, and thought how no matter what she said or did, it was always the thing he wanted her to do. He liked it because she did not tread the measures in stately dignity like the lady of a manor, but romped through them with the same gay abandon of the village girls who mended nets for thruppence. All Hog Island loved Nan Knight, but all their loves together, he thought, would not be so great as his. And he looked at her across the loud, hot, smoky room, and she slipped out of her partner's arms and came to him.

They did not speak to each other, but he put his hand under the crook of her elbow, and they walked out into the foggy moonlight that hung over all the ledges and the invisible sea. Wordless still, they climbed the craggy pathway to the top of the island, to her low house taller than the crab apple trees before it. Watch came running through the stiff, tattered flower stalks in the garden to welcome them, swinging his tail eagerly, but they did not even know he was there. On the threshold Nan stopped, the iron latch half lifted under her fingers, and turned to Will. She looked up, and he looked down, and there they stood together, not in Earth or Heaven or Hell, nor yet on Hog Island.

"Nan—what do you want me to do?"

"I want you to come in unto me after the manner of all the earth."

"Then—then, by God, I will."

They lay all night together in her bed, and at first they took much joy of the flesh, and then they went from that to the deeper joy of lying there wrapped in each other's arms, but so much one in spirit that they took no thought of the flesh at all. The soft golden air flowed through the gnarled trees outside, and the sea wind walked gently around the house, and Watch kept guard on the threshold. All the rivers had come home to the sea now, and all that ever parted had met again, met and come together for all time, in Will Scarlock and Nan Knight. But man lives by blood, and blood is only living water, with its own tides that ebb and flow and rise, and past the high purity of that moment, the flesh awoke again, and they gave themselves up again to its delight. And so they lay, one with the dust of the fields and the pure light of heaven all night long.

In the hard light of a cold daybreak, when the sea beyond the windows stretched out like a plain of flint, and the very trees seemed cut in stone on a stone sky, he looked at her across the wheat loaf and milk posset, untouched between them on the table.

"I feel terrible, Nan."

"I don't. I feel . . . I feel so . . . so much more *one* with everything than I've ever felt before. I was Nan Knight, and I had a good name, and I had money in my pocket, and I went like a holy image walking, and I had never stained my dress, or harmed any man or woman, and I'd always contained myself and always meant to. I was so proud and strong and sure. And now—I've been wicked, and I've fallen. I've lain abed with another woman's husband and loved doing it."

He couldn't help a wry smile at the forthrightness of her.

"I've been weak and I've yielded, and betrayed a girl who was my friend and never wronged me," Nan went on. "I meant to do right always, but the time came when I couldn't. I'm soiled, and mean as dust, and damned to hell forever. But now—I'm like all the rest of the earth."

"I wish . . . I wish I could feel like that," said Will. "But when I think of you . . . and of her . . . and of what I've done . . . it sort of stops my breath, Nan. As if God's good air doesn't want to go into me."

She smiled at him. "You'll have to learn to be humble too, my darling; to face the fact that you're no better than any other man. When we learn that . . . I think . . . I'm not sure yet . . . we can begin to be happy a little, in spite of hell."

He put his head down in his hands for a long time, and she sat silently across the table, waiting for him, wanting to touch him, but forbidding herself. By and by he stood up.

"I—I'm going home, Nan. We mustn't—again."

"No," she said levelly, "we musn't—but this we've had."

"I—I'll always remember, Nannie—how wonderful it was, with you."

And then he went quickly out of the door, headed nine miles off for trouble, and his footsteps died away on the bleak ledge, and there was nothing of him there any more. Nan put her head down then, thinking she would cry, but she could not, so she lifted it, and sat there staring at the wainscot in utter, dumb woe, trying to live again that beautiful golden night when all the rivers met, and knowing she never could.

23. The holly and the ivy

≋≋≋≋≋≋≋≋≋≋≋≋≋≋≋≋≋≋≋≋≋≋≋≋≋≋≋≋≋≋≋≋≋≋≋

THE WORD had gone out along the frozen river and snowy fields and pastures, up Dock Lane and from farm to farm in Piscataqua Country, that Will Scarlock and his wife Doll would keep Christmas tide after the old way, and wanted all the faithful to be there. Christmas Eve it was to be, after dark, when there was less chance of the Select Men and Mr. Moodey catching them at it and fining them five pounds and maybe other unpleasantness. Joan and Doll worked for a week, roasting, and baking, and stewing, and dressing the house, and Nan came in from Hog Island to be there and help. Will left the logging crews in the woods for a day or two and stayed at home to do the tasks that took a strong shoulder, for this was no simple merrymaking, as he saw it. It was a gesture of defiance, secret still, but what he hoped would be the beginnings of his plan—to set up the old way again, the old, simple, easygoing English way, when people lived by the Prayer Book, but not very close by it. He and his friends had done well with the masts that year—more hard money and English goods in all their houses, and the other side was beginning to watch their shillings closer, and it did his heart good to see it.

Nan and Will knew little of the high old feast day, but Joan remembered how it had been in her girlhood in Nottingham, and Doll's face lighted up as she told the other three of the London Christmases she had known, when green boughs were put out before all the houses, and mummers roamed the street, and the waits caroled half the holy night through.

"Oh, there are some wonderful songs for Christmas," she cried, the queer, lost elfin look that she wore most of the time nowadays

287

leaving her and a happy smile taking its place. "And I know them all! The church songs, and the country songs, and the song to sing when they bring in the Boar's Head . . . !"

Joan nodded, but Will questioned her. "Boar's Head? What's that?"

"Oh, the greatest pig that can be found. It's roasted whole and sprigged with rosemary and a lemon in its mouth, and they bring it to the table with a procession and a song—like the wassail bowl."

"We had a wassail bowl at the College, I remember."

"Oh, the Boar's Head," went on Doll, her eyes sparkling, "is all because of a queer old story. It seems that on Christmas Day there was once a scholar of Queens' gone walking in Shotover Forest conning his Aristotle. And when a wild boar rushed at him on a sudden to bite him, he ran forward and stuffed his book right into the beast's open mouth. And he shouted, 'Take Greek!' and killed it so."

Will smiled at her, not looking at Nan at all. He couldn't now. Not since that night on Hog Island. He knew that if he did he would go to her and take her in his arms in spite of hell. "Where'd you hear about that, Doll? It's not the kind of tale they told at Milady's when I was there."

"Oh—I knew an Oxford clerk once."

Her face did not change, but Nan, watching Will—all her life now a matter of looking at him, all a blind fog when he was not there—saw just the slightest question come in his grey eyes, and she could not understand it. Was he jealous? She did not know this was the second time he had heard Doll mention the old acquaintance, and he did wonder.

"I know what to put in the wassail bowl," said Joan. "It seems only yesterday I was stirring it up in Jack Gambrell's tavern." She had her hands in a poplar dish of bread dough, and kept on kneading it. "You fill your largest pewter bowl two-thirds full of ale, and put in spiced nutmeg, and sugar, and roasted apples . . ."

"I think the lads about here had rather have rum from Newbury-port," said Will dubiously. "Hot, with butter and maple in it. Let's get out Father's old Tusser, and see what he says to do."

So with Tusser's aid, and what Joan and Doll could remember, they went to work to set up an old English Christmas in their house by the black, half-frozen Piscataqua, where there was a good strong law against it, and few of the younger folk knew what it meant. Joan was the first to see that no matter how hard they tried, they could not make it quite the same. They roasted the pig, but there was no

lemon or rosemary, so they used apple and wild mint leaves from
the brook valley by Hogstye Cove. There was no holly or ivy, so they
hung up juniper sheaves, and pigeon berries and ground pine, and
for the Yule Log that should be ash because it was burning ash
wood that warmed the stable in Bethlehem, they had to turn to pine
again. They moved all the furnishings out of the big bedroom where
Will had been born and John had died, rested long deals on the kegs
to make a feasting table, and every guest was warned to bring his
own stool.

The high night came finally, after a dull week of iron-gray weather,
just the way it should come, with soft snow like wild goose feathers
spread over everything, and crisp air, and a dark blue sky shining
with great stars. Twilight was hardly down before the little boats
started edging out of the creeks and away from the river landings
and tacking down the Kittery side; and shadowy, secret figures moved
furtively in the lanes about the Bank, carrying stools half hidden in
their greatcoats. Johnny Crowther and his eldest boy did ferry duty,
setting everybody over to the island, and once there, people dared to
lift their voices a little as they tramped through Sam Fernald's snowy
field, and past the salt marsh, and up the headland to the weathered
house John Scarlock had built for his bride more than thirty years
ago. Not a crack of light shone out from anywhere to let the town
know what was going on, for Joan had strung up gay patchwork
quilts tightly over all the windows—like tapestries at Squire's back
home, she thought, when it was all done and she stood looking at
it. The house inside was all trimmed with greens and berries, and
the tall white Yule candles burning either side of the hearth, and half
a hundred little candles going on every shelf, and table, and
dresser top. Will and Doll stood just inside the door to make the
welcomes, she in her scarlet London dress, and he wearing a crown
of pine cones shoved to the back of his head. Nan had made the
crown under Joan's direction, so that he could be King Christmas,
old Lord of Misrule.

One moment the house had been swept and garnished and lighted,
but empty, and the next it seemed to be so crowded with people, and
talk, and laughter, that there wasn't an inch of space anywhere to
set your wassail cup down, but then, the cups were full of hot but-
tered rum from Newburyport—the only good thing that ever came
out of Massachusetts—so who wanted to set them down anyway?
The Frosts had come from Kittery, and Mary and Tam from Bloody

Point, and all the children; Francis Champernowne from Greenland; John and Ruth Billings, nine miles in from the sea, and Abraham Corbett just out of Boston Gaol; half a dozen Fernalds and their families; Beck and Henry Sherburne; old Edward Godfrie, and Sarah Scriggins, well nigh sober. As Joan Scarlock looked happily around, she saw more than one old neighbor who had been with her in the *Pied Cow*, and she saw their children and their grandchildren, everybody laughing, and talking, and drinking under the green boughs. "I wonder," she said to herself, "if when we came away we really left anything—if we didn't bring England with us, after all?"

They played hoodman blind, and shoe the wild mare, and hot cockles, and bob apple, and kissing games, and always they sang, and Will set Doll up on the rude mantel high over everyone's head, where she and her lute could lead them, for she had been the toast of Portsmouth ever since the day she stood in the pillory to save the mast trade. And then they all drew up to the bending tables and ate —roast wild turkey and goose and duck, and stuffed partridge and woodcock, pumpkin and squash and parched corn boiled in milk, and sweet spiced puddings, and stewed cranberry, and shred pies. And so the evening went, down to the time when people were so full of good food and drink that they wanted to do nothing but sit and enjoy the warm feel of it inside them.

"Now this is the way it should be," rumbled Francis Champernowne, gray and gruff with years. "And this, by God, is the way we'll have it hereafter. The way it was at home where a man's soul belonged to himself first and the parish after. There's a difference on it here—it's not quite the same—but it's good enough." And all the company agreed, pleased as a roomful of purring cats. Then they talked about England, those of them who could remember how it had been there, and those who had heard their fathers say. And then they tried to call up all the old Christmas lore so that next year they could make it more than ever the way it had been; so that the children would know. They told how the oxen kneel at midnight, and the bees sing in their hives, and all the trees bow down. Sarah Scriggins said that in Essex the lads would wrestle for the Boar's Head, the winner to take it home, and Abraham Corbett told how in Yorkshire the men would put on deer antlers and dance in the street, and how they used to toll the devil's death knell, as many bell strokes as the count of the year.

Then Will cried out that he was King Christmas, and he decreed that John Billings should go over to the Bank and break into the Meeting House and toll the bell sixteen hundred and sixty-seven times, but they talked him out of it, because they were not quite strong enough and rich enough yet to set up the new order of things in the open street.

Nan said then that her father used to tell her when she was a little girl, how in Devon they would march among the apple trees, and pour wassail punch on the roots of them, and fire their guns at the same time; but they couldn't do that here either, because the noise would bring the constable before the smell of powder'd cleared from the air. Jane Crowther remembered that in Somerset the men would float almonds in the wine, and light it, and drink it all aflame, and Kitty Scarlock's oldest boy tried it with shagbark nuts, but went astray and blistered the tip of his nose.

Then Joan filled up the wassail bowl again, and Nan and Doll and Joannie went round with marchpane and honey cakes.

"One thing my grandmother told me they did in all the eastern counties," said Ruth Billings shyly, "back to the days when the people there were not our people at all, but strange folk from over the sea —not this sea, I mean, but the one behind it. When the feasting was over, the women would all arise and go to scan the sky for a star called Virgo, and when it shone out, they knelt, for it meant that Christ was born."

The women of Piscataqua looked at each other, turning in their minds the old Angle custom. "Does Virgo shine in America?" "How'll we know it from any other?"

"We won't," said Nan softly, "but we can look for a bright star."

She went to the door and opened it, and stood in the cold, looking into the dark, starry night over the snow-covered ledges, and Ruth went to her, and old Sarah took her swaying way there, and Alice and Mary, and half a dozen others. Doll stood up and began, very, very softly, to sing and play the "Cherry Tree Carol."

Joan stood by herself in the kitchen, watching them, and then she looked at her tall son, and her daughter's children, and all her old, kind friends in their rough, strong country clothes, and at the worn walls of her home, and she thanked God that He had given her just the life He had, with only the one black day in it. The little group of women still waited in the open door and she turned to it again. Their faces were lifted and their heads back, Nan's golden, and Ruth's dark, and Sarah's all rusty gray. And the feasting table was hushed, and nobody spoke at all. In the pauses of Doll's music you could almost hear the candles burn. Suddenly it was too holy for Joan to bear, so she turned, and fumbled with her apron, and stepped into the tiny storeroom behind the stairs, all fragrant with apples and herbs and winter vegetables, thinking she would shed just a few happy tears out of gratefulness for it all.

But then came a rush of skirts, and fingers clutching her arm, and there stood Doll, her face drained white, and her blue eyes great with horror.

"Oh, Joan! Mother Joan!" she cried. "Nan's with child!"

Joan took the girl's shaking hands in hers and tried to collect her scattered wits, but found it slow work.

"Why . . . why, Doll! That . . . that's a terrible thing to say. Nannie's a good girl. Why do you think that? She's as slim as you be!"

"I—I know she is. But it was not in her body I saw it. It was her face that told me. She looked for the star, and I was singing:

> "*Let him pick thee cherries*
> *Who got thee with child . . .*"

And then she looked at *him*—and I saw."

"Doll, you can't be sure of this. You mustn't believe it. Nan and Will have always been fond. They lay in the same bed . . ."

"That's what I'm telling you!"

"I mean, when they were little," said Joan almost crossly, thinking back over the week Nan had been there, thinking over it with the mind of a woman who has borne four children, and fearing horribly that Doll was right. "Will's a good lad, and Nan wouldn't go to any man's bed unless she was married to him. It's all your fancy."

Doll pulled her hands out of Joan's and ran them through her dark hair. "I must think," she said, bowing her head, "I must think what to do."

"Doll! Doll!" Will began shouting. "We want you to sing!" Everybody had started to talk at once and they were all calling for her. She looked up at Joan, her piquant face drawn and terrible.

"What . . . shall . . . I do?" she asked simply, letting her hands fall limp on her scarlet skirt.

"You must go out there now and sing," said Joan grimly. "Now you must. No matter what's to happen after."

Doll turned without a word and stepped across the kitchen. Joan leaned her head against an upright timber her husband had hewn with his own hand when he built the house for her. She ran her hand over the dry, gnarled wood. "Oh, Johnny," she said, "Johnny. I need you more than I ever have—since it happened to you. Oh, Johnny, what shall I do? To help our Will and those two poor girls?"

And then Doll's voice rang out, sweet and clear, but deeper, and purer, and more beautiful than it had ever sounded before. It could always charm and please, but now it went into your heart and spoke to you—of things that Doll and the music did not know, of things that no one knew except yourself, and perhaps one other.

> "Oh, the holly and the ivy,
>   When they are both full grown,
> But of all the trees that are in the wood,
>   The holly bears the crown."

"Why . . . why . . ." said Joan wonderingly. "How does she come to sing that one—now? He called me his holly tree. Holly's lucky for men, they say, and ivy for women, and he said I was all his luck. He said it was the strongest tree in England. He . . . he means . . . I must be strong, he's telling me that."

> "Oh, the rising of the sun,
>   The running of the deer . . ."

sang Doll, and Joan remembered sunrise in the Trent Valley, and the deer of Sherwood Forest, smaller, and trimmer, and sweeter-fleshed than those in New Hampshire, shaking their twiggy antlers, and running in the red morning light across the snow. She remembered sweet things and bitter, things she hadn't thought of for years, old pauper women dying wretchedly in St. Nicholas' workhouse when she was a little girl, and all the sweetness with Johnny, in the hedges and on the stone stairs under the Bull's Head. Her heart grew seven spans in the moment—and Doll's singing had done it all.

She . . . she . . . she's more than any of us . . . if she can sing like that, thought Joan. More than Nannie, whose people came with me in the *Pied Cow* . . . more than Will, my own son. God loves her better than all to make her sing so.

And then the singing ended sharply and there was a moment of taut silence, broken only by a gasp or two. Something terrible must have happened. Joan felt a draft of cold air blowing on her and knew that someone had opened the outside door. She crossed the kitchen and looked into the feasting room. The company still sat over the broken meats and half-empty mugs, but their faces were no longer merry, only dismayed and frightened. Doll had sunk to a bench, and only Will stood up, his pine cone crown pushed over one ear. In the doorway loomed Anthony Wiggin, narrow and beaky, the godly pry-all who had caught Doll singing in Ben Leighton's tavern.

"I thought **there** was something afoot," he announced triumphantly. "Too much **passing** in the street, I told John Cutt and Richard. Too many boats **tied up** below the town. When the devil comes here we know whom he visits." He was looking at Will, and Will answered him.

"And what are we doing that we shouldn't do?"

"You're keeping Christmas."

"We're worshiping Christ and His Mother."

"You're feasting."

"We're having supper. We do it every night about this time."

"This will cost you five pounds to the church treasury. You and every man and woman here."

The Christmas guests looked helplessly at each other. Five pounds was so great a sum you lowered your voice when you mentioned it —and five pounds from every man there. Mr. Moodey could rebuild his church in pure gold.

"No," said Will Scarlock steadily. "I don't think it will."

"Oh! You don't think so? You know it's the law. I shall cry up the town, and send the constables and Mr. Moodey . . ."

"Want to wager . . ."

"Any money! How can you keep me from it? My word is taken as truth everywhere, and my name smells sweet among the just, and yours reeks of brimstone. I have the name of knowing all that goes on in Piscataqua Country."

"Yes, you do. You even know what goes on in the alders by Hogstye Cove on the dark of the moon when a certain deacon is out of town. When Deacon . . ." Will paused, with the air of one who will not pause long.

Anthony Wiggin's face had fallen with the swiftness of a wild duck shot out of the sky.

"Stop! Stop there!" he quavered. "I—I . . ."

"Go on back to town and stop bothering us," said the Lord of Misrule, straightening his crown a little, "unless you want to stay and share the wassail bowl. And don't bear any tales with you this time, Anthony. For whatever you tell, I can cap it with a better."

Wiggin bit his lip, turned on his heel, and walked out into the night.

"Mother," said Will, "have you got some more rum out back? There's time for one more round before midnight—and we need it, after that!"

People were thawing from their stiffness of fright, and beginning to talk again, and pick at the half-bare platters. His heart grew warm and reckless inside him, as he looked at his friends, and thought how he loved them, and how glad he was they had not come to trouble in his house. No doubt he should have felt like a whited sepulchre, one adulterer chiding the other, but sometimes it did the pot good to call the kettle black. And what he had done with Nannie was not the same. Safely across the room from her, he dared to look, expecting her to smile approval for what he had just done, and she did smile, but what was the matter that she looked so grave and sad? He turned to Doll, and Doll looked white and sick, and then his mother went by, carrying a tray of sweetmeats, and her mouth was tight and her face gray. Oh, what the devil was the matter with women anyway? So he went among the men, and laughed with them, and felt them slapping him on the shoulder from all sides, and he ladled himself a great helping of rum.

Then came the holy hour, and they opened the door to let the Christmas in, and the guests bowed their heads, and Will stood up to read from the Prayer Book, still feeling gay, and reckless, and very much his own man, and a hell of a good fellow, still wearing his crooked crown.

"Almighty God, Who hast given us Thy only begotten Son to take our nature upon Him, and as at this time to be born of a pure Virgin; Grant that we being regenerate, and made Thy children by adoption and grace, may daily be renewed by Thy Holy Spirit, through the same our Lord Jesus Christ, Who liveth and reigneth with Thee and the same Spirit, ever one God, world without end. *Amen.*"

He closed the book and flashed a quick, merry smile around the room, where people were beginning to shift, and stir, and part from each other. But Doll and Nan still stood with their heads down, and Joan clutched the wooden latch of the kitchen door and murmured over to herself, "Poor lad, poor lad." Holly was lucky for men, she thought, and ivy for women, and neither of them grew in Piscataqua.

24. It came with a lass

〰〰〰〰〰〰〰〰〰〰〰〰〰〰〰〰〰〰〰

IT WAS in March that Doll Scarlock watched the changes of the moon and waited desperately for Nan to act, but no word of her came ashore from Hog Island where she had gone on Christmas Day, any more than as if she had died and been buried under the gray rocks there—though of course that couldn't have happened without their knowing. Will stayed upriver with the masting crews, and Joan and Doll moved about the house, keeping the little Joan with them, not talking of the terrible thing that would be coming on as surely as the green grass of April and the buds to the gnarled, old trees. Once only they talked.

"Do you think *he* knows?" said Joan to her daughter-in-law.

"You've seen him—with his head back, laughing—and you think he could?"

"No. No, he doesn't then. That would be like Nan. She'd make no trouble for him. I—I suppose it's wicked to say, but it's been done before and will again. The boy from Boston—Truth Damerill—he loved her so. I think he'd marry her even now."

"She won't ever marry Truth Damerill."

"No . . . but this . . . oh, how do you think it happened?"

"The way it always happens," said Doll, her face white. "They loved each other, and they were alone . . . and it did. I . . . please . . . if you should ever wonder sometime . . . you've been kind to me and I thank you for it."

Joan did not understand at all. "What—what do you think will come of it?"

"I don't know. I don't know what Nan will do. I don't know what

I will do . . . but I must know soon. I think . . . oh, Mother Joan . . .
I think that maybe all will be well with us. I think I see. Only let
us wait for Nan a little while."

So they waited for Nan. The ice moved down from the brooks,
and the blue sky burned like summer over the brown hillsides and
dead grass. The country lanes were runnels of mud, and water swam
in all the furrows, and willow buds dipped white puffs of ermine in
the flooding streams.

"Do you think . . ." said Joan, "you could be wrong about Nan?"

"No," said Doll, "I wasn't wrong. What would you do—if you
were Nan?"

Joan did not even stop to think about it. "Why—why I'd go
away. I wouldn't stay here and be a trouble and a shame to him. I'd
go before anybody knew."

"I—I think I would do that too. I—I wonder if maybe she won't.
Do you think—maybe she's gone?"

"Oh—not on the winter sea. But there's a ship off the dock now
going for England, stopping by the Shoals, of course, as they all do.
And the spring's begun. She might go by that. She has friends there."

And Doll and Joan watched the ship, and one day they noticed
the men taking barrels of sweet water aboard, getting ready to sail.

"Mother Joan," said Doll, "I'm going with that ship. Out to Hog
Island—maybe further. I'll talk with her, and when it's over, there'll
be one of us you won't see again—one of us. Do you know what I'm
thinking?"

"Yes," said Joan sadly, "I do know. And I know this, Doll. Ever
since I heard you sing on Christmas Eve I knew you were more than
any of us. That's true, whatever happens, and I'll believe it all my
life, and I want you to believe it."

"Whatever I am, I'm not so fine as you . . . or so strong."

They did not say good-bye. Joan stood unmoving as the holly tree
and watched Doll out of sight.

It was a sharp, blue spring day with a great wind roistering all
about and cuffing whitecaps off the top of the river. Doll did not
turn as she walked out in it, wrapped in the sober cloak that she had
never felt she owned, that seemed to be something lent to her for a
little while. She crossed the fields, past Sam Fernald's, and waited
at the shore till the Crowther boys saw her, and came and fetched
her across. She went along Dock Lane then, like a girl walking in

a dream, down to where the river boats were moored, and she asked up and down the wharf till she found a man willing to row her out to the ship. That was not hard to do.

It was sunset when she walked up through Appledore Town to Nan Knight's house at the top of the stone ledges behind the stunted trees. The house had a blind look, for wooden shutters had been nailed across the windows, and Nan stood in the doorway wearing her cap and cloak with Watch quiet at her feet.

"Why—why, Doll?" she gasped, looking a little white and startled as her visitor drew near. "I—I didn't expect you. I was going away."

"Where are you going, Nannie?"

"To—to England. I've only been waiting for the winter to break." The brisk sea wind of March tore at their clothing and Doll's dark hair streamed backward, her white skin reddened a little from it, and she shivered. Nan saw.

"Come in. The fire's dead and all the house shut. I have only to lock the door when I go out of it—to sail with the night tide. It's cold indoors, but there's no wind blowing there."

She stepped into the darkened kitchen, and Doll followed her, and there they stood, simply, face to face, and all defenses down.

"You—you're going to England?"

"Yes."

"And what will you do there?"

"I—I'll go to Catherine Audley again. I've written and told her, and she's answered, and expects me."

"Oh, yes—to Whitehall?" And then Doll went on, not meaning to be cruel, but knowing she had to bring the thing out between them, and falling back on the practical speech of Milady's, "I suppose one more bastard will never be noticed there."

They were silent for a long moment. Doll stared into the low, smoky room behind Nan, and Nan stared outward at the bright sea all ruddy with sunset, and the ship anchored outside the cove, the ship she had a passage on.

Then she said, "I don't care whether it's noticed or not. I—I'm sorry, Doll. I—we—we couldn't help it. And it was only the once. I'm going away. I'm never coming back. He'll be yours always—and I pray you never to tell him this. How did you know?"

"I knew at Christmas, Nan. You couldn't keep it from your eyes when you looked at him."

"I—I—there's no need to tell you how I feel, about going from him forever, going from home. But about you—oh, Doll—I shall feel so, all my life—what I've done to you!"

Nan put her proud gold head down on the shoulder of her cloak. The garment whipped away from her now in the wind that reached everywhere, and Doll could see the slight thickening of the waist, could see what all Hog Island would see soon—if Nannie didn't go—but Nannie was going. Then she looked down at her own slight body.

She went close to Nan, and reached out her hand, put it against Nan's cheek and lifted her face up.

"Nan. Listen. I think—I think *I* am the one to go."

Light woke in Nan's gray eyes like tinder struck, and died as quickly. "You couldn't, Doll. You are his honest wife and have the right to stay with him always."

"But—but he doesn't love me. He loves you."

Again Nan bowed her head. "I—I—" She leaned, shaken and trembling against the salt-stained timbers that framed the door.

"Nannie. Listen. I think that he loves you, and that you love him, and that I should go away, so you two can marry . . . before . . ."

"But how can we marry? You are his true wife."

"No," said Doll evenly, her fingers clasping Nan's sleeve, firm and steady. "No, I'm not. And I never was."

"But he told me he married you—all honest and before the parson—at Nottingham at the Goose Fair. And he wouldn't lie . . . about that."

"But he didn't know, Nan. I had a husband before ever I saw him. He came to Milady's when I was a young girl. He was a clerk from Oxford in town for holiday; young, and swearing, and laughing, and treating the house the whole night long. He wanted to come into my bed, but I had promised my mother I would not be like the other girls there, so I would not let him unless he married me. And he did. We were not together long. Milady said I should forget, and live as if it had never been at all. And maybe it was wrong—but that was what I did. His father had a manor in Suffolk and he went back there, and has taken another girl in the church, I hear, which he should not have done, for our marriage still stands firm and is written down in the parish register of St. Magnus' by the Bridge Head. The book was saved from the fire, for I asked the clerk afterward. I can prove what I say by that. But I do know that he goes upright and alive and well, or did at the time of our Goose Fair wedding—and while he lives, your Will's a bachelor for all of me."

Suddenly Nan began to cry. She leaned there in the doorway and cried and cried, and Doll did not touch her, did not say anything, but waited while the night began to gather, and a hail came up from the shore.

"Oh, Nan! The tide's right! They want to sail!"

"Good-bye, Nan," said Doll, putting out her hand. "I'll take your place. I—I don't need to say anything more. You'll hold your head up in a minute and be Miss Nannie Knight—who's going to be Mistress Scarlock—and it'll all be well—with all of us."

Nan's limp shoulders stiffened. She tried to answer but she could not. She held out a small leather bag to Doll and Doll knew what was in it.

"No, Nannie. I don't need money. Never, while I have this." She flashed the lute from under her cloak. "And I think—I owe you more than you owe me."

"I owe you," said Nan, lifting her tear-stained face, "my life and blood and breath and all my soul forever—if this is true."

"There was something you said to me, Nan—last summer on the hill by Hogstye Cove. You said I loved to sing and have folk listen, more than anything. I did not know it till you told me, but I have thought since. And it is true. I have never loved any man so much as I loved this." Both girls looked at the lute. "I—I came the closest to loving him—but—but even that could not make up for all London—and the Old Serpent, and Moorfields, and all the clapping, shouting, gay, bright people who loved me. It's sweet to lie in bed with a man you love, Nan."

"Yes. I know."

"But it's not so sweet as that."

"Now that I don't know, and I'll never believe. For you . . . maybe . . ."

"Nan!" came the insistent bellow from the cove. "We're holding the ship!"

Doll smiled up into Nan's eyes. "He's yours—and you can have him true and honest in the Meeting House. I—I'm going now—back to England where I have a husband already, before I ever knew Will Scarlock—and I won't come back. Give him my love and tell him good-bye for me, and tell him I'm sorry it all happened the way it did."

"I suppose," said Nan brokenly, her gray eyes black through her tears, "I'll never know whether you're telling the truth or not?"

"I pray you, believe me."

Doll ran out of the house and lightly down the ledges to the shaly beach. A rough man whom she had never seen before was just about to shove off in a small boat, and none of the Hog Island men were by, except John Billings, for Nan had let no one else know of her plan to go away. He looked in surprise at Doll.

"Where's Nan?"

Doll waved toward the house. "Up there. I'm going instead." She turned to the man in the boat. "Wait, please. I'm coming. I'm ready now."

"Time, too. Be you the one? I thought 'twas a fair girl took passage."

"It was. But a dark one will go."

"Go where?" said Will Scarlock.

Doll turned swiftly. He had drawn his boat up across the cove and followed the curving beach to where she stood, and all the time she had not known he was there—she had thought he was miles away in the woods, felling the great mast pines along the Lampereel, and that she would never see him again.

"How—how did you come here?" And then her eyes clouded and her shoulders drooped, though it could not possibly matter now. "I suppose you came to see Nan."

"I didn't. I followed you. Tom Everie broke his leg and we had to bring him downriver. At the dock they told me you'd been hunting for a boat going to Hog Island and had just left for there. So I knew something was wrong—and I got my boat and came. Is—there's nothing wrong with Nan, is there?"

"Nannie'll tell you her own story, Will. But first—I have to tell you mine. I know that you love her, and I want you two to be happy. So I am going home."

"But—but you can't do that! You're my wife!" She watched his face, and just as with Nan there had been the bright gleam of hope, and then the sadness of knowing that it could never be.

"No, I'm not. I never was."

"What . . . ?"

"Because you can't marry another man's wife, Will. When I stood up with you in Nottingham, I was another man's wife already."

Hot words of denial and disbelief leaped to his mouth, but he held them there without saying them.

"Doll," he said, "I—I can't believe you."

"Don't you want to?"

He stood there with his head bowed; the purple shadows of evening poured over all the rocky island, and the faint line of the mainland glowing gold in the sunset far away, and the fresh sea wind troubling and catching at everything with unseen fingers.

"I—I suppose I do."

He put his hands on her shoulders, and she lifted her face up, and suddenly it was a face that he had not seen since that time in London when all the trouble came; sweetness and love were in it, but there was also something independent, and gay, and careless, and strong, something that said, "Do not fear for me. This will not be my end. No man can break Doll Trasper."

"I have my lute, Will. And you know—I think you knew before I did—that would always come first."

"I remember when I knew. It was that day in the rain at Boston when I sat with Nan in the Green Hound and watched you. You'd forgotten I was alive. But, Doll, I guess—I guess it's best that you go. But I'll always remember the fire that was between us —the greatest fire that ever was in London, not forgetting the fire I lost you in."

"Yes," said Doll, "it was a great fire. And I'm glad we had it. But it's ashes now, and what's between you and Nan is fire—but it's earth and air and water, too, and all the world— And it won't ever be ashes. It'll be sweet forever. Good-bye."

"Doll! Wait! I can't let you go like this with nothing! I know you have your lute. I know they'll welcome you back at Milady's. But some day—maybe you can't sing any more. You may be sick, and you will be old like all of us, and trouble may come on you. But there's Old Thorny. I'll never go back to it. They'll never see any more of me there. But I'll write to Kit Harroday, who thinks you're my wife, and tell him to give it over to you as quick as he would to me. You know where the deed is—in the chest in the root cellar—for I showed it to you and read it out loud. I'll tell him it's yours for all time. And maybe you'll take your husband there and have the boys a-plenty they've been asking for. And your boys can have that land. Mine will have enough to do here."

"I—I thank you, Will. I won't promise boys—not to any man. But that's as it may be—my going there."

She turned from him and stepped lightly into the little boat. The oarsman shoved off hastily, and they plowed outward through the purple sea toward the squat, white-sailed ship waiting beyond the reef. The tide welled powerfully under them, and Doll leaned her head against the pitch-coated planks, wet and rough with a film of barnacle.

She thought about the old parchment piece in the crumpled and yellow cow's horn, and how the claim it bore went back through Earl Peverell to Doomsday Book, because she had always meant to make a song about it. "It's like they said of the power of Scotland's throne once," she murmured to the boiling gray sea just beyond the waves of the little boat. " 'It came with a lass and it'll go with a lass.' It came to Scarlocks with the girl who fed the knight's heir, and he's letting it go—with me. But past all that—only six weeks or so of sailing, and then—Doll Trasper'll be singing in London again."

She held her head up proudly, not turning once to the still figure watching her from the shore, and the gruff oarsman rowed silently from the shelter of the dark island with the red sunset behind it, out into the darkening sea.

25. New Hampshire man

WILL SCARLOCK lay in bed beside his wife Nan, and dreamed a dream. He was tired to the bone when he flung himself down there, in the house by Hogstye Cove, for he'd been out prowling the woods half the night with Watch, trying to round up the drunken Indian who had been going from farm to farm on Dover Neck threatening him. Kin of Passaconaway, he was, a decent enough young buck when sober, but inclined to be mean and muttering over the bottle, and always holding a grudge about this particular land, though it seemed to Will his father had purchased it fair enough for him, and he had the deed in order. After all, it was Passaconaway had set the price, and John Scarlock had paid it.

The last three weeks had not been easy for Will in other ways. He and Nan had gone to the courthouse on Smutty Nose to be married by the magistrate there, and because she paid the parson's salary there hadn't been too much trouble about banns. They couldn't have stood up before Mr. Moodey in Portsmouth Meeting House —not Will Scarlock who'd been living among them peaceably with another wife, and Nan Knight, spinster, incapable of man. Tongues had clacked worse than spinning wheels as it was, and the Select Men had gone hot after Sarah Scriggins, waving her affidavit, but they got nowhere with that, for Sarah was not sober enough to talk sense. They charged her with drunkenness and bearing false witness, and she paid her fine—nobody understood how. And Nan, for her part, said she'd always believed Sarah's first opinion—till she'd visited a doctor on her trip to London, who told her things were otherwise. John Billings stood up and swore that he'd heard

Doll's confession about her husband back in England, so, much as they'd have liked to punish Will, there was nothing they could do. He'd married a strange girl he did not know, and been deceived by her. When he found out the truth—that he was really a single man—he had a right to choose another wife, though he'd done it with unseemly haste, even in a time of hasty marriages. No, regretfully they decided, they could not punish Will; they could not punish anybody. When Nannie bore a child in the late summer, maybe they'd have more to say. Well, he wasn't afraid. He'd stand up to them and face it down. He might have been shocked when she told him of its coming, that night on Hog Island when Doll left, except that he'd been through so much by then that he felt nothing could shock him any more. No. None of it had been easy.

The men were rafting the logs out of Great Bay now, floating them to the mast pools in the lower river for the spring arrival of the fleet, so it was here that he had to be all day, and he wanted Nan with him, not away on her island, nor even with his mother Joan in Portsmouth, where all the gossip was, and the nine days' wonder. On this soft, spring night, with the brook gurgling loudly through the mist that hung dripping about the budded trees, it was enough to know that she lay there beside him, warm, and safe, and ready to respond if he wanted it; that they would be secure always in each other's love.

"Oh, Nannie," he murmured, his eyes closing in spite of himself, "I'm so sleepy. I didn't find the ugly devil. He's mean, this time, Major Walderne says—with a great tomahawk like nobody's seen since the early days. But we'll be safe tonight. Watch is outside."

"Oh . . . I'm not frightened, dear. You get some sleep now."

And go to sleep he did, and he dreamed.

He dreamed that he stood by Bloody Point where the rivers parted, and the Back River flooded through the farms and marshlands west and south, and the Fore River went streaming north. And they looked the way they always had in his time—all green woods, with here and there a cornfield, or a pasture ledge, or a hay meadow, and the rough roofs of the farm houses, and the Meeting House on Dover Neck. And then, as he watched it, one river changed. The western river stayed the way it was—Piscataqua Country. But along the Fore River suddenly appeared the wharves, and spires, and gables that had bordered the Thames—before the fire, that was. There grew up before him, swiftly, as he watched it, London City,

all that was rich, and old, and crooked, and many-colored, and singing bright with human life, and gray with human pain and squalor,
and living as a man endowed with blood and breath, the blood and
breath of time. And then he saw beyond London City, the green
fields of England, and the curving thatch of Old Thorny, and the
hazels sweeping away from it toward Gamwell Chase, where deer
stalked down from the high wood, and there might always come the
ghostly flash of green.

There he stood, Will Scarlock, where the rivers parted, and he
faced the two rivers and felt a worse trouble come on him than when
he had said good-bye to Nan in the fens of Lincolnshire—and
that had been the worst moment of his life. He knew, even in his
dream, that his life was given for always to the green forest river,
but where his heart would choose, he did not know. Oh, rivers, he
thought, rivers parting! They part before a man, and he can only
follow one—and which one, not even God can show him how to tell!

Then the towers of London shimmered and dissolved, and all the
green banks seemed to be swept away and flooded over with green
water, and there was nothing but the green water everywhere, and
then he felt Nan's gentle fingers shaking him.

"Will—Will, it's early to wake you—but you're dreaming—not a
good dream."

"I—I—yes, I was dreaming. I'm glad you waked me, Nan."

He stretched out under the quilts, feeling heavy and dull, with
his eyes stuck together, and as if he hadn't slept at all, and much too
warm. The red sunrise beyond the window looked as if it would be
a warm day.

"I'll get breakfast," she said, and he closed his eyes again, hearing
her moving soft and sure about the room, and that made him feel
better somehow—it sounded just like his mother moving about
the kitchen at home when he was a little boy. Later they sat at the
table, licking their porridge spoons and smiling at each other.

"I'm going over to Blake Cotterill's cove for a little while," he
said, getting up from his stool. "We're thinning the masts out of
there pretty clean—he'll have a good tract of stumpage to make
over into meadow now. But I won't go down to the Bank with them.
I'll come back and beat the woods some more. Till then, you've got
Watch."

And he went down to Cotterill's cove, and saw the rafting crews
off toward Bloody Point, herding the docile, shaggy logs bound in

floes with crude chains, and he got back to his house a little past noon. Nan had bread and ale and bacon and stewed pease for him, and they sat and talked, the warm sunlight coming in through the open door, and all the budding oakwood stretched away beyond.

"Oh, Will—I know I shouldn't. Shouldn't ever ask it—it's better not—but I still wonder. Do you think Doll told the truth to us—or did she make it up—just like one of her songs?"

"I think, Nan, we better take her word."

"Well, I'm not going to take her word. I wrote to Catherine. I asked her to go to Saint Magnus and look in the parish register."

"You did?" Dismay looked out of his eyes first, and then the inevitable question. "Suppose—suppose, Nan, she can't find that Doll was ever married there? Suppose it is a lie? Would—would you want to go away from me?"

"Oh, no, Will! Never!"

"Then—no matter what's the truth of it, Nannie—we'll live together all our lives, and we'll have this child, and we'll have others. And if, if it is wrong at law—if I am married to Doll—and if ever we have to stand up and answer for it—to God or to General Court —we're not afraid, are we? Together?"

"Oh, no! Not ever of anything—together!"

They could not know that at that very moment Catherine Audley stood in the little vaulted room at the side of the ruined church, the sunlight of an English April falling across her hair, across the charred pages of the book spread open on a table, while her fingers traced the blunt characters that made their flesh and blood lawful for all time. "Ye 6th of January, 1662. Roger de Clavering, armiger, of Haveryll in Suffolk, to Dorothy Trasper, spinster, of London Bridge. In the presence of Tom Tacke and Audrey Moor."

He got up and kicked his stool back into a corner. "Now I'll have another look for that damned Indian. See if I can find out what he wants and settle with him."

"He wants these fields back—all the Hogstye Cove land. I heard Major Walderne say that when we were in Dover yesterday and he warned you."

"Well, he can't have it. I've known this land was mine ever since I was a little boy, and I'll never give it up. Maybe if he wants money, not too much . . ."

"Take your gun."

"I have it."

He went out into the sunlight, stepped around the house on the lower side toward the cove, and then started up the hill, following the full brook and dipping alders. He reached the black, swampy bog pool at the top, and then turned past the blackberry thicket and started into a grove of redbud maples. A great bull briar ran down into the blackberries, and scrub hemlock, and juniper, and tall thistles reaching up to the low trees made a cluster of little coverts he could not see into, and he thought he heard a noise in them. He stopped to listen, but there was nothing but silence under the sun, and the calling of the crows on the black, slanted field, and the shouts of a logging crew, below the oaks, toward Greenland. He crossed a ledge, and looking down he saw where something had scraped across the tiny, gray, flame-tipped lichens that covered it. Was this a track? An Indian would have more wits than that. Still, no man with hobnailed boots had been in here, as far as he knew, and an animal would not have made it. He shifted his gun from his shoulder, and leaned it against an elm tree, and bent down.

It was then that the Indian struck. Will only heard a little in-drawn breath, a fainter sound than an adder's hiss, but with the same malicious triumph in it. He caught a glimpse of faded blue breeches and a brown torso above him, and felt the bite of the tomahawk in his shoulder. With a desperate twist he writhed away from it, leaped backward, and took one look at the lithe figure that came on him again, with staring, inflamed eyes, its lips drawn back, and an ugly shout in its throat he could not understand. No use to reach for his gun now—he was too close in to use it. He turned and sprinted down hill for the house, his arm hanging numb, and drops of blood flying backward from his wild plunge, and he knew the Indian was racing after.

He's drunk, he thought. Drunk enough to fall over on his head if he trips a little. If I can get to the house—get the door between us—Oh God, make Nan have the door open!

In the oaks by the slate shore of the cove, he heard the deep bellow of the mastiff.

"Here, Watch!" he shouted. "Here, lad!" Watch was heavy as a mountain moving, but he was sure. His fangs could tear a man's throat out.

He stumbled across the furrows and the little strip of grass, and reached the blue slates he'd set like a pave in front of the door. The door stood open. He could see Nan inside, standing in the middle of the clean, sanded floor, looking startled. She must have heard him shout for Watch. He could almost feel the Indian at his back. One more leap and he would be inside and safe. And then his boot sole struck the treacherous, smooth slate, and he slipped, and came down in a heap, his shoulder striking the oak sill, throwing him back a little, his head coming to rest on the ground, his eyes staring straight at the soft, brown turf.

It was his last minute, he thought. He knew that the Indian had lifted his arm. He could not recover himself—it was all in a moment's flash—but it seemed to take an hour in time. He had never known before that it took so long to die. He saw, in that flash, the brown earth under him, and he saw, as he looked, the drops of his own blood fall there, and sink into it—and so—in his last moment—seeing his blood going into that brown earth—he knew. He knew that he and this earth were kin, with the old kinship and agreement that exists between any creature and the place where it is bred. He knew that he was a New Hampshire man, come of New Hampshire earth, and that he loved that earth, and he belonged to it, and it to him, the way his father had belonged to Old Thorny. And now—after living all his life away and a stranger —now only at his ending had he come home. And now the blade would fall.

And then there was a howl, and a curse broken by a gurgle, and a brown, sweaty, stinking body coming all down in a heap on top of him, and thrashing about there, and then going still.

He shrugged, and writhed, and pulled out from under the weight that held him pinned there, and struggled to his feet. He saw the blue river beyond the cove, and the little green border of farms across Great Bay, running down from Oyster River toward Exeter, and the budding oaks below, and the deep sky over all, and he felt that he had never seen such beauty or felt such love. It was not the love and beauty that you found at a woman's breast, and it would not take the place of that—it was a part of that, and beyond it. They were both a part of what a man meant when he said home.

He looked at the doorway of his house, and there stood Nan, her face ghastly, and her eyes gone deep and black, and blood all over her dress, and she was leaning weakly on a red hatchet.

"I—I—" she gasped. "I thought of you—not just our nights together—but the man you are—and how I couldn't bear that he should ever die! And I struck him!"

Silently they looked at the dead Indian lying sprawled between them, with Watch worrying at his throat.

"And then—I thought—I thought of our child—never to know its father! And then—and then I *really* struck him!"

"Oh, Nan!" he cried. He stumbled to her and took her in his arms, and they sank down on the bench just inside the door, holding to each other.

Will buried the Indian at the top of the field, below the black-berries where Doll had told Nan that she prayed to Venus. It was in the twilight that he finished, and there were stars over Stratham Hill, and a fresh wind coming out of the hills all purple behind the tree line on Great Bay's inner shore. Nan had washed his arm and bandaged it, but the blow had not gone deep, and it felt only a little sore and stiff. When the tide shifted in half an hour, they would go down to the Bank and sober up Sarah Scriggins, and get her to dress it for him with the proper herbs. He straightened up from prodding the last turf into place, and looked out over the dark water and shadowy fields that his father had bought for him—that no father could ever buy for him. Watch lumbered past, chasing a squirrel, and then gave up, and ran over to nuzzle against Will's thigh. He put his hand on the tawny, wrinkled head. The dog's father had come from an old country too, like his, and their fathers had fought in all England's wars for a thousand years, he thought, but the blood would fight no more for England. Will looked west-ward, to the rivers of Piscataqua, spread out like God's great hand upon the countryside, running into the green farm and forest land, shimmering in the evening light.

"It's a tough country, Watch, and it'll be harder to take than the Spanish Armada was. But we can do it. It's ours. It's home."

Watch turned and licked his hand companionably. Together they went down the hill to Nan.